Ballots and Blood

Ballots and Blood

RALPH REED

PUBLISHING GROUP

Nashville, Tennessee

978-1-4336-6925-5

Published by B&H Publishing Group,
Nashville, Tennessee

Dewey Decimal Classification: F
Subject Heading: MYSTERY FICTION \ POLITICAL
CORRUPTION—FICTION \ WASHINGTON (DC)—FICTION

Author is represented by the literary agency of Alive Communications,
Inc., 7680 Goddard Street, Suite 200, Colorado Springs, CO 80920,
www.alivecommunications.com.

1 2 3 4 5 6 7 8 • 15 14 13 12 11

To Christopher

An unmarked blue Ford Crown Victoria carrying a District of Columbia police detective pulled up in front of a pre-World War II, three-story redbrick townhouse in the upscale Georgetown section of Washington, DC. The detective slid out of the car, the summer heat hitting him like a furnace blast, the air heavy and almost choking. DC was like a paved swamp in the summertime, he thought. As he stepped to the curb, he glanced in either direction to survey the street for any suspicious persons (an instinctive response honed over twenty-two years of police work) and nodded at the patrolman standing on the sidewalk. He opened the iron gate to the small garden out front and descended to the basement.

Inside, his eyes adjusted to the semidarkness. A second patrolman stood in what appeared to be a reception area-living room, its floor covered with a bland industrial carpet.

"What do ya got?" asked the detective, dispensing with formalities.

"White male, approximately sixty," said the patrolman. "Based on the condition of the body, I'd say he's been dead for a while."

The detective nodded. "Show me."

The officer led him to a door and a second set of stairs, which creaked as they descended. A pungent smell filled their nostrils, a noxious mixture of sweat, blood, leather, and death. A fly buzzed. When they reached the bottom, the detective surveyed the room. An empty cage sat in the corner, a wooden table with leather straps at the ends, a wall rack with whips hanging from it—the equipment of a faux-torture chamber.

"It's a dungeon," said the officer.

"So I see," said the detective. He stooped and studied the body. The man's flesh was pale with a gray pallor, soft and cool to the touch. His hands and feet were bound with leather restraints. He wore a black leather mask. Had the victim accidentally suffocated? Reddish-purple contusions flecked his shoulders, back, and buttocks. The lower limbs were discolored, indicating a settling of blood. The victim had been dead for hours.

"What do you think? A whip, maybe?" asked the detective, pointing to the bruises.

"Looks like it," said the officer. "There's plenty of 'em. And riding crops. I didn't notice anything missing."

"We'll have to wait for the autopsy to find out how he died. I doubt a whip was the murder weapon. We'll get prints. That'll lead to whoever worked here. My hunch is there will be plenty of outstandings and priors," said the detective. "Find out who owns the building."

"Roger that, sir."

The detective stared at the body. "Any ID on this guy?"

"His clothes are in the changing room," replied the officer, pointing to the corner of the basement.

The detective walked to changing room. "Probably a lobbyist or corporate puke. Or a traveling businessman looking for a good time on the road."

"He got more than he bargained for," said the officer.

A crisp navy blue suit hung on a hook in front of a mirror, a red-and-blue striped tie draped over the hanger. A blue shirt in dry-cleaning plastic hung on a second hook. A pair of boxer shorts, meticulously folded, rested on the chair, navy blue socks lying across a pair of black wingtips. The detective patted the suit, feeling a bulge in the pants. He reached in and pulled out a wallet. Opening it, he found a Florida driver's license. Reading the name, he let out an expletive.

"What?" asked the officer.

"Well, now we have what we refer to as a situation." He reached into another suit pocket and pulled out some business cards, flipping through them, then closed the wallet and pulled his cell phone out of his pocket. He dialed a number, pausing while awaiting an answer, his gaze leveled at the officer. "I need the chief."

The chief of detectives came on the line. "What's so important that you're interrupting me?"

"I've got a white male, sixty-two, bound and gagged in a Georgetown apartment retrofitted as a torture chamber. Somebody beat him up pretty bad. It appears he either choked to death or had a heart attack during the act," said the detective. "I need a full crime scene unit stat. And I'm going to need a public affairs officer."

"Why?"

"The body is Senator Perry Miller."

"What? Are you absolutely sure?"

"Not exactly. His face is covered. But unless someone else is wearing his suit and carrying his driver's license, yeah, it's definitely Perry Miller."

The chief of detectives sighed. "This is going to be a cluster."

"Total."

"Sit tight," said the chief. "The CSU will be there in ten minutes. Secure the building. No one goes in or out until it's swept for prints. I mean no one. Pretty soon it'll be a police convention, with badges standing around with their thumbs up their noses and the media crawling everywhere. For now, I don't want a thread moved. Is that clear?"

"Done."

"We might as well call the FBI. They're going to show up anyway. Give them all the cooperation they need, if only to protect us, if you get my drift."

"Sadly, I do."

"What's your location?"

"321 M Street, NW."

"It's probably nothing beyond what it looks like. A guy was having a good time, things got out of control, next thing you know you've got a dead body."

"Nelson Rockefeller, call your office."

"Right. But you never know. And given the victim, we need to tread carefully. This is going to be on the front page of every newspaper in America by tomorrow morning."

The detective hung up and turned to the patrolman. "Congratulations, officer. You just bought yourself a front row seat to a sex scandal."

A BLACK LINCOLN TOWN CAR pulled up slowly to the back gate of the White House bearing Governor Kerry Cartwright of New Jersey. A uniformed guard scanned the driver's licenses of the driver, Cartwright, and a personal aide. He surveyed their faces to establish a visual ID.

"Good afternoon, Governor."

"Good afternoon," replied Cartwright, shooting the aide a knowing smile.

The guard waved the car through, the iron gates opening slowly with a creaking noise by remote control. The driver pulled into a spot just outside the West Wing with an orange cone placed in the center.

Jay Noble's assistant stood beneath the green awning of the entrance to the West Wing. She wore a smart blue skirt with a crisp white blouse, White House staff badge dangling conspicuously from her neck. As the car pulled up, she smiled officiously and greeted the governor.

"Governor, so glad you could come. Jay's with the president. He'll meet you in the mess shortly. He asked me to go ahead and take you to your table." She accompanied Cartwright and his aide down the narrow stairwell to the White House mess, greeting the host and leading the way to a private room.

David Thomas, White House political director and manager of Bob Long's presidential campaign, sat at a chair, head down, eyes peering at his BlackBerry screen, his fingers flying across the keyboard.

"Governor!" he boomed a little too loudly when Cartwright entered, flashing a warm and expansive smile. "David Thomas, political director. Welcome." He shook his hand vigorously.

Cartwright, a bowling ball of a man with stooped posture, loping gait, forty pounds of excess weight, and a look of permanent bemusement on his countenance (as if to say, "How did I get this far, this fast?"), gripped his hand tightly, their eyes locked. "Good to be here, David." He turned to his aide. "You know Bill Spadea on my team."

"Absolutely," said Thomas, shaking Spadea's hand. "He's one of the best political operatives in America. Bill, your reputation precedes you."

At that instant the door swung open and Jay breezed in, immediately changing the room's dynamics with his presence. Everyone wheeled to face him. "Is Thomas talking about himself again? I heard something about the best political operative in America." Jay never resisted a chance to get a playful dig in on Thomas.

Cartwright let out a belly laugh while Thomas and Spadea eyed each other warily, chuckling nervously. They all took their chairs as Jay waved over a white-coated waiter, who took drink orders.

"The president says hello," said Jay. "If you have time after lunch, we can swing by the Oval and see him before you leave."

"Terrific," said Cartwright a little too enthusiastically.

"So—how goes the Garden State?" asked Jay.

Cartwright nodded. "We finally got the budget done," he said with the relaxed sigh of an accountant after tax day. "It was a beast. The Democrats fought me to the bitter end."

Jay smiled knowingly. "We know the feeling, Governor."

"The session turned into a game of chicken with the Speaker of the House and the teachers' unions, who have him wrapped around their finger. We won because I refused to give in to their demands. I pledged when I ran for governor I wouldn't raise taxes, and I've kept it. In fact, I've cut property taxes three times."

"It's amazing," said Jay.

"The press—and especially the *New York Times*—is crucifying him," said Spadea as he took a sip of Diet Coke. "But all it does is remind people he's a man of his word. The governor's job approval is 68 percent. That's the highest number he's ever had."

"We know," interjected Thomas. "Why do you think we're having lunch?"

Everyone laughed. The waiter reappeared with drinks and took everyone's order. Cartwright ordered a cup of chicken noodle soup, clear evidence he was back on a diet in anticipation of another campaign.

"So have you figured out how to handle Sal Stanley yet?" joked Cartwright after the waiter left the table.

Everyone laughed again.

"Actually, we have," said Jay, leaning forward, his countenance radiating intensity. "We're gonna beat him."

Cartwright was stunned. "You really think you can beat Stanley?"

"Like a drum," said Jay.

"Nothing would make us happier," said Spadea. "The guy's negatives are high and he's a polarizing figure. But he's got eighteen million bucks in the bank and has a gun to the head of every lobbyist in town. It's a shake-down operation. No one wants to cross him because they know he plays dirty."

"That can be turned into a liability," said Thomas. "Washington insider, pay-to-play, corrupt deals."

Cartwright and Spadea nodded, their facial expressions telegraphing skepticism.

"You know, it's funny," said Cartwright. "I've always had a good relationship with Sal. Sure, he helped my opponent in the gubernatorial race, but he didn't like him, so he only did what he had to. He called me the morning after the election and said, 'Whatever you need for New Jersey, I'm a phone call away.' I can't say this publicly, but we've had a good working relationship for the most part."

"I'm glad somebody does," deadpanned Jay. "We sure don't."

"That's all about the presidential race," said Spadea.

"He can't let it go," added Thomas.

"We can beat him," said Jay. "He's seen as partisan. He's badly wounded after failing to stop Marco Diaz's nomination to the Supreme Court. If Mike Kaplan is convicted, his senior advisor will be going to prison." He popped a saltine cracker in his mouth, chewing it vigorously. "Besides, I've got the perfect candidate to run against him."

"Really? Who?" asked Cartwright.

"You."

Cartwright nearly spewed out chicken soup. Spadea visibly flinched. "Whoa, hold on a minute!" exclaimed Cartwright. "I'm running for reelection as governor."

"Why? You've already done that. You've got nothing left to prove," replied Jay with what was clearly a rehearsed line. "If you're reelected governor, you'll serve a second term and fade into the woodwork, your popularity declining by the day. But if you beat Sal Stanley and go to the U.S. Senate . . . well, you'll be a rock star."

"The voters will understand," said Thomas reassuringly. "They don't lose a governor, they gain a senator and a national figure. It's kind of like when your daughter gets married. You don't lose a daughter. You gain a son-in-law."

"I don't know if I want to be a senator," stammered Cartwright. "I've got the only job in politics I always wanted."

Jay leaned forward, his eyes locking on his target. "Governor, with all due respect, this isn't about you. It's about the country. You can beat Stanley. And when you do, you'll be a giant killer. You'll headline fund-raisers from coast to coast. I'm not asking you to say yes today. I'm asking you to think about it."

Cartwright stared back. He swallowed. "I'll think about it. But I don't want to give you any false encouragement."

"I don't need any, false or otherwise," volleyed Jay.

There were three quick raps on the door, and Jay's assistant appeared wearing an anxious expression on her face. "Jay, Charlie Hector needs to speak with you. You can take it here."

Jay picked up the receiver on a house phone on the credenza. "Charlie?"

"Jay, I'm afraid I have some sad news. Perry Miller was just found dead in a Georgetown apartment."

"What? How?"

"We don't know all the details yet, but it looks like a sexual encounter that went terribly awry. We just got the heads-up from the FBI."

Jay bent over, leaning on the credenza, absorbing the news. "Thanks for letting me know. I'm in the mess with Governor Cartwright. I'll call you back when I get out of this meeting." He hung up the phone.

"What was that?" asked Thomas.

"Oh, nothing," Jay lied. "Charlie just needed to check in on something." Before he could retake his seat, the phone rang again. Jay screwed up his face. "What is this, Grand Central Station?" he asked. He picked up the receiver. "Yes. Yes. Alright, we'll be right down." He placed the phone down and turned to Cartwright. "Want to see the president?"

"Sure," said Cartwright, oozing anticipation.

They left lunch half eaten and headed up the stairs and through the West Wing lobby on their way to the Oval. Jay walked shoulder to shoulder with Cartwright, who moved with a spring in his step. Jay's mind was already elsewhere, specifically Florida. A thought rattled around in his brain: with a little luck they might be able to pick up the Senate seat vacated by the death of Perry Miller.

N ews of Perry Miller's death rocketed across DC within minutes. Details were sketchy and sordid, fueled by bloggers monitoring police scanners. Miller's body landed like a whale in the Internet slime machine. Merryprankster.com's headline was typical and lurid: "Senator Dead in Bondage Game Gone Awry!"

The dispatch's lead reported breathlessly: "In a capital where people thought they had seen it all, the death of Senator Perry Miller in the basement of a Georgetown apartment retrofitted as a torture chamber in what appeared to be a bondage game shocked official Washington." Miller, the powerful chairman of the Senate Foreign Relations Committee, "was one of the most respected voices on foreign affairs in the world. Presidents and prime ministers counted him an advisor and friend. Now he is dead, apparently the victim of accidental asphyxiation at the hands of a dominatrix he secretly saw as often as once a week." Married to his college sweetheart for thirty-seven years, with four children and nine grandchildren, Miller was a centrist Democrat who seemingly practiced family values in his own life.

Politicians of both parties flooded media outlets with statements honoring Miller's memory and mourning his death. "Perry Miller's loss will be keenly felt by a saddened nation," said President Long in an official statement. "He was a courageous voice for human rights and democratic values around the world who opposed tyranny in all its ugly forms. I benefited often from his counsel, and our country will miss his leadership. Today America has lost a great leader and a selfless public servant."

But these eulogies competed with tabloid condemnation. To many Miller's death was yet another example of a politician revealed as a fraud. "Perry Miller is the latest in a string of politicians who claimed the mantle of family and values but proved to be a phony and a hypocrite," said the head of far-left advocacy group People for the Separation of Religion and Politics. Beyond the Monday-morning, maudlin moralizing lay a stark reality for Democrats: Miller's death put in play a Senate seat considered safe by both parties. Who might replace Miller and whether they could hold the seat in the next election would have huge implications for whether Democrats could maintain control of the U.S. Senate.

SALMON P. STANLEY SAT IN the majority leader's spacious, stately office in the Capitol, its view of the Mall stretching all the way to the Washington Monument. But Stanley was not soaking in the view. He was bonding with Yehuda Serwitz, Israeli ambassador to the U.S. and one of the savviest operators in DC.

"Yehuda, you gotta trust me on this one," said Stanley forcefully, stabbing the air with his index finger. "Do us both a favor and tell your friends at AIPAC to back off. I don't need 'dear colleague' letters demanding the Iran sanctions bill be reported out of committee." He sighed in disgust. "When is AIPAC going to get it? This makes it all about the Jews. It's bad optics. We need it to be about U.S. national security interests."

Serwitz chuckled, unfazed. "So they're *my* friends now, huh? Last time I checked, they were *your* friends."

Stanley laughed. "Of course they're my friends, but they're still a major pain. I can get the sanctions bill out of the Foreign Relations Committee and on the floor next week. What I need are your friends in the Jewish community to tell the Republicans not to offer a bunch of amendments authorizing a military strike or war. If everyone acts like adults, I can pass it in a day by unanimous consent and get it out of conference committee in two weeks."

"That's outstanding, Senator," cooed Serwitz. "I'll tell the prime minister."

"You do that. Give her my best. And make sure the heavy hitters in the Jewish community know I *personally* got this done. I've got a tough campaign coming up, and I need them on my team."

"You really think you'll have a difficult reelect?" asked Serwitz, surprised. "I would think people in New Jersey like the fact their senator is majority leader."

"Depends on what day it is," said Stanley with no hint of irony. "I always run scared and like I'm behind. Jay Noble and Bob Long are coming after me with hammer and tongs. They despise me." He paused. "And the feeling is mutual, I assure you."

"Sounds like Israeli politics," said Serwitz. "Everything is a grudge match, and the long knives are always out."

"Welcome to my world, my friend. Thanks for calling." Stanley hung up the phone. Two knocks came on the door. In walked his press secretary wearing a shocked facial expression. "What?" asked Stanley.

"Sir, I hate to be the bearer of bad news, but . . . Perry Miller's dead."

"My God! How?"

"They found his body in a townhouse in Georgetown. The news just hit the wires and the Web sites. The cable nets are going live with it right now."

"What was he doing in Georgetown? We have votes today."

"Unclear, sir. It looks like he was asphyxiated in some kind of sex game that got out of hand." He paused. "We're going to need to get out a statement."

Stanley slumped in his seat. "I . . . I can't believe it." He paused. "Don't allude to the cause of death. Say something like, 'Perry Miller was a close friend and colleague for over twenty years. He always put his country ahead of party and principle ahead of politics and served our nation with distinction and honor. My heart goes out to his wife Mabel and their four children as we mourn his loss with them.' Something like that."

"Yes, sir. I'll get you a draft."

The door closed behind the press aide. Stanley walked to the large floor-to-ceiling windows overlooking the Mall, lost in thought. The Iran sanctions bill was scheduled to go to the floor the following week, and it would now fall to Stanley to select a new chairman of Foreign Relations. His mind raced. The next ranking Democrat by seniority already chaired the Commerce Committee, so he was out. The second ranking was a lightweight and a self-righteous preener. With war clouds threatening with Iran, might he have to throw seniority out the window and muscle in his own choice as chairman? It was not something he wanted to contemplate.

KERRY CARTWRIGHT LOPED INTO THE Oval Office greeted by the smile and extended hand of President Robert W. Long and felt his knees buckle.

"Governor!" boomed Long affectionately. "Thanks for coming."

"So good to see you, Mr. President," replied Cartwright.

Long, beaming, directed him to sit in one of the wingback chairs at the head of the sitting area. Jay Noble sat down on the end of one of the two cream-colored couches to either side, his elbow on a throw pillow, his eyes studiously focused on notes written on the legal pad resting on his lap. As he settled into the chair, Cartwright felt his heart racing.

"Did you hear about Perry Miller?"

"No," said Cartwright. "What is it?"

"He died. Looks like he had a heart attack."

"In the act," interjected Jay. Long shot him a look of disapproval.

"Oh, no," replied Cartwright, a stunned expression on his face.

"He was a patriot," said Long. "I just talked to him for the last time the other day. We were working on the Iran sanctions bill. Johnny says he was a first-rate, stand-up guy, one of the finest men over there in the Senate."

"He was a rare breed. Those will be big shoes to fill."

"Yes, they will. And that's what I wanted to talk to you about," said Long, his eyes boring into Cartwright. "The Senate needs new blood. Sal Stanley has turned it into a partisan instrument of personal revenge and is trying to destroy my presidency. Look at the way he handled health care and the Diaz nomination. It's a disgrace."

"Mr. President, he's never recovered from losing the presidency."

"I understand that. Who can blame him?" said Long. "The convention credentials fight, the Dele-gate scandal, Kaplan's indictment, the House election. It was tough for everyone. But somebody has to lose. You have to move on."

"We don't move on real well in New Jersey," said Cartwright jokingly. "We tend not to forget our friends or our enemies."

"Look, I bear Sal no ill will," Long said, not entirely convincingly. "This isn't personal. It's about restoring the integrity of the U.S. Senate. Right now it's being corrupted by Sal. The man has got to go. That's why you should run. You've got name ID; you can raise the money. And you'd win." He flashed a smile. "I'll back you 100 percent."

Cartwright shifted uncomfortably in his chair. "Mr. President, the fact this is coming from you means a lot. I have a tremendous amount of respect for you, I really do."

"But?"

"But I have the temperament of an executive. I like making decisions, not hanging around for roll-call votes until midnight. I've got the only job in politics I ever wanted, other than U.S. attorney."

Long nodded. "That's why you'd be perfect," he said, swatting away the objection. "Look, I've been a governor. I get it. A lot of people thought I was nuts when I walked away from the governorship of California to run for president as an independent." He smiled. "Come to think of it, Jay thought I was nuts."

Jay grinned like a Cheshire cat but said nothing.

"But in the final analysis this isn't about you or me, Kerry. It's about the country. You'll be an impact player the minute you get to the Senate. You'll be a national figure overnight by defeating Stanley."

"I'll give it full consideration, sir," said Cartwright noncommitally.

Long leaned forward until their faces were no more than six inches apart. "Have you ever thought about being attorney general?"

"Not especially," replied Cartwright, flustered. He glanced over at Jay nervously as if to say, *I thought I was here to get love-bombed for U.S. Senate.*

"I think you'd make a great AG. Or a Supreme Court justice." He tapped Cartwright on the arm and winked. "The Senate is just the beginning. The sky's the limit."

Cartwright squirmed in his seat, unsure of what to say.

"Kerry, this race is winnable. The partisan role Sal's assumed as majority leader is not playing well in New Jersey." Long turned to Jay. "What are his numbers?"

"Forty-five fav; forty-five unfav," said Jay, reading from the legal pad. "His reelect is forty-three; new person is forty-seven."

Long arched his eyebrows. "There you go."

"My job approval is 68 percent," said Cartwright.

"Trust me, we know," replied Long. Everyone laughed. "Sal's numbers are only going to get worse once Kaplan goes on trial. The headlines are going to be ugly."

"You're a good salesman, Mr. President," said Cartwright, swallowing hard. "I like what I hear. I'd like to talk to my wife before I make a decision."

"Sure, of course," said Long with fatherly concern. "I tell candidates they shouldn't run without the approval of their spouse or their employer. The first time I thought running for president as an independent was possible was when Claire said she thought I should do it."

Jay smiled knowingly.

"I'm honored by your confidence," replied Cartwright.

"If you jump in, we'll put together fund-raisers in California and every major city in the country. We've got thirty-two million e-mail addresses and cell phone numbers. They'll all be at your disposal."

Cartwright's eyes widened. "That would be great!" he exclaimed.

"Plus our 527 and c4," offered Jay, the first time he spoke without being spoken to first. "This will be our highest national priority."

"All of the above," said Long. He rose from his chair and guided Cartwright to the door. "I hope you do it, Kerry. You'll be glad you did." He shot Jay a wink. Cartwright got the feeling he was not the only U.S. Senate prospect being tag-teamed by Jay and the president. He wondered: if he ran and won, would he be able to get a set of those special presidential cuff links Long gave only to his closest friends? He hoped so.

FBI SPECIAL AGENT PATRICK MAHONEY stood in the foyer of the redbrick townhouse on M Street and watched the controlled chaos of a crime scene investigation unfold under his watchful eye. Mahoney didn't look like the typical clean-cut, well put-together FBI guy. He was thick around the middle, a shock of black hair combed above a pale face, with deep blue eyes and beetle eyebrows that darted when he talked. He could pass for a street cop, but appearances were deceiving, for Mahoney was one of the best agents in the Bureau. Which is why when the body in the townhouse turned out to belong to Perry Miller, he got the call.

Roadblocks were placed a block in either direction, snarling traffic. Bomb squad units with dogs checked every car, checking the undersides of the chassis of each vehicle with mirrors. Ten FBI vehicles and an equal number of DC police squad cars lined the street. A dozen federal agents, including four in protective suits, scoured the building for evidence, removing items in evidence bags. At the end of the block, camera crews and reporters performed live stand-ups beneath television lights. Spectators leaned over the police barricades, craning their necks and gawking, hoping to catch a glimpse of precisely what was hard to determine. The sound of police sirens, honking horns, and barking dogs filled the air.

Miller's body was transported to GWU Hospital, where a team of forensic pathologists readied for an autopsy. Police interviewed the owner of the building and identified the renter of the basement apartment as a woman who operated a dominatrix service on the Internet. She had a rap sheet two pages long, including previous arrests for income tax evasion, cocaine possession, and solicitation. A federal judge approved warrants for her phone records, e-mail accounts, and a search of her home and computer hard drive.

Mahoney ordered a complete review of the phone numbers, e-mail accounts, and credit card transactions of every client. The body language of the higher-ups in the Bureau was not good. What was the point? Miller was dead, and whoever else patronized the service was irrelevant. The suits on the seventh floor didn't like investigations that veered off the beaten track—they called them "rabbit trails" within the Bureau—especially when it was likely the dominatrix service's client list would include prominent individuals with expensive lawyers and friends in high places.

But Mahoney was a grizzled veteran who played by old-school rules. If a U.S. senator was dead in suspicious circumstances, he wanted to know why. He stood with his hands in his pockets, a practiced scowl on his face, occasionally barking a directive. One of the other FBI agents approached.

"Tell me something I don't already know," grunted Mahoney.

"We found the girl who saw Miller," said the agent. "DC cops just picked her up."

"And?"

"It's bizarre," replied the agent. "She's the girl next door: Phi Beta Kappa, UCLA undergrad, second year at Georgetown law. Law student by night, dominatrix by day. Grew up in southern California. Apparently she's been in the business for four years."

Mahoney shook his head. "It just doesn't add up."

"You mean golden girl lawyer in training murders prominent senator?"

Mahoney shrugged. "I don't know . . . it doesn't fit."

"She's got an attorney and she's been Mirandized. So I don't know how much help she'll be."

"She'll talk. Either that or she'll walk the plank on a second-degree murder charge. No amount of daddy's money will save her from a DC jury."

"Her lawyer told police Miller was a regular customer of hers. She claims he was alive when she last saw him."

"We'll know soon enough based on the autopsy whether she's telling the truth. But parts of this don't add up," said Mahoney.

"What do you mean?"

"He's got bruises all over his body."

"So?"

"Miller's married. The sex workers don't leave marks on married clients because at night they go home to their wives."

"Maybe she lost control."

"Maybe. But she's a pro. And even if she did kill him, she didn't have to beat him up. The guy was tied up. All she had to do was choke him to death. And these bruises were made before he died. Why?"

"I don't know."

"Look at this place. It looks like your grandmother lives here. Nothing out of place, nothing stolen or missing, clothes neatly folded, no sign of a struggle, no clothing hurriedly discarded. That's odd, given how he supposedly died."

"So what are you saying?"

"I'm saying maybe someone wanted him dead."

"Who?"

"Lots of people. Terrorists, hate groups, Islamic extremists, the mob, any number of people. If someone wanted him dead and they knew he was a client here, they could have killed him and brought his body back here and everyone would assume he died at the hands of someone else."

"Like our Girl Scout in leather."

"Exactly."

"Good luck selling that to a DA. What's next? Shots fired from a grassy knoll. . . . Lee Harvey Oswald worked for the Russians?"

"That was LBJ, not the Russians," said Mahoney with a sly smile. "I'm just asking questions. And so far I'm not finding answers."

"DOJ doesn't like it when there are questions with no answers."

"Neither do I."

Mahoney walked back out on the front porch and looked down the street. He suspected someone (or something?) far more sinister than a twenty-four-year-old Georgetown law student was behind the death of Perry Miller. But who? Before Mahoney could pursue his hunch, he needed to convince the suits in the Bureau. To do that, he would need a powerful ally, . . . and he thought he knew where to find one.

3

Governor Mike Birch sat on the back terrace of the Governor's Mansion in Tallahassee sipping black coffee from bone china as he surveyed his fourth newspaper of the day. He spooned granola and strawberries from a bowl and occasionally sucked a soy milk protein shake through a straw. Birch consumed as much protein a day as a body builder. He had the metabolism of a hummingbird and the daily carbohydrate intake of a runway model. He read the *Miami Herald*, *Orlando Sentinel*, the *St. Petersburg Times,* and the *New York Times* each morning and also scanned news Web sites and political blogs incessantly. He was primarily interested in stories about himself, and today there was no shortage of them. Everyone wanted to know who he would appoint to the Senate seat made vacant by the death of Perry Miller.

With closely cropped silver hair, a deep tan, and penetrating black eyes, he had the wiry build of a marathon runner. He recently declined Bob Long's offer to serve on the U.S. Supreme Court, thoroughly embarrassing Long in the process. Birch then supported

Diaz—the Hispanic vote was the golden ticket of Florida politics. Widely considered the front-runner for the Republican nomination for president, Birch prepared for a general election contest pitting him against Long and an as-yet-to-be-determined Democratic nominee.

Which was why he was stunned when a butler appeared holding a phone. "Governor, President Long is on the line."

Birch dropped the newspaper and raised his chin, snapping off his reading glasses. "Well, what do you know. I wonder what he's offering me this time." The two had not spoken since the icy call in which Birch rejected the Supreme Court appointment. He picked up the receiver.

"THIS IS MIKE BIRCH."

"Mike, Bob Long," said the president.

"Mr. President, good to hear from you. To what do I owe this honor?"

"The honor's all mine, Mike," said Long smoothly. "I only wish the circumstances were better. I'm referring of course to Perry Miller dying."

"Everyone's in shock down here, Mr. President," said Birch. "Not just by the suddenness of his death but by the circumstances. I'm still trying to wrap my mind around it. The guy was a Boy Scout."

"I know," said Long, tiptoeing around the elephant in the room. "He was leading the charge on the Iran sanctions bill, which may be our last chance to avoid a military conflict with Iran. I don't know who can fill Perry's shoes."

An awkward silence ensued, which Birch declined to fill. Long continued: "As with me when Peter Corbin Franklin died, you've got a big decision to make, my friend. I don't envy you."

"Yes, I do. Of course in the case of Franklin, the House started the process of replacing him before he was even gone," said Birch, twisting the knife, alluding to Speaker Gerry Jimmerson and the right-wing Republicans trying to impeach Franklin while he lay in a coma. It was a wicked shot—and a reminder of why Birch rejected Long's offer.

"Yes, well, emotions run high in the House, I'm afraid," demurred Long, refusing to be drawn into rehashing the past. "Anyway, I just wanted to tell you I'm thinking of you as you mull it over. If there's anything I can do to help, just let me know."

"Such as?"

"Such as discussing possible replacements—off the record."

"I appreciate the offer," said Birch in a hollow voice. "But in general I've found it's best to keep one's own counsel. Too many people talk. No offense intended."

"None taken. Are you thinking of appointing a placeholder or someone who will run next November?"

"I haven't thought about it. To be honest, I'm still absorbing the news," lied Birch. He thought to himself: *Long is shameless! He didn't even wait for the body to get cold.* "My plan is to appoint the best person and let him or her decide. At the end of the day, if I'm able to appoint a real strong person, it would be best if they ran and got elected because they'd carry their seniority into the new Congress. That would be good for Florida."

"Mmmm-mmmm," said Long. "Speaking of what's best for Florida, why not appoint yourself? I can't think of anyone who could do a better job than you."

Birch was floored. "I haven't really thought about it," he said curtly.

"You should. You've got the two vital qualities needed in the Senate. You're capable, and you won't caucus with Sal Stanley." He let out a wicked laugh.

"Well, if I were going to appoint myself, I sure wouldn't tell you," said Birch, chuckling.

Long laughed, shaking off the insult. "Well, I don't care who you appoint as long as it's a Republican. One less vote in Stanley's back pocket will be good for America. I think there's a chance the Democrats will lose control of the Senate. If they do, you'll be a hero."

"My concern is not to be a hero," Birch replied with false modesty. "My only concern is appointing the right person. And I will look at Democrats as well as Republicans, especially given the fact the voters of Florida elected a Democrat to the seat." He could almost feel Long recoiling over the phone line.

"I see your predicament," said Long abruptly. "I'm sure you'll do the right thing. Just wanted to check in with you. Good luck." He couldn't get off the phone fast enough.

"Thank you, Mr. President."

Birch hung up the phone and shook his head in wonder. Did Long really want him to appoint himself, thinking it might weaken him in the presidential race? Or was he just playing head games?

He picked up the phone again and quickly dialed the cell phone of Nick Furhman, his chief political advisor and sounding board on all things.

"Good morning, Governor," said Furhman, who was on his way to the office.

"Guess who just called me about the Senate seat?"

"Let me guess . . . Don Jefferson," said Furhman in a drawl laced with contempt. Jefferson was a famously ambitious wingnut from central Florida. It was an inside joke that Birch wouldn't appoint him if he was the last man alive.

"Nope. It wasn't Don, though I'm sure he'll be calling both of us soon."

"Okay, I give up. Who?"

"Bob Long."

"What?! Who's staffing his calls?"

"Apparently no one! It was one of the most awkward conversations I've had in my life. He was on his knees begging me to take his advice on the appointment."

"He's wetting his pants at the thought you might appoint a Democrat."

"Oh, it's better than that. He suggested I appoint myself."

Furhman burst out laughing. "Fat chance."

"I'd be committing political suicide. Which is why he urged me to do it."

"The guy's infatuated with you." Furhman was getting worked up. "What did you tell him? I hope nothing."

Birch chuckled. "Not a thing. I was very careful."

"I wonder: should we leak this? This is highly inappropriate, almost icky. I think people should know he tried to influence who you appointed before Miller had a decent burial."

Birch paused. "Let me think on it. Don't get me wrong—I don't mind burning him. I just don't want to get burned at the same time, you get my drift?"

"Yes, I get it. But I can feed this to Marvin Myers, and he'll be my lap dog for six months," laughed Furhman. "I can't wait until you announce the appointment. In a sense it'll be the first shot fired in the presidential campaign."

Birch hung up, turning it all over in his mind. Bob Long begging him to appoint himself was beyond comical. In truth Birch loved the attention, thrived on it, needed it like most people needed oxygen. To keep everyone talking about him, he intended to drag it out a bit. Yes, Birch thought, he would take his sweet time.

IN A CRAMPED, WINDOWLESS INTERVIEW room painted a bland, putrid green on the sixth floor of the industrial-looking, antiseptic Metropolitan police headquarters building on Indiana Avenue, a visibly frightened Amber Abica fidgeted in a metal-backed chair. She hardly fit the profile of a murder suspect. Demure and striking, with soft, jet-black hair that fell to her shoulders, she wore black pants, towering heels, and a clinging top. Her curvaceous figure proved irresistible to the police officers. A slash of ruby-red lipstick highlighted luscious, full lips, creamy white skin and sparkling blue eyes. Also present were her attorney, Patrick Mahoney from the FBI, Metropolitan police detective Paul Browne, and an attorney from the district attorney's office.

"Alright, just to dispense with formalities prior to conducting today's interview," said Browne, "Ms. Abica is here voluntarily and has been informed of her Miranda rights. She is not here under coercion and has not been tendered any offer with respect to any subsequent charges in exchange for her appearing here today. Correct?"

"Correct," said Abica's attorney.

"Alright, Ms. Abica, please tell us your current legal residence."

"417 Eight Street, NE, the District of Columbia."

"How long have you lived there?"

"A year and half."

"And your current occupation?"

"I'm a law student at Georgetown University, in the night school program, in my third year. I also work at Adult Alternatives."

"How long have you been in that occupation?"

"Four years."

"How did you first come into that kind of work?"

"I had a roommate who had a friend who advertised her services on the Internet. One night she came over to the apartment, and we talked. I asked her if the money was good. She said it was. She referred me to Adult Alternatives."

"You went there for an interview?"

"Yes."

"And you were hired."

"Correct."

"How many clients do you have?"

"Hundreds. But my regulars are about thirty." She seemed to bristle with pride. "I'm one of the more popular girls."

"How long had Senator Miller been your client?"

"I think the first time I had a session with him was last April. So roughly fifteen months."

"How did he first contact you?"

"Through the Web site."

The attorney from the DA's office made a note on her legal pad.

"Did he say what he wanted in terms of your services?"

"Role-playing, mostly. You know, playing nurse and schoolteacher. Sometimes we would reverse roles. He had me dress up like one of his staff members, and he would spank me." She paused as the men's eyes widened. "Over time he got more into bondage and domination. He became more willing to take risks and be adventurous. He was comfortable with me."

"Did he ever say why he wanted to avail himself of your services?"

She shrugged. "Men with as much power as he had like being powerless. When he was with me, he was my submissive, and I was completely in charge. It was a rush for him."

"I see," deadpanned Browne. "How much did he pay per session? Was it an hourly charge? Was there a set rate?"

"Five hundred dollars for an hour session. I kept half, the rest went to the service. He was a good tipper. He usually gave me a $250 tip, sometimes more."

"How did he pay?"

"Cash. Always cash. That's how most of them paid."

"Did you and Senator Miller ever have intimate relations?"

"You mean did we have sex?"

"Yes."

Abica turned to her attorney. He nodded. "No," she said firmly. "It wasn't about sex. It was about power."

The attorney from the DA's office and Browne made eye contact, seemingly unconvinced. "How often did you see him?" asked Browne.

"Two or three times a month. Less when Congress was out of session."

"Did you know who he was?"

"Not at first. But a few months after he started coming in, I saw him on television."

"Did you tell him you saw him on TV and knew who he was?"

"No."

"Did he ever express concern his relationship with you would become known?"

"No. He knew he could trust me to be discreet. And I was . . . until this happened. He was hardly the only well-known man I've had as client. I've had a lot of them."

"But none more so than him?" asked Browne. "Was he the most prominent client you had?"

Amber pursed her lips. "Perhaps." She turned to her attorney. "I don't have to get specific about members of Congress or the administration, do I?"

"I don't think so," said her attorney, leveling his gaze at Browne. "That hasn't come up in our discussions in preparing for this interview."

"Not at this time," answered Mahoney. "Right now we're interested in your relationship with Senator Miller."

"How physical were these sessions? Did you inflict pain?" asked Browne.

"Yes. He wanted that more and more. But I never hurt him." She looked directly into Browne's eyes. "I never hurt one of my clients, and I never would."

"Tell us what happened this past Wednesday."

"He came for a previously scheduled session. He changed. We role-played. I put him in restraints. . . . He liked that. I did the usual stuff."

"Can you be more specific?"

Abica dropped her eyes. "I whipped him. I spanked him. After the session was over, I cleaned up, and he went into the dressing room to change back into his suit. I left because I was meeting a friend for a drink. That's the last time I saw him."

"Was it normal for you to leave the apartment before a client departed?"

"No. But he was a longtime client, he knew how to let himself out, and I was running late."

Mahoney leaned forward. "One question: did you and Senator Miller ever play asphyxiation games in which he was temporarily deprived of oxygen?"

"No. We did plenty of other stuff but not that."

"Did you ever play asphyxiation games with other clients?"

Abica lowered her eyes, averting Mahoney's penetrating gaze. "Yes."

"How often?"

"Not a lot. Maybe a half dozen times. It's not my thing really. But if a client wanted it done, I did it." Her eyes teared up. "I did a lot of things that made me sick. I could tell you things that would make you want to throw up. It's not glamorous work, you know."

Browne resumed his line of questioning. "So the last time you saw Senator Miller, he was doing exactly what?"

"He was stepping into the changing room and I told him he could let himself out when he was done. I knew there were no more sessions scheduled at that location for the rest of the day. So I went up the stairs and left the townhouse."

"Do you remember what time that was?"

"It was twenty after six. I was meeting my friend for a drink at 6:30 p.m. I was worried I'd be late, which is why I remember."

"As you left the building, did you encounter anyone who could place you there at that time?" asked Browne. "A street vendor, a parking garage attendant, someone like that?"

"No," said Amber morosely. "I didn't drive so there's no parking garage. I took the Metro."

The prosecutor made more notes. "Metro security cameras might have captured her going through the turnstiles," said Abica's attorney helpfully.

"Don't worry," said Browne dismissively. "We know how to conduct investigations. Just make sure your client answers the questions honestly." He turned back to Abica. "Did you see anything or anyone out of the ordinary as you left the townhouse?"

"Like what?"

"Someone who might have been following Senator Miller or you."

"Not that I noticed."

"What was the name of the person you met for drinks?" asked the prosecutor.

"Daniel Blatt. He's a friend from law school."

"We'll want his contact information."

"Of course," said Abica's attorney. "We can get you that."

"Alright, let's take a brief break. Ms. Abica, you're welcome to use the restroom or grab something to drink if you want," said Browne. "We'll be back in a few minutes."

They left the room and walked down the hall in a single file to Browne's office. Closing the door behind them, Browne slumped in the chair behind his desk, rubbing his chin. The prosecutor stood in the corner, arms crossed, tapping the toe of her high heel on the linoleum tile. Mahoney sprawled out in a chair, studying his fingernails.

"What do you guys think?" asked Browne.

"Her fingerprints are all over the restraints, and she left marks on the body. There's no question she asphyxiated Miller," said the prosecutor. "The physical evidence is damning. I think we can get a second-degree murder conviction based on that alone."

Browne nodded. "I agree. She's got no one who can verify she wasn't there at the time of death other than this friend, who could be lying. Her alibi has holes in it big enough to drive a Mack truck through."

Mahoney rose in his chair. "If she was gonna kill him, why do it at the regular time of his appointment and leave fingerprints everywhere? And why not at least try to dispose of the evidence? She's a third-year law student. . . . She's taken criminal procedure."

"Maybe she skipped those classes," joked the prosecutor.

"You mean like you did?" chuckled Browne.

"She didn't act like someone trying to get away with murder," said Mahoney. "She left the building, met a friend for drinks, and went about her business. I think she's telling the truth: he was alive when she left the townhouse."

"That may be true, but the physical evidence is incontrovertible," said the prosecutor.

"Where's the motive?" asked Mahoney, throwing up his hands.

"Who knows, maybe she snapped," said Browne. "You heard what she said: the clients made her do disgusting things that made her sick to her stomach. Maybe that included Miller. Maybe he pushed her button one time too many, and she lost it."

"She's hiding something," said the prosecutor.

"Like what?" asked Mahoney.

"For starters, she didn't take the Metro because there's not a station in Georgetown. If she's lying about how she left the townhouse, she's lying about other things, too."

The three sat in silence for a moment. "So what do you think . . . should we go ahead and arrest her for murder?" asked Browne.

"No. Not yet," said the prosecutor. "If we do, we've got to present charges within twenty-four hours. She's not a flight risk. She's talking. We're still gathering evidence. Let her go."

"I'm good with that," said Browne. "Let's go back in there and see what else we can get out of her. She may hang herself yet."

They walked back to the conference room. But something kept nagging at Mahoney, and it wasn't just the fact no one could explain why a professional like Abica would leave marks all over Miller's body that directly implicated her. It was also that Miller was supposed to be the floor manager of the Iran sanctions bill the next week, with war drums beating in the Middle East. Suddenly he turned up dead. Mahoney thought the timing suspicious. He wondered if the same Iranian-funded terrorists who assassinated Vice President Harrison Flaherty in the previous campaign exchanged shoulder-fired missiles for whips and chains. He was going to find out, and he wasn't going to let a bunch of bureaucrats in the DC police department or the Justice Department get in the way.

4

Two thousand mourners packed into First Baptist of Jacksonville for Perry Miller's funeral, which resembled that of a head of state. The political establishment of Florida filled the pews, joined by three dozen members of the U.S. Senate, as well as numerous foreign dignitaries and members of the diplomatic corps. Three former secretaries of state sat on the front pew, including David Petty, the Republican presidential nominee who lost to Bob Long. With Sal Stanley in attendance, both men Long defeated were there to honor Miller's memory. Long was represented by Vice President Johnny Whitehead, Secretary of State Candace Sanders, and National Security Advisor Truman Greenglass.

The funeral had awaited Miller's autopsy, which concluded the cause of death was asphyxiation. Some who tracked in conspiracy theories claimed Miller was killed by terrorists. But leaks from the DC police suggested an open-and-shut case against Amber Abica, the law student/dominatrix. The only question was whether she would be charged with second-degree murder of voluntary manslaughter.

After a series of Scripture readings and the singing of hymns, Vice President Whitehead walked slowly to the pulpit. His posture slightly stooped, he walked in a determined gait, his white hair perfectly coiffed, his face stretched like putty with sadness.

"This week our nation lost a giant," said Whitehead, his voice growing firmer as he spoke. "The Senate chamber can barely contain the egos of its members." (Knowing chuckles.) "But such was not the case with Perry. He was a workhorse, not a show horse, never a self-promoter, a man who did not seek his own glory. He worked mostly behind the scenes. But when he spoke, everyone listened."

Whitehead gripped the edges of the podium. He spoke in a flat voice that nonetheless resonated with emotion. "We all have stories about Perry. This is mine: prior to the recent vote on the confirmation of Marco Diaz to the Supreme Court, the Senate held a private session in the old Senate chamber in the Capitol. Only members of the Senate were in attendance, and the proceedings were confidential. After various senators spoke their minds, Perry took the floor." Every eye in the sanctuary was on Whitehead. "Perry told us, 'We must never forget that we are Americans first. We must remain true to our beliefs as Republicans and Democrats. But more important than advancing those beliefs is doing so in a way that strengthens our country and our democracy.'"

Whitehead gazed out over the sanctuary, his eyes glistening. "I believe that would be Perry's message to us today. The U.S. Senate he loved and the country he served with such distinction will no longer have him to show us the way. But if his appeal becomes our calling, we will honor his memory and finish the work to which he devoted his life."

Andy Stanton sat beside the pastor of First Baptist in one of the thronelike chairs behind the pulpit, legs as large as tree trunks crossed, huge hands resting in his lap, listening intently. A former Golden Gloves boxer with a cherubic face and salt-and-pepper hair, Stanton was the godfather of religious conservatives, an unlikely eulogist at the funeral of a Democrat. But Andy was the son of a Democratic Congressman from Georgia and a former Democrat himself. It was one of the reasons he had few qualms about abandoning the Republican Party to back Long in the previous campaign. He and Miller bonded over their mutual support for Israel. When Miller's widow called him and asked him to speak, he never hesitated. As he approached the pulpit, everyone snapped to attention. Reporters leaned forward, anticipating news. How would the nation's leading pastor and religious broadcaster handle the death of the chairman of the Foreign Relations Committee in an S-and-M tryst?

Stanton's blue eyes surveyed the crowd. "It was my privilege to get to know Senator Perry Miller over many years," he began slowly. "We traveled to Israel together. We worked on issues of mutual concern. We came from different parties, but I learned the things we shared in common were far greater than the things that separated us." He paused for dramatic effect. "In all our countless hours of conversation, in meetings in his Senate office, on the phone, or as we flew in a helicopter together over the Golan Heights, I never once heard him say an unkind or hurtful word about anyone. He was an even better man than he was a politician."

He looked down in front of the sanctuary, making eye contact with Miller's widow and adult children. "I want to speak directly to the family. I know how much you loved him. Where the world saw a politician, you saw a husband, a dad, a grandfather, a friend. And I know today there is one question that echoes in your mind and soul: why?" He lifted his eyes, pulling the rest of the congregation into his spell. "Why? How could one of the world's most distinguished statesmen die this way? A life this great just wasn't supposed to end like this."

Not a single person moved. Silence enveloped the sanctuary.

"There are two answers to that question. The first is found in the book of Genesis, when man defied God in the garden of Eden. From that time until today, all of us on one level or another seeks to do what *we* want to do, not what *God* wants us to do." In Stanton's delivery, *God* came out as, "Gaaawd." "Some sins are known, others are not until after we are gone. But we are all sinners. We live in a broken world with broken people and broken lives. That brokenness is all around us, and today it takes the form of a flag-draped coffin."

Stanton rose on his heels, raising his arms to heaven. "But there is a second answer. It is the glorious answer, the transcendent answer, the transformative answer, and it is the cross," Andy said, his voice booming. "Life is broken without Jesus. Not just Perry Miller's life, but all our lives. Think back on your own life before you gave yourself to Jesus Christ. The pain, the hurt, the grief, the betrayal, the loneliness. We still experience heartache after we become Christians, but Jesus heals the brokenness, makes sense of our loss. He takes the broken shards of glass that are our lives and remakes them into stained-glass that reflects His glory."

Heads nodded throughout the sanctuary. "Amen," someone said in a low voice. The sound of sniffles filled the air.

"We can trust the Lord to do that when it comes to our friend Perry," said Stanton, his voice firm. "God used him to do great things. I believe He holds Perry in the palm of His hand today and has welcomed him into the bosom of Abraham. And for those of us who loved him, and especially to his family today"—Stanton again fixed his gaze on the family pews—"know that Perry is in a better place, and the questions you have will all be answered according to the timing and will of Almighty God." He paused, gazing down at the casket. "May God bless Perry Miller. We will miss you, friend." He bowed his head and walked back to his chair.

A woman sang the final song, "It Is Well (With My Soul)." Her voice filled the sanctuary, bringing many mourners to tears. After she finished, the pallbearers, two of whom were fellow senators, returned to the front of the church. They lifted the casket off its catafalque and carried it slowly down the center aisle. The Miller family rose from their pews and walked behind the casket, exiting the church.

SHADING HIMSELF BENEATH A PINE tree from the north Florida sun, Patrick Mahoney stood outside the church watching the crowd stream to their cars. His eyes scanned each face, looking for anything out of the ordinary. Nearby Governor Mike Birch held forth before a clutch of television cameras, saying something sappy about Miller. *What a grandstander,* thought Mahoney. Out of the corner of his eye, he saw Truman Greenglass, President Long's national security advisor, talking to someone. On a lark he walked over.

"Mr. Greenglass, forgive me for interrupting," he said. "I'm Patrick Mahoney. Good to see you here representing the administration."

"Wouldn't have missed it," said Greenglass, shaking Mahoney's hand. "Do you know Senator Leo Lubar from Illinois?"

"I don't believe we've met, but of course I know who you are. Good to meet you, Senator," said Mahoney, nodding in Lubar's direction.

"So are you a friend of the family, Mr. Mahoney?" asked Greenglass.

"No. I work for the FBI. I'm investigating Perry Miller's death."

Greenglass's looked as if someone had punched him in the stomach. "I see."

"I left a message with your office the other day."

"I'm sorry, I don't recall seeing it," said Greenglass. "Why would you want to talk to me?"

Senator Lubar stepped back. "Truman, I'll catch you back in Washington," he said, beating a hasty retreat.

"Checking boxes, mostly. We're contacting everyone who knew Senator Miller to make sure we're not missing anything. Standard operating procedure." Mahoney smiled weakly.

"That's a big job. Perry knew a lot of people. Is that why you're here at the funeral?"

Mahoney shrugged somewhat sheepishly. "Perpetrators sometimes attend the funeral of the deceased. They get a thrill seeing the suffering caused by their handiwork, if you will."

Greenglass looked surprised. "You're still looking for the perpetrator?" he asked. "But I thought the woman who killed him was already in police custody."

"She's a person of interest."

"So there are other suspects?"

"The investigation is ongoing," replied Mahoney obliquely. He shifted gears. "You worked closely with Senator Miller, didn't you?"

"Yes, I did," replied Greenglass. "He was a good man and a patriot."

"So I'm told," said Mahoney. "I'm curious given the unusual circumstances surrounding his death if perhaps there might have been a connection to foreign policy."

Greenglass pulled back. "Not that I know of. Like what?"

"Oh, I dunno. Iran, maybe Rassem el Zafarshan." The latter organized the terrorist cell that assassinated the late Vice President Harrison Flaherty.

"So you think you've turned up evidence of a terrorist connection?"

"I'm afraid I'm not at liberty to discuss the investigation," said Mahoney. "But I know Senator Miller sponsored the Iran sanctions bill. Supposedly it included a 'trigger mechanism' authorizing military action if the sanctions did not have the desired effect within a specified time frame." He moved in closer, lowering his voice. "I hear that language was drafted by your office. Is that true?"

Greenglass grabbed Mahoney by the arm and pulled him away from the crowd. "Listen," he said through gritted teeth. "This isn't a good time. I don't see what I have to do with any of this. But if you want to discuss Perry's murder with me, you'll need to clear it with the White House counsel. That's *our* standard operating procedure."

"I'll do that, sir."

Greenglass spun on his heel, two Secret Service agents in tow and lowered himself into a black Town Car. "Good luck with your investigation, Agent Mahoney."

"Let's do lunch," said Mahoney half jokingly as the car pulled away.

ANDY STANTON BURROWED INTO THE backseat of a Cadillac Escalade as the driver crept slowly out of the parking lot. Occasionally a dignitary or well-wisher recognized him and walked over to the car. Andy would roll down the window and extend a hand or sign an autograph. Accompanying him in the backseat was Ross Lombardy, the political *wunderkind* who headed the Faith and Family Federation, his grassroots lobby group. Andy's VP for public relations sat in the front seat.

"That was rough," said Andy to one in particular once they were on the road.

"I don't know how you did it," the VP fairly gushed. He was in full suck-up mode, which was his default posture. "I knew you were good, Andy, but turning the murder of a U.S. senator at the hands of a sex worker into a vehicle for the gospel message was something I didn't think was possible. There was not a dry eye in the place. Your message was *amazing!*"

Andy drank in the praise from his subordinate. "God is sovereign, brother. His hand is in everything, even tragedy." He thought a moment. "*Especially* in tragedy."

"Boy, Miller was the last guy on earth I would have expected to go that way," said Ross. "I guess it just shows you never really know, do you?"

"Ross, 'Some men's sins are obvious, reaching the place of judgment before them, while others trail behind them,'" said Andy, reciting a Bible verse from memory. "First Timothy, chapter 5, verse 24. Just make sure it doesn't happen to you."

"Oh, don't worry," replied Ross. "If I ever did, it wouldn't be the dominatrix who killed me. It would be my wife. You know what

I mean?" Andy laughed, slapping his knee. "Speaking of sin, I'm hearing Birch may appoint a Democrat."

"What!?" exclaimed Andy. "A *Democrat*? If he does that, he's dead man walking. He can kiss the Republican presidential nomination *good-bye*."

"If we have anything to say about it, he's dead man walking no matter who he appoints. He's a RINO. Totally worthless. I can't believe Long wanted to put him on the Supreme Court. We dodged a bullet there."

"Indeed," Andy agreed. "The good Lord spared us. Now we need to make sure Birch appoints an R."

"From what I hear, he's not listening to anyone. He's flying solo on this one."

Andy thought for a moment, watching the cars whiz by on the highway as they rushed to the airport. "Should I call him? I could offer to give him a little boost with our people if he does the right thing."

Ross recoiled in horror. "I wouldn't call him. Number one, you can't trust him. Number two, if it leaks you lobbied him and he does appoint a conservative, then people will claim he caved to the religious right. So we're darned if we do and darned if we don't."

Andy looked despondent. "So you're telling me with control of the U.S. Senate on the line, I just have to sit here and let it play out? This is in a state where we have how many members?"

"Four hundred thousand."

"This is nuts," Andy complained. "What good is it to have power if I can't use it?"

"Power is a little like sex, Andy," said Ross, a smirk on his face.

"You don't say," Andy giggled. "How so?"

"It's best done behind closed doors. Remember the love scenes in the old movies when they had to keep their feet on the floor? It's the same with power—subtle is always better."

"Perry Miller should have remembered that," said the ministry vice president, joining in the fun.

"Perry thought he could do whatever he wanted to as long as it stayed secret," said Andy. "That's the nature of sin, brothers. We don't realize God sees everything."

"Precisely," said Ross. "Your conversation with Birch wouldn't remain secret either."

"So what are you saying. . . . You don't want me to get in bed with Mike Birch?" asked Andy, his eyes dancing with mirth.

"He's a black widow." He leaned into Andy. "*Stay away.*"

"I don't want to get in bed with Birch. I just want him to appoint a conservative Republican to the U.S. Senate," said Andy. "Why can't I just tell him that?"

"He apparently already got that message from a higher source."

"Who?"

"Long. He called Birch the other day. Now Birch's people are shopping a story to the national media that Long tried to get him to appoint himself."

"No!" exclaimed Andy. "Did Long really do that? What is he . . . stupid?"

"A hundred percent. So when I tell you to stay away from the guy, I'm looking out for you."

The car pulled up to Andy's Gulfstream, its jet engines running with a loud hissing noise, the stairs lowered, a red carpet on the tarmac. Andy would use the short flight to Atlanta to plot how to get Birch to do the right thing. There might be another Supreme Court appointment and Andy wanted a Republican U.S. Senate. If they got it, there was no limit to the legislation they could pass and the judges they could confirm. He smiled at the thought.

5

Jay Noble held on for dear life in the jump seat of a staff van as the president's motorcade hurtled down the 110 freeway in LA at 85 miles an hour. He never liked how fast they drove, fearing it was only a matter of time before the motorcade was involved in an accident. The president was about to appear at a fund-raiser at the Beverly Hilton for his third-way independent political organization after a "message event" with small business leaders in Ventura. Jay's cell phone went off. He glanced down and saw the number belonged to Marvin Myers, the big foot syndicated columnist who struck fear in the hearts of his sources and terror in the hearts of his targets. Jay did his best to remain in the former camp.

"It's M and M time!" exclaimed Jay, using his handle for Myers.

"Hello, Jay," said Myers in his syrupy baritone. "Are you with the president in Caly?"

"I am indeed. We're out here vacuuming up the dough."

"How much will you raise today?"

"$3.8 million. But don't attribute that to me."

Myers let out a whistle. "Impressive."

"It is; $3.8 down and 250 million more to go."

"You're raising a quarter of a billion dollars just for the Senate races?"

"Yep," said Jay. "It's a different world, pal. This is not your daddy's political party. Between the 527s, c4s, PACs, the party committees, and the labor unions, we're going to have the first three-billion-dollar midterm election in history."

"Incredible," said Myers. "Actually, I'm calling about one of those Senate races."

"Which one?"

"Florida."

"We're staying away from that one . . . for now."

"That's not what I'm hearing," said Myers, moving in for the kill. "My information is Long called Mike Birch last week and suggested he appoint himself to the Senate seat."

Jay felt the blood rush from his skull. *Myers had the story!* His mind raced: *Who was leaking?* "Not true," he lied.

"Long didn't call Birch?"

"I didn't say that."

"Jaaaay, stop playing games."

"I'm not," Jay stammered. "What I'm saying—and this is on very deep background . . ."

"Feed the beast, Jay."

"I *am* feeding the beast," Jay protested. "Look, I was with the president in the residence when he called Birch," he said, embellishing the lie. "It was two days after the cops found Miller's body. All Long did was offer his condolences and say he wished appointing a new senator had not fallen to Birch under such difficult circumstances. That's it."

"He never said anything about Birch appointing himself?"

"He said something about how it was too bad Birch couldn't appoint himself because he was the most qualified guy for the job. It was a throwaway line."

"Birch took it differently. Suggesting a governor appoint himself to the U.S. Senate doesn't sound like a throwaway line to me."

"Come on, Marvin, the guy's running for president! He's using you to make us look bad." Jay shot forward in his seat, pounding the dashboard with the palm of his hand. "Do you think we'd be dumb enough to call Birch of all people and suggest he do something so idiotic? It's insane! Give me more credit than that."

"Calm down. But they did talk? You can confirm that?"

"Yes, but the characterization of the conversation you relate bears no resemblance to what the president said."

"Duly noted. If I do something, I'll say a White House official said it was a courtesy call."

"That's all it was. Birch is just trying to be more important than he is."

"So . . . who do you think he'll appoint?"

"Honestly, Marvin, I don't know. We're hearing all kinds of rumors. If he goes with a D, he'll blow himself up. I think Miller was the only Democrat who could hold the seat. Any other D goes in with no mandate, no money, and they have to face the voters in thirteen months. Birch knows that, so my hunch is it'll be an R."

"Who do you think is the strongest Republican?"

"A member of Congress along the I-4 corridor. It won't be Don Jefferson—Birch hates his guts. Birch loathes the legislature, so it won't be a state legislator. His LG is weak, so he can't go there. In the end, it's all about Birch."

"Well, it's working so far," said Myers, chuckling. "One more thing. The FBI is broadening the Perry Miller investigation. Word is they have the client list of Adult Alternatives and more shoes are going to drop."

"Spike-heeled shoes. Lots of collateral damage."

"Any names?"

"Nothing beyond rumors. How 'bout you?"

"Nothing yet, but I'm digging. And I'm not alone. The *National Enquirer*, TMZ, and Merryprankster are all over it."

"That doesn't end well."

"No. If you hear anything, I'd appreciate a heads-up."

"Heads-up!? Are you kidding?" bellowed Jay good-naturedly. "Marvin, I feed you so many stories I should share your byline!" Laughing, he hung up. He hoped the schmaltz and lies limited the damage from the president's ill-advised call to Birch. He wondered how Long could have done something so dumb. For the moment he had bigger worries. He hoped no one in the administration turned up on the client list. Jay shuddered at the thought.

PATRICK MAHONEY STEPPED INTO THE guardhouse on the Pennsylvania Avenue side of the White House, slipping off his FBI identification and sliding it under the Plexiglas window to the officer. He lifted his coat, revealing his FBI-issued .38 revolver. The officer looked over the ID and nodded.

"He's good," he said to the other officer working the metal detector.

Mahoney walked through the metal detector and strolled up the driveway toward the West Wing lobby. A guard opened the door. White House deputy counsel Maureen McConnell was waiting for him.

"Agent Mahoney, welcome," said McConnell. A former JAG officer, McConnell had short, wavy brown hair, intense eyes staring out from behind rimless glasses, a pug nose, and a sharp jaw. She exuded the efficiency and discipline of a reform-school headmaster. "Mr. Battaglia sends his regards. He's sorry he couldn't join us."

Sure he is, thought Mahoney.

McConnell led Mahoney across the alley to the Eisenhower Executive Office Building. As she walked down the shiny green-and-white linoleum floor, her heels clicked on the tiles. They rounded a corner, and she opened the door to an unmarked conference room.

Truman Greenglass stepped forward and shook Mahoney's hand, their eyes locking. With a compact build and a shock of dark hair, Greenglass's five-o'clock shadow and pale skin were the most visible signs of the stress and exhaustion of his job. Seated at the table in a dark gray pinstripe suit and Charvet custom shirt and silk tie was Walter Shapiro, one of the top criminal lawyers in the nation. No stranger to the FBI, he most recently represented G. G. Hoterman in the Dele-gate scandal, helping the uber-lobbyist avoid indictment.

Smart, thought Mahoney to himself when he saw Shapiro.

"Just to make sure we're all clear on who's who, Walt is representing Truman in his personal capacity," said McConnell. "I represent the White House."

"That's what I assumed, but thanks for the clarification." He smiled weakly. "Sorry to be the cause of so much lawyering."

"No apology necessary," said Shapiro with a chuckle. "The FBI helped me put three kids through college. So on behalf of my wife and children, thank you."

"You're welcome," replied Mahoney, laughing. "Shall we get started?"

"The floor is yours," said McConnell, leveling her gaze.

"I'm here to ask questions related to the FBI's investigation of Perry Miller's death. While there is some evidence pointing to his being killed by an employee of Adult Alternatives, we are pursuing every possible lead." He paused. "That includes the senator's professional responsibilities. Mr. Greenglass is not a subject or a target at this time. He is considered a witness. We hope he can help us understand Senator Miller's work as chairman of the Senate Foreign Relations Committee."

"At the president's direction, every member of the EOP will cooperate fully," replied McConnell, using the acronym for Executive Office of the President.

Mahoney pulled out a legal pad from his satchel and placed it on the table. It already held series of written notations. "First, Mr. Greenglass, on the Iran sanctions legislation. We understand you requested and Senator Miller agreed to a trigger mechanism that authorized military action in the event the sanctions failed to disarm Iran's nuclear weapons program. Is that correct?"

"Not entirely."

"Okay, can you educate me on the Iran sanctions bill?"

"Well, the bill is still in the committee, so the process is underway," said Greenglass officiously. "The chairman's mark included language stating the NSC would report to the president and the DNI would report to Congress within twelve months on the efficacy of the sanctions," said Greenglass. "So it was NSC *and* the DNI."

"DNI being Director of National Intelligence. What about the trigger mechanism?"

"I would not use that phrase."

"What phrase would you use?"

"If NSC and the DNI concluded the sanctions hadn't ended Iran's nuclear weapons program, the president was authorized to take additional measures to render it inoperable."

"Including military action?"

"It did not specify. But all options are on the table."

"Who drafted the legislative language?"

"We drafted it and provided it to the committee."

"Who actually wrote it?"

"Excuse me," growled Shapiro, his lips pressed into a thin line, fingers fidgeting, the jowly flesh under his neck vibrating with anger. "Is this a seminar on how a bill becomes a law, or are we trying to solve a murder here?"

Mahoney shot Shapiro a withering look. "Miller was killed the week before he was to bring the Iran sanctions bill to the floor. We're looking into whether there's a connection."

"Fair enough. But what does that have to do with my client?"

"I think that will become apparent in fairly short order if I can ask questions without being interrupted," said Mahoney, his eyes smoldering.

"I'm not here for the fun of it, Agent Mahoney," fired back Shapiro. "I'm here to represent my client."

"It's okay, Walter," said Greenglass. "I've got no problem answering."

"Who else knew about the existence of this language besides you and Senator Miller?"

"The president, Candace Sanders, Bill Jacobs at CIA, and the ranking Republican on Foreign Relations. That's it."

"Were you hoping no one found out about it until you had the votes to pass it?"

Greenglass leaned back in his chair and sighed. "No. But we didn't want it out there until we had everyone in the administration on board."

"And did you?"

"For the most part, some more than others," said Greenglass with a wry smile.

Mahoney reached into his satchel and pulled a sheet of Xerox paper containing a newspaper clipping. "Have you seen this article before?"

Greenglass scanned the page. "Yes."

"It's a report in a German newspaper claiming you told the German ambassador it was too late for sanctions to work and the U.S. was preparing to take military action," said Mahoney. "It says Senator Miller agreed and that is why he planned to include language authorizing military action in the sanctions bill."

"Obviously we were not happy about this article."

"At the time it appeared, Lisa Robinson was asked about it during a White House press briefing. She denied it. But you're telling me today it was accurate?"

"Not every detail, but yes, it was essentially accurate."

"This report ran two weeks before Senator Miller was killed."

"Are you suggesting someone murdered Miller because he supported military action against Iran?" asked McConnell, incredulous.

"I'm just asking questions," said Mahoney, his eyes unblinking.

"To what end?" volleyed back McConnell. "You're weaving a theory that someone killed Miller to stop the Iran sanctions bill. But the bill is going to pass anyway, so that theory is not supported by the facts. Moreover, the president needs no legislative authority to take military action against Iran. It is inherent in his powers as commander in chief."

"Thanks for the primer," deadpanned Mahoney.

"Agent Mahoney, I don't have a problem answering these questions," said Greenglass, trying to diffuse the situation. "But we knew the authorization would be hotly debated in the Senate. We weren't trying to hide anything. This is no state secret."

"Then why did the NSC mislead the president's press secretary and cause her to lie to the press and the American people?" fired back Mahoney.

Greenglass averted his eyes. "We never denied I had a conversation with the German ambassador expressing my concern about whether there was enough time left for sanctions. We denied we were readying plans for military strikes. The reason for that is obvious."

"Let me ask you something else," said Mahoney, loaded for bear. "Last year's State Department budget included funds for an initiative to promote democracy in the Middle East. Are you familiar with that budget?"

"Yes."

"What is involved in that initiative?"

"A variety of things. Conferences with democratic and women's rights activists, training for human rights advocates, building a network of dissident leaders. Things of that nature."

"Does it include aid to the Green Movement in Iran?"

Greenglass shifted in his chair. "The Green Movement was included in the overall outreach to pro-democracy activists."

"How much of this funding went to the Green Movement?"

"The entire program was four hundred million dollars."

"And the share that went to the Green Movement?"

"I'm not sure the exact number."

"Ballpark?"

"I think it was between $125 and $150 million."

"That's a lot of money, isn't it?"

"Not in the grand scheme of things, but it's not peanuts."

"Do you know what it paid for?"

"Training, logistical support, infrastructure."

"Senator Miller inserted these funds in the State Department budget?"

"Yes."

"One person told us Senator Miller was infatuated with the U.S. providing support to the Green Movement. Did you find that to be the case?"

Greenglass smiled. "I wouldn't say he was infatuated. But he believed in it deeply, and he felt a moral obligation to support the Green Movement leaders, who courageously opposed the regime at the risk of their own lives."

"To the best of your knowledge, was any of that funding used for technology transfers or military materiel to the Green Movement, such as bomb-making equipment, night-vision goggles, satellites, cell phones, PDAs, and laptops?"

Greenglass made eye contact with McConnell. Mahoney knew a government official as seasoned as Greenglass would be familiar with 18 USC. Section 1001, which made it a felony knowingly and willfully to make a materially false statement to a government agent. As he anticipated, Greenglass blinked.

"I'm not sure I can answer that."

"Why not?"

"Because those activities are classified."

McConnell cleared her throat and jumped in. "Since this involves potentially highly classified information, I'm going to recommend Truman tell you everything he can today, and then let's hold the rest in abeyance pending an opinion from the White House counsel."

"That's fine. I've only got one more question," said Mahoney. His eyes bore into Greenglass. "Were the funds Senator Miller inserted in the State Department budget used to pay for black ops inside Iran?"

Greenglass looked like he had been hit across the face with a hammer. "My answer to that is identical to the previous one."

"So you can't answer it?"

"No."

Mahoney gathered up his papers and shoved them back into his satchel. "That's all I have for today," he said crisply.

"I'm not going to make any promises on the issue of classified information," said McConnell. "But I'll take it up with Phil."

Mahoney grunted his acknowledgement. Together, he and McConnell left the conference room, the door closing with a bang.

Greenglass looked at Shapiro, his eyes like saucers. "This guy's crazy."

"No kidding. Why do you think I jumped down his throat?" said Shapiro. "If someone at the FBI doesn't get him back in his cage, he could destroy a lot of careers."

"He could do worse than that," said Greenglass. "He's about to blow up a covert op. That'll get major assets in Iran *killed*. He could set us back a decade."

"What's so hard to figure out here?" asked Shapiro, throwing up his hands. "Arrest the chick who asphyxiated Miller, let her plead to involuntary manslaughter, she does two years in minimum-security prison, and this thing is *over*."

"Should someone reach out to Golden?" Greenglass asked, referring to Attorney General Keith Golden.

"Absolutely not," said Shapiro, horrified. "The media will claim the White House tried to obstruct an FBI investigation. That's a felony."

"But someone has to shut this down," said Greenglass. "Lives are at stake. The future of the Middle East is at stake, for goodness sake."

"I agree. But the person who steps up to the plate can't be you, Truman. Protect yourself."

Greenglass knew Shapiro was right. But he knew of someone who could shut it down. It would be dicey, but it might work. One thing he wasn't going to let happen was some rogue FBI agent unraveling the government's top secret strategy to bring about regime change in Iran.

6

The president's eyes were tired. It had been a long day, and he was jet-lagged. "Are we really going to do this?" he asked. Long sat slumped in a chair in the presidential suite of the St. Regis in Beverly Hills, the age lines in his face creviced, the bags under his eyes dark. The room was dimly lit, the curtains closed on orders of the Secret Service, who worried about snipers getting a shot at the president through the windows.

"Yes, sir," said Jay. "We have to win this seat. It's home cookin'. We've tested the top-tier candidates, and he polls the best."

"Polls, always the polls," said Long, sighing. "Alright, bring him in."

Jay walked to the door of the suite and opened it. In breezed Governor Macauley "Mack" Caulfield, who served as Long's lieutenant governor and rose to the governorship when Long won the presidency. Eager to please, with a lanky build, ready smile, and a male bouffant of boyish brown hair, Caulfield looked like he won the lottery.

"Mr. President, that was a *terrific* speech," he fairly gushed as he loped across the huge Oriental rug in the living room, blue eyes dancing. "Never heard you better, sir."

Long grinned. "I got in a few licks."

"The shot at Stanley was classic!" He glanced at Jay like a puppy in full wag. "What was it again? 'I know the majority leader calls me the enemy. I only wish he got as worked up about opposing al Qaeda and Rassem el Zafarshan as he does me.'"

"Do you realize only two of my fourteen appellate court nominees have even had a hearing?" asked Long.

"Outrageous!"

"Mr. President, I'm going to let you two visit in private," said Jay, backing out of the room on cue.

"Have a seat, Mack," said Long. "Pull up a chair." It was bonding time.

A White House photographer snapped a rapid-fire series of shots. As he captured the scene for posterity, the president and Caulfield caught up on political gossip.

"Any truth to the rumor that Peg Lipscomb is going to run for governor?" asked Long, eyebrows arched. Lipscomb was the former CEO of a Silicon Valley software firm with a personal fortune of over $700 million.

"She's looking hard at it. As you can imagine, the Republican Governor's Association is salivating because she can self-fund."

"Ego with a checkbook," said Long, waving his hand as if swatting a fly. "She's Meg Whitman without the charisma."

Caulfield chuckled. "We've already got an oppo file on her six inches thick. She's used undocumented aliens to mow the lawn of her mansion. She got fined by the SEC for backdating stock options."

"Really? I think you'll beat her convincingly. She's got money but no policy chops."

"Zero," agreed Caulfield. "She did the *LA Times* ed board, and someone asked her about how she could balance the budget and cut the state income tax at the same time. You know what her answer was?"

"What?"

"Lowering tax rates will increase revenue. She cited the Laffer curve."

Long laughed, slapping his knee. "That's great for a Heritage Foundation lecture, but it won't fly in Sacramento. Governors have to balance the budget."

"Don't I know it," said Caulfield, rolling his eyes.

Long crossed his legs, reloading. "Mack, I want to talk about your future."

"Okay," said Caulfield with a hint of reticence.

"Look, I know your inclination is to run for governor, and I don't blame you," said the president. "It's a great job. But I think you should keep all your options open. I think the country might need you in another capacity."

"Such as?"

"U.S. Senate."

Caulfield's face fell. "You really think I should run against Kate?" Katherine "Kate" Covitz was a former congresswoman and two-term senator. Married to a wealthy real estate developer, she was a prodigious fund-raiser and true-blue liberal, far to the left of Long.

"She doesn't even want to be a senator," said Long, sliding to the edge of his seat. "She traded her vote for a committee chairmanship. Now she votes however Stanley tells her to. She's checked out. Unless you're the sultan of Brunei, you can't even get a meeting with her."

"That's funny . . . I've heard the same thing from our people in DC."

"It's true. I'm telling you, California's only has one United States senator for all practical purposes. Kate's the third senator from New Jersey. She's *got* to go."

"But Mr. President, she'll have strong support in a Democratic primary," Caulfield objected. "She's got the feminists, the labor unions, the Jewish community, and the Latino community wrapped around her finger."

"I'm not talking about the primary," replied Long, his eyes hooded.

"What do you mean?"

"Run as an independent."

Caulfield looked like he had been punched in the gut. "Are you serious?"

"As a heart attack."

"You're about to give *me* a heart attack."

Long laughed. His fish about to jump the hook, he decided to put some slack in the line. "Mack, I know it's a lot to consider. Take some time to think on it. But the wave I rode to the White House is still cresting. People are tired of partisanship, career politicians, and business as usual. They want to throw the bums out. They want to tear down the system and start over."

"Kate's a tough customer," said Caulfield.

"I know, but she's the past. You're the future. You'd beat her like a drum."

Caulfield's eyes narrowed. "It would be the first really tough race she's ever had, that's for sure." He leaned forward. Long sensed he was ready to deal. "Mr. President, nothing in politics is guaranteed. If I ran, I could lose. If that were to happen, I'm assuming there would be an opportunity to serve in some other capacity?"

Long raised one corner of his mouth. "If for any reason you didn't make it, we'll come up with a Plan B. Frankly, I think you'll win, and my preference would be for you to be in the Senate. But if that didn't work out, I'd find a place for you."

A smile spread across Caulfield's face. "Glad to hear it. If I walk away from the governorship, I'd just like to know it would be remembered."

"You bet," said Long, signaling the meeting was over as he rose to his feet. "Give Charlie Hector a call and work out the specifics. Let him know your areas of interest. You'll be on our short list if this doesn't pan out for some reason." Taking the cue, Caulfield stood up. Long grabbed his right hand and pumped with both hands. He pulled Caulfield close, their faces inches apart. "You'd be a heckuva senator. Impact player from day one."

"Thank you, Mr. President. Coming from you, that means a lot."

Long walked him to the door, his hand gently on Caulfield's elbow as though he were guiding a quarter horse. "Give my love to the missus."

The door swung open. Jay stood in the hall chatting it up with the Secret Service agents.

"Jay, you missed all the fireworks!" joked Caulfield.

"Oh really?" asked Jay, playing dumb. "How so?"

Long put his arm around Caulfield's shoulder. "Mack has agreed to run for the United States Senate."

"That's terrific, governor!" exclaimed Jay.

"Well, not exactly," said Caulfield, stunned. "I think I said I'd think about it."

"Okay, you've thought about it," said Long. "Now it's time to say yes."

"I need more than five minutes to decide, Mr. President."

"No you don't. It's all about the gut." Long patted Caulfield's midsection with the palm of his hand. "When you know, you just *know.*"

Caulfield began shuffling for the door, trying to break away from Long's embrace. "I promise, I'll get back to you soon, Mr. President." He scampered down the hallway toward the elevator, a California state trooper in tow.

The Secret Service agent pulled the door closed, leaving Jay and the president alone.

"How did it go?" asked Jay.

"I worked him hard. I think he's 50–50. He's a governor, for crying out loud. It's a pretty good gig, and we're asking him to give that up for a wing and a prayer."

"We need to get him to a better place."

"He asked me about a consolation prize. I may need to offer him a Cabinet post."

"That's doable, don't you think?"

"Yes. It's a small price to pay to get the Senate."

"The truth is, he may not make it," said Jay. "But we can't tell him that."

"No way."

"Getting the Senate is about spreading the field. We need Stanley and the Democrats to have more seats in play than ours. We need them on defense."

"And tie him down in New Jersey with a tough challenger. If we don't take it to Sal, he'll spend all his time campaigning and raising money for other Democrats."

"That's why we need Cartwright," said Jay, nodding. "So if Mack doesn't go, what's our Plan B?"

"I don't even want to think about it," said Long. "My next choice would be Hector."

"That solves one problem but creates another. We need Mack to go."

"I did my part," replied Long. "You need to do yours. Get him on board."

"Yes, sir," said Jay. With that he turned and exited the suite. They had an early wake-up call, but Jay had work to do if where he was going next could be called work.

MAUREEN MCCONNELL KNOCKED ON THE door with three firm raps.

"Come in," came a voice behind the door. She walked in to find Phil Battaglia, her boss and White House counsel, coatless in a striped shirt and matching tie and suspenders, jet-black hair combed over his bald spot, studying some papers on his desk. McConnell was his star associate and protégé, a real comer.

"How did it go?" asked Battaglia, leaning back in his chair.

McConnell took the chair directly opposite his desk. "We have a problem."

"I know *that*," said Phil. "The FBI is in the White House asking about the murder of a U.S. senator."

"I'm afraid it's far worse than that."

"How can it be worse than that?"

"The lead FBI agent, Patrick Mahoney, is asking a lot of questions leading to classified information. I don't have all the facts, but it seems to involve a covert operation in Iran involving funding the Green Movement."

Battaglia wore a poker face. "What's that got to do with Miller's murder?"

"The FBI thinks the Iranians had him killed. They think the language authorizing military action against Iran in Miller's sanctions bill was the precipitating event."

"This guy sounds like Inspector Clouseau meets Patrick Fitzgerald."

McConnell shrugged. "I checked him out. Hard-nosed, no-nonsense, take-no-prisoners agent. He's got a background in counterterrorism. I'm just wondering if he knows something we don't know. Maybe the physical evidence is pointing him in this direction?"

"Give me the blow by blow. I need specifics."

McConnell opened her leather-bound legal pad and began to flip through the pages, reviewing her notes. "He asked whether or not the classified portion of the State Department budget provided military materiel, night-vision goggles, satellite phones, laptops, GPS, and other technology to the Green Movement."

Battaglia let out a long sigh. "This investigation is going places it shouldn't go. Believe me, Miller was up to his armpits in all kinds of things. The guy was like a shadow government. But even if the

Iranians or Rassem el Zafarshan or someone else was involved in Miller's murder, we can't let that compromise a presidential finding."

"But we have to cooperate."

"There's cooperation and then there's cooperation."

"What if the FBI decides to play hardball?"

"Two can play that game," replied Battaglia, his eyes unblinking.

McConnell felt her stomach tighten. It had never occurred to her that Miller's personal scandal and tragic death would land like a grenade in the West Wing. Up until now DC gossip centered around the client list of the dominatrix service, which everyone assumed included some big names, among them members of Congress. Now it was clear there was far more at stake, not the least of which appeared to be a top secret plan to bring about regime change in Iran.

JAY RODE THE ELEVATOR TO the rooftop of The Standard Hotel just off Figueroa Street downtown. It was just after 11:00 p.m., and he was meeting Satcha Sanchez, the Latino news anchor from Univision and "It" girl of broadcast journalism for a nightcap. A beefy security guard with a shaved head and beefy arms wearing black Prada and an ear piece accompanied him.

When the elevator door opened, a wall of sound and light hit Jay, causing his brain to go into overdrive. Spinning blue directional lights illuminated the rooftop lounge, hundreds of partiers in skinny jeans, hot pants, and minidresses sprawled across couches and lounge chairs, the *thump-thump* of club music filled the air. Waiters bustled to and fro carrying trays of drinks.

"Mr. Noble, welcome to The Standard," said the club manager. "Ms. Sanchez asked me to tell you she's on her way. She'll be here shortly."

Jay nodded. "Sounds good," he said.

"Allow me to take you to your table."

The club manager escorted Jay past the bar, which was jammed with dozens of partiers waving their hands, trying to get the attention of harried bartenders throwing bottles of vodka and gin. A DJ at a turntable bobbed his head as though in a trance, headphones wrapped around his head. A swirl of bodies bumped and grinded to the music. Jay followed the manager up some steps to the pool area, where a row of metallic red and blue egg-shaped containers with beds were stuffed with nimble bodies of both genders, their arms and legs entangled, lips locked. A group of young women splashed about in the pool in string bikinis, tossing a beach ball back and forth, absorbing the stares of male spectators. The place was a meat market.

"This is quite a party you've got here!" Jay shouted over the music.

"Best in LA," replied the manager with a sly smile.

They arrived at the VIP section, guarded by another security guard wearing wraparound Gucci sunglasses. The club manager lifted the velvet rope and escorted Jay to a back table with a couch and two chairs. A woman with dark brown skin in red shorts with long legs, black pumps, and a black top sat on the couch. She eyed Jay seductively.

"You must be Jay Noble," said the woman in a low purr, extending her hand. She wore a white gold and black onyx bondage ring and a yellow gold and black rhodium pyramid bracelet with multicolored diamonds.

"That's me," said Jay, shaking her hand. "Who are you?"

"I'm Satcha's friend." Jay took note of her brown skin, angular face, espresso eyes, and curly hair pulled back to reveal a long neck. "Let me buy you a drink," she said.

"Sure."

"What can I get you?"

A waitress appeared in a low-cut cocktail dress. Jay thought a moment and ordered a vodka on the rocks. He sat down and leaned back on the couch. "So tell me your name."

"Samah," she said extending her hand. "But all my friends call me Layla."

Jay shook her hand. He noticed how soft it was. Her skin was almost the color of caramel mixed with cream, with perfect white teeth.

"My father is Italian, my mother is Somali," said Layla. "It's quite the conversation-starter."

"Wow! Where in Italy? I just got back a few months ago from running a campaign in Italy, so I got to know the country pretty well."

"Cortona."

The waitress appeared, handing Jay his drink. "Here's to Cortona . . . and Italy and Somalia." They clinked their glasses and drank, their eyes never losing contact. "What do you do, Layla?"

"I'm in public relations," she said, leaning forward, her hand brushing Jay's knee. He felt a jolt of sexual tension shoot through him. He was supposed to be hanging with Satcha, but he found himself entranced by Layla. "Is that vague enough for you?"

Jay laughed. "Works for me. People ask me what I do, and I just say I'm a consultant. Or at least I did. Now I have to say I work for the president." He took a sip of vodka, which burned as it went down. "So my cover's blown."

"Well, you don't need to worry about that tonight," said Layla, taking a sip of white wine. "You're safe with me. So relax . . . enjoy yourself." She smiled suggestively.

"I think I'll do that."

Layla glanced in the direction of the dance floor. "Do you like to dance?"

"I'm not much of a dancer, but I can hold my own."

"Then let's dance." She grabbed him by the hand, their fingers interlocked, and led him out on to the dance floor, which was jammed. As they moved to the music, their bodies pressed against each other.

Thump-thump-thump.

He felt her warm breath on his neck. Then, suddenly, she wrapped her arms around his waist, their bodies swaying as one. He hoped no one had a cell phone camera.

"Are you having a good time?" shouted Layla over the music, her breath tickling his ear.

"Yes," said Jay over the beat.

Thump-thump-thump.

"You're so handsome. I don't know if it's your hair or if it's your eyes, or your nose, but there's something about you. You've got a perfect nose and beautiful eyes. Don't ever let anyone tell you different."

Welcome to LA, Jay thought. Apparently for Layla power was an aphrodisiac. Jay was willing to play along and see where it went. The song ended, and they walked back toward the table, holding hands. That was when Jay saw Satcha. She was sitting on the couch working her way through a blue-colored drink in a martini glass, checking her BlackBerry. As usual, she looked like a million bucks. She wore white skinny jeans, a form-fitting black silk top, and six-inch heels with white bows.

"Satcha! Layla was keeping me company until you got here," said Jay mischievously.

"Sorry I'm late, honey," said Satcha, rising to hug him. She shot Layla a mock dirty look. "Did you steal my date?"

Layla giggled. "I didn't steal him. I only borrowed him." Jay felt her tickle him from behind with her fingers.

"So tell me about the fund-raiser," asked Satcha. "You had a big day?"

"We banked almost four million bucks."

Satcha's eyes grew wide. "Not bad. Everyone knows you and Long are either going to take out Stanley or die trying."

"We'll either beat Sal in New Jersey or win the Senate back, or both. I think we have a decent chance of achieving both objectives," said Jay as he took a swig of vodka. "It just never ends. All we do is raise money. To the president's credit, he never complains."

"Is it true you're trying to recruit someone to run against Kate Covitz? That's the word around town."

Jay grinned sheepishly. "Perhaps. Perhaps not."

Satcha leaned forward, smiling. "So how is it that the strategic genius who helped elect Democrats for twenty years in California is now trying to defeat them?"

Jay laughed. "I've always had the same enemies," he said. "I've spent my career fighting the Democratic establishment. They were never for Long. The only difference now is I used to do it with Democrats. Now I'm doing it with independents and Republicans."

Satcha shook her head admiringly. "You're too much fun!"

"I still hate the same people. I'm just hating them from a different place now."

Layla leaned over and draped her arm through Jay's. "I just have one request," she said in a low voice.

"What's that?"

"Come with me tonight. Satcha can have you any time. But tonight I want you."

Jay looked over at Satcha, unsure if she overheard. Satcha just winked. Layla batted her lashes, awaiting an answer.

"So I guess I'm not going to get much sleep tonight," Jay deadpanned.

"I guess not," replied Layla with a wicked smile.

Jay wondered how in the world he was going to make the 7:00 a.m. flight on Air Force One. The advance guys would be picking up his luggage outside his hotel room in four hours.

T he most closely guarded secret in the country was the client
list for Adult Alternatives, LLC, the dominatrix service Perry
Miller patronized. Reporters hovered around the FBI and
the Justice Department like buzzards, working every source they had,
while tabloids waved cash in front of former employees, asking them
to divulge the names of their clients. All the networks love-bombed
Amber Abica's media-hound attorney, offering a prime-time slot for
her first televised interview. But Abica was for all practical purposes
working for the FBI, and for now the list could not be obtained at any
price.

In truth, there was no "list," just a series of digital fingerprints:
computer records, e-mails, phone records, credit card transactions, and
wire transfers. Mahoney and an army of agents pored through them in
the hope the clients might hold the clue to the Miller's killer, or killers.
All they turned up were the usual hedge-fund high flyers, traveling
businessmen, preachers, rabbis, and politicians.

That was why Mahoney nearly came out of his chair when he got the call about a client from one of his investigators.

"What have you got?" Mahoney asked. It was his normal conversation starter.

"I don't know exactly yet, but it looks promising," said the investigators. "We ran one of the cell phone numbers from the incoming calls through our databases. It belongs to a Saudi Arabian national living in Towson, Maryland."

"What about an e-mail account?" Mahoney pressed. "We need more for probable cause."

"Got it. This guy visited the Web site of the service and searched around. We traced the cookie to his Gmail account."

"Who is he?"

"Hassan Qatani. Single male, twenty-six years old. Here's the best part: he turned up on a watch list of individuals with known ties to Islamic extremist groups. His passport records indicate he spent time in Pakistan two years ago."

"Say no more," said Mahoney.

"He fits the profile. Highly educated, comes from a prominent family, his father was an influential banker close to the Saudi royal family. He came to the U.S. six years ago to go to business school and stayed. We can't tell right now what he's doing for employment."

"We know he was a client?"

"Yes," said the investigator. "Always paid cash."

"How long?"

"Six weeks."

"Does anybody remember him?"

"That's where it really gets interesting. He was a client of Amber Abica's. Saw her every week for five weeks, always on the same day as Miller. The day Miller died, he missed his scheduled appointment."

"Get a surveillance team over to his residence in Maryland," directed Mahoney, his adrenal glands opening. "Watch his movements. See where he goes and who he sees. Be ready to move in."

"Yes, sir."

"Do you think it's just a coincidence, or do you smell a rat?"

"Don't know yet," said the investigator. "We need to pick him up and find out known associates, where his money came from, review phone and e-mail records. If there's something tying him to Miller, it'll turn up."

"Yeah, well, a guy with no known source of income who drops $2,500 to get spanked had to be up to something."

"No question. If there's something there, we'll find it."

"Do it fast."

Mahoney hung up and rubbed his chin, his fingers scratching his beard, deep in thought. The suits at the Bureau were asking lots of questions about the investigation. Colleagues averted their eyes when they passed in the hall. People didn't like it when the FBI became the issue, and Mahoney's investigation was putting the Bureau in the crosshairs. As was usually the case, good police work might save the day. Mahoney sure hoped so. Because if this lead didn't go somewhere, he might be forced to shut it down.

Impulsively, he picked up the phone and dialed the number of Bing Williams, deputy director of the FBI, the number two person in the Bureau. He answered on the second ring.

"Bing, it's Pat. We may have a development in the Miller investigation."

"Talk to me," said Williams.

"We traced an e-mail account and cell phone from the client list to a Saudi national living in a rental home in Towson, Maryland. He's got known ties to Islamic radical organizations and suspected terrorist connections. He spent time in Pakistan."

"Okay. What does that have to do with the price of eggs in China?" asked Williams.

"He always paid cash, saw the same girl as Miller, didn't show up for his last scheduled appointment the day Miller was killed."

"Can you place him at the scene?"

"Not yet. We're pulling the video from all the cameras in and around the Georgetown apartment and doing a facial recognition search now."

"Let me conference in Art Morris at Justice," said Williams. Morris was deputy attorney general and ran DOJ on a day-to-day basis. Williams briefly placed Mahoney on hold, then came back on the line. "Pat, I've got Art Morris on the line. Tell him what you just told me."

"Hello, Mr. Morris, Pat Mahoney with the FBI. I'm leading the investigation into the murder of Senator—"

"I know who you are, Agent. What have you got? This better be good," said Morris. "I'm getting a lot of push back on this investigation."

"Our team just traced a cell phone number to a Saudi national with known ties to extremist groups who was a client of the woman Senator Miller patronized. He failed to show up for his last appointment. He hasn't been heard from since."

"I hope you've got more than that. Don't you think any man who frequented the service headed for the exits once a senator's body turned up in the basement?" asked Morris.

"Of course. But this is a questionable character who shows up out of nowhere, no known source of income, no job that we know of, and he's paying $500 a week for an appointment and going in right before or right after Miller every time. Where's he getting the money?"

"What do you want, Pat?" asked Williams.

"Full surveillance team to track this guy, total interagency cooperation, a complete data dump of every digital footprint he's left on the planet in the last six months, search warrant of his residence, and the backing of the AG. We need to flood the zone."

"Bing, what do you think?" asked Morris.

Williams paused, thinking as he tapped the keyboard on his computer. "He may be a one off, he may be tied into el Zafarshan, he may have had nothing to do with it. But even if he didn't, we ought to err on the side of caution. I'd say do it."

"Alright, you've got our full backing," said Morris, his voice clipped. "I'll alert the attorney general, and we'll give a heads-up to Charlie Hector at the White House. If this guy was involved, I don't want the president hearing about it on the evening news."

"Thanks. We'll report back on a real-time basis," said Mahoney.

"You do that, Agent," replied Morris. "Don't let him get away."

"Yes, sir."

Mahoney hung up and grabbed his coat, flying out the door and calling out to his deputy as he headed for the elevator. His deputy hustled to his side.

"Alright, listen up," said Mahoney. "I need a full surveillance team on Hassan Qatani, multiple vehicles, scramble a chopper if you have to. I need to know every Web site he's visited, every phone call he's made, every credit or debit card transaction he's made in the past six months. I want a complete list of known associates. And we need a search warrant for his rental house and vehicle."

The deputy walked beside him, taking notes. "We'll do."

"And get your hands on all the video from street cameras within a six-block radius of the Georgetown apartment. If you need a subpoena, get one."

He stepped onto the elevator.

"Where are you going to be?"

"The Justice Department. If this thing goes down, that's where the action will be."

"Should I call anybody and let them know you're coming?"

Mahoney smiled. "They'll know soon enough." The doors to the elevator closed and Mahoney was gone.

THE PRESIDENT'S ASSISTANT USHERED VICE President Whitehead into the Oval Office for his weekly lunch with the president, her pleated skirt billowing as she walked. Long stood in front of his desk, the silvery streaks in his brown hair more prominent than when he took office, standing erect in a tailored dark brown suit with a deep red Ferragamo tie, ostrich cowboy boots polished to a brilliant shine. *The man has gradually become president before my very eyes,* thought Whitehead.

"Johnny, my main man! What's the word?" asked Long. He was a sponge, always absorbing information, sucking people dry, searching for gossip, the more salacious the better.

"Fighting the good fight, Mr. President," said Whitehead. "Trying to keep Sal Stanley from destroying the country."

"That's a big job," chuckled Long. They walked into the small dining room off the Oval and sat down. A waiter poured an iced tea for Long, sparkling water for Whitehead. He laid down china salad plates containing Caesar salad. The president picked up his napkin and popped it open with a snap of his wrist, laying it across his lap. Whitehead let the waiter lay his napkin on his lap. The president tore into his salad, talking as he chewed.

"What are you hearing on the Miller vacancy?"

"Radio silence," said Whitehead. "Birch is holding his cards close to his vest."

"He's a snake," said Long, grimacing. "I called him to make nice and express my condolences after Miller's death. The guy tells the press I was trying to get him to appoint himself to the U.S. Senate." His eyes smoldered as he punctuated his words by jabbing the air with a salad fork. "That was a low-down, gutless, duplicitous thing to do."

"It's all about the next election for him, Mr. President."

"You think so? He's that much of a weasel?"

"Oh, he's running. As in right now."

"I think he was running when I offered him the Supreme Court seat."

"I think he was running when he was in high school."

Long laughed. Finished with his salad, he pushed the plate away. The waiter picked it up from the table and scraped the crumbs from the tablecloth with a metal scooper. "The guy has no core, no convictions. He's an empty suit."

"Totally calculating," agreed Whitehead. "Which in this case may coincidentally serve our interests as well. We need him to appoint a Republican who can hold the seat in November. That also happens to be in Birch's interest as he gets ready to run for the GOP nomination for president."

"You'd think he'll tack right to try to bring the social conservatives back into the Republican fold," observed Long.

"That's what I would do. But I don't think he can pull him away after the Diaz nomination."

"I agree. You know, these Senate appointments are complicated. They don't always go the way you plan them." Long paused as the waiter laid down the entrée, grilled salmon with sautéed asparagus. "Everyone who doesn't get it becomes an enemy. If you pick an enemy, your friends are mad. If you pick a friend, everyone says you appointed a stooge."

Whitehead laid his napkin on the table, ignoring the entrée. "Mr. President, I had a couple of things I wanted to talk to you about."

"Sure. Fire away, Johnny."

"The FBI came by here the other day and interviewed Truman Greenglass," said Whitehead. "Asked all kinds of questions about covert aid to the Green Movement in Iran. Truman begged off, saying it was classified. But we're between a rock and hard place because the counsel's office has directed everyone to cooperate."

"Why would the FBI be asking about that?"

"They've got a theory that Miller was murdered by the Zafarshan network, perhaps with Iranian funding."

Long's eyes widened. "I thought he was accidentally strangled to death in some bondage game." He shook his head. "Poor guy. I hate he went that way. What was he thinking?"

"The FBI thinks Miller's plan to include a military authorization trigger in the sanctions legislation might have made him a target for assassination."

"They think it was a terrorist operation?" asked Long.

"Maybe." Whitehead leaned forward. "The problem is if they keep turning over rocks, it will cripple our regime change covert ops in Iran. Between State and CIA, we're putting hundreds of millions of dollars into pro-democracy groups, including the Green Movement. We're doing technology transfers, military supplies, and black ops. If that becomes publicly known, it will destroy the credibility of the democracy activists and compromise sources and methods."

Long nodded.

"Mr. President, we can't let that happen. Let's say Miller was killed by Iranian-funded terrorists. We still don't want the Iranians to know that we know. If they murdered Miller, we can take care of that without it being publicly reported."

"If Zafarshan or the Iranians killed Miller, I'll make them pay," said Long, tapping the table with his index finger. "It'll be an eye for an eye."

"No question. Of course, they may be trying to pay us back for some of the people we're taking out in Iran."

"So be it," said Long with a shrug. "They'll find out they're messing with the wrong guy in me, believe me. The main thing is we can't have covert operations in Iran compromised."

"So how do we handle the FBI?"

"Someone over there in a position of responsibility has to know what's at stake. I certainly shouldn't talk to Golden about it," said Long. "Battaglia could."

"The problem is those two don't get along."

"Tell me about it," said Long, rolling his eyes. He thought a moment. "What about Jacobs? He could talk to the FBI." Long referred to William Jacobs, director of the CIA.

"Probably better if he talks to either Golden or, even better, Art Morris at DOJ. Let them handle it with an appropriate level of discretion. They've got career counterterrorism prosecutors over there."

"That's far preferable to a communication from the White House."

"Big time. We don't need a bunch of interrogatories from some Senate committee asking us who talked to whom at DOJ."

"Tell me about it. Stanley and the press would have a field day with that."

The waiter placed a slice of key lime pie with whipped cream, a lime garnish, and strawberries on the table in front of the two men.

"What are you trying to do, kill me?" joked Long as the waiter smiled. "Don't you know I'm trying to watch my weight?"

"There's one other thing, Mr. President," said Whitehead. "I need to make you aware of it in the interest of full disclosure."

"Sure, Johnny. What is it?"

"Well, sir, this is a bit embarrassing, but . . ." His voice trailed off. Long sat staring in anticipation, a bite of key lime pie suspended in midair on his fork. "I visited Adult Alternatives." He averted his eyes from Long's. "Not recently. It was a long time ago, five years ago. It was only a few times. I was going through a tough time and was sort of lost after I left the Senate. I guess it was a midlife crisis. I don't even know if there'd be a record of it. Hopefully, there isn't. I wanted you to know that so you didn't think I was raising this issue to protect myself, because I'm not."

Long put the fork down on his plate, stunned. "Well, Johnny, I appreciate you telling me. You've done the right thing."

Whitehead hung his head. "I feel like I've let you down, Mr. President."

"I don't feel that way, Johnny." Whitehead raised his eyes. Long noticed they were watery. "If it comes out, we'll deal with it."

"If it comes out, it's going to be bad," said Whitehead. "It could make it very difficult for me to continue to serve as vice president." He took a sip of coffee. "Mr. President, I'm prepared to offer my resignation."

Long was stunned. "Johnny, I think you're overreacting. Let's see how it plays out first. I'll think about it, but as of now I don't think that will be necessary."

"Should I just try to get in front of it by releasing a statement saying I briefly visited this service years ago, it's in the past, and I've moved on?"

"I wouldn't do that either," said Long firmly. "Don't hang yourself in order to pacify the mob. If I were you, I'd give a speech in which you basically say you've made mistakes in the past, you're not claiming to be a moral example, and express humility." He arched his eyebrows, admiring his own strategy. "Then, if it ever does come out, you can point back to the statement and say you publicly admitted to unspecified instances of falling short."

"I just wanted you to know in case it comes out."

"You've got no issue with me, Johnny," said Long, trying to reassure him. He put his hand on his shoulder. "I've got your back."

"I appreciate that more than you know, Mr. President."

The lunch was over, and they walked to the door of the Oval Office. Whitehead greeted the president's assistant and then headed down the hall back to his own office. As he walked, he felt his chest tighten, the butterflies in his stomach fluttering. He felt as though he might throw up. If and when it became known he was on the dominatrix service's client list, it was going to be a media firestorm; and the president's assurances notwithstanding, he knew he might not survive.

8

Ross Lombardy hung up his cell phone and turned to Andy Stanton in the green room of the Washington Hilton. Andy, who grew irritable whenever he was about to be in the presence of presidents or heads of state, chewed nervously on a throat lozenge, his blue blazer pinched at the waist, pressed gray slacks tapered at his black cowboy boots, salt-and-pepper hair coifed into a male bouffant. He pored over the text of his introduction, printed in large type so he would not need his reading glasses.

"That was Jay from the motorcade. POTUS's ETA is three minutes," said Ross.

"I hope he's ready," said Andy. "Because this crowd is loaded for bear."

"He is. I had a planning meeting with Jay and the speech writers to go over themes and language. You will like."

Andy's eyes danced with glee, his massive skull bouncing like a bobble-head doll. "Now we're talkin', brother," he said. A makeup artist patted his nose with a powder puff, touching up his hair with a blast of hair spray. "Enough with the hair spray," said Andy, swatting her away with the palm of his hand. "I'm one YouTube video away from being John Edwards."

"I'm just trying to get rid of the live wires," the makeup artist said.

In the hotel's cavernous ballroom, seven thousand screaming, stomping, shouting, and singing members of the Faith and Family Federation awaited the arrival of the president. He was the keynote speaker of the "America-Israel Solidarity Conference," an educational and lobbying conference sponsored by Andy's grassroots group, the leading Christian Zionist organization in the country. A country music star whose best days were behind him sang a stirring rendition of "God Bless America," bringing the crowd to their feet. They sang the final stanza more as a prayer than a lyric.

"God bless America! Land that I love/Stand beside her/And guide her/Through the night with the light from above!"

When the song ended, the hall went dark, and the crowd stood to their feet, clapping and chanting. People waved neon wands and American and Israeli flags. It resembled a rock concert more than a political rally.

"We want Long! We want Long!"

Andy and Ross could hear the roar from the green room. Suddenly, the door flew open and in walked Long, beaming, trailed by Jay Noble and Truman Greenglass.

"Mr. President!" said Andy effusively.

"Andy," said Long, clearly energized, his face and movements animated. He wrapped Andy in a bear hug. "Great to see you, friend."

"Thank you for coming."

"Wouldn't miss it. I'm honored to be here, really."

Jay stepped forward. "Mr. President, just wanted to make sure you knew Yehuda Serwitz is in the audience."

Long nodded.

"There are also a dozen members of the Senate and House," said Andy, his voice rising an octave. "They're here to show their support for the Iran sanctions bill."

"Make sure anyone in leadership or chairing a committee is added to my remarks," directed Long. "You guys ready?" He wanted to get the show on the road. An aide handed him a leather binder with the presidential seal on it containing his remarks. "Let's go."

They headed down the hall toward the stage, Andy and Long in a power clutch, the noise from the crowd wafting over them.

"Ladies and gentlemen," said an offstage announcer. "The President of the United States, accompanied by Reverend Andy Stanton, the chairman of the Faith and Family Federation."

Andy and Long bounded onto the stage to a loud roar. Long stood to his right on a tape mark on the carpet, acknowledging the applause with a bob of his chin. Andy beamed.

"Ladies and gentlemen, every now and again a leader comes along who is the perfect marriage of a man and a moment in history," Andy began as the crowd fell to a hush. "Washington after America won its independence, Lincoln during the Civil War, Franklin Roosevelt during World War II, or Ronald Reagan during the Cold War. We now face a similarly perilous time of both great opportunity and great danger. I believe the man of the hour is President Robert W. Long."

Loud cheers and applause.

"Bob Long is a man of courage, with moral clarity and conviction. As the United States and the civilized world face threats from terrorist networks like those of Rassem el Zafarshan, Hamas, and Hezbollah, state sponsors of terrorism like Iran, and the timidity and vacillation of the United Nations, we can say of President Long, as was once said of Esther, he has come into the kingdom for such a time as this." (Applause.) "My friends, please welcome our friend, a friend of democracies around the world, and a friend of Israel, President Bob Long."

Long pumped Andy's hand and leaned in, whispering something in his ear, then bounded up the steps to the elevated podium. Teleprompters rose as if by magic from either side.

"Thank you for that warm introduction, Andy," said Long as the applause died and people took their seats. Long went through the list of introductions of senators, members of Congress, and the Israeli ambassador, paying the obligatory obeisance to the Faith and Family Federation.

"Israel was founded, providing a place of refuge for a people who suffered for centuries from the persecution of pogroms, the bigotry of anti-Semitism, and the horrors of the Holocaust," said Long. "It was the fulfillment of a dream, one might say a miraculous fulfillment, that turned the promises of God and the predictions of prophets of old into a modern-day reality."

Long rose on his toes, ramping to his topic. "Since that time, Israel has been a beacon of hope and democracy in a region that knew only bloodshed and violence. Until recently it was the only functioning democracy in the Middle East, where tyranny, authoritarianism, and terror was the norm." He paused, raising his chin, signaling a rhetorical high point. "For all these reasons the United States has had a special relationship with Israel, one based on shared democratic values and strategic interests, and that relationship is nonnegotiable and inviolable."

The crowd leaped to their feet in a standing ovation that lasted a full minute. Flashbulbs exploded, recording the moment as Andy smiled with approval.

"Today one of the greatest threats to that relationship and to peace-loving people throughout the Middle East and around the world, is the pursuit of nuclear weapons by Iran, the leading state sponsor of terrorism in the world." Everyone knew Iran obtained a nuclear weapon, but neither Iran nor the U.S. would publicly acknowledge that fact. It was useful fiction. "Iran sponsors terrorist organizations like Hamas and Hezbollah, pays cash bounties to homicide bombers, funded Islamist militias that killed U.S. soldiers in Basra and Baghdad, trained terrorists who killed innocent civilians in Buenos Aires, and harbored and funded Rassem el Zafarshan, the murderer of an American vice president." The catalog of Iran's sins complete, Long moved in for the money line. "In the 1930s, some said Hitler's rhetoric was only for domestic consumption. It led to the West's surrender at Munich. If we allow the regime in Iran to threaten the world with nuclear weapons, fifty years from now those who survive the inevitable cataclysm that follows will turn to those of us who could have stopped it and ask, 'How could you have let this happen?'" Long stabbed the air with an index finger for emphasis. "We must vow together that they will never have to ask us that question."

The crowd rose to their feet in a throaty roar that rolled across Long in waves of adoration. They elected him! He would not let them down.

"The Senate has before it legislation containing crippling sanctions against Iran unless it abandons its nuclear weapons program," Long continued. "It includes an embargo on exports of refined gasoline to Iran, insurance of vessels traveling to and from Iran, loans by the Export-Import Bank to companies doing business with Iran, and banking and financial services to Iranian entities." Long leaned into the podium, his mouth closer to the microphone, raising his voice a decibel. "I ask the Senate to send me this bill forthwith for my signature. And if these sanctions have not had the desired effect, I ask the Senate to authorize my administration in consultation with other nations to take the necessary steps to end Iran's threat to the civilized world."

The crowd leaped to their feet yet again. A guttural, ear-splitting roar filled the ballroom. Long stepped back, nodding, basking in the applause.

Truman Greenglass and Jay Noble stood backstage in the dark, watching Long from the side. Greenglass looked on the front row and saw tears of joy streaming down the face of Yehuda Serwitz.

"Check out Yehuda," said Greenglass.

Jay glanced over. "I guess he's glad he's finally got a U.S. president with the kahunas to take on Iran."

"Yeah," whispered Greenglass. "Wait until he finds out if the sanctions don't work—and they probably won't—it's going to be the Israelis, not us, who have to take out Iran's nuclear program."

Jay looked at Greenglass and gulped.

A MOB OF REPORTERS WAITED in the rotunda of the state Capitol in Tallahassee for the news conference to begin. A podium was rolled into the center, a clutch of microphones attached to it. Beams of sunlight streamed in from the windows above, giving the cavernous room an ambient glow.

"Here they come!" someone said in a stage whisper.

Heads turned to see Governor Mike Birch strolling down the marble stairs, chatting amiably with another man wearing a blue suit, white dress shirt, and red tie.

"Who is it?' someone asked. It didn't appear to be one of the Congressmen on the short list.

"Is that . . . Dolph Lightfoot?" asked the *Orlando Sentinel*.

"Nah, it couldn't be," said the *Florida Times-Union*.

"It is!" replied the *Sentinel*.

Birch approached the podium with his arm around Lightfoot, a former governor who left office because he was limited to two terms. Lightfoot, sixty-nine, was a chamber of commerce centrist like Birch, no friend of either the Tea Party or the religious right. His appointment was guaranteed to send tingles down the legs of the press corps.

"Thank you all for coming," said Birch, wearing a satisfied smile. "When the Senate seat held for over two decades by my friend Perry Miller became vacant because of his untimely death, I thought long and hard about who would make the best U.S. senator for the people of Florida. Perry Miller was irreplaceable. These are big shoes to fill.

But I believe I've found the man who can fill them. Dolph Lightfoot was one of the most successful governors in the modern history of Florida. He has great experience, a remarkable breadth of policy knowledge, and he is a man of principle who is a consensus builder, not an ideologue." Birch looked up from his notes, raising his chin. "I believe he is the most qualified person I could have chosen at this time to represent Florida in the U.S. Senate. Ladies and gentlemen, please join me in welcoming U.S. Senator Dolph Lightfoot."

Lightfoot shook Birch's hand and bowed slightly at the waist in thanks. Birch gave an abbreviated bow of his own. "Thank you, Governor," said Lightfoot, staring out at the faces wearing expressions ranging from shock to disbelief. Most assumed Lightfoot was enjoying retired life and had no interest in running again. "Let me first of all thank Governor Birch for the opportunity to serve the people of Florida again. As the governor said, no one can replace Perry Miller, and I will not even attempt to do so. But Perry and I were close friends, and we worked together over many years. I will work hard to live up to the example Perry set in his time in the Senate."

Cameras snapped, flashes exploded, and print reporters scribbled on steno pads. "While it is too early to lay out my legislative priorities, let me just say my main concerns will be economic growth and job creation, especially in the area of trade and tourism, which are so vital to our state. Second, given the looming specter of Iran's nuclear weapons program, I will give high priority to national security. Assuming my appointment is certified by the secretary of state and I am seated in time, I will vote for the sanctions legislation currently pending before the Senate." His words echoed off the stone walls of the Capitol, giving them an apparently increased gravity. "I also plan to request a seat on the Foreign Relations Committee, where I can contribute to the ongoing issues to which Senator Miller devoted his life. Let me say to the people of Florida how deeply honored I am by this opportunity. I look forward to serving them and earning their trust and support."

Lightfoot took two steps back, yielding to Birch. "Any questions?"

"Just a few," joked the *Miami Herald* to laughter. "Governor, by appointing a Republican, you have ensured the Senate now has only fifty-one Democrats. The GOP will likely gain control by picking up only one seat in November, assuming Vice President Whitehead breaks the tie. Given the speculation surrounding your seeking the presidency in the next election, did this factor at all into your calculus?"

"I haven't done calculus since college," said Birch smoothly, cracking a relaxed smile. The reporters chuckled. "The short answer is no. This appointment was not influenced at all by partisan or political considerations. I appointed the best person to represent Florida in the Senate and that person is Dolph Lightfoot."

"Senator Lightfoot, what do you say to critics who say you're too moderate?" asked AP.

Lightfoot glowered defensively. "I was elected in my own right three times statewide, including governor twice," he said, jutting out his jaw. "I think that says something about whether or not my views are in synch with the people of Florida. They were before and I think they are today."

"But you previously criticized what you called 'the extremist wing' of the GOP," said the *St. Petersburg Times*.

"I think we need to focus on the issues voters care about. Right now that's jobs and economic growth. I recommend we declare a temporary truce in the so-called culture wars and focus on putting people back to work." Reporters scribbled the words furiously on their steno pads.

"Are you planning to run for a full term in the Senate?" asked a television reporter.

"I have not made a decision on that at this point," replied Lightfoot. "I will make a decision in due course. I believe Florida will be best served by the person with the greatest seniority in the Senate. So I would generally lean in that direction, but I don't want to make a final decision until I consult with my family and others in the state."

Birch stood to the side, beaming like a proud father. The brief news conference over, Birch put his hand on Lightfoot's back, and they walked slowly up the marble staircase to the governor's office, the press watching them depart like royalty.

"So Birch appointed himself after all," joked the *Miami Herald*.

"Now the only question is, can he keep the seat?" said the *Orlando Sentinel*.

"And if he doesn't, how will that affect his presidential run?" asked AP to no one in particular.

"If Lightfoot doesn't win the nomination and the general," shot back the *Herald*, "Birch's presidential bid is over before it started."

ROSS LOMBARDY CALLED ANDY STANTON'S office, where his assistant patched him through to the dressing room. A makeup artist was methodically removing makeup from Andy's face with a wet washcloth when the phone rang. The makeup artist handed the phone to Andy.

"What's up?"

"Guess who Mike Birch just appointed to the Miller seat in Florida?" asked Ross.

"Who?"

"Dolph Lightfoot."

"What?" exclaimed Andy. "The guy's a dinosaur."

"Totally. And a RINO."

"It's unbelievable. Birch just doesn't get it," said Andy, agitated.

"And get this: Lightfoot said at the news conference at the Capitol that we should declare a truce in the culture wars."

"The guy's waving a white flag of surrender on life and marriage, and he hasn't even gotten to the Senate yet! Where's the calcium in the guy's spine?"

"Let's face it. Lightfoot is yesterday's news. He's washed up. Birch wanted a moderate so he reached back in time."

"Birch sure gave us the back of his hand," said Andy, his voice laced with disgust.

"More like his middle finger," said Ross with a chuckle.

"That's it!" exclaimed Andy, rising out of his chair. "This is not the head of the parks and recreation department! It's a U.S. Senate seat, and he appoints some RINO tyrannosaurus rex."

"It's an insult. I'm telling you, this torpedoes Birch's presidential ambitions."

"He's dead tan walking," said Andy, a reference to Birch's permatan. "Can you get on the phone with our friend?"

"Don Jefferson?" asked Ross.

"Yes. Tell Jefferson he should run. Tell him we'll mobilize the troops."

"He'd be fantastic."

"Get him in," directed Andy.

"Will do." Ross hung up. It was going to cost the Faith and Family Federation a boatload of cash, but there was nothing Ross loved more than a fight for the soul of the Grand Old Party.

IN THE SOLARIUM ON THE top floor of the residence, Jonah Popilopos asked if there were any prayer requests. Shafts of sunlight broke in through the glass ceiling, creating a spiritual aura altogether fitting given the occasion. It was the weekly meeting of Claire Long's women's discipleship group, and she invited her new friend and spiritual mentor, the itinerant evangelist Popilopos to lead the discussion. His message that day was about Esther and the biblical models of a righteous woman. Popilopos preached in revivals all over the globe, filling soccer and football stadiums from Mumbai and London to Glasgow and New York City. Raised Greek orthodox but an evangelical convert, he preached an unconventional mix of charismatic Christian perfectionism—that regenerate believers could achieve holiness through the power of the Holy Spirit. Known for his white Nehru jackets, silk pants, and shaved head, his deep and authoritative voice commanded a television and radio audience estimated at thirty million worldwide.

"I have one," said Marilyn McLean, wife of the junior senator from Virginia. "We're dealing with some serious parenting issues with my sixteen-year-old daughter. Her hormones are raging, and she's in a rebellious phase where everything we say is wrong."

The women nodded around the coffee table, encouraging her with knowing moans.

"She's in a relationship with a young man who I just don't think is right for her," continued McLean, her face etched with anxiety. "He's not a Christian and he's a bad influence. But I know if I try to force her to end it, it will only cause her to get even closer to him."

"Sounds like we just need to pray against that romantic attachment," said Popilopos, his fleshy face breaking into an angelic grin.

"Is it okay to do that?"

"Absolutely!" fired back Popilopos. "As a parent, it's your moral duty to pray a hedge of protection around your children." The women nodded in assent.

As others offered their prayer requests, the list grew: a child going through a bitter divorce, a friend suffering from cancer, a non-ambulatory elderly father being admitted to a nursing home over his objections, a son-in-law who needed a job, a woman with her house on the market praying it will sell. Throughout, Claire hung back, silently taking notes. Finally, she spoke up.

"I can't go into a lot of details about this," she said haltingly. "It's a little awkward because some of it I'm not even supposed to know." Everyone leaned forward as the First Lady seemed about to share classified information. "I have to be a little vague about it. But there are terrorist threats against our country, against our leaders, and against Bob. So I just ask that you all pray for his protection and for my peace of mind." Her eyes began to fill with tears. "I knew this job was going to carry with it the usual security threats. But I wasn't prepared for something like this, even after what happened to Harris Flaherty." Vice President Flaherty, at the time the Republican nominee for president, was assassinated by terrorists in an attack on his helicopter as it departed the Republican National Convention the previous year.

One of the women leaned over and placed her hand on Claire's shoulder. Regaining her composure, Claire wiped a tear from her eyes.

"Let's pray for all these requests," said Popilopos. "And let's lay hands on Claire and pray for special protection over her and the president."

"Amen," several of the women murmured. They stood up and gathered around Claire, placing hands on her shoulders and back.

Popilopos stood behind them. "Father God," he began. "We lift up all these requests to You and place them at Your altar. So many needs, Lord. So many people hurting. We thank You that we can come boldly to Your throne of grace and lay these at Your feet."

"Amen," one of the women said. "Thank You, Lord."

Claire hung her head, deep in prayer. She felt a peace fall over her. She prayed earnestly that God would protect Bob from Rassem el Zafarshan, who killed Flaherty and probably Perry Miller. She wondered who was next.

9

A black SUV, trailed by a staff car and a chaser car, pulled into the West Wing parking lot at 7:22 a.m. as heavy rain pelted the nation's capital. In the backseat sat William Jacobs, director of the Central Intelligence Agency, talking on a secure phone with the team responsible for intelligence gathering at Langley, receiving a final verbal update before he briefed the president. Hanging up, he stepped out of the car in a blue pin-striped suit and beige London Fog raincoat, ducking under the awning of the West Wing entrance to protect himself from the rain. A CIA briefer followed him. He carried in his briefcase a copy of one of the most top secret documents in the government, the president's daily brief (PDF), a daily synopsis of intelligence gathered by leading U.S. and foreign spy agencies.

As Jacobs walked in long strides down the hall to the Oval Office, he saw Truman Greenglass, Charlie Hector, and Vice President Whitehead standing outside the door. Whitehead rarely sat in on the president's daily intelligence briefing. Something was up.

"Mr. Vice President, good to see you," said Jacobs. "You joining us?"

"Morning, Bill," said Whitehead. "Yes, I am."

"Shall we go in?" asked Greenglass. He opened the door. Long sat at his desk, reading glasses on the end of his nose, flipping through his copy of the PDF.

"Bill, what's the word?" asked Long.

"We live in interesting times, Mr. President."

"Don't I know it."

Jacobs took a seat directly to the right of the president's desk, the CIA briefer to the immediate left. Greenglass and Whitehead sat in chairs directly across from Long. The president nodded at Jacobs, who signaled the briefer to begin.

"Mr. President, the Iranians continue to prepare for a possible military strike. We have satellite photographic evidence of increased truck traffic around the nuclear facilities in Natanz and Ifsahan. They appear to be dispersing their infrastructure to make it more difficult for a strike on a single facility to debilitate their nuclear program."

Long furrowed his brow. "Can we track this stuff?"

"Yes and no," replied the briefer. "We can track it up until it goes into the mountains. But inside them they have an extensive network of caves, roads, and tunnels."

"How much time do we have?"

"Before they have all this materiel dispersed and fortified underground?" asked the briefer. "I'd say ninety days. Maybe 120 days tops."

Long shot a worried look at Greenglass. "They'll have everything spread around the country in the caves before we can get military authorization."

"Technically, Mr. President, you don't need congressional authorization," said Greenglass.

"I don't?"

"Not according to the lawyers."

"How would that play on the Hill, Johnny?" asked Long, turning to Whitehead.

"Depends on how much of this we can share with the leadership," said Whitehead. He leaned forward, his eyes locking with Long's. "If you brought in the leaders of both parties from the House and Senate and showed them these satellite photographs, I think you'd get solid bipartisan support."

Long turned to Jacobs. "Can we take this stuff out with bunker-busting bombs? Or is it too deep?"

"Sir, that's a question for the Pentagon and the Joint Chiefs. I don't do military strategy." It was a brush-back pitch. Jacobs was a stickler for treating the White House and DOD as clients of intel and let them make the final call. He didn't want Langley to take the fall if things went wrong.

"Can we declassify this stuff?"

Jacobs looked like someone shot him in the chest. He cleared his throat. "That's a presidential call. But if you're asking for my judgment, I would keep classified information limited to only those with the highest level security clearance."

Long nodded, clearly not pacified.

"If it comes to a military strike, whether it's us or the Israelis, we'll have to do more than offer assurances," said Greenglass. "After the intelligence failures in Iraq, the bar is higher now."

Jacobs stared back unblinking. He turned to Long. "Mr. President, once you start declassifying intelligence, you're disclosing sources and methods. It's hard to get the genie back in the bottle."

Long nodded. "Okay, what else have you got?"

"On a related topic, an Iranian scientist who was one of the top architects of the nuclear program was found dead from gunshots at close range in a hotel room in Damascus the day before yesterday," said the briefer. "The Israelis took him out. They found out he frequented a particular brothel and paid one of the prostitutes to tip them off when he was coming."

"Shot him in the act," said Jacobs, knowing the president loved gossip. "Double tap in the skull."

"In the act, huh?" said Long. "Well, he died with a smile on his face."

Greenglass cracked a smile. No one else laughed.

"How many is that now?" asked Long.

"I think that's eight or nine between us and the Israelis," replied Jacobs.

"Is it making any difference?" asked Long.

"We think so, Mr. President. Certainly the Iranians know we're playing hardball."

"Good," said Long. He closed his briefing book. "Any chance Perry Miller was killed as payback for us taking out these Iranians?"

"Miller murdered by the Iranians?" asked Jacobs. Long nodded. "I guess anything's possible, but that's the first I've heard anything about it."

Charlie Hector spoke up. "The FBI is pushing the theory. . . . There's nothing tangible, but Miller was funding the Green Movement, pushing military strikes against Iran, so they're kicking the tires, asking around. It's typical Bureau stuff." He nodded in the direction of Greenglass. "When they interviewed Truman, they asked about military supplies and technology transfers to the Green Movement."

"Mmmmm," said Jacobs. "What'd you tell them?"

"I told them it was classified," said Greenglass. "But I don't know if that satisfied them. They'll be back for more."

"It's not beyond the realm of possibility. Stupid, though. It won't stop us. But if the Iranians murdered Miller, we need to know," said Jacobs. "There could potentially be other targets, including the secretary of defense, secretary of state, even you, Mr. President."

Long's eyes grew wide.

"We can't have the FBI blowing the cover on our black ops in Iran," said Whitehead, speaking up for the first time. "We obviously don't want to circumscribe the investigation into Miller's murder. But we need to quarantine it so it doesn't compromise what we're doing in Iran."

"I don't know how one does that," said Jacobs. "It's an ongoing investigation."

"Can you go to the FBI and say, 'This is leading into places that involve a sensitive and ongoing CIA operation'?" asked Long. "Tell them it's a national security issue involving regime change."

"I think I'd have to be more specific than that," said Jacobs, his slumped posture telegraphing discomfort with the entire topic. "There are strict protocols governing communication among the agencies within CTC." He used the acronym for the multiagency Counter Terrorism Center.

"Fine. Follow all the protocols. Right, Charlie?" asked Long, looking for a lifeline.

"Sure," said Hector. "No one's asking anyone to violate protocols."

"I'll look into it, but the FBI tends to guard," said Jacobs. "They don't like being told to put their agents on a short leash."

"I understand," said Long.

"If I may, Mr. President," said Whitehead. "If the FBI screws this up and what we're doing in Iran leaks, Agency assets will be eliminated. Pro-democracy activists have put their lives in our hands. This is like giving up Solidarity organizers to the Soviets at the height of the Cold War. We can't leave soldiers on the battlefield, or no one in that part of the world will ever trust us again."

"We can have our FBI liaison at CTC find out the status of the investigation," said Jacobs in a dull monotone. "If it's moving into areas of covert activity, we have procedures for bringing that to the attention of the director and the AG."

"Good," said Long. "I knew you'd know how to handle it."

Jacobs now knew why Whitehead showed up for the meeting: he was playing bad cop to Long's good cop. Greenglass scripted the entire meeting, hoping to protect himself from taking the fall for funneling covert military aid to the Green Movement. Rather than calling the

Justice Department itself, the White House wanted the CIA to do its dirty work. As the meeting wrapped and Jacobs headed back to his car, something gnawed at him: what if the Iranians really did murder Perry Miller?

"I NEED REAL-TIME UPDATES!" shouted Kris Howard, assistant attorney general for national security, her voice jagged with frustration. "What am I, a potted plant? Somebody talk to me." Howard, surrounded by FBI agents and DOJ officials, was on the seventh floor of the Robert F. Kennedy headquarters building of the Justice Department, in the bunker at the National Security Division's SCIF (Sensitive Compartmentalized Information Facility), the top secret, limited-access nerve center where federal law enforcement tracked terror suspects. Wearing a crisp white blouse and a navy blue skirt with matching jacket, she paced back and forth among the desks, arms crossed, riding herd.

"We lost him," said one of the agents.

"What?!" Howard exclaimed. "How do you lose a suspect when he's being trailed with an FBI surveillance van, a SWAT team, and a chopper? I've got fifty boots on the ground out there, and we can't find a ham sandwich?"

"We don't know what happened, ma'am," said the agent, frantically scanning a bank of screens displaying video feeds from the helicopter's cameras. "We had him five minutes ago. We might have lost him at a red light, or he turned onto a side street."

"Find him. Now." Howard walked over to Pat Mahoney, who stood in the semidarkness doing a slow burn. Her eyes smoldered. "If you lose this suspect and he gets away, I swear someone will pay. Can't you guys run a surveil?"

"We'll get him," said Mahoney, nonplussed.

"You better, or heads will roll. Starting with yours." She stomped off.

Mahoney said nothing in reply. He signaled to one of the agents, who scrambled over, his face a picture of high stress. They had been tracking Qatani for three days. It was time to end the party. "Hit the residence," said Mahoney.

"Now? We've got everyone trying to find him. I don't want to pull people off that in order to take down the guy's house."

"Just do it. If he slipped the surveil team, we may need clues as to where he's going next. He may be going to a safe house . . . or trying to leave the country."

"Alright," said the agent. "I'll send in a second SWAT team."

For his part Mahoney was a picture of calm. Unlike the preening egos at DOJ, he had full confidence in his team. But the window to get Qatani was closing fast. As he often did in situations like this, he tried to put himself in the place of the suspect. Had he figured out he had a tail? If so, where would he go? Certainly not back to the house where a SWAT team waited. He might go underground—no credit cards or cell phone traffic. Or he might try to leave the country by car or plane. Mahoney pulled out a cell phone and dialed the direct number for his deputy, who was at FBI headquarters.

"Have TSA put out an alert to all the airlines. We need them to be on the look out for any young male fitting Hassan Qatani's description. Make sure it includes a physical description and possible disguises. ASAP."

"What's up?" asked his deputy.

"We lost him. He disappeared like Tinkerbell."

His deputy let out an expletive.

"Don't worry. I ordered the SWAT team to take down his house. Now we need to lock down the airports." Mahoney turned his back to Howard, who noticed he was on his cell phone, cupping his hand over the phone and lowering his voice to a half whisper. "If this guy boards a flight and disappears into Pakistan or Yemen, this gets a lot more complicated."

"We're already getting heat from upstairs. If he gets away, we're done," said the deputy. "I'll also tell Homeland we have a high priority surveil underway and we need air marshals on every flight carrying passengers connecting to Arab capitals."

"Good. Don't let him get away." Mahoney hung up his phone. He hoped they caught a break.

LISA ROBINSON CAME INTO JAY'S office and closed the door. With raven-like hair, doe eyes, and the svelte figure of an athlete, she wore a black spectator jacket with white buttons, white pants, and black-and-white heels. Jay's earlier crush on her mellowed into professional cordiality, with a pinch of West Wing infighting. Once her mentor, he was now her rival. The press labeled them "beauty and the beast." There wasn't any question about who the beast was.

"What's the ticktock on Iran?" asked Lisa.

"Hey, I'm the political guy," said Jay. "Ask Truman. He's in charge of the world."

"I mean politically."

"Oh, that," said Jay. "Every member of Congress is going to have to go on the record on this sanctions bill, which will include a military authorization or else the president will veto it. It has to have real teeth, not gums. The Democrats will be their usual profiles in cowardice, playing up to their antiwar base. They'll vote against it, and we'll hang that around their necks like a burning tire in November."

"And then?"

Jay leveled his gaze. "Then my guess is the NSC and DNI will report the sanctions have failed. There will be a short pause before the bombs start dropping. Shock and awe. Real video game-type stuff.

Precision-guided munitions will level every military and government building in Iran."

"Wow."

"Yeah. After that, we'll see. I assume Iran is crippled and the UN condemns us."

"Don't you think Hezbollah and/or Hamas invade Israel? I can't imagine Iran just laying back and letting us or the Israelis bomb them without a counterattack."

Jay shrugged. "Hard to say. But if they do, the Pentagon says we can counter their counterattack. At that point we can offer the Israelis anything they need."

"When's all this going to happen?"

"Honestly, I don't know. The president still hasn't decided. But the war plan calls for us to be ready in four to six months."

"So it could theoretically happen before the congressional election."

"It could."

Lisa nodded, absorbing the information. "If we're at war during the midterm election, is that a good thing or a bad thing?"

"Depends on how it's going. If it's going well, it helps us. If it's going badly, it helps them. If it's a muddle, it's probably a wash, but that helps them more than it does us."

"On another topic, we're getting press calls about the Senate Finance Committee subpoenaing you to appear about allegedly interfering with an IRS audit of Andy Stanton's ministry."

"That's just Sal Stanley trying to distract me from my number one job in life, which is defeating him," said Jay with a smirk.

"Media reports say they're calling in the commissioner of the IRS and the head of the exempt division to testify."

"So what," said Jay dismissively. "I didn't do anything wrong."

"The question is, are we going to cooperate?"

"It's up to the lawyers, Lisa."

"I can't say *that*," Lisa replied.

"Can't you just say the White House counsel is reviewing the subpoena?"

"I've been saying that for two weeks. At some point we've got to say more."

"Okay," said Jay. He wheeled around in his chair and picked up the phone. "Get me Phil Battaglia, please. Right away if he's available." He hung up the phone, spinning back around to face Lisa. "Look, I've got no problem testifying. Phil says he doesn't want the 'money shot' of me standing up there with my arm raised being sworn in. So I'm at his mercy."

His assistant knocked, then cracked the door open. "Phil's on line one."

Jay pivoted in his chair and punched the line, putting it on speaker. "Phil, it's Jay. I have Lisa in my office. She's getting media inquiries about the Senate Finance Committee investigation of the IRS matter. What should she say?"

"Tell them we're still reviewing the subpoena," said Battaglia.

"Phil, I can't keep using the same line," said Lisa. "The natives are getting restless. When are we going to answer the question of whether or not we're cooperating? Throw me a bone here."

"We're going to cooperate as much as possible without surrendering executive privilege," said Battaglia. "This is a fishing expedition. It's an infringement on the president's constitutional prerogative to confidential advice. It's a politically motivated witch hunt. We're not going to let Stanley and the Dems haul Jay or any other member of the president's staff down to the Capitol anytime there's a story in the *New York Times* suggesting somebody did something wrong."

"So our position is Jay is not going to testify?"

"Correct," said Battaglia. "But don't say that. At least not yet."

"I think they'll burn us alive if that's our position," said Lisa. She made eye contact again with Jay. He threw up his hands to signal his disapproval. She ignored him. "This is a question of an alleged interference by a top aide to the president with an IRS investigation of the leading conservative religious broadcaster in the country. The agent in charge says he felt pressured. He's going to testify. If we crouch in the bunker on this, it's going to get ugly."

"It's ugly either way, Lisa," said Battaglia. "We can't surrender executive privilege."

"You can waive it."

"Over my dead body."

"Fine. But I'm on the record saying this is a bad idea. I respect your legal judgment, Phil, but I'm sending a memo to Charlie Hector stating my view."

"You're entitled to your opinion, Lisa. Have a good day." Battaglia hung up.

Jay shook his head. "Why are you hanging me out to dry? There's nothing there. This is a trumped-up political charge by the *Times* and Sal Stanley."

"Jay, the hearings are going to be a circus," said Lisa. "I honestly believe the pressure will be so great you're going to have to testify. So let's make necessity a virtue and just waive privilege and get it over with now."

"Like I said, I'm fine either way," said Jay. "I'm just doing what I'm told by the lawyers."

Lisa turned to leave, then stopped. "Oh, by the way, we got a call from someone at Merryprankster.com. They claim witnesses saw you at a VIP table at The Standard in LA the other night doing shots and dirty dancing with Satcha Sanchez and some party girls."

"I was not!" lied Jay. "I met Satcha for a drink. The other chick was a PR flak." He gave her a sheepish look. "I don't even know her name."

Lisa lowered her chin and gave Jay a dirty look. "You're off message, Jay. Always remember their names." She turned to go.

Jay laughed. "I'd never forget yours!"

Lisa rolled her eyes with disgust and left the office, closing the door behind her.

10

Truman Greenglass was on the phone with the number two official at the Defense Intelligence Agency discussing the latest Intel on the dispersal of Iranian nuclear material. The DIA official was explaining the HUMINT regarding the Iranian operation. Basically, there was none. What else was new? Just then Greenglass received an e-mail on his desk computer, which made a characteristic *bong* noise. He rotated the mouse over the e-mail and highlighted it, clicking the mouse. It was from Bill Jacobs at the CIA. Anxious to read it, he wrapped up his call.

"Truman, per our conversation the other morning during the daily intelligence briefing, I have attached a memorandum regarding communication between the CIA and the FBI on the subject of the investigation of Senator Perry Miller's murder. Call me if you have any further questions."

Opening the memo, he scanned the text, his eyes darting, his curiosity curdling to anger. He could not believe Jacobs would stab him in the back in such a systematic fashion. The memo was a classic

CIA maneuver by one of the wiliest officials in the government. It read in part:

TOP SECRET: EYES ONLY
MEMORANDUM OF CONVERSATION
FROM: WILLIAM JACOBS
TO: TRUMAN GREENGLASS
CC: CHARLES HECTOR

This is to reduce to writing our conversation on Tuesday regarding the FBI's ongoing investigation into the death of Senator Perry Miller and its potential impact on national security. Specifically, you asked whether the investigation could compromise CIA covert operations in Iran designed to destabilize the current regime. Further, you asked whether or not the CIA could communicate our concerns through appropriate channels to the FBI.

The previous administration issued a presidential finding authorizing Operation Code Green, a multiagency effort that included monetary aid to democratic organizations, technology transfers, military supplies, paramilitary operations, and the targeted elimination of certain elements within the country.

There is no evidence at this time that the FBI's investigation will lead to public disclosure of the operational details of Operation Code Green. We conclude the FBI is seeking to ascertain whether Rassem el Zafarshan or some other terror network, perhaps funded by elements within the Iranian government, was involved in Senator Miller's death in retaliation for his role in supporting regime change. To our knowledge this investigation in no way threatens to compromise covert activities in Iran.

As you know, 24 USC 2008 prohibits direct operational involvement with domestic law enforcement investigations by foreign intelligence agencies. This statutory delineation of lines of responsibility has been essential to the prosecution of the war on terror. However, the Patriot Act authorizes the sharing of intelligence between the

FBI and the CIA, and we will certainly ensure that that is the case with the Miller investigation.

GREENGLASS MUTTERED AN EXPLETIVE UNDER his breath. He always considered Jacobs a patriot, but it now turned out he was just another spy with a briefcase and a pension, a bureaucrat, and a gutless wonder. This kind of careerism by high-ranking government officials allowed Iran to get the nuke in the first place. Forget him and the Agency, Greenglass decided. They were worthless. And when it came to dealing with the FBI, there was more than one way to skin that cat.

PAT MAHONEY STOOD IN FRONT of a bank of video screens in the SCIF, talking to the SWAT team captain at Hassan Qatani's rental house on his headset. "Please tell me you've got something. We still can't find him. He shook the tail, and we can't locate his vehicle."

"We found a laptop, several prepaid cellphones, and an iPod," said the SWAT team captain. "We also found some fake passports, forged immigration papers, and fake driver's licenses. This guy's on the move and someone's supplying him."

"Get the laptop and the cell phones back to headquarters right away so our technicians can do a full data dump off the hard drive and the SIM cards," ordered Mahoney. "Maybe we can see if he's been visiting any travel Web sites to research airline flights. If he's got fake passports, he's planning to travel under an assumed name and probably a disguise."

"I'd say sooner rather than later."

"Okay, good work. Keep a surveillance team on site in case he comes back." Mahoney hung up the phone, walking over to Kris Howard.

"Who was that?" she asked.

"The SWAT team captain over at Hassan's house. They found a laptop, prepaid cell phones, and some fake passports," replied Mahoney. "Looks like he's planning a long vacation."

"Yeah, but to where? And from where?"

"My guess is Dulles, BWI, or Philly. It's too far to New York."

"He'll likely be on a direct flight to the Middle East," said Howard. "Make sure we have air marshals on all those flights."

"Already done. The problem is, we can't rely on his name popping up on the terrorist watch list if he's traveling with a false passport. We'll have to rely on facial recognition software."

"What about biometrics?"

"That's when they come into the country."

"We should search the database of incoming passengers," suggested Howard.

"Also, we're targeting anyone traveling alone on a one-way ticket."

"I hope you still have the surveil team looking for him."

"Absolutely. Nothing so far. But one way or the other he's going to hit the grid."

"I hope you're right. If he does, we can't lose him again."

"We won't. We've got thirty-two flights to European or Middle East destinations out of those three airports we're monitoring. We've pulled the passenger lists, and we're running all those names through the various databases. We've also got real-time feeds of video from airport security cameras."

Howard nodded and walked away, deep in thought.

A BEARDED MAN OF ARAB descent wearing a Boston Red Sox hat approached the SpanAir ticket counter at Dulles International Airport at 4:40 p.m. and bought a one-way ticket to Madrid on Flight 106, departing at 7:00 p.m. He paid in cash. His passport said he was Diego Garcia and had entered the U.S. on a student visa nine months earlier.

The walk-up fare for the ticket was $752. He pulled a wad of bills out of his pocket and counted out seven $100 bills, a fifty, and two ones. The woman working behind the counter printed out the ticket and handed him his boarding pass.

As the man left the counter and headed for security, she noticed he looked a little old for a student and assumed he must be in graduate school.

AT A COMPUTER TERMINAL AT FBI headquarters, an agent scanned video from several cameras stationed at the main security check-point at Dulles airport. He looked for anyone remotely matching the description of Qatani or, alternatively, a male wearing a lot of clothing, sunglasses, and a hat who might be trying to disguise his appearance.

As his eyes scanned the screen, he saw a man going through a metal detector who appeared to be in his mid-twenties. He wore a baseball cap pulled low over his eyes, which he removed at the direction of the TSA agent as he stepped through the magnetometer.

"Gotcha," said the agent. He froze the footage, zoomed in on image, and clicked an icon in the corner activating the FBI's proprietary facial recognition software, the most sophisticated such technology in the world. It instantly matched the photograph against databases containing hundreds of thousands of pictures of known and suspected terrorists, as well as Islamic extremists with ties to terrorist organizations. The software flashed a symbol showing it identified a match. The agent clicked on the symbol with his mouse, pulling up the matching photograph. It was a picture of Hassan Qatani taken just days earlier by an FBI surveillance camera.

"It's him!" exclaimed the agent. He excitedly picked up the phone and dialed Patrick Mahoney's cell phone.

"Mahoney here," came the voice on the other line.

"I just did a facial recognition match on a guy going through security at Dulles," said the agent. "It's him."

"Qatani?"

"Yes."

"When?"

"Thirty minutes ago."

"We have to figure out what flight he's on," said Mahoney.

"Hold on," said the agent. He tapped on the keyboard, pulling up a list of all the international flights leaving Dulles. "I got a British Airways flight to London, United flights to Munich, Paris, Dubai, and Cairo, and a SpanAir flight to Madrid. That's all in the next ninety minutes."

"Can we check cash purchases on those flights?"

"You bet."

"Do it. All hands on deck. Call me back immediately. We'll call airport security from here and alert them that we have a major situation." Mahoney hung up. Making eye contact with Howard, he said in a raised voice: "Alright, everybody, listen up: Hassan Qatani went through security at Dulles thirty minutes ago. He's probably boarding right now, so let's pull the passenger manifests for every international flight departing in the next ten to ninety minutes. Keep in mind he's using a false passport. We're looking for males between the ages of twenty and forty years old, traveling alone on a foreign passport, probably paying cash."

"What about the air marshals?" asked an agent.

"Alert every air marshal on an international flight via e-mail. Tell them we've positively ID'd Qatani, and we have reason to believe he's boarding a flight shortly. Given the situation, they may need to apprehend him themselves."

"I'm on it," said one of the agents.

ATTORNEY GENERAL KEITH GOLDEN WAS at his home in Alexandria having dinner with his family when the phone rang. His wife answered it. "It's for you," she said. When he picked up the receiver, he heard the voice of Kris Howard.

"General, sorry to bother you at home, but we're closing in on Qatani, the Miller murder suspect," she said.

"Good. I thought the FBI lost him."

"They did. But half an hour ago he went through security at Dulles. The FBI and TSA have been monitoring those video feeds. They ID'd him using facial recognition software."

"Where's he heading?" asked Golden.

"We don't know," said Howard. "He's using a fake passport. We're doing a search of the passenger manifests to find any male passenger who fits the profile."

"Do we have time to do that before those international flights take off?"

"Not all of them, but most of them."

"Let's hope we find him before the plane takes off," said Golden.

"Just wanted to let you know what's going on. If it looks like we're going to get him in custody, you probably want to be here when it goes down."

"Absolutely. Keep me posted."

Golden hung up the phone. If they nabbed Qatani, it would blow the Miller investigation wide open, and Golden would be the one making the announcement at a news conference from the DOJ press briefing room. How sweet would that be?

AT SCIF AN AGENT RAISED his hand and snapped his fingers, signaling he had something. Mahoney strode over.

"What is it?"

"I got a male passenger by the name of Diego Garcia on a student visa from Spain flying back to Madrid on a one-way ticket," he said. "Paid cash at the airport, two hours before departure."

"Can you pull up the scan of his passport."

"Hold on, I've got to access the ICE database," he said, referring to the Immigration and Customs Enforcement. He pulled up a Web site, clicked an icon, and typed in a password, then quickly did a search on the name. Four matches came up. The first one was an eighteen-year-old student at UCLA. The second came up with a photo that was clearly Qatani. "There's your man," he said, tapping the screen with his finger. "He's going to Madrid. I'm sure that's just a stop-off point."

"What time does that flight take off?"

"Seven p.m."

"We're too late," said Mahoney, glancing anxiously at one of the clocks on the wall that tracked the time in different time zones. It read 7:17 p.m. "I'm sure they've left the gate by now, but they're probably still taxiing on the runway. Can we notify the pilot to go back to the gate?"

The agent quickly dialed a number to the Homeland Security Control Center the Federal Aviation Administration. "I'm calling for Agent Mahoney at the FBI," he said. "There's a high-level terrorist suspect traveling on a fake passport on SpanAir flight 106 to Madrid. Can you tell me the status of that plane. Is it still on the ground?"

"Checking," said the FAA. There was a brief pause. "No, afraid not. Flight 106 has been in the air for eleven minutes."

The agent let out an expletive and banged his fist on his desk. He turned to Mahoney. "We lost him. They're airborne."

"Divert the aircraft," ordered Mahoney.

"You don't want to pick him up in Madrid?" asked the agent.

"No way," said Mahoney. "I'm not going to deal with the politics of getting him back here from Spain. That could take days. Divert the aircraft."

The agent returned to the FAA, which was still on the phone. "Please order the pilot to turn around and return to the airport."

"Negative," said Mahoney. "Tell him to go to JFK in New York." "JFK?"

"Darn right. At least initially I want him in custody in the Southern District of New York. They'll know how to handle him. Best prosecutors and judges for a terrorist case in the country."

"Can you tell the pilot to land at JFK?" asked the agent.

"Roger that," said the FAA. "We'll make direct contact with the pilot and get you an ETA pronto."

Mahoney allowed himself a smile and slapped the agent on the back. He turned to Kris Howard and gave her a thumbs-up. "Tell the AG he can schedule his press conference," he said with a touch of sarcasm. "He's on a flight to Madrid we just diverted to JFK. We'll have him in FBI custody within the hour."

"Good job," said Howard. "I want you standing up there when we announce we got him. You guys deserve all the credit."

"Thanks for the offer, but I'm out of here," said Mahoney. He pointed with his index finger at two fellow agents and motioned for them to follow him.

"Where are you going?"

"New York." With that he was gone.

THE PILOT AT THE CONTROLS of SpanAir flight 106 had just completed a slow climb to thirty-five thousand feet. The aircraft was sixty-four miles due east of Washington, DC, over the Atlantic Ocean, when air traffic control broke in with an emergency communication for the cockpit. The FAA was diverting the flight to JFK due to the fact that a suspicious individual with known terrorist ties was on board.

Following standard operating procedure, the pilot got on the intercom and informed the passengers that the plane had a mechanical issue involving the navigation system that required them to go to JFK Airport, where a needed part was available. He apologized for the inconvenience and promised to provide more updates as they became available. Then he signed off, turning to his copilot and raising his eyebrows.

In the coach section of the aircraft, an armed FAA air marshal wearing an army fatigue jacket, jeans, and a scruffy beard noticed a young man wearing a baseball cap called the stewardess over, engaging her in an animated conversation. He appeared to be highly agitated by the pilot's announcement. The marshal wondered if he was the guy, or just another overly excited tourist. He decided to keep a close eye on him in case he tried to do something stupid.

AT THE FBO AT REAGAN National Airport, Patrick Mahoney and two other agents screamed up in government sedans, blue smoke rising from the tires, the smell of burning oil thick, and pulled in front of one of the FBI's G-4 private jets, its engines warming on the tarmac. They scrambled up the stairs.

As he boarded, Mahoney stuck his head in the cockpit. "Let's get out of here as quickly as we can, gentlemen. We need to get to JFK within the hour if we can."

One of the pilots flashed a thumbs-up. "We know. We got the word."

"Good," said Mahoney. He walked to the back of the cabin and sat in one of the captain's chairs, buckling his seat belt, shifting about in his seat like a ten-year-old boy who had to use the restroom. "Let's get this bird in the air," he said to no one in particular.

"Why didn't you stay at DOJ for the news conference?" inquired one of the agents on board. "It would have been good publicity for the Bureau."

"PR is for wimps," sniffed Mahoney, lips twisted with contempt. "I'm not gonna stand behind Keith Golden like a mannequin." He tore open a foil bag of peanuts, throwing a handful in his mouth and chewing. "The terrorists never sleep, pal. Neither do I."

The agent nodded and smiled. "Let's hope he talks."

"He'll talk," said Mahoney mysteriously as he glanced out the window at the Jefferson Memorial, White House, and Washington Monument against the orange-red haze of dusk. "This isn't about who murdered Perry Miller. This is about finding Zafarshan."

The G-4 taxied down the runway slowly at first, then with a burst of speed barreled down the runway, its nose rising until the wheels lifted and they were airborne.

THE SPANAIR BOEING 747 SLOWED to a stop in front of a jetway at JFK Airport in New York at a little after 8:30 p.m. An FBI agent accompanied by two detectives from the counterterrorism unit of the New York Police Department and an airline maintenance employee stood at the edge of the jetway.

"Open the door," one of the detectives said to the airline employee. The employee banged on the door three times with the palm of his hand.

The door swung open and the FBI agent and the detectives walked down the near aisle in a single file, stopping at Row 29. They paused before a male passenger wearing a baseball cap pulled low over his face. Other passengers turned around and craned their necks to see what was happening.

The agent flashed his badge. "Hassan Qatani? I'm with the FBI. These two men are with the New York City Police Department. Come with us."

The man looked up, cracking a half smile. "I've been expecting you," he said.

11

Attorney General Keith Golden's Town Car barreled across the Fourteenth Street bridge at a high rate of speed, accompanied by a chaser car carrying a personal aide and two machine-gun-toting FBI agents, and two Metropolitan police squad cars, blue lights blazing, their sirens silent. Golden was pumped with adrenalin like a juiced-up body builder, his knees bouncing, strumming his fingers with his thumbs nervously. When the news reached him of Hassan Qatani's arrest, he excused himself from the dinner table with his family, retired to the bedroom, and practiced his lines in front of the mirror. "We got him!" he said, shoulders thrown back, chin raised. Then: "Tonight's arrest is a big leap in the investigation of the murder of Senator Perry Miller and a major stride forward in the ongoing war on terror." It would lead every newscast in the country, of that Golden was confident.

The secure phone in the car rang. Golden answered it.

"General, how are you? Truman here," came the voice of Truman Greenglass.

Golden wondered why Greenglass was calling him at this late hour. He hoped the White House wasn't planning on stealing his glory by having the announcement of Qatani's arrest made from there. This was an FBI and DOJ operation from start to finish, and they deserved the credit.

"I'm good . . . very good. I assume you heard the news?" asked Golden.

"You mean about the suspect in the Miller's murder? Yes."

"We've got FBI agents with a strong background in counter-terrorism landing in New York as we speak," said Golden proudly. "He'll be detained as an enemy combatant. He's not a U.S. citizen, so there's no issue of Miranda rights. We'll start interrogating him immediately."

Greenglass grunted, seemingly unimpressed. "What's this I hear about a news conference?"

The question landed with a thud. Golden hoped Greenglass wasn't trying to rain on his parade. "It's more of a press briefing," he said, backpedaling. "We're announcing Qatani's apprehension."

Greenglass was silent for what seemed like an eternity. "The president doesn't think that's a good idea," he said at last.

"I'm afraid I don't understand."

"The president's not a fan of grandstanding, Keith," replied Greenglass. "It's not his style. More to the point, this is an ongoing investigation. The CIA feels we should not let our enemies know we have Qatani in custody."

"Look, Truman, I'm a team player," said Golden, feeling as though someone punched him the stomach. "But the terrorists know he boarded the flight to Madrid because they planned to pick him up. When he's not on the plane when it lands—and especially when it's delayed four hours—they're going to know."

"Keith, this press briefing is a bad idea and not just for the Miller investigation. It's bad for you. Do you want me to draw you a picture?"

"No," said Golden, his voice drained of energy. "But the press is not going to like the fact we cancel it."

"Forget the press," said Greenglass. The line went dead.

Golden put down the receiver, anger boiling up inside him. The car pulled into the motor entrance of DOJ headquarters. He decided to go directly to the Secure Information Center and show the flag. But the truth was, no matter how much of a brave front he put up, he was persona non grata at the White House. It was no longer a question of if he would go, only whether he jumped or was pushed.

THE SUN BROKE THROUGH THE windows of the presidential suite of the Gaylord Hotel in Orlando, not far from Disney World, where Andy Stanton preached at Sonshine Church, one of the largest megachurches in the nation. Normally, he would have jumped on his plane and flown straight home, but he still had some important business.

A brunch spread fit for a king sat on the dining room table: scrambled eggs, bacon, sausages, cheese blintzes covered with strawberry sauce, fresh fruit, grits, eggs Benedict, and salmon lox. Several knocks came on the door. Andy's security aide, a squat man with a thick torso, legs like tree trunks, and a .38 police revolver on his belt, opened the door. It was Ross Lombardy accompanied by the man of the hour, Congressman Don Jefferson.

"Senator!" bellowed Andy.

"Not yet, not yet," said Jefferson as he loped toward Andy with a crooked grin. He practically oozed servile devotion, silver helmet hair sprayed to the rough texture of white granite, his face slightly puffy and pink, his lanky body wrapped in a nondescript gray suit with a blue-and-red striped tie.

Andy stepped forward and enveloped Jefferson in a bear hug. Jefferson's nostrils filled with the musky scent of his cologne and

Andy's beard stubble rubbed against his cheek like sandpaper. "Come on over here and get something to eat," he said.

Jefferson gazed at the buffet spread, his eyes like saucers. "I don't know if I want to be a senator," he joked. "I think I want to be *you*, Andy. How do I get your life?"

Andy cackled, placing his hand on Jefferson's shoulder. "I'm afraid the creature comforts of a televangelist do beat those of the garden variety member of Congress!" He roared with laughter. "Of course, it's not all sweetness and light. Did you see that vicious editorial the *New York Times* wrote about me last week? They *hate* me."

"No, I didn't see that one. What was it about?" asked Jefferson as he ladled scrambled eggs on his plate.

"They got upset because I spoke to a Jewish synagogue in New York and called on Israel to strike Iran. Called me a warmonger," replied Andy, wearing a scowl.

"They hate it when Andy makes inroads into the Jewish community," said Ross. "Drives them nuts."

"It's not you they hate, Andy," said Jefferson, his plate piled high with food, a piece of bacon hanging off. "It's politically active Christians. Your crime is organizing them."

Andy settled into a chair at the head of the dining room table, motioning Jefferson to take a seat to his right. Ross pulled up the chair to Andy's left. "Speaking of which, what's your current thinking on the U.S. Senate seat?" asked Andy as he took a swig of orange juice.

Jefferson leaned back in his chair and exhaled slowly, assuming a reflective repose. "I ran for Congress so I could be well positioned for a statewide run if the opportunity came. I'm on good committees from a fund-raising standpoint. I have a financial and geographical base." Andy nodded approvingly. "It's happening a little quicker than I would have liked because of Miller's death. And whereas any time I ran there would have been a crowded field, now I'd be running against Birch's handpicked candidate. So we're not just talking about running *for* the Senate; we're talking about running *against* the governor." He flashed a smile. "Not that I'm afraid of Birch. I'm not. It's still not clear to me he can take a punch. My hunch is he's got a glass jaw. The guy's never really had a serious challenge from within his own party." He paused, leaning in closer. "But I have to raise enough money to be competitive."

"Money's the mother's milk of politics, no question about it," said Andy. "That's what my father always told me. He used to say, 'Son, show me a politician who can't raise money, and I'll show you a politician who's a loser.'" Andy's father served in Congress for fourteen years before losing a bitter U.S. Senate primary.

"How much do you need?" asked Ross.

Jefferson turned down his mouth. "I'd like to have ten million for the primary, but six million is the floor. For the general, another thirty million."

"Forty million dollars for a Senate seat?" shrieked Andy.

"Oh, it's more than that, Andy," replied Ross.

Andy looked horrified.

"That's just Don's campaign," said Ross. "Lightfoot will raise $20 million. The Democrat will have $30 to $40 million. Then you've got the state parties, the outside groups like us and the trial lawyers, and the national party committees. You add all that in, it's probably closer to $125 million."

Andy let out a long whistle.

"Florida's an expensive state. You've got six media markets, including two big ones: Orlando and Miami," said Jefferson. "One week of statewide TV is a million dollars."

"Don, how much do you have in your congressional account?" asked Ross.

"I have $1.3 million," replied Jefferson. "We think we can probably push that up near $2 million."

"Good. Flip that into a Senate account and get all those donors to max again."

"That's legal?" asked Andy, surprised.

"It's not just legal; it's practically encouraged," said Jefferson with a smile. Andy laughed in a little-boy giggle.

"So that's between three and $3.5 million out of the chute," said Ross, pushing his plate aside. He pulled out a legal pad and began to make a series of calculations.

"Then the question is, how aggressively will Birch twist arms of the lobbyists and corporate types to give to Lightfoot?" asked Jefferson.

"He'll twist them so hard you'll hear bones breaking," said Andy.

"I'm not sure," said Jefferson. "Don't get me wrong, Birch can't stand the thought of me beating his fair-haired boy. But he also knows Lightfoot's got no base, and his financial support is entirely derivative. So Birch has to be careful how he plays, if he plays at all."

Ross and Andy exchanged disbelieving glances.

"So what's the bottom line, Don?" asked Andy, pushing himself away from the table and crossing his massive legs. "What do you need from us?"

Jefferson wore the expressionless mask of a high-stakes poker player. "Three things," he said, raising three fingers. "One, I'd like your PAC to endorse me, max out, and bundle contributions from your members."

"That's three things right there," joked Ross.

"No, that's just one," laughed Jefferson. "Second, I'd like you to have me on the radio and the television show whenever you can."

"I can do that," said Andy. "The IRS is all over me, so we'll have to do as much of it as we can before you formally announce. Afterward, we can book you as a member of Congress talking about a legislative issue."

"You can have him on to talk about the campaign as long as it's legitimate news," said Ross.

"I know . . . we just have to be careful," said Andy. "I've got to get this cotton-picking IRS audit behind me. It's a bear." He turned to Jefferson. "Alright, what's the third thing?"

"I'd like Faith and Family Federation to play in the primary, with voter guides, phone banks, door knockers, the whole nine yards."

Andy turned to Ross. "Can we do that?"

"We can," said Ross. "But I don't recommend we talk about it with Don. Legally we can't coordinate. There has to be strict separation of church and state."

Andy's face fell, but Jefferson nodded knowingly. "Once we get up and running, we'll post all the facts on Lightfoot's record on a Web site so it can be publicly accessed by any third party group who wants to play," said Jefferson. "That's perfectly legal."

"Beautiful," said Ross.

"Lightfoot's a RINO," sneered Andy. "I want him in the primary. Do whatever you have to do. The thought of that guy in the Senate makes me sick to my stomach."

Jefferson reached for the pot of coffee and poured, freshening his cup. He took a swig, letting the dead air hang. "So what do you say, Andy? Can I count on you?"

"Brother, you can do more than count on me," said Andy with a smile. "Trust me, the cavalry's coming."

"That's what I like to hear," said Jefferson. He looked across the table at Ross. "Talk to you soon . . . or maybe not."

"Don't worry, we don't need to talk. We know what to do. This ain't our first rodeo." Ross glanced at his watch in a prearranged cue. "Andy, you have a plane to catch."

Andy rose from the table. Jefferson stood as well, extending his hand. Andy clasped it and pulled him close. "You're gonna make a great senator."

"Thank you, friend," said Jefferson, his eyes sparkling.

Andy and Ross walked Jefferson to the door, exchanging small talk. Then he opened the door and departed.

"Well, what do you think?" asked Andy, eyes dancing, hands clasped behind his back.

"I think we have ourselves a U.S. Senate candidate."

Andy rocked on his heels, grinning from ear to ear.

IN THE CAVE ALONG THE Pakistan-China border that served as temporary headquarters for Rassem el Zafarshan and his top lieutenants, a man in his late twenties extended his arms and spread his legs as a member of Zafarshan's personal security detail searched him for weapons. After a thorough strip search, the guard nodded.

"He's clean," he said.

The other guard escorted the young man down a tunnel with a torch, stooping to avoid stalactites and protruding rock formations. They rounded a corner, and he turned to the right into a cool chamber illuminated by lamps and candles. In the semidarkness sat Zafarshan cross-legged on a Persian rug, wearing a turban and a dark beard, his olive-colored skin shining in the flickering light.

"God is great," said the young man. "It is a great honor to be in your presence, great leader."

"Sit down," said Zafarshan. The man complied, sitting cross-legged on the dirt floor. The guard remained standing, his finger on the trigger of a Russian-made Kalashnikov machine gun. "Who are you?"

"I am Afzaal Hakim. I am foot soldier in Pakistani Taliban."

Zafarshan nodded. "What do you have for me, son?"

"I was sent to tell you that Hassan Qatani has been arrested. The FBI has him in custody. He was detained after boarding a flight from Washington to Madrid."

"How do you know this?"

"My cousin was to meet him in Madrid and help him get to Islamabad. From there we hoped to transport him to one of our safe villages in Waziristan."

"When did this happen?"

"Four days ago."

Zafarshan's black eyes flashed with concern. "Thank you for coming," he said. "God is great."

The young man rose. "God is great." The guard escorted him out.

Zafarshan's aide emerged from the shadows. "If they have him, they have not announced it. That is a not a good sign."

"Very bad," said Zafarshan. "He will be tortured. He will talk."

"What do we do?"

"We move ahead with our plans. Nothing changes except the urgency with which we must carry out our mission. America, the Great Satan, will pay. This time the price will be far higher than before."

"May Allah be glorified," said the aide.

Zafarshan pulled on his beard, which he often did when anxious. He hoped the mullahs in Iran did not blink in the face of what was coming. For his part he intended to strike a blow so great America would wish for what happened to Harrison Flaherty and Perry Miller.

12

Hassan Qatani sat strapped in a metal chair in front of a table in the bowels of the Federal Detention Center in midtown Manhattan, leather bindings buckling his ankles and wrists to the chair. He stared straight ahead at his CIA interrogator, eyes shooting darts, beads of sweat on his upper lip. A series of photographs was spread out on the table. A two-way mirror on the wall allowed assembled CIA and FBI personnel to view the interrogation. A video camera mounted in the upper right-hand corner of the ceiling recorded the proceedings.

"Hassan, you can make this as hard on yourself as you want," said the interrogator. "We know you murdered Senator Perry Miller. We intercepted the cell phone calls between you and your handler in Madrid." It was a lie, told convincingly.

Hassan's eyes widened with recognition.

The CIA agent pointed to one of the photographs. It was a shot of a senior member of Zafarshan's terror network captured on a security camera at a hotel in Dubai. "Who is this man? Do you know him?"

"Hell will freeze over before I give up my brothers."

"Suit yourself," said the interrogator. "But your comrades don't seem to share your same devotion to the struggle. In fact, you're the fall guy." He moved forward in his chair, clasping his hands on the table. "We have your Madrid handler in custody, and he's singing like a canary," he lied. "He's not been nearly as reticent as you in telling us what he knows. In fact, he gave you up in about ten minutes. Fingered you so fast your head would spin. And that's not all. He's told us a great deal about Zafarshan's network."

Hassan stared back, unblinking. "I will not betray my brothers, you infidel."

The CIA interrogator's face hardened. "Have it your way." He got up and walked to the door, exiting the room, and closing it behind him.

In the tight quarters of the viewing room sat two of the interrogator's CIA superiors, Patrick Mahoney, an FBI attorney, and a stenographer. The CIA agents sat slumped in chairs, watching impassively. Mahoney leaned against a wall, arms folded across his chest, wearing a scowl.

"He's not talking," said the interrogator.

"So we gather," said one of his superiors. He glanced around at the others. "I wonder how valuable he really is. He's the trigger man, to be sure. But you don't assign that job to someone indispensable."

"He's a chump," said Mahoney, stepping away from the wall. "An extremely valuable chump. He can lead us to others, both here in the U.S. and abroad. We need to get whatever information he has out of him by whatever means necessary."

"Meaning?" asked the interrogator.

"Exactly that," replied Mahoney. "Enhanced interrogation techniques. Sleep deprivation. If necessary, we waterboard him."

The interrogator looked queasy. "That's going to require approval of the director."

"I don't know if it'll be approved for a suspect this low on the org chart of Zafarshan's network," said the interrogator's superior. "Khalid Sheikh Mohammed he is not."

"You'll get the approval, or I'll get it for you," snapped Mahoney. "This is an FBI case involving the murder of a U.S. senator that leads directly back to Zafarshan, who assassinated a U.S. vice president and currently possesses enough enriched uranium to detonate a dirty bomb in every major city in the country." The veins in his neck bulged with anger. "If you don't waterboard him, I will."

The interrogator looked at his CIA superior. The superior nodded. "I'll call Langley," he said. "This will require a decision at the director level." Exhaling loudly, he got up and left the room. Mahoney walked to the door of the interrogation room and put his hand on the doorknob.

"What are you doing?" asked the interrogator.

"I'm going to talk to Qatani."

"You can't do that."

"Watch me," said Mahoney.

"You walk in there, and I'll file a formal complaint with the DNI," said the interrogator, referring to the director of National Intelligence, the senior official in the intelligence community, who supervised the Counter-Terrorism Center. "You'll never work a covert investigation again."

"You do that," said Mahoney through clenched teeth. "Golden and Whitehead have both been briefed on this investigation, and they'll back me 100 percent." He turned the doorknob, opened the door, and stepped into the interrogation room. Qatani looked up, his eyes flashing with anxiety.

"Hassan, I'm Pat Mahoney with the Federal Bureau of Investigation. I'd like to ask you a few questions. I should warn you I'm not as patient as the CIA when it comes to getting answers. Do we understand each other?"

Qatani stared back, his black eyes unmoving.

"I want to know who ordered the murder of Senator Miller."

Qatani pressed his lips together and pulled at the straps around his wrists.

"I'm only going to ask one more time: who ordered the murder of Senator Miller?" He reached across the table and grabbed Qatani by the back of the head, pulling on his hair and yanking his skull forward until it was inches away. "Answer me!" Silence. Mahoney leaned over and whispered in Hassan's ear. "You will either tell me who ordered Miller's killing, or I swear I will make you wish you never heard his name." Letting go of his hair, he grabbed him around his neck with his hand in a modified chokehold. "Tell me now!"

BEHIND THE TWO-WAY MIRROR, ONE of the CIA interrogators became agitated. "Get Mahoney out of there," he said. "He's losing it."

"No he's not," said one of his colleagues. "He's making Qatani think he'll do anything to get the information from him."

"And if Qatani gets a lawyer and claims he was tortured, this whole interrogation is going to be subjected to congressional inquiry. Someone's going to get blamed."

"Better Mahoney than us."

QATANI'S EYES BULGED AND HIS face turned red from the pressure Mahoney exerted on his throat, but he still said nothing. Mahoney let go of his neck. Qatani gasped for air, his breathing labored. Mahoney walked over to the door and knocked twice. The door opened and a detention facility guard appeared.

"Take him to EIC," said Mahoney, referring to the Enhanced Interrogation Center. "Put him on the waterboard."

"Yes, sir," said the guard. "But I'll need authorization before proceeding."

"You'll have authorization."

A second guard entered the room, and they began slowly to unstrap Qatani from the chair, then had him stand up, handcuffing his hands behind him. A third guard stood to the side, his sidearm holster unsnapped, index finger on the gun handle. The guards pulled out shackles and attached them to Qatani's ankles. They led him away, his ankle shackles clanking on the concrete floor as they departed.

IT WAS 8:10 A.M. AND the senior staff meeting was wrapping up in a conference room off the West Wing lobby. Charlie Hector kept his watch propped up in front of him as he ticked through the agenda like a NASA astronaut doing his final checklist before launch.

"Okay, go to the order," said Hector, the bags under his eyes dark against his brown skin, nearly matching his shock of black hair. "Anybody got anything?"

"I've gotten a few questions about a terrorist detainee named Hassan Qatani," said Lisa, her blue eyes intense. "Is he being interrogated? Does he have counsel? Those kinds of things. What should I say?"

A look of concern crossed Hector's face as if to say, "No one is supposed to know about this." He turned to Truman Greenglass. "Can you get Lisa some guidance?"

"Not much," said Greenglass with a sigh. "We're not yet publicly acknowledging he's in custody, though we will at some point. Legally, he's an enemy combatant, and he's being questioned about his involvement in the murder of Perry Miller as well as his connections to Rassem el Zafarshan."

"Can I say the interrogation procedures utilized by the FBI have been reviewed and signed off on by DOJ?" asked Lisa hopefully.

"If it makes you feel better, sure," joked Greenglass. Chuckles rumbled up and down the table.

"Guys, come on," said Lisa, throwing up her hands in frustration. "I've got Amnesty International all over me and State like a banshee in heat. They've got the *New York Times* eating out of their hands. Give me something—*anything*."

"Alright," replied Greenglass. "Without acknowledging Qatani is in custody, say our agents act consistent with established protocols governing the interrogation of enemy combatants and abide by all relevant statutes. Anything beyond that, refer them to DOJ."

Lisa nodded, not entirely convinced, jotting notes on her pad.

"What else?" asked Hector, picking up his Rolex and putting it back on his wrist.

"There's a story in the *New York Post* claiming POTUS met with Kerry Cartwright to recruit him to run against Sal Stanley," said Jay in a flat montone.

"I believe the headline is, 'Grudge Match,'" said Lisa, her lip curling in a sardonic grin.

"Something like that. Anyway, if anyone gets asked about it, the ticktock is Cartwright came by to meet with the intergovernmental affairs folks about law-enforcement grants, the usual drill," said Jay. "David and I met with him. He briefly met with the president in the Oval Office. No agenda. It was a courtesy call."

"There are a lot of courtesy calls with potential U.S. Senate candidates these days," joked Hector.

"Purely coincidental," said David Thomas.

Jay's eyes twinkled. "David is the Sergeant Schultz of the West Wing. He sees nothing . . . *nothing*."

"How did the *Post* find out about it?" asked Lisa.

Thomas shrugged. "People talk."

"Anyway," Jay continued. "Cartwright is coasting to reelection, which is in two weeks. We suspect Stanley's people leaked this to ding him. We need to deny we tried to recruit him—which we did not—while leaving him running room if he does decide to go."

Hector lowered his chin, staring down the table with mock disapproval. "Jaaaay," he said. "Are you causing problems again?"

"Just doin' my job, Charlie."

"That's what worries me." Hector rose from his chair. "Alright, meeting adjourned."

Everyone gathered up their pads and memos and headed for the door. When Jay reached the threshold, the president's assistant was waiting.

"Jay, the president wants to see you."

"Now?"

"Yes." She also corralled Phil Battaglia and the two headed down the hall, shoulders brushing against each other, toward the Oval Office. Jay wondered: *POTUS wants to see me and his counsel . . . together? Something must be up.* Battaglia opened the peephole to make sure the president was alone, rapped on the door twice, and walked in, Jay trailing behind.

Long sat at the HMS *Resolute* desk, reading glasses on the end of his nose, eyes scanning some papers. When he saw them, he turned his head and snapped off his glasses. "Hey, guys. I needed to see my legal eagle and my one-man brain trust." He motioned for them to sit down in the chairs on either side of the desk. "Have a seat."

They both obliged, bathing in the warm glow of presidential attention but also questioning the import and purpose of the impromptu meeting.

The president's face turned serious. Jay noticed his face seemed grayer, the lines in his forehead deeper, his eyes tired. "I need to tell you both about something that cannot leave this room under any circumstances. Those are the ground rules."

"Of course, Mr. President," said Phil.

"You know that dominatrix service Perry Miller patronized?" asked Long.

"Sure," said Jay, startled by the question.

"Well, brace yourselves," said Long, leaning forward across the desk. "Our own Johnny Whitehead was a client, too."

Battaglia went white. Jay felt he had been hit in the chest by a cannonball. It took a moment before he could breathe. Long read their shocked facial expressions.

"I know," he said, shaking his head. "Johnny's the last guy on earth I would have guessed was involved in something like this. I mean, the guy's a Boy Scout."

Battaglia recovered sufficiently to get his brain and mouth working. "We've got two tracks to deal with here," he said, synapses firing. "The first is the criminal track. The woman who operated the dominatrix service is going to be charged—no way around it, not with a dead U.S. senator in her basement. She either cops a plea and gives up her clients or keeps her mouth shut. My guess is the former. Hopefully the statute of limitations has passed and the vice president isn't charged. The second track—"

"Let me stop you there," interrupted Long. "Any chance Johnny's name doesn't come out? It was five years ago. Maybe they didn't keep records that long."

"Mr. President, this is the FBI we're talking about," said Phil. "It's going to come out."

"Yeah, you're right."

"The second track is political. Can he survive? This isn't going to be a one- or two-day story. It's a mushroom cloud."

The president turned to Jay. "What do you think, Jay?" Long asked. "Can Johnny survive it?"

"Depends," said Jay. "If it's an isolated incident, perhaps. If this Amber Abica chick turns up on *60 Minutes* describing Johnny's leather fetish, he's done. We just can't have that. He'd probably have to announce he wasn't running again. If it gets bad enough, he might have to resign."

The president flinched. He was visibly uncomfortable at the suggestion he might have to throw Whitehead under the bus.

"Johnny's a valued member of my team," Long said firmly, eyes narrowing, jutting out his jaw. "I know they say if you want a friend in Washington, get a dog. But he's my friend and colleague. Besides, I'm a Christian, and I think if someone has repented and been forgiven by the good Lord, who am I to judge? Mercy begets mercy."

Jay was intrigued by Long's response, even moved. He wished he had whatever faith led Long to be so forgiving. But as far as he was concerned, Long could not make a decision based on Christian compassion when the situation called for cold-eyed politics.

"Sir, you're not Johnny's pastor; you're the president," said Jay. "There's a difference between being forgiven and being effective. This is going to be extremely damaging, and especially given your profile with the faith community, we have to preserve your brand." He gestured with his hands for emphasis. "Look, we're going to have a tough reelect. The Republicans are not gonna choose a pro-choice nominee again. They saw how that turned out, and they've learned their lesson. The Democrats won't be hobbled by a scandal. We've got no margin for error." He paused. "Something like this is more than the system can bear."

Long looked sad. "I hear you. But I don't want to tell Johnny to fall on his sword." He looked plaintively at Battaglia, eyes searching. "Phil, can you talk to him?"

Battaglia recoiled. "Mr. President, I think that should be Charlie or Jay. I'm conflicted here because I'm interfacing with the FBI and DOJ on the Miller investigation."

Long nodded. "I don't think Jay should do it. Bad optics."

"Charlie's better," said Jay. "But I'll do it if you need me to."

Long shook his head in sadness. "This is just *brutal*, isn't it?"

"Unbelievable," said Jay. "But it is what it is. Mr. President, if we don't get in front of this story and take control of it, it will spin out of control."

"Alright," said Long, sighing. "I'll ask Charlie to talk to Johnny. Maybe he'll decide to announce he's not planning on running again. He's getting up there. He can blame his health and age. Then, if and when this hits, it's anticlimactic."

"That's the best outcome for everyone, Johnny included," said Jay.

"Charlie should have come to the meeting. Then he wouldn't have drawn the short straw," joked Long.

"That's why I never miss a meeting," volleyed Battaglia.

Long chuckled morbidly, standing up. "I ought to make you do it, Jay. You're the one who recommended him in the first place."

"It helped get you elected, sir. Johnny helped us carry Kentucky and West Virginia, just like I predicted."

"Yeah, it worked for a while, didn't it?" Long turned to Battaglia. "Phil, why didn't we turn this up in the vetting process?" It was a veiled shot; as the campaign's chief counsel, Battaglia handled the vetting of vice-presidential candidates.

Battaglia's face flushed. "I don't know. I'd have to go back and look at it. I know he was asked if he had any girlfriends or had an affair."

"Well, I guess he didn't consider a dominatrix to be a girlfriend," said Long. The president stood up, heading toward the door and the living quarters. "I think we've got a plan. Let's hope it doesn't break before we get our ducks in a row. You guys get on it."

Jay and Phil turned to leave. Jay acknowledged the president's assistant with a wink and a wave as he departed. But outward signs of ease disguised an inner turmoil. He felt physically ill. He could not believe they were going to have to shoot Johnny Whitehead in the back of the head. His mind raced with another question: who could they find on short notice to take his place as veep?

13

Congressman Don Jefferson walked briskly into the conference center at The Villages, the retirement community outside Orlando that was a veritable honeypot of votes and campaign contributions for GOP statewide candidates. The parking lot was packed with golf carts, the favored mode of transportation inside The Villages—it looked like a good crowd, which put a spring in Jefferson's step. A body man opened the door, the soggy 90-degree humidity giving way to the frigid air and Ethan Allen furnishings of the lobby. Jefferson was scheduled to address the monthly meeting of the Conservative Republican Women's Club, a breakaway from the state Republican women's federation, which these true believers considered too moderate and an apparatchik of the party establishment.

A short, energetic woman with a deep tan and a gray pageboy haircut approached in lime-green slacks and a white cotton blouse. "Don! Don!" she shouted, waving frantically.

"Yes?" he asked.

"I'm the president of the club." She smiled brightly, her dentures sparkling in the bright light. "Welcome! We're so excited you're here."

"Well, I'm glad to be here," said Jefferson in his best aw-shucks baritone. His blue suit was a half size too large and slightly wrinkled from the campaign trail. His coat had an American flag lapel pin prominently displayed. "Thanks for having me."

A clutch of women approached like bees buzzing around a daffodil, fairly trembling with excitement. "It's him!" one of them whispered to her friends.

"He's more handsome in person," said another.

"Don, I've already got your bumper sticker on my golf cart," said a third. (No one called him "Congressman." He was their friend and no titles were required.) She smiled proudly.

Jefferson laughed. "Well, I'm honored, but I haven't announced if I'm going to run or not!" he faux protested. "I don't even have a bumper sticker yet."

"Yes you do!" she replied. She pulled a batch out of her purse and waved them. "See? I had them printed myself?"

"Oooooh! I want one!"

"Me too!"

A woman with a bubble of hair dyed fire-truck red mixed with tangerine approached. "Don, can I get a picture?" she asked.

"Why, of course," said Jefferson. "Be happy to."

The woman handed her camera to her husband. Jefferson buttoned his coat and plastered on a smile. He felt the woman's hand wrap around his torso, her left side pressed against his rib cage. "Be sure to get my good side," she joked to her husband as he snapped the picture, the flash lighting up the room. "I'll put that on my Facebook page!"

A spontaneous click line formed, with women brandishing cameras, cell phones, and BlackBerries to get a photo with the man of the hour. Jefferson dutifully stood there, his body man grabbing business cards, notes, and pamphlets from those who wanted to get involved in the as-yet-unannounced campaign. After about ten minutes, the event's organizer approached.

"Don, we have to get started. Follow me," she said. They walked to a head table together as the crowed worked their way to their tables. "This is the biggest crowd we've had since Bob Long came here for one of his final appearances of the presidential campaign," she said out of the corner of her mouth. "We usually have two hundred people for our monthly meeting. Today, because you're here, we'll have almost 850." She paused for dramatic effect. "They don't just want you to run; they're *demanding* you run."

Jefferson's eyes grew wide.

After a prayer from a local pastor, the pledge, and the national anthem, the meal was served. As they worked their way through a plate of rubber chicken and cold yellow rice, various local elected officials and party activists approached the head table to greet Jefferson, some of them handing him business cards or getting photos. Whenever they handed him something, Jefferson passed it to the body man, who stood to the side, a look of bemused anonymity etched on his face.

After a former state representative and failed state senate candidate offered to host a fund-raiser, Jefferson leaned over to the club president.

"If I decide to run, should I get her involved?" he asked.

The woman pursed her lips. "She's a sweet lady who means well, and I would certainly get her involved, but between us, she can't organize a two-car parade."

"Got it," said Jefferson, smiling.

"Ready?" she asked.

"You bet. Let's get the show on the road."

The club president walked to the podium, beaming. Table conversations petered out as the room fell silent. The crowd crackled with anticipation.

"Well, this is the moment we've been waiting for," she said with brio.

"Here, here!" someone shouted.

"It is my great pleasure and a tremendous honor to introduce a man who truly needs no introduction to this audience. He was recently rated by the *National Journal* as the third most conservative member of the House of Representatives in the entire country." The room broke into applause as Jefferson smiled. "How did you only come in third, Don? What are you doing wrong?" she joked to gales of laughter. "As chairman of the Republican Study Committee, he helps to set the agenda for the Republican majority in Congress. A member of the Budget Committee, he has fought for lower taxes and balanced budgets. He is a man who believes in the Reagan philosophy of limited government and a national defense second to none." She paused, glancing down at Jefferson. "And he's good looking, which never hurts, does it, ladies?" Jefferson blushed as the women tittered. "He's long been talked about for higher leadership in the House. But if what I read in the papers is accurate, you just may be able to vote for him for U.S. Senate next year!"

The room exploded in a standing ovation. "Ladies, please welcome our friend and a conservative hero, Congressman Don Jefferson!"

Jefferson approached the podium, head bowed, wearing a restrained smile, his rubbery face a picture of humble pie. "Thank you, thank you," he said. "Please be seated."

The crowd slowly took their seats.

"Thank you for that warm introduction," Jefferson began. "As we gather here today, I want you to contemplate this fact about our nation: from the dawn of human civilization, down through the millennia, through wars and bloody convulsions, all the way until today, there has been only one nation whose explicit and sole reason for existence was to serve as a refuge from tyranny, and that is the United States of America."

The women were transfixed. They were under his spell, and he knew it.

"Whether it was the first Pilgrim settlers of the New World who fled religious persecution, the Irish who came when their farms were turned into wastelands by famine, the Jews who fled the pogroms of the motherland, or more recently, the refugees from Castro's Cuba, Chavez's Venezuela, and the Ayatollah's Iran, America, unique among all nations, has welcomed those who fled tyranny and terror because they wanted to be free." He raised his chin, cocking his head to the side. "And I want to begin with a question: if America is not free, where will these people go? The truth is, there is nowhere else for them to go."

Heads nodded throughout the room. "That's right," someone said in a low voice.

"We can only remain free with the right policies and visionary leadership. And as long as Salmon Stanley is in charge—"

"Boo! Hiss!" replied the crowd.

"I thought you might react that way," joked Jefferson. Everyone laughed.

"As long as Sal Stanley controls the U.S. Senate with an iron grip, enabled by the special interests and the labor unions, that body will be the graveyard of every conservative, commonsense policy we propose." He rocked on his toes, preparing for the roundhouse punch. "We're doing our job in the House. We passed a tax cut. It died in the Senate. We passed an energy bill to put us on the path to energy independence. It died in the Senate. We have passed crippling sanctions against Iran. It still awaits Senate action." He paused for dramatic effect. "So maybe what we need is to take some of the leaders and reformers in the House and move them over to the Senate and give Sal Stanley his walking papers."

The crowd leaped to their feet, exploding in applause. "Run, Don, Run! Run, Don, Run!" they chanted.

Jefferson wore a look of unrestrained satisfaction. He glanced over at the club president, who wore the sinister grin of a Tammany Hall ward boss. She winked. He winked back.

"You're tempting me," said Jefferson a little too loud into microphone.

"RUN, DON, RUN!! RUN, DON, RUN!! RUN, DON, RUN!!"

Jefferson stepped back from the podium, basking in their love. He wondered: *Was this enough to propel him past the party establishment, lobbyists, an incumbent governor, and the smart money that would bet against him?* His head said no, but his heart said yes.

In the back of the room, the state chairman of the Faith and Family Federation watched the scene with a mixture of excitement and awe. He pulled out his BlackBerry and punched out an e-mail to Ross Lombardy: "At Villages. Jefferson just told GOP women he might run. Standing O."

Thirty seconds later, Ross fired back: "Super. Can he win?"

"Think so," the state chairman fired back. "Grassroots r on fire."

Ross replied: "He needs $."

The state chair put his BlackBerry in his pocket. He thought to himself, *Didn't it always come back to the dough?*

AN AIDE ESCORTED TRUMAN GREENGLASS through the Mansfield reception room, named after former Democratic Majority Leader Mike Mansfield, with its Oriental rug, period furniture, and portraits of former majority leaders, who stared down from the walls like a great cloud of witnesses. As the aide pulled open the door, Greenglass found Sal Stanley seated in a thronelike wingback chair, with Senator Tom Reynolds of Oklahoma and Senator Susan Warren of Nevada, the new chairman of the Foreign Relations Committee, seated on the couch in front of him.

"Truman, come on in," said Stanley with a wave of his hand. As Greenglass approached, he rose from his chair and greeted him with a firm if perfunctory handshake.

Reynolds and Warren stood as well. Greenglass sized her up. She wore a yellow St. John outfit and matching pumps with a David Yurman gold necklace and earrings. Her short black hair had brown highlights, Greenglass guessed to hide the gray. Her milky skin showed the fading beauty of a still-striking woman, the wrinkled flesh of her neck betraying the years traveled to the pinnacle of power. The book on Warren was simple: smart, tough, liberal but not a wacko, obsessed with her own image in the press. Stanley elevated her over a more senior member of the committee who he saw as unreliable. She owed him. Greenglass would have to tread lightly.

"Truman, we'd like to move forward on the Iran sanctions bill," began Stanley, crossing his legs and leaning in his direction. "We've looked at the language of the House bill as well as the draft Perry put together before his death. Assuming we can all agree, we think we can get it out of Foreign Relations promptly and get it to the floor next week."

Truman nodded. He opened his leather-bound legal pad. "I brought some draft language for you." He glanced about. "Should I give it to you, Madam Chair?"

Stanley nodded. "Sure, give it to Sue."

Greenglass extended his hand across the coffee table. Warren took it from him and held the paper in her hands, scanning the text. Everyone else was silent as she read, her eyes widening in apparent shock.

"I'll run this up the flagpole with other members of the committee," she said coldly. "But I don't want to mislead you. I'm not a fan of including a trigger for military action."

Stanley shifted in his seat, chortling. "Absolutely not," he said. "That won't fly."

"But Senator Miller and I agreed on this language," said Greenglass. "We had a deal."

"Senator Miller is dead," replied Warren. "I'm the chairman of the committee now. I've discussed it with our members, and they're not buying. Tom can introduce it as an amendment, but we've whipped it, and I can promise you it won't pass." She leaned back in her chair, a smug look on her face.

Greenglass did a slow burn. He leaned forward, elbows resting on his knees, staring down Warren. "Senator, the president feels very strongly about this. Time is running out. Iran has weaponized a nuclear device. We don't have the luxury of trying sanctions for six months and then coming back with a second resolution authorizing military action that will take weeks or months to move through Congress. This is for all the marbles."

"Truman, I'm not opposed to military action if and when it comes to that," shot back Warren, her steely blue eyes steady. "But I won't mix the two. This is a sanctions bill. If we're going to authorize the president to go to war, it has to be a stand-alone bill."

"Why?" asked Greenglass. "There's no procedural or constitutional reason to do that."

"Because I'm chairman of the committee, and that's the way I want to proceed," said Warren. "Period."

"Sue's right," said Stanley. "The votes aren't there on our side of the aisle for a trigger. So I really don't know why this keeps coming up."

Reynolds remained silent up to that point, simmering with barely repressed anger. "Sue, if you do that, I will introduce a competing sanctions bill with bipartisan support," he said, his eyes shooting darts. "I've got a commitment from Kravitz to be a lead sponsor. He thinks he can bring half a dozen Democrats with him. The bottom line is, you may win in committee, but you'll lose on the floor." He paused, letting the dead air hang. "Do you really want to lose the most important foreign policy vote since the Iraq war?"

Warren's face hardened. "Is that a threat, Tom?"

"No, it's a promise."

Stanley crossed his arms, assuming a defensive posture. "Tom, you're playing with fire. If we do what Sue and I recommend, we can pass this bill with bipartisan support, strengthening the president's hand with Russia, China, the UN, and the EU. If we go your route, this becomes a partisan issue."

"It doesn't have to be a partisan issue, Sal," said Reynolds. "Perry Miller was on board. We ought to honor his memory by doing what he wanted."

"It doesn't work that way," shot back Stanley. "We don't go to war to honor someone's memory."

Warren turned to Greenglass. "What's the administration's position going to be, Truman? Are you going to support a competing bill?"

Greenglass hooded his eyelids. "We would prefer not to go in that direction. But if it comes to that, we'll make it clear we support authorization for additional measures if the NSC and DNI conclude the sanctions are insufficient. That's always been our position."

"I'm disappointed but not surprised," said Stanley, disgusted. "We're getting nowhere. Tell the president the consequences will be a divisive process and delay."

Greenglass's eyes smoldered. "Senator, I hope we can disagree without being disagreeable."

"I do, too, but given the emotions on both sides, I'd be lying if I said I was optimistic," said Warren.

"One last thing," said Greenglass, pulling out another piece of paper. "Here's some language that we'd like included that has nothing to do with the so-called trigger." He handed it to Warren.

"What is it?" she asked, eyes scanning the text.

"It blesses technology transfers to Iran for organizations promoting democracy and human rights," said Greenglass. "Basically it allows us to provide them with cell phones, satellites, secure broadband access, et cetera so the Green Movement can organize free from detection by the current regime."

Warren narrowed her eyes. "Do we want to telegraph that we're doing that?"

"We need clear statutory authority."

"Alright, we'll look at it."

"Anything else?" asked Stanley.

"Not that I know of," replied Greenglass.

"Alright then," said Stanley. He rose and shook Greenglass's hand. "Looks like we're going to cross swords again. Tell the president this is a matter of principle."

"As it is with us, Senator," said Greenglass in a hollow voice.

He and Reynolds walked out together, accompanied by an aide who led them through the reception area. When they reached the hallway outside, Greenglass turned to Reynolds and pulled him close in a power clutch.

"Can you roll 'em?" he asked, his voice urgent.

"I think so," said Reynolds, puffing up like a poison toad. "A number of Democratic senators don't want to look weak on national defense right before the elections. They don't want to vote against challenging Iran."

Greenglass nodded. "I need you to cut that deal on technology transfers. It's critical."

"I'll do what I can. But Sue's in Sal's clutches."

Greenglass shook his head. "Gotta have it. We're kind of pregnant on this one, if you get my drift."

"Alright. I get it."

Greenglass turned and headed down the hall, heading toward the exit and his car and driver, which was waiting to take him back to the White House. His stomach was in a knot. Not only was he facing a battle royale in the Senate over the sanctions bill, but the technology transfer language now hung by a thread. If it failed to pass, all the work he did to equip the Green Movement would be in legal limbo, and his career would hang in the balance.

G. G. Hoterman stood on the eighteenth tee box at the Badlands course in northern Las Vegas, staring at a lake on his right and a desert hazard twisted with rocks, cactus, and sagebrush. The carry over the desert was 241 yards. Walking to the ball, carrying the massive girth of an aging former high school offensive lineman on spindly legs with much effort, he stared down the fairway, waggling the clubhead of his $750 TaylorMade driver. Pulling the club head back, his eye glued to the Titleist logo, he pulled the shaft down and turned his wrists over, rocketing the ball high in the air with a slight draw. It headed right for the desert.

"Get up! Get up!" he shouted with flourish.

The ball cleared the sagebrush by no more than a yard, bouncing high and exploding down the fairway.

"Safe!" exclaimed G. G. "I made it!" He giggled like a little boy.

"You like to live dangerously, don't you, G. G.," said Fred Elrod, his playing partner.

"It's clean living," joked G. G.

"I know that's not true," replied Elrod. G. G. cackled. Elrod, flat belly and narrow waist highlighted by a white Adidas belt, bow legs balancing his frame, took his cap off and wiped his brow, revealing a deeply tanned face and gray hair turning slowly white. Only the top of his head had hints of black. Elrod leaned over his ball and made a rapid, jerky swing, sending his ball in a low slice toward a trap by the lake. The ball cleared the desert, bounded across the fairway, and skipped into the trap. He let out an expletive. "I hate it when you do this to me on the final hole," he said, leaning down and snatching the tee up, breaking it with his fingers and hurling it into the rocks.

G. G. was feeling good not only about his match with Elrod but also life in general. One of the top Democratic lobbyists and rainmakers in DC, he was bonding with Elrod, one of his favorite (and richest) clients. Elrod was at the top of the food chain at Hoterman and Schiff, G. G.'s law and lobbying firm, primarily because he paid the firm $100,000 a month to act as his inside-the-Beltway fixers and courtroom attack dogs. He also knew how to have a good time, shared G. G.'s nose for the jugular, had a gorgeous wife, and had plenty of problems needing solutions (but not too quickly!). Elrod owned a thirty-thousand-square-foot Mediterranean-style mansion in northern Las Vegas with its own home theater, fitness center and spa, an Olympian pool featuring statutes of Caesar and Napolean, poolroom, game room, and smoking room. G. G. was always welcome as a houseguest. To make matters even more satisfying, G. G.'s drive all but assured Elrod would owe him $10,000, half of which was for winning five net holes at $1,000 each, with $5,000 more for winning the match.

Not that Elrod would miss it. The former owner of El Capitan casino on the Strip, he sold out for an estimated $150 million. He took the money and bought Ultimate Wrestling Federation, which featured a hybrid of wrestling, boxing, and karate. It was consistently one of the top five highest rated cable programs in the country. Television revenue alone from UWF brought Elrod $175 million a year, with the gate, concessions, and collateral revenue brining in another $130 million.

As they jumped in the golf cart, Elrod turned to G. G. "So what's the date for the Stanley fund-raiser again?" he asked.

"Right after Labor Day. We don't want to do it during the holidays."

Elrod nodded. "And am I the chair or a cochair?"

"You tell me," said G. G. "How much can you give or raise?"

"What's the limit again, $6,200 per couple?"

"Correct. But that's just for the primary, so double it when you include the general."

Elrod stared into the distance, turning the question over in his mind. "Total, I think I can do $75,000 between me, my family, my companies, and my vendors." He turned to G. G. "Is that enough?"

"It's a good start," said G. G. "I'd love to be able to tell Sal you can do that in hard money and then hopefully do a nice contribution to the Democratic Senatorial Committee and our 527."

"Sure, I can do that," said Elrod. "Put me down for the max to the senatorial committee." He paused. "I'll do a half a million to the 527. How does that grab you?"

G. G. tried not to appear too excited. He came to view Elrod as a virtual cash machine, always good for the maximum, whenever he asked. Elrod was the kind of donor who only asked one question: how do I make out the check? G. G. did a quick calculation: his fund-raising company, which had a contract with both Stanley's campaign committee and the DSCC as well as Committee for a Better America, would make 15 percent off Elrod's contributions, or $67,500, above and beyond the 100K he paid the law firm each month. He decided $625,000 deserved a dog biscuit.

"Hey, why don't we call Sal?" he said, black eyes darting.

"Right now? "

"Sure," replied G. G. He glanced at his watch. "It's not too early on the East Coast." He reached into the golf cart and pulled out his

BlackBerry, scrolling to Stanley's cell phone number. He hit the dial button. Turning to Elrod, he whispered, "It's ringing." He paused. "Mr. Leader, good morning, it's G. G. Hope I'm not catching you at a bad time." He laughed. Cupping his hand over the phone, he said, "He just stepped out of the shower. He's standing in the bathroom with a towel, dripping wet."

Elrod wrapped his mind around the sight of the Senate majority leader standing nude in his bathroom, clutching a towel in one hand a cell phone in the other. His eyes widened, visibly impressed, the precise reaction G. G. intended.

"Senator, I'm here in Las Vegas with your good friend Fred Elrod." He paused, listening. "Yes, he's a big fan of yours as well." He winked at Elrod. "Anyway, he's agreed to cochair your Vegas event, and he just asked me to put him down for 75K hard for the event and the max to the Senate committee." He paused again. "That doesn't count the half million he just agreed to give to my 527, which you know nothing about." He laughed, throwing back his head. "Sal wants to say 'hi,'" he said, handing the phone to Elrod.

"Senator, how are you?" asked Elrod.

"Very well, Fred," replied Stanley. "Just wanted to say thanks for agreeing to help out on the upcoming Las Vegas event. I'm thrilled by your generosity and truly humbled by your support. That is just terrific news."

"Happy to do it, Senator," said Elrod, suck-up juices flowing. "You know, I'm one of those rare breeds in politics. I don't ever want to run for office myself. I don't want to be appointed to anything. I'm interested in only one thing, and that's good government. And I'm happy to help folks like you who help deliver it."

"We'll keep at it," said Stanley. "I'm afraid the current administration is quite a burden to bear, but we'll keep fighting the good fight."

"I know you will," said Elrod. "And thanks again for your support of Sue Warren as chair of Foreign Relations. She's a solid woman. I've been supporting her for years."

"She is indeed. She'll do a top-notch job. Thanks again for your help, Fred."

Elrod handed the phone back to G. G. "Alright, Senator, you can dry off and shave now," joked G. G., preparing to sign off. "I promise I won't ask you to fund-raise from the shower again!"

Stanley laughed. "Before I let you go, G. G., I assume you know Long and Noble are gunning for me big time."

"So I've heard."

"They're trying to recruit Cartwright to run against me," said Stanley. "They're denying it, but we know from our sources in Trenton that it's true."

"Do you think he'll do it?" asked G. G.

"Dunno. His numbers are good, he's gotten a free ride from the *Times,* and he's got a huge ego. With Long blowing in his ear and Noble stroking his thigh, you never know."

"The guy's never been in a street fight. Not like this."

"No, he hasn't," agreed Stanley. "But he can raise money, and the White House will bring the Long national finance operation into play, so it's going to be a knock-down, drag-out, bloodletting if he goes."

"How much will you need?" asked G. G.

"Believe it or not, $75 million. I'm counting on you to be a key member of the team."

Hoterman let out a long whistle. "Wow. Count me in."

"One last thing: I heard you might testify in Mike's trial. Is that accurate?"

Hoterman felt a palpitation in his chest. How could Stanley have possibly learned such a closely guarded secret? As far as he knew, only the Justice Department and his attorneys knew he might become a prosecution witness. The impending criminal trial for perjury and obstruction of justice of Michael Kaplan, former campaign chair for Stanley, who went down in flames in the Dele-gate cash-for-votes scandal in the previous presidential election, was now just weeks away. G. G. barely avoided being indicted himself, and his lawyer was talking to the public integrity division at Justice about his possible testimony.

"We don't know yet," lied G. G. "My attorneys have been talking to them for a year and a half. I had to testify before the grand jury *twice*. So did Dierdre, my former deputy. I'm hoping like the dickens that'll be the end of it."

"Who's your lawyer?" asked Stanley.

"Walt Shapiro."

"Tell Shapiro to tell the Justice Department that you're not a favorable witness for them," said Stanley firmly. "If you testify against Mike, it puts me in a bad place."

Hoterman nearly passed out. He wasn't a real lawyer, having barely passed the bar, but even he knew this was witness tampering—and by the Senate Majority Leader, no less. "I know, I know, Senator," he heard himself say.

"Ketih Golden timed this trial deliberately so it damages my reelection," said Stanley, spitting out the words. "They're criminalizing a political dispute. It's payback, pure and simple, and it's corrupt as the day is long."

"It's a disgrace," agreed G. G.

"Well, Shapiro's good. If he needs to talk to my counsel, let me know."

"Yes, sir."

Hoterman hung up the phone. Elrod had been listening to only one side of the conversation, awed that the Senate Majority Leader was G. G.'s phone pal. "What was that all about?" he asked.

"Oh, nothing. Just Dele-gate." He sighed. "It's the gift that keeps on giving."

"Mike Kaplan's trial?"

"Yeah," said G. G. "Poor Mike did nothing illegal, but he made some dumb mistakes, including shredding some documents. He's in real trouble, and it's tearing Sal up inside." He brightened, his thoughts returning to Elrod's large contribution and his 275-yard drive. "Hey, let's hit our shots!"

"Now you're talking," said Elrod, stepping from the cart and walking to his ball.

Hoterman glanced back at the tee box, where a group had been standing around waiting while he wrapped up his phone call. They had their hands on their waists, clearly annoyed. They clearly didn't know how important he was. He approached his ball, which to his astonishment cleared the desert by only a few yards and then bounced hard left, giving him barely enough room for a stance on the fairway. He addressed the ball, his back heels on the desert floor, and tried to balance his weight and focus on the target. But his mind was a jumble, and he kept returning to Stanley's phone call. What if he did testify and helped send Kaplan to prison? How could he live with himself? Would Stanley ever forgive him?

He tried to focus, ripping a five iron low into the wind toward the green. But a combination of a poor stance and his distracted mind forced the ball to the right, where it skipped into a greenside bunker. G. G. let out an expletive and slammed his club on the ground. His phone call to Stanley, intended to impress Elrod, backfired and now threatened to cost him the match. Elrod, meanwhile, hit a spectacular hybrid club out of the fairway bunker with a slight draw that bounced toward the green and skipped onto the putting surface, rolling to a stop just twelve feet from the pin.

"I got you now, G. G.!" Elrod shouted, pointing with his index finger. "What a difference a shot makes."

The men heard some shouting behind them. Was it those jerks back on the tee box, wondered G. G. But when he turned around, he saw Elrod's wife Ling and Dierdre, G. G.'s girlfriend, standing on the deck of Elrod's massive home on the eighteenth fairway, waving. They wore bikini tops and skirts, their bodies glistening with lotion, holding umbrella drinks.

"Hey, girls, did you see my shot?" shouted Elrod.

"Good shot, honey!" replied Ling.

"Hey, Ling, he hasn't won yet," said G. G. playfully. "I've seen him putt. He'll probably three putt from there."

"Get up and down, G. G.!" cried Dierdre.

"Fred, why don't you and G. G. join us by the pool for a drink when you're done? I make your favorite mohito," said Ling.

"Great idea," replied Fred. "Thanks, baby!"

By now the exasperation of the foursome on the tee box had reached the snapping point. One of them threw his hands in the air in frustration, turning to the others and jawing about their slow play. *Tough,* thought G. G. *I'm playing the final hole for $10,000 with a billionaire whose gorgeous wife is making us a homemade mohito.*

As they pulled away in their cart and headed for the green, G. G. turned to Fred. "Ling seems to be a very good fit for you," he said. Elrod married Ling a little more than a year earlier after going through a messy divorce.

"She's fantastic," Elrod fairly gushed. "She's naturally submissive. She's Korean. . . . She aims to please."

G. G. smiled admiringly. "Good for you, Fred."

"You know, I probably never should have married an American woman."

"Why?"

"They're too demanding," Elrod, replied, making a face. "Too much complaining, too much take, not enough give. I'm telling you, if you want a wife who'll take care of you, go Asian."

"How did you meet Ling?" asked G. G. as they got out of the cart.

"An online dating site," said Elrod. "It specialized in Asian women."

"Really?" said G. G. "I didn't know there were sites specializing in ethnic backgrounds."

"Is this a great country or what?" exclaimed Elrod.

G. G. twisted his feet into the trap until the sand covered the soles of his shoes, giving himself a solid stance for the bunker shot.

He stared at the pin, which was only five paces on the green from the edge of the lake, a foreboding steep drop into the water just beyond it. If he was short, he could not make the putt and tie Elrod; if he was long, he would go in the water and lose the match. *What the heck,* he thought. *I've got nothing to lose.* With a full swing, he blasted the ball out of the trap, sending it about fifteen yards onto the green, where it rolled rapidly toward the hole as if drawn by a magnet, hitting the pin dead center and dropping into the cup.

G. G. threw his arms in the air in a celebratory fit, pumping his fists in the air and shaking his torso. "I can't believe it went in! Now the pressure is really on you, Fred."

Elrod let out an expletive, disgusted. "You never give up. I guess that's why I pay the big bucks for you to represent me in DC." As the caddy accompanying them raked the trap, Elrod paced around the hole, kneeling with his hand cupped over his eyes, reading his putt from every angle. Then, with a firm stroke, he hit the ball to his right, and it fell in the right side of the hole. "Take that!" he cried.

G. G. walked over, grinning from ear to ear, shaking his head. "After all that, no blood."

"Let's go have a drink with the girls," said Elrod. "Then I'll have Ling give me a deep tissue massage. She walks on my back!" He winked.

They walked off the green, arm in arm, oblivious to the poor foursome that had waited behind them all day, now standing in the fairway shaking their heads with a mixture of manly respect and thorough disgust.

15

S atcha Sanchez walked through the lobby of the Ritz-Carlton
Residences on Twenty-third Street, NW, one of the premier
power addresses in DC and home away from home for Jay
Noble. Poured into skinny jeans, Christian Louboutin pumps, an
embroidered Bebe white tee and blue jacket, Satcha drew the stares of
the bellhops as she fairly pranced, her bouncing bouffant of black hair,
ruby red lips, and molasses skin even more striking in person than on
TV.

Approaching a house phone, she dialed the hotel operator with her
index finger, her enamel-red fingernail clicking on the button, asking
for Jay's apartment.

"Hel-loooo," he answered.

"Hey, sugar, it's me," said Satcha.

"Come on up. Apartment 1202."

After riding the elevator to the twelfth floor, she stepped into the
hallway, walked to the door, and rang the doorbell. Jay opened the
door.

"You look mah-velous, darling," he said, his hungry eyes sizing her up from head to toe. "As always!" He felt a surge of desire rush through him. He hoped it wasn't too obvious.

"Thank you," said Satcha. She pulled a green bottle from behind her back. "Look what I brought."

"Champagne?"

"Not just champagne. It's Dom," she said.

Jay made a mock frown. "Darn, I already opened a bottle of wine."

"No problem," said Satcha with an alluring smile. "We'll have the champagne first, then the wine."

Jay apologized profusely for leaving her standing in the hallway. He opened the door wide and motioned her into the apartment. As she breezed past, her body brushed against his chest. He felt a surge of sexual tension. He wondered: *Was she feeling it, too?*

"Oh, I *love* your apartment," gushed Satcha. "Who decorated it?"

"This is how it came. Honestly, I didn't change a thing," said Jay. He gave her a quick tour of the eighteen-hundred-square-foot unit, pointing out the oak paneling in the library, the Sub-Zero refrigerator, gas range and espresso maker in the kitchen, and the cozy master bedroom with a terrace. "When the president asked me to come to the White House, I told my real estate agent I had to find a place no more than ten minutes from work that was low maintenance. I signed the contract the next day."

"It's wonderful," she said. "I *love* it."

"Come here. . . . I'll show you the balcony." He walked to the kitchen, grabbing two fluted champagne glasses from the bar, and led her outside. As they stepped onto the balcony, they drank in the panoramic view, the White House to their right, the illuminated Capitol dome visible beyond it, the twinkling lights of downtown DC to their left, the National Cathedral, and spires of Georgetown University farther in the distance.

"Oh, what a view," said Satcha.

"It's nice," said Jay. He opened the champagne, the cork flying off with a loud pop, and poured the bubbly lovingly into the glasses. He handed Satcha a glass, then lifted his aloft, proposing a toast. "To victory in November . . . for me at the ballot box and you-slash-Univision in the ratings."

"I'll drink to that," said Satcha, giggling. They clinked glasses and drank, never losing eye contact. "Alright, can we talk business?"

"Business before pleasure is my motto."

"I want you to help me book all the top U.S. Senate candidates on my show to debate their opponents," said Satcha. "It'll be *Meet the Press* meets *El Nuevo Herald*. I'll have a panel of Latino journalists, and I'll moderate." She batted her eyes. "Will you help me?"

"Sure, I think it's terrific," said Jay. "But why would they take time away from feeding the local press to do a national Latino cable show?"

"Are you kidding?" asked Satcha, eyes widening. "I get higher ratings than the networks in Miami, LA, and Houston in prime time. Think about that! Between the Cubans in Florida, the Mexicans in California, and the Ricans in New Jersey, the Hispanics are going to be the swing vote in all three of the top Senate races in the country." She shook her tush, jutting her hips back and forth. "Latinos are the hottest thing in politics."

Jay raised his glass. "And you're their ambassador."

"Not ambassador, baby. I'm the queen bee."

"Well, your highness," said Jay, bowing low from the waist. "I'll help you get all our guys. But I want something in return."

"What's that?"

"You know," he said mischievously, leaning into her, their faces no more than six inches apart. He felt her breath on his chin, the smell of the fresh champagne intoxicating.

"Oh, you naughty boy," she said, raising her mouth to his.

"Quid pro quo," said Jay in a low baritone. Before their lips could touch, Jay's cell phone went off.

"Ignore it," said Satcha, her eyes closed, her lips puckered.

"I can't," said Jay. "I think it's a reporter under deadline." He pulled out the phone and looked at the display, rolling his eyes. "It's worse than that: Marvin Myers."

Satcha lowered her chin, speaking in a mocking tone, imitating Myers' trademark baritone: "Feed the beast."

Jay put his index finger to his lips, requesting quiet, and answered the phone. "Double M! Which am I today: the source or the target?"

"You're always the source, Jay," purred Marvin in a syrupy voice. "One of the best."

"I bet you say that to all your dates."

Myers let out a wheezy, rat-tat-tat laugh. "Listen, I heard through the grapevine Long met with Mack Caulfield when he was in LA and asked him to consider running for the U.S. Senate against Kate Covitz," said Myers, dropping a grenade in the middle of Jay's date night. "I'm sure you don't want to go on the record, but is there anything you can tell me on background?"

Jay nearly dropped the phone. His mind raced: who was running their big mouth? If it was Caulfield, he would wring his neck. "We've talked to a lot of people about the California Senate race," said Jay. "Caulfield is just one among many. The list is longer than the LA phone book."

"I've got it confirmed by two sources," said Myers, holding his ground.

"He and the president are friends. It was a wide-ranging discussion about Mack's future. The Senate race came up, but only in passing."

"What's wrong with Mike Hammer?" Myers pressed, referring to the Orange County supervisor who was a favorite of the Faith and Family Federation.

"Off the record? He's an Orange County wingnut," said Jay. "He'll get the Faith and Family vote and the gun nuts and the Howard Jarvis society crowd, but that's it. What's that worth—38 percent of the vote? Besides, Hammer won't talk to the press, doesn't take questions at events, won't do ed boards. Heck, he won't even work a rope line for fear of getting picked up on a boom mike! They've got him in a witness protection program."

"But if the goal is for the Republicans to take the Senate, why kick the base in the teeth?"

"He can't win, Marvin."

"Well, my sources tell me Caulfield is a no go."

Jay wanted to scream into the phone: *Why are Caulfield's handlers talking to you instead of me?* He was livid but kept his emotions in check. "Don't be too sure, Marvin. This casserole is not fully baked."

"Suit yourself," said Myers. "Hey, by the way, I hear Satcha Sanchez is in town. That can only mean one thing, which is she's trolling for an exclusive. You're not giving her a sit-down with the president, I hope. You promised me the next one, remember?"

Jay suppressed an expletive. Myers was uncanny—the guy had sources all over town. He put his hand over the receiver and moved his lips silently, mouthing to Satcha: "He knows you're here."

Satcha read Jay's lips, and her eyes grew into saucers. She frantically waved her arms as though warning a jet off a carrier deck. "I'm NOT here," she whispered.

"No, nothing like that," said Jay into the receiver. "I think the next media avail for POTUS will be in the briefing room or the East Room. No one-on-ones are in the works, at least not to my knowledge."

"Well, don't let her have him or the Senate candidates until I get a chance to make my pitch," said Myers. "You know my ratings on Sunday morning are the highest on cable."

"How well I know, Marvin," said Jay. "We watch the numbers every week. You're at the top of the heap, and don't think we don't notice."

"Good. I want the Senate debates. Forget about Satcha. She's yesterday's news."

"You're at the top of the list," Jay lied. He hung up the phone and turned to Satcha. "I don't believe this guy! He's wrapped around the axle with Caulfield, and he's gunning for the Senate debates just like you. He wants an exclusive."

"I hope you're not going to give it to him," said Satcha, her mouth forming a pout.

"Of course not, but I'm not the only one making the decision. Lisa's going to have a lot of say. So will the candidates for that matter."

"Lisa hates me."

"No, she doesn't. She's just competitive, that's all."

"Jay, she doesn't even return my phone calls."

Jay stared into his champagne. "I guess you're right. She does hate you." He let out an uproarious laugh.

Satcha drained her champagne and set it down on the iron and glass table. A red line from the setting sun silhouetted the skyline as night fell across the nation's capital. She moved in and pressed her body against Jay, wrapping her arms around his waist. He could smell her Brioni perfume, the scent of which was intoxicating. "Get me the Senate candidates, Jay," she said. "You won't regret it."

"Now you're not playing fair," he protested. "We agreed we wouldn't mix business with pleasure."

"That was before Myers tried to move in on my turf."

"So all's fair in love and war?" Jay asked, raising an eyebrow.

"Yes. And in the pursuit of higher ratings," she cooed, rubbing the small of his back with her fingers. Jay felt his lower back relax and his knees go weak.

"Whatever you say," he heard himself answer.

NINE BLOCKS AWAY ON THE second floor of a nondescript gray townhouse on F Street, Sal Stanley presided over a strategy session with some of the most important minds—and wallets—in the national Democratic Party. Dubbed "F Troop" after the 1960s' sitcom of the same name, the assembled heavyweights gathered over pizza, beer, red wine, and Chinese takeout once or twice a month. They pored over polling data, traded intelligence on candidates and races, and plotted how to beat back the assault of the Long administration and the far right against the Democratic Senate.

They assembled at the request of Salmon Stanley, who brought a single-minded focus to the task. Among those joining him were Christy Love, the president of Pro Choice PAC; uber-lobbyist and rainmaker G. G. Hoterman, the Service Employees International Union (SEIU) president, officials from MoveOn.org, and an assortment of Democratic consultants and pollsters. In a happier time the meetings were run by Michael Kaplan, Stanley's long-time campaign advisor and consigliere. But with Kaplan's criminal trial scheduled to begin in two weeks, he was otherwise occupied.

Stanley sat at the head of the table wrapped in a blue suit and striped tie, his reddish hair now blondish gray, his ruddy complexion a mottle of freckles, sun spots, and worry lines. He looked weary but determined, his blue eyes intense. He was thoroughly in his element, issuing directives in crisp sentences, cutting people off when he thought they were getting long-winded, and occasionally falling silent as he listened to the sometimes combatively offered and conflicting views of his advisors.

"I asked Tom Jensen to join us. He's one of the smartest guys in the party. Tom, tell us what's going on in the country," said Stanley, pushing away a plate of cold pizza.

Jensen's face lit up like a fluorescent light, a day's worth of beard stubble flecking his chin, his face glistening with sweat from a full day of intellectual exertions. A bowling ball of a man with a thick neck and a tiny head, he looked as if he might burst out of his blue button-down shirt and blue blazer. Walking to the foot of the table, he pecked on the keyboard of a laptop until the first slide of a PowerPoint appeared on a screen.

"The key to this election and the nonnegotiable variable in preserving our majority in the Senate is who does a better job getting their voters to the polls," said Jensen, darting eyes surveying his rapt audience, with an occasional adoring gaze in Stanley's direction. "Overall, voter participation in by-elections declines by 30 to 40 percent from the level in presidential elections. Whoever gets more of their presidential voters to turn out two years later, wins. Simple as that." He clicked the cursor with his hand, bringing up a slide that read: "Long's Right-Wing Coalition." People chuckled as it came up. "Long and the Republicans will be focusing on four main voter groups: white men, evangelicals, rural voters, and conservative independents in the suburbs and exburbs." He clicked a slide over showing the percentages of the electorate. "Obviously, there's some overlap here, but these four groups constitute about 45 percent of the electorate, all in." He paused, eyes scanning the slide. "That's the good news: their team does not make up a majority in the electorate."

"What's the bad news?" asked Stanley.

"The not-so-good news for us is these voters can comprise a majority if our voters stay home or they turn out in unusually high numbers," replied Jensen. He clicked the next slide, which listed exit polling data for previous elections. "That's what happened in 1994, 2002, and 2010. White males, evangelicals, and rural voters went to the polls in record numbers. We lost the House or the Senate, or both, in each of those elections. If it happens this year, the Senate is on the bubble."

"What's your prognosis?" asked Stanley. "What do the tea leaves say today?"

"Their base is more fired up right now than ours. The current average among the last ten published polls is a twelve-point intensity gap favoring them. If we don't get our side more fired up, we could have a rough election."

"That's why Andy Stanton and Ross Lombardy are trying to recruit far-right candidates in the model of Don Jefferson in Florida," said Hoterman. "They're trying to turn out the church people and the Tea Party crowd. They're throwing red meat into the shark tank."

"That cuts both ways," said Stanley. "Jefferson wants to privatize Social Security. We'll *kill* him with that if he's their nominee in Florida."

"We can only hope they're that stupid," joked G. G. to a chorus of laughter.

"So what's our strategy?" asked Jensen. He surveyed their anxious faces. His presentation was having the desired effect: they were petrified.

"Turnout," said Christy Love.

"Correct," said Jensen. "But not just any old turnout. It has to be targeted. They have their groups. We have ours: young people, union households, single women, African-Americans, Hispanics." He threw another slide up on the screen showing turnout figures for the four demographic groups. "When we have won in the past, those four groups have comprised 52 percent of the electorate. That's in a presidential year. But their turnout has historically declined during off-years more than conservative voters. We call them drop-off voters. The most important to reenergize is our eighteen- to twenty-nine-year-olds and minorities."

"Don't forget about union households," said Dick Puck, the president of SEIU, a thatch of black hair and thick moustache highlighting beady eyes and a bulbous nose that looked like it was broken in three places. "That's 15 percent of the vote."

"Yes, *very* important," said Jensen, scrambling to pacify the union chief. "Especially in places like Ohio, Michigan, Pennsylvania, and California."

"How do we turn them out?" asked Christy, lips pressed into a thin line. "They've got talk radio, FOX News, the vast right-wing conspiracy."

"Three ways," replied Jensen. "The ground game is key, but it's only part of the answer. We need better candidates and a favorable issue mix."

"We need to be talking about jobs and health care," said Puck. "Right now we're talking about Iran, nukes, and terrorism. That plays right into their hands."

"How much longer will the sanctions bill tie up the Senate?" asked G. G., his facial expression telegraphing concern.

"I'm afraid two weeks," said Stanley, a scowl plastered on his face. "I had hoped to move more quickly, but the Republicans are going to offer a trigger mechanism amendment, and that basically turns it into a military authorization vote."

"We still have time," said Jensen. "But if we're talking about Iran in October, we're dead."

"Somebody needs to tell that whack job Salami he's strengthening Long's hand politically," said Christy, picking at a plate of cold Chinese takeout.

"I don't think Salami is receptive to rational persuasion," deadpanned Stanley. Everyone laughed.

"There's another aspect of turnout that is essential," said Jensen, pulling the conversation back on track. "Hatred and fear are more powerful in motivating voters than simply enthusiasm for our team. We need to demonize the right and tie Long to the most extremist elements of his coalition in order to excite our voters."

Stanley's face assumed a putty-like plasticity. He seemed ambivalent about Jensen's brutal honesty.

"That's exactly right," said Christy, always up for a fight, her eyes aflame. "We can't let Long continue the charade that he's independent. He's a religious right, Wall Street, tea-bagger Republican. He's a fraud."

"Tell us what you really think," quipped Stanley, to laughter.

"Push him right," offered G. G. "Morph him and his candidates into Andy Stanton. Hang the extremism and bigotry of the tea baggers around his neck."

"In 1946 Arthur Vandenberg told Harry Truman if he wanted to pass a bill giving aid to Greece and Turkey, he'd have to scare the hell out of the American people," said Jensen, turning off the PowerPoint to eliminate the visual distraction and give his words full impact. "The passage of that bill effectively laid the seeds of McCarthyism. The right is better at frightening their people than we are. If we let them do it this time, Andy Stanton won't just control the White House and the Supreme Court. He'll control the entire government."

"Now that's a message my guys can get excited about," said Puck in a gravely baritone, leaning forward and tapping the table with his finger for emphasis. "This is about having a check on the far right and Long."

Stanley stood up and walked around behind his chair, his hands grasping its edges. "Great presentation, Tom," he said. He glanced at every face. "I think Tom has laid out very clearly what we need to do between now and November. We'll do our part in the Senate. Once we get past this Iran sanctions vote, we're going to get the Republicans on record on a slew of tough votes. Christy, I need you and Dick and the minority groups to get that message out and turn out your people."

Christy and Puck both nodded. Stanley walked around the table shaking hands and hugging necks, his body aide hovering at his side. As he departed the room, he signaled for Jensen to walk out with him. "Excellent," he said. Jensen beamed, walking step for step with Stanley. "Can you do this same PowerPoint at the caucus lunch next week?"

"Absolutely," said Jensen.

"Good. I think every member of our caucus needs to hear this." He stopped, his eyes boring into Jensen. "What keeps you awake at night?"

Jensen thought a moment. "A military strike against Iran. It would rally the country the way the Cuban Missile Crisis did for JFK in 1962. The Democrats were going to lose ten House seats. Instead, JFK's job- approval rating shot up, and they gained two."

Stanley nodded. "Me too. And I wouldn't put it past Long and Noble to do it so it was timed for maximum political benefit."

"He won't think twice," said Jensen. "First he puts Marco Diaz on the Supreme Court. Now he's threatening to start another war in the Middle East. This guy has got to be stopped."

"I tried, remember?" replied Stanley morbidly. With that, he was gone.

16

In a warehouse somewhere outside Newark, New Jersey, one of the CIA's so-called "black sites" for the interrogation of terrorist suspects, Pat Mahoney lowered the wooden board on which a blindfolded Hassan Qatani's was strapped, his legs and arms immobilized by leather restraints, and laid a wet towel over his face. He leaned forward, his mouth inches from Qatani's face.

"You either tell me what I want to know, or you're going to drown to death right here and now," he said through clenched teeth. "I'm only going to ask one more time: who else was part of your cell in the United States?"

Qatani breathed with great difficulty, the wet towel sucking against his mouth each time he inhaled. His fists were clenched tightly, his body shaking with fear, his brow furrowed. He was in great distress. Mahoney glanced at the CIA operative who was assisting him and nodded. "Do it," he said.

The operative held a metal pitcher filled with water up at a distance of about two feet and began slowly to pour it over the cloth enveloping Qatani's face. He tried to shake his head from side to side to no avail, his screams muffled by the towel. The operative poured half the pitcher over the towel, creating the sensation for Qatani that he was drowning. After about ninety seconds of screaming and crying, Mahoney raised the board back to an upright position.

"Have you had enough yet, Hassan?" He paused as Qatani choked and gasped for air. "Because I'm just getting going. And don't think for a minute I'm going to stop until you start talking. Because I *enjoy* this. I *relish* watching you suffer. That's what you did to Perry Miller, and that's what you and your compatriots want to do to as many Americans as you can."

Qatani remained silent except for his labored breathing. The veins in his neck bulged, his vena cava protruding, his nostrils flared, every fiber in his body straining for oxygen. Mahoney walked to the other side of the room and looked through the glass into the observation chamber, where the CIA black-site supervisor and a colleague observed the proceedings. He shrugged his shoulders as if to ask, "Do I keep going here?" The supervisor stared back impassively, raising a mug of black coffee to his lips. They were reaching the end of their rope in terms of CIA protocols governing EITs, or enhanced interrogation techniques.

Mahoney made an executive decision. He pulled his gun out of its holster and put the cold, nickel-plated barrel against Qatani's temple.

"Tell me what I want to know, NOW!" he shouted. "Who are the other members of your cell? Who are your handlers? Tell me, or I swear I'm going to kill you by either drowning you or pulling this trigger!"

Qatani's facial muscles twitched involuntarily. The CIA operative running the water board looked at Mahoney with a mixture of genuine concern for his physical safety and professional detachment. Mahoney knew neither the operative nor the Agency was happy with the way things were going. *I'm living on the edge,* he thought. But this was his interrogation, and it was sanctioned at the highest levels of the government, including the White House.

"Drown him," he muttered.

The operative began to lower the board back in a reclined position. He took the damp towel, methodically folded it, and began to lay it across Qatani's nose and mouth.

"*Istanna, istanna,*" said Qatani in Arabic. "Wait, wait!" His voice was muffled through the wet towel.

"Are you ready to talk?" asked Mahoney, putting his revolver back in its holster.

Qatani nodded his head violently; the motion restricted the restraints holding his skull to the board. Mahoney looked at the operative and nodded. The CIA operative removed the towel from Qatani's face.

"*Naam aaywa,*" Qatani replied. "I will talk. Just please don't put me under the water again."

Mahoney glanced back at the glass separating the observation room. He allowed himself a little smile. The CIA guys stared back, their faces like stone. They didn't like Mahoney's tactics. But they liked the results.

IN A SEEDY, SMOKE-FILLED BAR in a seedy section of Damascus, not far from the old city, a middle-aged Iranian man ordered another shot of vodka, tapping the top of his glass with his index finger. The bartender nodded and pulled down a bottle of Russian vodka, which had become the drink of choice during the Cold War, and poured. The glass filled slowly with the clear liquid.

Just then a petite woman in a short black dress, fishnet stockings, and stiletto heels walked from the end of the bar and slid onto the stool next to the Iranian. She had been eyeing him for some time, their eyes occasionally locking. Her dyed blonde hair was teased into the mop top of a Kewpie doll, her large red lips projecting a sensual allure, the rose tattoo on her left shoulder blade suggesting exotic wanderings. She opened her small black purse and pulled out a cigarette, placing it between two fingers.

"Where are you from?" she asked as the bartender placed the glass of beer down.

"Tehran," said the man.

"And what do you do in Tehran?"

"I'm an engineer."

She placed the cigarette in her mouth and leaned forward, inviting him to light it. He picked up a pack of matches out of a nearby ashtray and lit her cigarette. She inhaled deeply, blowing the smoke into the air above his head. "An engineer. That sounds important. What kind of engineer?"

"I could tell you, but then I'd have to kill you," said the man, smiling.

The woman raised her eyebrows. "Aaaah, a secret! So tell me your name, Mr. Secret Agent Man."

He extended his hand. "Nasrin."

"Good to meet you, Nasrin. My name is Marlin."

"Marlin?" he asked.

"Yes, as in the fish."

The man became aware of a presence to his right. He turned to see a thin, wiry woman in a black lace dress, jet-black hair pulled back into a ponytail, her eyes covered with mascara so thick she resembled a raccoon. She crossed her legs and leaned in his direction, her black pump tickling the back of his calf.

"This is my friend, Jasmine," said Marlin.

The man shook Jasmine's hand. She giggled.

"So . . . would you like to party with us?" asked Marlin.

"What kind of party do you have in mind?"

"Whatever you like," she said. "We can dance for you. I can give you a massage. We can do whatever we want." She looked over at her friend, who giggled again.

"Sounds good. Where can we go?"

"Where are you staying?"

"The Beit Al Mamlouka."

"I know it. Very charming. Why don't you get a check, and we'll go there together." The man agreed. She pulled up her dress, allowing him to gaze briefly at the garter belt holding up her stocking. "Like what you see?"

"Yes," he replied. Having seen the goods, he waved for the tab and paid for their drinks. They stumbled out of the bar, the man thoroughly inebriated, and walked arm in arm to the hotel, cruising through the lobby and up the stairs to his room. Once inside the room, they raided the minibar, and he uncorked a champagne bottle, filling three plastic cups.

Marlin stood on the bed and began to do a slow dance, rubbing her hands up and down her body. "Put on some music," she said. Jasmine kicked off her shoes and lay back on the bed, stroking Nasrin's leg.

Nasrin swung his legs over the bed and reached across the bedstand to turn on the radio, fiddling with the dial. As he leaned forward, the closet door slid slightly open. The barrel of a .45-caliber pistol with a silencer held in a gloved hand peeked out. He never saw it.

Two shots were fired. Both bullets hit the victim in the back of the head, blowing the top of his skull off and pulling back a flap of his scalp, spraying the wall with blood, bone chips, and gray matter. His body lurched forward and slammed into the wall, crumpling to the floor, lifeless. His legs were splayed awkwardly to the side, his torso twisted away from the wall, his eyes stared unseeing, his head turned at an impossible angle.

Marlin let out a scream, panicked. Tiny flecks of blood covered her face. "Why did you do that?"

A man with short-cropped black hair came out of the closet and unzipped a green body suit. His feet were clad with green surgical shoe covers. He walked over to the body and wordlessly placed two fingers on the neck, checking for a pulse.

"I couldn't take a chance on him seeing me. He stuck the pistol in his belt and pulled out a wallet, counting out bills with his gloved hands and laying them on the bed. "That's $2,000," he said. "One thousand each."

The women stared at the money, still in shock. The man said, "What—you don't want the money?"

"Yes," said Marlin in a quiet voice. She picked up the bills with trembling fingers and shoved her portion into her bra, handing the rest to her friend.

"Pleasure doing business with you, ladies," said the man. "If you become aware of any other customers who might be of interest to my clients, let me know."

He walked out the door, leaving them alone with the body.

TRUMAN GREENGLASS CAME OUT OF his office and walked to his assistant's desk. "What have we got this afternoon?" he asked.

"You've got Tom Friedman doing another think piece on the Middle East peace process," she said, her voice flat.

"Again?"

"Then the ambassador of Ghana, followed by a video hookup with General Slayton from Afghanistan."

Greenglass screwed up his face. "Reschedule everything. Get Bill Jacobs on the phone. And find out when I can brief the president and the war cabinet."

His assistant immediately dialed Jacobs's number and put him on hold. "Bill's on line one," she said.

Greenglass walked into his office and closed the door. As he stepped toward the phone, he glanced at the image of a photo of his wife and children he used for a screen saver. A thought rattled around in his brain: should he have his family relocated to a safer place, maybe the Dakotas or somewhere else in the Rocky Mountain West?

"Bill, how are you?" he asked as he picked up the receiver.

"As good as can be expected."

"How soon can you get over here for a meeting?"

"I'm already en route," said Jacobs. "Ten minutes tops."

"Good. I've cleared my calendar for the afternoon. We'll work around the president's schedule."

"I need to give you a heads-up on something."

"What?"

"I'm bringing Pat Mahoney with me."

"That's a no go. It violates protocol," fired back Greenglass. He despised Mahoney and had no intention of letting him in the Sit Room. Mahoney forced him to hire a criminal attorney and run up a $50,000 legal bill (so far) to deal with his fishing expedition into covert ops in Iran. DOJ and Phil Battaglia were currently in a royal spitting match over whether Greenglass would have to share classified information with the FBI.

"Too late. He's with me," said Jacobs. "If you exclude him now, it'll make *you* look bad. And I'm going to insist he join us for the debrief because Mahoney is the one who broke Qatani." He paused, reloading. "If you still want to try to stop it, you should know Keith Golden agrees with me."

"Fine," said Greenglass, his voice jagged. "But only for the debrief on the Qatani interrogation. After that, he leaves."

"Okay, that works for me."

Greenglass hung up the phone and stared at the photograph of his children, deep in thought. Mahoney was out of control, he reflected, and this latest development was only going to strengthen his hand. To make matters worse, Jacobs was giving the little weasel a guided tour of the West Wing. The whole investigation was turning into a nightmare for the White House.

TWENTY MINUTES LATER THE DOOR to the Situation Room opened, and the president strode into the room. Everyone at the table snapped to attention. Gathering for the meeting in addition to Greenglass and Jacobs were other members of the National Security principals committee: Johnny Whitehead, Charlie Hector, Secretary of State Candace Sanders, Secretary of Defense Alan Sweet, and Attorney General Keith Golden. Aides from NSC, CIA, and DOD lined the walls, witnesses to history. Also present was Pat Mahoney, his face on high beam. He and Greenglass sat as far apart as possible, having failed to even acknowledge the other when they entered the room prior to the president's arrival.

All business, Long sat in his captain's chair at the head of the table and spun in the direction of Jacobs. "I understand we've got information from this guy who killed Perry Miller. . . . What's his name again . . . Qatani?"

"Hassan Qatani, Mr. President," said Jacobs, opening a leather-bound briefing book in front of him. "We've been utilizing EITs and they have yielded extremely valuable intel. With your permission I'd like to go ahead with what Qatani has told us."

Greenglass could hardly believe his ears. Jacobs and the Agency dragged their feet on using EITs on Qatani, and did so only when DOJ, the Pentagon, and the White House insisted. In a typical CIA maneuver, Jacobs demanded a presidential authorization to do so . . . and now he was taking credit for their success!

"Proceed," said Long, all business.

Jacobs clicked a remote control with his thumb, illuminating the screen on the wall opposite the president with a photograph of Qatani. With black hair, a beard, and hollow eyes, he looked disheveled, his stare vacant. "Qatani is a Saudi national who trained in Yemen with an offshoot of al Qaeda. The underworld of Islamic terrorism is rife with personal rivalries and schisms tactical and theological. It looks like he switched teams after the assassination of Harrison Flaherty, believing Rassem el Zafarshan was more creative—and had more financial resources with which to fight."

"That's been the problem with the fixation of the intelligence community on al Qaeda," said Long firmly. "It's not the organization that is the enemy; the real enemy is Islamic radicalism."

Heads nodded around the table.

"So how did this Qatani guy get into the country?" asked Long.

"Student visa," said Jacobs.

"Unbelievable," said Long, shaking his head. "I can't believe we're not catching these guys when they enter the country." He caught Greenglass's eye, who shook his head in disbelief.

"They're getting more creative about who they recruit," said Jacobs. "Qatani was an ideal candidate. He came from a prominent Saudi family and had no known terrorist ties."

"They're also going aggressively after Americans," said Golden. "They're trying to puncture our security cordon."

"What's Qatani saying?" asked Long.

Greenglass jumped in. "He's confessed to the murder of Senator Miller. He claims he acted with the full knowledge and funding of Zafarshan. He said the original plan was to kill Miller when he arrived home one night. Qatani said it was only after he saw Miller leaving the townhouse in Georgetown that he went back to his handlers and recommended staging it there."

"You're telling me Qatani was going to the same dominatrix and just bumped into Miller one day?" asked Long, incredulous. "This was a total coincidence?"

"Yes. He never physically encountered Miller but saw him leaving the townhouse."

"Incredible!" exclaimed the president.

"If I may, Mr. President," said Jacobs, "I'd like Special Agent Pat Mahoney with the FBI to take it from here. He participated in the interrogation of Qatani."

"Tell us what you've found out, Mahoney," said Long.

Mahoney stood to his feet, buttoning his blue suit coat. "Mr. President, we at the FBI felt from the beginning there were aspects of Senator Miller's death that simply didn't add up. We began by checking the client list of the dominatrix service, which was how we traced Qatani. We found him from disposable cell phone calls. He also visited the service's Web site, so we traced the cookies to his laptop."

"What's a cookie?" asked Long.

"It's a digital fingerprint that allows us to track where someone goes on the Internet," said Mahoney. "Anyway, we ID'd Qatani but still had no motive. We never thought the sex worker did it. And once we began to delve into Miller's involvement in funding covert activity in Iran, we had the motive for what we now know was a political assassination."

"Just like Harrison Flaherty," said Golden.

"Yes, sir," said Mahoney, deferring to his boss. "Zafarshan's MO is to strike fear into political leaders by making it clear there will be retribution if they act against regimes favorable to radical Islam. Where feasible, that means murder."

"Well, it won't work with me," said Long.

"He's murdered two prominent U.S. politicians already. I can't imagine he's going to stop there," said Secretary of State Sanders, her blondish-brown hair pulled back from her face.

"Qatani says there are other targets," said Mahoney. He clicked a remote control and a slide came up with a list of names. "Truman, Speaker Jimmerson, Secretary Sweet, the chairman of AIPAC, Reverend Andy Stanton." He paused. "Mr. President, both you and Vice President Whitehead are targets."

"Is he serious?" said Long, his eyes searching the faces around the table.

"Dead serious, sir," replied Mahoney.

"Well, Keith, we need to alert these targets and provide them with enhanced security," said Long, pointing at Golden.

"We're on it, sir," replied Golden. "Every target is being notified as we speak."

"Zafarshan's ambitions don't stop there," said Mahoney, clicking another slide in the PowerPoint, this one showing the journey of enriched uranium from Iraq that a Zafarshan-funded crew of pirates hijacked. "Qatani indicates Zafarshan plans to smuggle the enriched uranium stolen from the tanker last summer into the United States and detonate a dirty bomb in either New York or Washington, DC."

"Is it here yet?" asked Golden.

"Qatani says he doesn't know. He says these operations are highly compartmentalized," answered Mahoney.

"When?" asked Long.

"Not clear. But Qatani says it won't happen in isolation," replied Mahoney. "He says it will be detonated in retaliation for a U.S. or Israeli strike against Iran's nuclear facilities."

The room fell silent as everyone around the table absorbed the news.

Long turned to Jacobs. "Bill, does Zafarshan have the technical ability to build and detonate a bomb?"

"We don't know for certain, Mr. President," said Jacobs. "But the information on how to construct a dirty bomb is readily available on the Internet. He has the fissile material. It's not a big leap from there to a weapon carried in a suitcase, a briefcase, or the trunk of a car."

"Like the Times Square bomber, only competent," offered Hector.

"Exactly," said Jacobs.

"Well, the United States cannot be blackmailed by some rogue terrorist into not taking military action against Iran," said Long, his facial features hardened. "We're going to have to do whatever is necessary to cripple Iran's offensive nuclear capability. We need to harden all targets and protect the homeland. Because assuming Qatani's not lying, that's when Zafarshan will hit us."

"We do have some good news on the Iran front, sir," said Jacobs.

"What's that?" asked Long.

"Two nights ago in Damascus, we took out Nasrin Bahmani, the number-two engineer on the Iran nuclear program. He was a major player in Iran. They will feel his loss sorely."

The corner of Golden's mouth turned up. "Any truth to the rumor he was lured into a trap by two prostitutes working for the Agency?"

"Oldest trick in the book," replied Jacobs with a smile. "It works every time."

"Good job, Bill," replied Long. "Keep it up. If we're lucky, maybe we can slow down or cripple the program enough so sanctions can work. Otherwise, it's us or the Israelis taking them out by force."

Greenglass glanced at the pensive expressions on every face. It struck him that what started as the death of a senator in a Georgetown dungeon had turned into a lot more than anyone bargained for . . . and might yet lead to World War III.

17

At a mansion in the Pelican Beach neighborhood of Newport Beach jutting out from a cliff and offering spectacular views of Newport Bay and the Pacific, the Orange County monied set lavished love and cash on the new "It" girl of California politics. Heidi Hughes was the former minority leader in the California Assembly who was now a state senator and was challenging the most despised Democrat in the Golden State, Senator Kate Covitz. An antitax, Tea Party, bomb thrower who counted Ronald Reagan and Sarah Palin among her heroes, Hughes was locked in a bitter primary with two nondescript white guys in suits. She was the hottest political commodity in the country among conservatives, as hot as the sun that hung in the late-afternoon sky, its rays burning through the mist blowing in off the Pacific.

The back deck and pool area were filled with tanned men in blue suits and polo shirts, accompanied by bejeweled, botoxed women in low-cut, sleeveless cocktail dresses, showing off their ripped biceps and calves chiseled by a daily regimen of yoga and Pilates. They towered in their designer heels, flashing jewelry and implants, some hiding recent eye jobs behind Prada or Chanel sunglasses. Everyone paid $2,000 a couple for the right to attend the reception and valet park their Mercedes, Range Rovers, and an occasional Lamborghini. The host committee raised or gave $10,000.

Hughes worked the room like a seasoned pro, standing by the pool in a striking off-shoulder yellow Bottega dress with black trim and open-toed black heels, hemline properly just above the knee, chatting up the donors and posing for photographs. Two decorative Styrofoam floats filled with orchids and lilies skimmed across the surface of the pool, blown about by a steady ocean breeze. A makeshift click line snaked across the patio and into the house. Inside, wide-eyed revelers roamed through the twenty-six-thousand-square-foot house, gazing at the expensive art on the walls and admiring the state-of-the-art appliances in the kitchen and the breakfast nook overlooking the ocean.

Out on the terrace, female bartenders with movie-star looks, blinding white teeth, and dark tans pushed mango mojitos and basil martinis, lubricating the already joyful crowd with the booze. Waiters moved through the crowd with trays filled with appetizers of tuna tartar, pineapple-glazed salmon, Kobe beef kabobs, miniature red velvet cupcakes, and chocolate-espresso lollipops.

In the click line, a former Democratic House speaker who served with Hughes and now lobbied in LA and Sacramento approached. A large, fare-thee-well fellow with a large mop of brown hair, beady eyes, swarthy skin, and insufferable grin extended his arms, balancing a glass of chardonnay. "Heidi!" he fairly shouted. "How are you, darling!" He wrapped her in a bear hug, his sweaty cheek and shoulder rubbing against her face, leaving a smear of base-makeup on his suit coat.

"Bob, what are you doing here?" asked Hughes in mock surprise. "You're a Democrat."

"I know *that*," he replied, his face stretched like putty. "Listen, we always got along when you were minority leader and I was Speaker. Remember how mad my caucus was when I gave you a larger office and let you hire additional staff? I told them to stuff it!" The crowd stood around eavesdropping, enjoying the story. "Most of the time, you and I sat down and cut the deal and got things done. There was never a budget stalemate when you and I did business!"

"Yeah, until you rammed through an income tax hike," deadpanned Hughes, flashing her teeth in a wicked smile.

"It wasn't a general tax increase, Heidi," bellowed the lobbyist. "It was a temporary millionaire surcharge."

The crowd roared with laughter. Hughes turned to them, playing to the crowd. "That's Democrat-speak for, 'Hold on to your wallet'!"

"That's right, Heidi! You tell him," said a local real-estate developer, egging her on.

"So did you bring a check, Bob, or are your freeloading?" asked Heidi. "If you turn up on my report, Kate's head will explode." More laughter.

"I didn't bring a check, but I brought a lot of PAC checks from clients," said the lobbyist.

"Of course you did," volleyed back Hughes. The photographer hovered, shooting a series of rapid-fire shots, her strobe light flashing. "Make sure to get one of these photographs over to the *Orange County Register*. I can't wait to see Bob explain this."

"No problem," said the lobbyist. "My clients are pulling for you, and I'm telling them to max out now. And I tell my Democrat friends you were the best minority leader ever."

"That's just because you got to run the show," joked Hughes.

The long-serving chairman of the Orange County Republican Party approached. "Heidi, it's almost time to head over to the gala dinner," he said. "Are you ready to speak?"

"Sure," said Hughes, brightening. "Where do you want me to stand?"

"By the gazebo."

They walked together with her husband, a former San Diego Charger backup quarterback, broad shouldered with thick arms and tree-trunk legs, tall and handsome, clad in tan slacks and a double-breasted blue blazer with a dress shirt and silk tie, walking with a slight gait.

"Could I have everyone's attention, please?" said the GOP chairman in a loud voice, pulling off his sunglasses. He and Hughes stood under the gazebo, the deep blue of the Pacific behind them, the sun slowly descending into the ocean mist as the hour approached sunset. "I want to thank all of you for coming. This has been a great event. I'm pleased to report that we have raised over $100,000 for Heidi tonight, doubling our goal."

The crowd applauded lustily. Hughes extended her hands outward in an appreciative clap directed at the donors.

"Heidi doesn't really need an introduction," he continued. "She's been a stalwart friend of the taxpayer, a principled conservative who stood firm for creating a more business-friendly climate in the state and reforming our broken public pension system. I'm happy to report she has never voted for a tax increase in twelve years in Sacramento." (Loud applause.) "She's going to beat Kate Covitz like a drum in November. Please give a warm Orange County welcome to our next United States Senator, Heidi Hughes."

Hughes stepped forward to loud cheers, whistles, and applause. Her beauty was deceptively striking. Her white porcelain skin, wave of brown hair, espresso eyes, and bright smile made her appear fifteen years younger than her fifty years. She projected feminine toughness and bubbled with an effervescent enthusiasm.

"Thank you, thank you," she said, bowing from the waist. "They say Orange County is God's country, and I can certainly see why." She extended her arm in a sweeping motion, pointing to the view of the ocean. "Of course, it's not so bad in San Diego either," she said mischievously to appreciative laughter.

"When I got in this race, no one thought I could win outside of my own household, and four of them weren't yet old enough to vote," she joked, referring to her children. "But I decided that I could not look my children in the eye someday and have to explain why at the tipping point when the United States fell from its status as the richest, most powerful, and most prosperous superpower the world has ever known to a third-rate power like Greece or Portugal, I did nothing." The crowd fell silent, sensing the raw emotion in her voice. "My apologies to the Greeks and the Portugese in the audience." (Laughter.) "How could I choose my own comfort over saving our country and redeeming its promise?" She paused, her dark eyes flashing. "There were plenty of people who wanted me to run for a lower office that would be easier to win, such as lieutenant governor or attorney general. And perhaps I would have won. But I decided the stakes were too high, and saving America from the failed policies in Washington was too important for me to play it safe. So I decided to run for the U.S. Senate, even though my chances did not look good, and Kate Covitz looked unbeatable."

"We're glad you did!" someone shouted.

"So am I," said Hughes, not skipping a beat. "At the beginning I trailed in the polls by thirty points. And that was just among Republicans." (More laughter.) "But as I've gotten around the state of California and gotten my message out, people have really responded. Today I'm leading the Republican Primary by twenty points and the latest Field Poll shows me virtually tied with Kate Covitz." She pointed her finger in the air for emphasis, the muscles in her jaw tightening. "We're going to defeat Kate and send her back to California once and for all. She may have to get a real job for the first time in thirty years." (Loud applause.)

The blue sky seemed to melt into the ocean behind her in a tableau of water, mist, fading sunlight, and white foam. Her intensity radiated. "Now I've been a conservative Republican since I was knee-high," she said, holding her hand out to the approximate height of a child. "But this election is about more than simply trading a Democrat for a Republican, a liberal for a conservative, or one politician for another politician. For the first time in my life, what's on the ballot is whether the American dream will continue or whether it will fade away and survive only in what Abraham Lincoln called the 'mystic chords of memory.'"

She paused, readying a roundabout punch. "Because in the end, this campaign isn't about me. Tonight I am up here speaking to you, and you are out there listening. But in an earlier time, and in the future, it may be one of you up here, and I'll be out there listening. Because this campaign is ultimately about what kind of America we leave for our children and grandchildren. I want to give them an America that is still proud, strong, and free, with a government limited and confined to specific, enumerated purposes, and a virtuous citizenry free to rise as high and as far as their talents can carry them." She bobbed her head, signaling she was done. "Thank you and God bless you all."

The crowd applauded loudly and lustily, men reaching for their checkbooks and women opening their purses to give the maximum amount. Hughes inspired them.

"Many of you already paid to come here tonight, and I appreciate it," said the Orange County GOP chairman, his eyes misting. "I have to tell you what I heard here tonight gives me hope. I've gotten cynical at times, but I must tell you, I'm inspired." (A smattering of applause.) He reached into his pocket and pulled out a piece of paper. "I'm so inspired I just wrote the largest check I've ever written to a federal candidate." He held the check aloft. "This check is for $9,600, the legal maximum for me and my wife for the primary and the general election." A chorus of "oohs" and "aahs" mixed with clapping. He looked in the direction of his wife, a stage grin on his face. "Honey, can we afford this?"

"Yes!" shouted his wife.

"Alright, I now have official permission from my better half. So who wants to join me at the legal maximum?"

Two hands went up.

"Alright, I see two more right there." He paused, surveying the crowd. "Anybody else? Okay, how about $5,000? Who can do $5?" Six more hands shot up. "Now we're talking!"

"Can you accept corporate contributions?" asked a disembodied voice in the back.

"No, that is for party contributions, not federal candidates," said the chairman, swatting away the question with a wave of his hand. "How about $2,000?" Two dozen hands shot up. Aides to Hughes hustled through the crowd passing out preprinted contribution envelopes. "That's good! Now how about $1,000." More hands. He pointed with his fingers, adding up the figure in his head. "That's another $124,000 from this crowd above and beyond the one hundred we raised coming into the reception! Give yourselves a big hand!"

The crowd broke into loud cheering and applause. Hughes tentatively stepped forward, her facial muscles slightly twitching with emotion. She patted her chest with her hand, imitating a fluttering heart.

"I am so touched by your generosity, I don't know what to say," she said, brown eyes open and inviting. "Thank you from the bottom of my heart. When I go to the Senate, I will not forget who sent me there, and I will never turn my back on you or our values."

Applause followed her as she stepped down from the gazebo, walking through the crowd, shaking hands and air-kissing, camera flashes accompanying her every move.

"Heidi! Heidi! Heidi!" they changed as she walked into the house.

ONCE INSIDE, HUGHES MOVED SWIFTLY up the stairs to the second floor. She opened a door to an upstairs study for a prearranged, off-the-record meeting. Sitting in a leather chair behind the mahogany desk, his fingers forming a church steeple, sat Jay Noble, who was whisked upstairs while the crowd listened to her speech. Hughes knew him by reputation from years of California political wars, but until Long bolted from the Democratic Party to become a center-right independent, she had never worked with him, or even met him. He struck her as smaller than he looked on television.

"Mr. Noble, good to meet you," she said, striding confidently and extending her hand, gripping his hand firmly. "It's a pleasure after all these years of being on different sides."

"The honor is all mine," purred Jay, surveying his prey. "Please, call me Jay."

Hughes sat on the burgundy leather couch, sliding her legs underneath her in feminine repose. They both paused for a beat, waiting for the other to start.

"The president sends his best," said Jay. It was one of his favorite conversation-starters, certain to impress the listener. "We've been watching your campaign. It's impressive."

"Impressive enough that you no longer want to recruit Caulfield into the race?" she asked, her eyes twinkling. It was a brush-back pitch.

Jay flashed a relaxed smile. "We don't have a lot of use for Covitz, so we've been in the market for a candidate. She went above and beyond the call of duty in opposing our health care plan from the left and opposing Diaz for Supreme Court." He shrugged. "The president has a soft spot for Caulfield. But he's over that, I assure you."

"I understand that," said Hughes. "I wouldn't have expected anything less from him. But Caulfield can't beat Kate in a primary." She dropped her chin, leveling her eyes on Jay. "I, on the other hand, can beat her in the general. Her numbers are soft."

"We know," said Jay. "My only question to you is: do you run as a cookie-cutter, southern California conservative, or as a broad-gauged candidate who appeals beyond your conservative base? You can't win statewide carrying San Diego and Orange County."

Hughes's back stiffened. "No. But you can't win without them. I can carry Orange and San Diego by a large margin, hold my own in LA, especially in the Valley, *and* appeal to women, independents, and middle-class voters."

Her confidence seemed to startle Jay. "Kate's tough. She's meaner than a snake. She's downright vicious. You sure you're up for this?"

"Yes. This time she's met her match," said Hughes, her face like flint. "I'm not intimidated by her. In fact, I can't wait to debate her. She uses the tough exterior to scare off strong opponents. She's never really been tested like I'm going to test her."

Jay nodded slowly. "I'd like for you to meet with some of the grassroots leaders who got Long on the ballot here. They are amazing activists. If they like you, then it won't look like we're trying to impose something from the White House."

"Absolutely," said Hughes brightly. "I'd love to meet them."

"It would also be helpful if you could align with Long on some part of his agenda," suggested Jay.

"I voted against Long's health care plan. I can't move on that," she said matter-of-factly. "If I flip-flop now, I'll lose all credibility."

Jay waved his hands. "One hundred percent. But you can say you would have voted for Diaz. You can take our side on authorizing military action against Iran if sanctions fail." He crossed his legs. "You don't have to eat everything on the buffet. Order a la carte."

Hughes smiled. "I like the way you think."

"And I, you. I think we could make some beautiful music together."

"I would look forward to that." Hughes stood, extending her hand. As they shook hands, their eyes locked. Hughes saw Jay's eyes widen, mesmerized by her charisma. She was having that effect on a lot of people she encountered lately. In fact, she was getting used to it.

The door opened. Hughes's travel aide stood in the doorway, pointing at his watch. She ignored him. "Get me the names of your California organizers," she said as she headed for the door. "I'll have my staff set something up right away."

"You'll have the list tonight," Jay replied.

As Hughes turned to go, her heels clicked on the hardwood floor, a new spring in her step. She had just raised another $225,000, and with a little luck she might have bagged the backing of the most feared and ruthless political strategist on the planet—not to mention his boss, the president of the United States. *Not bad for an afternoon's work,* she thought.

18

A wooden Adirondack boat glided up to the dock, the bow cutting through the water, small waves rippling out across the glassy surface. Tall pines cast shadows across the lake as the sun's fading rays lit up the mountains in a lush palette of green, blue, and yellow. G. G. Hoterman helped Dierdre out of the boat and walked up the lawn to the Lake Placid Lodge. The peaceful setting provided a needed escape from the turmoil roiling G. G.'s world. In spite of Walt Shapiro's herculean efforts, he was on the final witness list for Mike Kaplan's trial, which was scheduled to start the following week.

Washington was riveted by the Kaplan trial. *Politico* headlined its story, "Kaplan Watch: The Witness List," citing sources close to the defense, who vowed on background to go after G. G. if he turned on Kaplan. *Roll Call* reported Nicole Dearborn, the striking brunette who spied on the Stanley campaign, might testify as well.

That was why G. G. and Dierdre escaped to Higher Ground, his home in the Adirondacks. As he often did at times like this, G. G.

anesthetized his pain with booze. He ordered a double bourbon on the rocks for himself and a chardonnay for Deirdre. Suddenly a single-engine seaplane buzzed overhead, floating to a perfect landing on the lake, its pontoons leaving a small wake as it taxied toward the dock. The propeller churned to a stop as the plane glided into its berth. The pilot, a short, balding man in his fifties wearing a blue blazer and tan slacks, climbed out of the cockpit and assisted a tall brunette onto the dock.

"Dan certainly knows how to arrive in style, doesn't he?" chuckled G. G.

Dan Friedman, the pilot and president of ABC News, was accompanied by his wife, Elizabeth, who everyone called by her nickname, "Bitsy." A raven-haired beauty with an impossibly thin figure, fair skin, and full lips, Bitsy was known for her cutting wit, flirty repartee, and fashion sense. Tonight was no exception: she wore white Chanel pants, a blue tank with a brown leather Dolce & Gabbana aviator jacket, and Dior heels.

"I come to dinner by Adirondack boat, and you top me with a sea-plane!" exclaimed G. G. when they reached the table. He air-kissed Bitsy. "Bitsy, you look stunning as always."

"Thank you, darling," she replied as she slid into her seat and removed her jacket.

"The plane is fun," said Dan, warming to the topic. "I got my pilot's license when I was flying around the country visiting local stations as head of the ABC O & O division. Started with a single-engine Cessna, then bought an Aero Commander, then a King Air."

Bitsy leaned forward as if to share a confidence. "The seaplane is *perfect* for picnics and moonlit dinners." She shot a knowing glance at Dierdre. "Very romantic, dear."

"But the cockpit isn't big enough for extracurricular activity," needled G. G.

"I've performed in smaller quarters than *that*, honey," volleyed Bitsy, patting G. G.'s hand. "Right, baby?"

Dan sat silently, grinning from ear to ear.

G. G. laughed, but the mirth masked an inner funk. Dan's poise and Bitsy's beauty and effervescence filled him with self-pity. He was jealous of Dan's wealth, career, gorgeous (second) wife, seaplane—heck, his entire disgustingly charmed existence. By contrast G. G.'s life was unraveling. Edwina was divorcing him, his legal bills totaled $1 million and counting, and he was about to testify in the biggest criminal trial in DC in decades.

The trial eventually reared its ugly head. "Word is Kaplan's going to call Sal Stanley as a witness," said Dan. "That might help Mike, but it sure won't help Stanley's reelect."

"They've been friends for a quarter century, so I don't see how Sal can avoid it," G. G. replied. "He looks bad if he testifies; he looks worse if he doesn't because he'd be turning his back on a friend. The good news is it's still early enough in the campaign for Sal to recover."

"Not if Mike is convicted, right?" asked Bitsy, running her fingers through her hair.

"I don't know. He *is* the Senate Majority Leader. Beating him won't be easy."

"Stick a fork in Stanley," said Dan. "Kaplan's going to be convicted of perjury at a minimum. He might as well get measured for the orange jumpsuit now."

"How can you be so sure, Dan?" asked G. G.

"I've got a friend, one of the top criminal attorneys in the country, who interviewed with Kaplan to represent him," replied Dan, lowering his voice to keep from being overheard. "According to him, when Mike sat down with the FBI, he had the campaign's attorneys sit in on the interview. He didn't even show up with a criminal lawyer. The guy walked into a gunfight with a knife." He held up his knife, pointing it. "He made misstatements of fact. That's a felony, pal. Section 1001."

"How well I know," said G. G. morbidly.

"Of course you do!" exclaimed Dan. "You lawyered up, right?"

"Big time. My lawyer is Walt Shapiro. He's a killer. Never lost a case."

"There you go," said Dan, popping another bite of steak into his mouth and chewing.

"Didn't Shapiro represent that ex-senator in a paternity suit with the bimbo?" asked Bitsy.

"Yep. Walt forced her to recant her story in a videotaped deposition. Reduced her to tears. It was on YouTube within twenty-four hours," said Hoterman. "They don't call Shapiro the Hannibal Lecter of the courtroom for nothing."

To G. G.'s relief, the conversation, lubricated with red wine, turned to other topics. They covered the usual subjects: who was sleeping with whom, who was getting divorced (awkward!), whose career had gone up in flames, who lost their shirts on the stock market. But after dinner, over coffee, Dan returned to the Kaplan trial. "G. G., I hope you're going to be all right if you have to testify. I know the lead defense attorney. He represented us in a libel case once years ago. He's a barracuda. A regular flesh eater."

G. G. gamely pretended not to be worried. "Is that so?" he asked.

"Oh, yeah. The guy's a cannibal."

"Dan, please!" said Bitsy, cutting him a dirty look.

"I'm ready," vowed G. G. in his best manly baritone. "Like Walt always says, tell the truth and let the chips fall where they may. That's what I intend to do."

Dierdre had hung back until now, letting G. G. spar with Dan. "I don't know the attorney, but I wouldn't want to see him after he goes twelve rounds with G. G."

"Here, here!" said Bitsy, trying to buck up G. G. "You'll do just fine, doll."

"I'll drink to that," laughed Friedman, raising his glass. They all lifted their glasses and clinked them in a toast.

Under the table Dierdre placed a hand on G. G.'s leg, which sent an electric shock through his body. He decided it was time to go and waved for the check. They rose from the table, and Dan and Bitsy walked down the dock to their plane. G. G. and Deirdre watched as the seaplane taxied, its pontoons streaking across the water, then rose into the pitch-black sky, blue taillight blinking, its propeller buzzing in the distance.

G. G. wrapped his arm around Deirdre and started walking back up the hill to the Lodge.

"Where are you taking me now?" she asked, surprised. "Aren't we going home?"

"It's too dark to take the boat back." He winked. "I reserved a cabin. This way we can sleep in late and have breakfast in bed . . . in a feather bed."

"Is it breakfast in bed you want . . . or something else?"

"I'm open to suggestions," joked G. G.

"I'll just bet you are," giggled Deirdre. She slipped her hand under his coat, hooking her index finger through a belt loop, and pulled him along the gravel path leading to the cabin.

WHEN IT BECAME CLEAR DON Jefferson planned to jump into the Republican U.S. Senate primary, Dolph Lightfoot's campaign team went into full-blown panic mode. Jefferson, a favorite of the Tea Party crowd and the religious right, posed a threat. Florida's closed primary permitted only registered Republicans to vote. Lightfoot's advisors decided it was time to burnish their candidate's right-wing street cred by booking him on FOX News.

Lightfoot sat in a chair under hot television lights. The clock read 7:12 a.m. He would be live in six minutes.

"This show is pure softball," said a media advisor, wearing jeans and a polo shirt. "It's a coffee clatch. Just be sunny and inject humor."

"How am I supposed to be funny when Jefferson is out there engaging in personal attacks?" groused Lightfoot, sucking on black coffee from a Styrofoam cup. "Did you see the video they posted on the Internet?"

The animated short portrayed Lightfoot as a broken-down, old thoroughbred who was put out to pasture, only to be saddled up by the party bosses to run one last race. As a caricature of a frenzied Mike Birch (playing the jockey) whipped the horse mercilessly, urging it to run faster, the horse turned around and said, "I didn't know I actually had to run. I thought all I had to do was show!" Up in the stands the lobbyists and special interest bosses bet furiously on the horse named Dolph, only to curse him when he couldn't run.

"Okay, he's got a Web site. Let's see if he can actually get on TV with real points behind it," said the media adviser dismissively.

"Amateurish," said Lightfoot with disgust. He took another swig of coffee. "Childish!"

"He's desperate," said the advisor, stroking his client.

"My wife saw him on television the other day. She said, 'What's with the hair?'" He laughed. "What's he using . . . shoe polish?" He chuckled. "I mean, it's practically blue."

The advisor laughed. "It's either Grecian Formula or black ink."

"He claims to be as pure as the driven snow," said Lightfoot, his voice dripping with contempt. "That's crap. He was a lobbyist after he left the state legislature." He paused. "A lobbyist!"

The floor director walked over. "Um, sir, that mike is live," he whispered.

The media advisor's eyes grew wide. He made a cutting motion across his neck with his hand.

"What?" asked Lightfoot, narrowing his eyes, which were blinded by the klieg lights.

"Your mike," whispered the media advisor.

Lightfoot nodded in recognition.

At that moment the host of the FOX morning show appeared on the screen of the monitor. "Mr. Lightfoot, thank you for joining us," he said politely.

"Thank you for having me," said Lightfoot.

"Do you prefer to be addressed as senator or governor?" he asked. "You've been both, now," he said with a chuckle.

"Senator is fine. That's my current job."

"We're coming to you in just a moment," said the director in Lightfoot's ear. He heard the sound of theme music, and then they were live.

"Joining us this morning from Orlando, Florida, is former governor Dolph Lightfoot, the new United States Senator from the Sunshine State. He was appointed by Florida Governor Mike Birch to serve out the remainder of the term of the late Perry Miller, and he is currently running for election in his own right. Good morning, Senator!"

"Good morning," said Lightfoot.

"So, you've been in the Senate for a month now. Have you found the bathroom yet?" joked the host.

"Oh, I've found a lot more than that," replied Lightfoot, laughing nervously. "I've hired staff, been workin' hard to get to know my colleagues, gotten fully immersed in my committees. I'm very grateful to have been appointed to the Foreign Relations Committee, as well as transportation, both of which are important to the people of Florida." He dropped his *g*s to sound more friendly.

"Senator, you just missed participating in the confirmation of Marco Diaz to the U.S. Supreme Court," noted the host, his face animated. "Your predecessor voted against confirming Justice Diaz. How would you have voted had you been a senator, or do you know?"

"I wasn't there to review every aspect of Justice Diaz's record, so I can't really say. He seemed qualified from where I sat, but having not been there, I couldn't really say for certain."

The media advisor visibly flinched. Diaz was only the second Hispanic justice in U.S. history, and Florida had one of the largest Hispanic populations in the country.

"Well, let me turn to Iran, a topic before you now," said the host. "The Senate is about to begin debate on a bill slapping some pretty stiff sanctions on Iran to try to stop its pursuit of nuclear weapons. Do you think that will be effective? Do you support it?"

"I support doing whatever we can through diplomatic pressure with our European allies to stop Iran from threatening its neighbors and other civilized nations with nuclear weapons," said Lightfoot, his voice steady, rattling off his talking points. "We cannot allow the world's most dangerous regime to obtain the world's most dangerous weapons."

"What about the so-called trigger mechanism that would authorize military action against Iran if the sanctions don't work?" asked the host. "Where do you stand on that issue?"

"Military action is a separate matter," said Lightfoot. "If it can be effective, that's one thing. But many experts believe the Iranians have buried many of their nuclear installations underground, meaning a bombing raid similar to that which the Israelis did against nuclear plants in Iraq in 1981 and in Syria in 2007 may not be effective."

"So you're not in favor of military action?"

"I am if it has a reasonable prospect of working," said Lightfoot. "I think the jury's out on that. I'm not sure I support putting ground forces in Iran when our guard and reserve troops are stretched thin in Iraq and Afghanistan. We can't be the policeman of the world."

"But on Iran, it sounds like you favor sanctions but oppose military action," said the host, moving in for the kill.

"Well, here again, I'd have to know more than just a 'trigger.' What are we talking about?" said Lightfoot. "As governor I was the commander in chief of the Florida National Guard, and many families saw their loved ones go to Iraq and Afghanistan on repeated deployments. If we're planning to take military action against Iran, we need to get serious about increasing the size of our regular Army forces."

"Alright, Senator, that's all the time we have today," said the host. "Thanks again for being with us."

"Thank you," said Lightfoot.

As the floor director removed his microphone and handed him a wet cloth to remove his makeup, Lightfoot glanced at his media advisor. He looked crestfallen.

"What?" asked Lightfoot.

"We're going to get calls about the Diaz comment," he said.

"Yeah," said Lightfoot. "Probably. I said he was qualified as far as I knew."

The media advisor nodded. It was going to be a long day.

19

A "money bomb" blast e-mail from the Faith and Family Fund—Andy Stanton's political action committee—on behalf of Don Jefferson for U.S. Senate went out to its 4.2 million-member e-mail list at 6:00 a.m. on Monday morning, two days after Jefferson formally announced his candidacy for the Republican Senate nomination in Florida. Text messages were blasted to a million mobile phones simultaneously. The e-mail was strategically timed to benefit from the earned media over Jefferson's entrance to the race and take advantage of higher open rates on Monday mornings. The conventional wisdom: Jefferson had a strong following among evangelicals and the Tea Party crowd, but he couldn't raise the dough. Thus the money bomb.

Ross Lombardy pulled into his reserved parking place at the Faith and Family Federation headquarters in Alpharetta, a prosperous suburb on the north side of Atlanta, in his silver Lexus 450 at 8:40 a.m., strolling to his office carrying a Starbucks Café Americano in one hand and his laptop in the other hand, breezing past his assistant, and sitting behind his desk. Not more than two minutes transpired before his PAC director, brown hair mussed with a cowlick at the back of his skull, appeared at his door in a pair of pressed khakis and blue blazer, eyes wide open, body twitching, visibly excited. He held a sheaf of papers in his hands.

"What's up?" asked Lombardy. "You look like you're about to wet your pants."

"You remember the Jefferson money bomb?" asked the PAC director.

"Remember it? I wrote it," joked Lombardy. "How's it doing? We need to give Don a big, fat, wet kiss, if you know what I mean."

"We're doing more than kissing him," said the PAC director. "He's going to have our baby. This thing is blowing the doors off!"

"Really? That's great."

"Way better than great," he added. He glanced down at some figures on the papers he held. "We're sitting at $1,272,325 so far. That's after only two and a half hours."

Lombardy let out a long whistle. "That's insane. That's just nuts. Are you sure?"

"You bet. We're already at a 15 percent open rate and half of those people are linking to Jefferson's campaign Web site. This thing could end up with an open rate north of 50 percent."

Lombardy shook his head in wonderment. "That's mind-boggling. What's the industry standard open rate again?"

"Twenty percent. We're usually around 30 to 32 percent because we have such an engaged and active membership. But we've never seen anything like this in any endorsement e-mail soliciting contributions for a candidate. Not even Long."

"Let's call Andy and give him the good news." Lombardy hit the speaker phone. He punched in the number for the dressing room at New Life Ministries, where he knew Andy would be preparing for his daily television show, a folksy mix of commentary, news, and celebrity chat resembling the *Today* show with a sprinkling of the gospel.

The makeup artist answered on the first ring. She put Andy on the phone.

"Ross, what's up?" asked Andy abruptly. He generally didn't like to be bothered right before he went on the air.

"Andy, remember I told you we were going to send out the money bomb for Don Jefferson?" asked Ross.

"Yes. And?" asked Andy, his voice rising an octave with anticipation.

"Well, we're already north of a million bucks, and the e-mail only went out two hours ago," reported Ross. He glanced at his PAC director, who fidgeted like a ten-year-old boy who had to use the restroom and winked.

"Brother, this is *fantastic!*" said Andy, his voice raised to a squeal. "This is a major shot across Mike Birch's bow."

Ross leaned into the speaker phone. "Try a torpedo fired at close range."

Andy giggled with manly mischief. "Birch is going to spew his coffee!" He paused. "I'd like to mention it on my show. But I don't know if I can report it directly without running afoul of the tax lawyers."

Ross knew all too well the dangers of a tax-exempt ministry endorsing candidates. "Why don't I leak it to Merryprankster or *Politico*? Then you cite them and report it as straight news."

"I love it," said Andy. "But hurry . . . I go on the air in twelve minutes."

"When I feed this to the barracudas at Merryprankster, it's going to go viral."

"Brother, put the pedal to the metal. I'd put banner ads on Drudge, Merryprankster, National Review, Newsmax, the works. We shouldn't limit this to our members. There are going to be a lot of Christians and conservatives who want to give money to Jefferson."

"That's brilliant, Andy," gushed Ross, always amazed that a preacher and talking head usually had more good ideas than a political operative. He turned to his PAC director. "Can we get those ads up quickly?"

The PAC director nodded vigorously, an irrepressible grin on his face, his eyes like saucers. He was running on pure adrenalin.

"Once it goes live, get that story from *Politico* or Merryprankster over to my news director," ordered Andy. "We'll report it in the news segment, and we'll flash the Federation Web site address. I'll do it on my radio show, too."

"Yes, sir!" said Ross with sycophantic brio.

"Tell your IT guys to reserve back-up server capacity," said Andy with a chuckle. "You're about to get deluged."

Ross hung up the phone and pulled up the Web site with the click of his mouse. The money bomb display appeared on the home page, a graphic of a bag of cash with a photo of Jefferson, a ticker displaying the current running total. "Holy smoke . . . we're up to 1.6 million!"

The PAC director leaned across the desk, gazing at the screen. "It's a tidal wave," he muttered to himself. "A freakin' tsunami."

Ross whipped around in his chair. "You heard Andy . . . get those banner ads up. Make it happen!"

The PAC director turned and scampered from the room. Ross stared at the ticker as it continued to spin, counting the cash pouring in over the Internet like water rushing over a waterfall. His mind raced. They were riding a wave, and his name was Don Jefferson. He hoped they didn't get thrown off their surfboard.

IN A BLACK LINCOLN NAVIGATOR with smoked windows (donated by one of the largest car dealers in Tampa-St. Pete) heading north on the Sawgrass Expressway, Dolph Lightfoot cradled a cell phone to his ear, listening to his high-paid strategists offer him expensive and thoroughly useless advice, doing a slow burn.

"The guy's gonna have his day in the sun. No way around it," offered his laconic campaign manager. "The media wants a race. Now they've got it."

Just great, thought Lightfoot. *I pay you $20 grand a month to state the obvious.*

"I think we say something like, 'One day does not a campaign make,'" chirped the finance director, a chain-smoking veteran of six statewide campaigns. "We'll see who raises more on their next finance report."

"Too inside baseball," said the campaign manager.

"Point to the published polls," said the pollster, who was on the conference call from DC. "We're leading by 22 points in the Mason-Dixon. The guy's a congressman from Ocala, which in a state the size of Florida is practically a state legislator. He's a *nobody.* Don't blow helium into the guy."

"Make it about outside special interest groups versus Florida," offered the general consultant, who assisted Lightfoot in his victorious gubernatorial campaigns. "This is an outside group led by a cable talk-show host trying to choose Florida's U.S. senator."

"You have to be careful," cautioned the campaign manager. "Faith and Family Federation has 250,000 members in Florida. We don't want triple-F to be able to do a mailing saying we trashed Andy Stanton."

Lightfoot had heard enough. "Folks, I hate to ruin this discussion by injecting a dose of reality. But Don has raised almost $2 million in less than three hours on the Internet with no fund-raising costs," he said with more than a trace of impatience. "This is a big hairy deal. It's going to be a national story. We better come up with more than spin."

The line went silent. Lightfoot's frustration was palpable. He viewed the Republican primary, if not the general election, as a virtual coronation. Now this?

"What are we going to show on our first finance report?" asked the campaign manager.

"Our goal is $7 million," answered the finance director. "I think we'll make it."

"How much from Florida?" asked Lightfoot.

"I don't know . . . maybe 90 percent," said the finance director.

"So our funds come from mainstream Floridians, not some special interest groups led by an out-of-state flake and right-wing preacher," said Lightfoot in a firm voice.

"Stress that you've never taken any campaign for granted and you don't intend to start now," offered the consultant, speaking in the falsetto voice of an imaginary candidate. "We take Don Jefferson's challenge seriously. We look forward to a vigorous campaign."

"People are getting more than a little sick and tired of Andy Stanton thinking he's the chairman of the Republican Party," said Lightfoot, his voice dripping with disdain. "Who does this guy think he is? I was governor of this state for *eight* years. I built this party. How dare he tell me I'm not a good Republican. It's outrageous."

"Stanton's not on the ballot. You're running against Jefferson," cautioned the consultant.

"The heck I am!" shouted Lightfoot. "I'm running against FOX News, Andy Stanton, Hannity, Beck, Limbaugh, and the stinking Tea Party."

"We need to test Stanton on the next poll," said the pollster. "If his numbers are as bad as I think they are, we may want to do an ad morphing Jefferson into Stanton."

The car exited the expressway. They were minutes away from the community center where Lightfoot was to address a gathering in the vote-rich suburbs of western Broward County. A call broke in on the phone. Lightfoot glanced at the screen of his phone. It was Governor Mike Birch.

"Gotta go, guys." He hung up and answered the incoming call. "Hello?"

"Dolph, it's Mike Birch."

"Morning, Governor," said Lightfoot, trying not to sound rattled.

"I assume you saw the Faith and Family Federation sent out a fund-raising e-mail for Don Jefferson?" asked Birch.

"Oh, yes, I saw it."

"That's Andy Stanton trying to hurt me by pounding you," said Birch. "He's a bad guy. Claims I'm a RINO. Sorry his dislike of me is complicating things for you."

"Looks like I've got half your friends and all your enemies," joked Lightfoot.

Birch laughed. "The good news is I've got a lot of friends."

"Well, Stanton's an enemy of all of us who believe in a broad-based, inclusive party," said Lightfoot with an edge in his voice. "The guy's practically issuing fatwahs. I for one am not intimidated in the least. And I'm gonna beat his fair-haired boy like a drum."

"Now you're talkin'," said Birch, hate juices flowing. "Keep doing what you're doing. You're doing great. I just wanted to call and tell you to hang in there."

"Thanks, Mike. You're a great friend." Lightfoot hung up the phone as the car pulled up in front of the community center. A clutch of television and print reporters from local news outlets gathered on the sidewalks, microphones and tape recorders poised.

"Governor Lightfoot, I wonder if you have any reaction to the nearly $2 million raised so far on Don Jefferson's behalf by the Faith and Family Federation?" asked the local CBS affiliate.

"Well, I've never taken any race for granted, and I certainly don't intend to start now," said Lightfoot, squinting in the sun, the crow's feet around his blue eyes evident. "I expect this to be a vigorously contested primary, and I'm looking forward to the debate."

"You didn't expect more support given your past service as governor?" pressed the Ft. Lauderdale *Sun Sentinel*.

"I'm leading by a large margin. I've got the support of Floridians," said Lightfoot, jutting out his chin, his jaw firm. "I'm confident I'll raise more than my opponent, and we estimate 90 percent of our contributions come from within the state of Florida. Most of my opponent's donors don't even live in the state. I think the next senator from Florida should be chosen by Floridians, not outsiders with their own agenda."

"So you object to fund-raising over the Internet?" asked AP.

"No," said Birch, his eyes ablaze. "What I object to is a special interest group run by a self-styled ayatollah trying to dictate the next United States senator from Florida." He wagged his head back and forth, punctuating each syllable with a head bob, a smirk on his face.

The reporters chuckled. "So Andy Stanton's an ayatollah?" asked the *Miami Herald*.

"That's for the voters to decide." Lightfoot turned on his heel and headed into the community center, reporters in tow. His communications director, her face drained white, looked like she had been hit by a bus.

MERRYPRANKSTER'S HEADLINE IN TWENTY-TWO-POINT TYPE screamed just below side-by-side photos of Lightfoot and Andy Stanton. "Ayatollah Andy! Lightfoot Compares Stanton to Radical Clerics!" To add insult to injury, the story ran just beneath a flashing ad featuring the Jefferson money bomb. Faith and Family Federation was both making news and raising money hand over fist.

Sitting in his office off Georgia Highway 400, which split the Atlanta suburbs like a long knife, Ross Lombardy stared at his computer screen with a mixture of awe and ecstasy. He speed-dialed Andy's cell phone.

"Hello?" came Andy's voice.

"Andy, it's Ross. Lightfoot just got clotheslined by some reporters in Ft. Lauderdale, and they asked about our money bomb. He called you a 'self-styled ayatollah.'"

"He called me *what?!*" squealed Andy.

"An ayatollah."

"As in Khomeini? This guy is comparing *me* to someone who executes women who don't wear a burka? This guy is an anti-Christian bigot. Does he have a death wish?"

"Sure looks like it. I just wanted you to know about it before you went on the radio."

"I need that sound bite" said Andy, wheels turning. "I'll play it all day."

"This is going to be like Howard Dean's scream," said Ross excitedly.

Andy giggled. "It really is, brother. Maybe I can have Jefferson on my show. This is big news now. Can you run him down?"

"Sure. I've got his cell phone."

"Call him. Tell him I'd love to have him on in the third hour. That's when I have the biggest audience."

"On second thought, I better give it to your producers. I can't talk to him when we're doing an independent expenditure for him."

"Good idea," agreed Andy. "Hey, what's the money bomb up to?"

"It's up to $2.9 million dollars."

Andy let out a long whistle. "It'll be more by the time I get done on the radio."

"Lightfoot is an idiot," said Ross. "He was put out to pasture years ago, and he's been sitting on his porch chewing his cud, eating hay, and they bring him back and ask him to run the Kentucky Derby, and he breaks a leg on turn number two."

"It isn't smart to attack one of the country's most respected religious leaders," said Andy. "He's not gay, is he?"

"No," said Ross, taken aback by the question.

"Just wondering." Andy hung up the phone so he could finish his show prep for radio. Ross speed-dialed Don Jefferson's cell phone. In the space of eight hours, a little-known congressman from central Florida became one of the biggest political stories in the nation. *What a funny business we're in,* thought Ross.

20

Mack Caulfield remained publicly silent on whether he planned to run for U.S. Senate or governor, setting the California political class on edge. Rumor in Sacramento claimed public employee unions dangled the prospect of a $40 million independent expenditure campaign if he ran for governor, thus sparing the Democrats a bloodbath Senate primary. For his part Caulfield played Hamlet, milking the speculation for all it was worth.

But Jay Noble had grown tired of the game. That was why at 10:30 a.m. EST, 7:30 a.m. Pacific time, his assistant placed a call to Caulfield at the governor's mansion.

The butler approached with a remote phone. "Jay Noble from the White House, sir." Caulfield snapped to attention, grabbing the phone from the butler.

"Hello?" he said in an expectant voice. He was wrapping up breakfast, taking a final swig of coffee and wiping his mouth with a linen napkin as the kitchen staff cleared the plates.

"Governor, hold for Jay Noble," said the assistant. It was the ultimate insult, making a sitting governor wait for a White House aide. Caulfield waited for a good thirty seconds.

"Governor, good morning," said Jay when he came on the line, all business.

"Hello, Jay," said Caulfield in a clipped voice, irritated at having to hold.

"Governor, I saw the item in *Hotline* about you negotiating with the public employee unions about an independent expenditure if you run for governor," said Jay. He let the dead air hang.

"Yeah, I was going to call you about that, Jay," said Caulfield, his heart racing. "That was an exaggeration. It was really a negotiation about reforming the pension system."

"So the report is false?" asked Jay.

"The Senate race came up," backpedaled Caulfield. "But there was no quid pro quo. That's just not accurate."

"Well, the president is not happy," said Jay. "There were only two people in the room when he talked to you in LA last month. We've now had a dozen stories claiming the president urged you to run and offered to raise money." He leaned forward, putting his elbows on his desk, fairly shouting into his headset. "The president and I had what we *believed* was a private conversation with someone we *thought* was a friend. I'm the one who recommended you to the president as a possible Senate candidate, and this is how you pay you back? Do you have any idea how embarrassing this is for me, much less you?"

Caulfield sat down at the dining room table, trying to steady himself as he absorbed Jay's blast. "Hold on before you jump to conclusions, Jay. The only call I got was from the *LA Times,* and I didn't tell them anything specific. I told them I was looking at both options."

"Mack, I got a call from Marvin Myers, who had the whole story. Do you think I'm *stupid*? Do you think I'm an *idiot*?"

"No," stammered Caulfield. "But everyone knows the president can't stand Kate. That's hardly news."

"Let me tell you where we are, Mack," said Jay. "These stories are hopelessly compromising. You do what is best for you and your family. But whatever you decide now, you're on your own. Don't expect any help from here for governor *or* Senate. From now on, you're *naked*."

Caulfield felt the blood rush from his head. He felt light-headed and thought for a moment he might pass out. "Jay, I understand why you're upset, but I think you're overreacting," he heard himself say.

"I don't think so, Mack. I'm sorry I went to bat for you. But this is just not going to work. We're grabbing our parachutes. Good luck."

The line went dead. Caulfield's head spun. He thought of calling Long directly, but he knew Jay would block the call. In a sense it didn't matter: he had always planned on running for governor anyway. But if Jay had him in his crosshairs, it was going to get ugly. He was now going to have to fight a two-front war against the Republicans and the White House.

ROSS LOMBARDY PULLED INTO HIS driveway after another trip for the Faith and Family Federation, this one to California. Jet-lagged and weary, he rolled into the garage and turned off the ignition, swinging his legs out of the driver's seat. He heard a characteristic *ping* indicating he had a new text message. It was from his Florida chairman. He opened it. It read: "Shocker poll: Lightfoot 39, Jefferson 42."

"Wow!" exclaimed Ross to himself. He dialed Jay Noble. This was big news.

"Hi, Ross," said Jay's assistant. "Someone's with him in his office, but let me see if I can get him for you."

Thirty seconds later, Jay came on the line. "Hey, dude, what's rocking your world?"

"Did you see the new numbers in Florida?" asked Ross excitedly.

"No, I've been in meetings. What are they?"

"Lightfoot 39, Jefferson 42. Mason-Dixon poll released within the hour."

"Amazing." Jay paused. "Do you believe it?"

"We do. You know we raised $3.5 million with our money bomb for Jefferson." Ross was working Jay hard. He wanted the White House to help Jefferson, if only to knee-cap Birch, who they both despised.

"I saw that. It's a start. But you think a Congressman can defeat a popular former governor like Lightfoot?"

"Lightfoot is a has-been. How old is he . . . seventy-two? The guy belongs in a museum. The party has passed him by."

"If he loses, it's a black eye for Birch."

"Big time. It's the first primary . . . and in his own back yard."

"Hey, I've got something else that's time sensitive," said Jay, shifting gears. "I'm sitting here with David Thomas, and we're talking California. Our original guy, Mack Caulfield, jumped the shark, so we're probably going to try to help Heidi Hughes, if only because she's the only game in town."

"She's our girl," said Ross effusively.

"We like her. But she can't beat Covitz straight-up. We need a third-party candidate to split the Democratic vote."

"Alright. What's the plan?"

"We need a c4 to contribute to the Green Party in California to pay for petitions to qualify their Senate candidate for the ballot," said Jay. "It's going to cost about $4 a signature, and we need 100,000 signatures. We've got a c4 that will make the contribution, but we can't give it to the Green Party. Do you have a c4 that can take the money and pay for the petitions? It'll be an in-kind contribution to the Greens."

"Is that reportable?" asked Ross.

"Yes."

Ross thought for a moment. "That's dicey. I can't explain why I'm helping to qualify a liberal candidate."

"I understand," said Jay, his voice even. "The clock's ticking. So if you know of a c4 we can use, get it to Thomas ASAP. Keep in mind you don't have to report where you get the money from, just that you did the job."

"Okay," said Ross. "I think I know someone who might want to play. Can they get a piece of the action on the petition drive and make a little money?"

"I can't commit to that, but, sure, we're open to it."

"On a less enjoyable topic, we got a call from a reporter with the *New York Times* today," said Ross. "I was traveling back from the West Coast so I was in the air when he called. My press secretary said he was asking questions about the IRS audit of New Life Ministries. He said the guy who was leading the audit was reassigned, and he now claims it was due to White House pressure. Says the White House forced him off Andy's case."

"What did you tell him?" asked Jay.

"I didn't talk to him. My press secretary told him we made the White House aware of our concerns about selective IRS enforcement but asked for no special treatment."

"Good," said Jay. "You handled it just right."

"It sounds like it's going to be an ugly story."

"The guy quit his job at the IRS and is shopping a book," said Jay, nonplussed. "It is what it is."

Ross hung up the phone, glad Jay wasn't mad at him for mentioning their conversations with the White House to the *Times* reporter. He hoped it didn't cause Jay any indigestion. He scrolled through his BlackBerry for the contact of the Arizona operative who had a c4 and liked to play on ballot petitions. Ross thought, they might just put the California U.S. Senate seat in play after all. That would be an unexpected gift.

JONAH POPILOPOS STOOD BEFORE A glass pulpit emblazoned with a lily-white cross, gazing out at his third consecutive sold-out revival at Madison Square Garden. He wore his trademark white waistcoat, black silk pants, and Beatle boots that added three inches to his five-foot, seven-inch frame. His bald head glowed like an incandescent flesh-bulb beneath the hot klieg lights. Some compared the controversial evangelist's invasion of New York City, bringing his gospel message to the belly of the secular liberal beast, to Billy Graham's 1947 crusade in Los Angeles that landed him on front pages of newspapers and made him a star. Even as the crowd hung on his every word and dozens of reporters crouched before him recorded the scene, Popilopos seemed strangely serene, apparently oblivious to the effect he had on people.

"My friends, I was born in Greece, and I have traveled all over the world, so I know of which I speak," said Popilopos, his sonorous voice echoing off the rafters. "We are uniquely blessed among all peoples in the world to be here in America."

The crowd clapped and cheered.

"Can you say amen?"

"Amen!" they roared.

"The Bible says when the righteous are in authority, the people rejoice," he continued. "And we are especially blessed to have leading our nation at this critical moment Bob and Claire Long, a couple who love the Lord with all their hearts, minds, and souls." (Loud applause.) "They are not ashamed of the gospel."

"Hallelujah!" someone shouted from the back.

"I am very honored one of them has blessed us with their presence here tonight." The hall fell to a hush as the crowd waited with anticipation. "This person came simply to worship the Lord. There was no plan to speak to you. But I asked this person to say a few words. So please join me in welcoming the First Lady of the United States, Claire Long."

As the crowd erupted in a standing ovation, Claire walked on to the stage in a white chiffon dress, waving to the crowd. Popilopos shook her hand and stepped into the shadows as she approached the Plexiglas pulpit.

"Thank you, thank you," said Claire, smiling demurely. The crowd would not stop, their applause sustained, the noise rising in volume. "Please . . . you're taking up my time," joked Claire. They dutifully took their seats. "Thank you, Jonah, for that introduction, and thank you for that warm welcome. I'm not here tonight to make any kind of political statement. I leave that to my husband." (Laughter.) "I am here tonight for one reason only and that is to testify that Jesus Christ is Lord, and if you will accept Him into your heart as your Savior, you will find a peace that surpasses all understanding and life eternal."

The crowd cheered and applauded.

"Whatever you are facing in life, Jesus is the answer," said Claire. "I know I have found that in my life. and I hope you will find it in yours. God bless you all." With that she was gone, exiting the stage as quickly as she entered, the roar of the crowd sending her on her way.

Popilopos stepped back to the podium. "Aren't we blessed to have a First Lady like that?" he asked.

"Yes!" shouted the crowd.

In the back of the hall, Dan Dorman leaned over to the White House reporter for CBS News.

"What was with the dress?" he asked. "Is she channeling Aimee Semple McPherson?"

"I don't know, but whatever she's doing, it sure is smart."

"How's that?" asked Dorman.

"She just locked up the Christian vote for Kerry Cartwright and every other candidate Long is backing in the midterms," said CBS News. "And she did it without appearing at a political event or endorsing a candidate. It's brilliant."

"I don't know," replied Dorman. "Popilopos is a nut. When the American people figure out he's Claire Long's spiritual mentor, they're going to wonder if there are séances going on in the White House." He made a mental note to do some digging around on Popilopos's ministry. *That might turn up some interesting nuggets,* he thought.

OUTSIDE A RUN-DOWN TENEMENT BUILDING in Jersey City, New Jersey, a dark blue van inched down a side street, trailed by two unmarked squad cars. From the roofs of surrounding buildings, police snipers crouched on their bellies, high-powered rifles with scopes poised. Nearby, some middle-school children kicked a soccer ball on a makeshift field of dirt and brown grass littered with aluminum cans and Hefty bags filled with rotting garbage. A stray dog scampered by.

The van came to a stop, and its back doors swung open. Out piled a dozen FBI SWAT team members wearing Kevlar vests, combat boots, and black helmets, carrying semiautomatic rifles, barrels pointing in the air. The police cruisers disgorged another eight Jersey City police detectives and FBI agents with sidearms drawn. The latter wore body armor under blue Windbreakers with yellow letters that read "FBI." The SWAT team leader opened a metal door and led them inside.

In the semidarkness of the stairwell, their eyes adjusted. As they walked up the first flight of stairs, a little girl who appeared to be approximately ten years old chased a kitten down the hallway. They continued up the stairs until they reached the sixth floor, where the SWAT team leader cracked the door to the hall and glanced in either direction. They hustled into the hall and moved quickly to the end, where they stopped short of the door to apartment 627.

The SWAT team leader turned to the lead FBI agent. He nodded. The SWAT team leader banged on the door with his fist. "Open the door! Come out with your hands up! Police and FBI!"

No response came from behind the door. The SWAT team leader banged on the door again. As he did, they heard the sound of people running around in the apartment.

"Let's go," said the lead FBI agent. "Go, go, go!"

The SWAT team leader pulled his semiautomatic rifle across his chest and kicked in the door, almost knocking it off its hinges. "Go!" he shouted.

They poured into the apartment, their boots banging on the floor and rifles cocking as they exploded through the doorway. A small man of Arab descent in his twenties stood in the middle of the living room, his hands in the air, shaking like a leaf.

"Don't shoot! Don't shoot!" he cried.

One of the detectives spun him around and threw him to the floor, placing a knee in the small of his back and pulling his hands behind and cuffing him.

They moved on to the back bedroom. The SWAT team leader pointed to his men, directing one group to check under the bed and in the closet while the other proceeded to the bathroom. One of the SWAT team members opened the bathroom door, where a man with a shock of black hair and a beard, wearing jeans and a V-neck T-shirt stood wide-eyed, holding a .38 Magnum pistol, his hands trembling.

"Put down your weapon," ordered the SWAT team member.

Suddenly the young man got off a shot, which missed. The SWAT team member fired three rapid shots from his M4 rifle, hitting the man in the chest and blowing him backward into the bathtub. As his body crumpled lifeless in the tub, the shower curtain fell and draped over him like a plastic funeral veil.

At that moment the closet door slid open slightly. Six automatic rifle barrels pointed at the cracked door.

"Come out with your hands up, or we'll do to you what we just did to your friend," barked the SWAT team leader.

A short, squat man in bare feet wearing jeans and a grungy polo shirt crawled out of the closet on his hands and knees, then rose on his knees to put his hands in the air. "Don't kill me, cops!" he cried.

The SWAT team leader grabbed his arms and pulled them behind his back, handcuffing him with plastic cuffs. The raid completed, they took two out of three members of a terrorist cell alive. Hassan Qatani's interrogation was beginning to yield tangible results.

21

G. Hoterman sat in a conference room in the Federal Court Building waiting to testify in the trial of Michael Kaplan. After a seemingly endless jury selection that dragged on for eight weeks, with defense lawyers striking the maximum number of jurors and using polls, focus groups, and jury consultants to seed the jury with the most favorable candidates (professional African-American women between the ages of twenty-five and forty-nine years), the much-anticipated trial was finally underway. It had been nineteen months since a grand jury indicted Kaplan on seven counts of perjury and obstruction of justice in the Dele-gate scandal. In that sense the trial was like a time capsule, hurtling official DC back to the scandal-plagued and acrimonious presidential campaign of two years earlier, when Long won as an independent in the first contest thrown into the House of Representatives in nearly two hundred years.

Hoterman was conflicted to say the least. As one of the most important prosecution witnesses (he cooperated with the investigation to avoid being indicted himself), he feared sending Kaplan to prison and dashing Sal Stanley's reelection hopes.

Journalists packed into the courtroom, including media celebrities like Marvin Myers, who had a bit part in the drama because Kaplan was a source of leaks to him, an embarrassing fact for both that emerged during discovery. Court sketch artists sat in the audience, charcoal pencils poised. Kaplan sat at the defense table, not a strand of his jet-black hair out of place, wearing a gray suit, blue tie, and a look of steely determination.

"Alright, let's review what we discussed," said Walt Shapiro, Hoterman's attorney. "Don't try to remember something you don't recall. Answer only the question as asked. Don't volunteer anything."

Hoterman nodded, his Adam's apple bobbing. Dierdre reached over and took his hand.

"If defense counsel claims you're testifying as part of a deal with the prosecution, don't let him get under your skin," Shapiro instructed. "Stay calm. Tone is critical."

G. G. nodded. "I'm afraid he's going to attack Dierdre."

Shapiro's poker face betrayed no emotion. "He probably will," he said matter-of-factly. "Be prepared for it. Don't lose your cool. That's what they want. Their entire objective is to undermine your credibility." He turned to Dierdre, leveling his gaze. "I know it's difficult, but you need to do the same. The jurors will be watching you, too."

Dierdre gazed through fearful eyes, nodding.

Two knocks came on the door. A court bailiff stuck his head in the door. "Mr. Hoterman, they're ready."

G. G. followed the bailiff down the hall and into the courtroom, walking down the center aisle, every eye following him. He felt the weight of Kaplan's accusatory stare but kept looking straight ahead. Stepping into the witness stand, he heard the presiding judge ask him to remain standing to be sworn.

"Do you swear to tell the truth, the whole truth, and nothing but the truth, so help you God?" asked the bailiff.

"I do," said Hoterman in a firm voice.

"You may be seated."

The lead prosecutor for the Justice Department approached Hoterman, his face expansive and welcoming. "Mr. Hoterman, how long have you known the defendant?"

"Seventeen years," said Hoterman.

"You and he were friends."

"Yes."

"Describe how you came to form the Committee for a Better America."

"Well," said G. G., his tone deliberate. "After Super Tuesday, the race for the Democratic presidential nomination was very close. I was supporting Sal Stanley. I got a call from Mike in early April, as the last primaries began to wind down. I think Stanley then had a lead of only about ten delegates. Mike was worried about conventions coming up in states where the primary was a beauty contest and the convention chose the delegates. He said they needed an outside group to run an independent expenditure for pro-Kaplan delegates."

"What did he ask you to do?"

"Raise the money."

"How much did he say he needed?" asked the prosecutor.

"One million dollars."

The prosecutor paused, letting the amount sink in. "Which states did he mention?"

"Virginia and Minnesota."

"Was it your understanding Mr. Kaplan would direct how CBA expended funds to achieve this objective?"

"Not exactly," said Hoterman. "But my impression was he had veto power."

The prosecutor walked in the direction of the defense table, standing no more than three feet from Kaplan, whose eyes smoldered. "The entire operation was an extension of the Stanley for President campaign, directed by Michael Kaplan, isn't that correct?"

The defense counsel jumped to his feet. "Objection, your honor. The prosecution is leading the witness."

"Overruled," said the presiding judge. "You may answer the question, Mr. Hoterman."

"Not entirely. But CBA would not have been formed without Mike's encouragement, and certainly its primary objective was to elect delegates who would vote for Sal Stanley at the national convention in Chicago."

"Mr. Hoterman, I'd like for you to look at an e-mail and attached document." The prosecutor took a piece of paper from the hand of one of the other prosecutors and handed it to G. G. "Your honor, for the court's record, the witness has been handed Exhibit 124-B."

Hoterman studied the piece of paper.

"Do you recognize it?"

"Yes."

"What is it?"

"These are my notes from a meeting held in the conference room of Hoterman and Schiff the week after I got the first phone call from Mike about the convention operation."

"Who attended that meeting?"

"Me, Dierdre Rahall, my deputy at the law firm, the executive director of the Stanley campaign in Virginia, and Melinda Lipper, who was the chief fund-raiser for the Stanley campaign."

"Can you please read the highlighted sentence in your notes?" asked the prosecutor.

"MK will provide list of approved vendors/contractors."

"And does MK stand for Michael Kaplan?"

"Yes."

The prosecutor handed G. G. another piece of paper. "Mr. Hoterman, I wonder if you can tell me if you recognize this document? Your honor, the witness has been handed Exhibit 144-C and D." At the defense table the attorneys flipped through their evidence books to the correct page, studying its contents.

"Yes. This is an e-mail from Mike Kaplan with an attached list of Virginia convention delegates and party officials to be paid by CBA."

"Who else received this e-mail?"

"Melinda Lipper."

The prosecutor bobbed his head with pride. He turned on his heel and said to the defense, "Your witness."

The lead defense counsel stood up slowly, his face a portrait of practiced disdain. He moved around from behind the table methodically like a lynx tracking its prey. In a slow lope, he glided in front of the jury box, stopping six feet short of the witness stand.

"Mr. Hoterman, you told the FBI the first time you were interviewed that you didn't recall receiving a phone call from Mike Kaplan . . . isn't that correct, sir?"

"That is correct," said Hoterman, his voice level. His collar felt tighter and his heart raced. He braced for the coming attack.

"Now you tell this jury, under oath and facing penalty of imprisonment if you commit perjury, not only that you can pinpoint when the call took place, but that Mr. Kaplan was allegedly anxious and upset. Which time were you lying, Mr. Hoterman, then or now?"

G. G. physically recoiled from the charge, pulling his head back sharply. "My memory was jogged by notes I found later," he said slowly, struggling to maintain his composure. "Once I remembered, the details came rushing back to my mind."

"How convenient," sneered the defense counsel, shooting a glance in the jury's direction and stretching his face into a sarcastic smile. "Are you sure it didn't have anything to do with the fact that you faced federal money-laundering charges for using your tax-exempt organization as a conduit for cash from donors like hedge-fund manager Stephen Fox?"

"No," said G. G., his face hardening.

"That is in fact what you did, is it not, Mr. Hoterman?"

G. G. ignored the defense lawyer and turned to face the jury, exactly as he had been instructed by Shapiro. "I believed the funds raised by CBA would be used to turn out grassroots activists to attend Democratic state conventions in Virginia and Minnesota," he said firmly, eyes unblinking. "That is a party-building activity and is well within the purview of a social welfare organization under Section 501(c)(4) of the Internal Revenue code."

"Unless!" shouted the defense counsel, raising his hands in the air dramatically. "*Unless* those funds were raised and expended in coordination with a federal campaign committee, according to the Federal Election Campaign Act—in this case the Stanley for President campaign." He stepped in the direction of Hoterman. "That's what you claim happened in your own testimony, is it not, Mr. Hoterman?"

Hoterman's face fell, the color draining from his face. He walked right into the trap. "That was not my intent. But it is what occurred."

"So according to you, the contributions to CBA constituted illegal and excessive corporate contributions to a federal campaign, correct?"

Hoterman pursed his lips. "Again, not my intent. But as it turned out, yes."

"Isn't it true that *you* were in charge of the Committee for a Better America, not Michael Kaplan?"

"I raised the money. I didn't decide where the money went."

"Oh, you didn't? Even though you served as chairman? Even thought you are an attorney whose law firm advises candidates on federal election law?" The prosecutor turned back to the jury, making eye contact. "If you were so clueless, why did you continue to participate?"

"Mike was a friend, I wanted Senator Stanley to win, and I believed we took the necessary steps to comply with the law."

"Are you sure it was Mike's assurances and not your desire to protect your mistress from prosecution?" asked the defense counsel, twisting the knife.

"Yes, I'm sure."

"Your deputy Dierdre Rahall recruited Stanley delegates in Virginia, isn't that correct?"

"Yes."

"Including her brother."

"Yes."

The defense lawyer paced to the front of the jury box, his back to Hoterman. Their eyes followed his every move, enraptured. Suddenly he wheeled to face the witness. "You were in this up to your armpits, weren't you, Mr. Hoterman?"

"That's not the way I would characterize it," said G. G., his eyes smoldering. He wanted to lunge over the barrister and strangle the attorney but restrained himself.

"Sounds like it to me," said the defense counsel in a sarcastic lilt. "Your law firm is advising the Stanley campaign, you're raising money for a tax-exempt group that is paying money to Stanley delegates, your mistress is running the delegate operation. . . . What, pray tell, do you call it, sir?"

"I was trying to help a friend," said G. G., his voice jagged and weary.

The defense counsel threw his hands up. "Well, you certainly did a *fine* job of that, Mr. Hoterman! Look around you!"

The courtroom broke out into laughter. The judge banged his gavel. "Order in the court! Order in the court." The laughter descended to muffled chuckles, then silence.

"Mr. Hoterman, you're here today because you and your mistress cut a deal to avoid prosecution in exchange for your testimony against Mr. Kaplan, isn't that right? You were willing to feed Mr. Kaplan to the wolves to save your own hide."

"No," said G. G. "I was informed early on I was neither a subject nor a target of the investigation. I was never accused of any wrongdoing, and I am here today for the same reason I have cooperated from the beginning—to tell the truth."

"I know the truth was painful for your wife and your children and your law firm and its clients whose money you laundered, Mr. Hoterman," said the defense counsel. "But sending an innocent man to prison is something else entirely."

"Objection!" shouted the lead Department of Justice attorney.

"Sustained," said the judge. "Counselor, I'm striking that comment from the record and instructing the jury to ignore it. I'm also warning you not to make a similar personal comment about a witness in the future or face the sanction of this court."

"I apologize, your honor," said the defense counsel. He stared at G. G. with a look of contempt. "No further questions." He walked back to the defense table.

"The witness is dismissed. Thank you for your time, Mr. Hoterman," said the judge.

G. G. Hoterman stepped down from the stand, his legs rubbery, his bum knee aching, his head spinning. He felt drained and flop sweat ran from his armpits and down his torso to his waist. To make matters worse, he accidentally made eye contact with Kaplan as he left the courtroom. Kaplan's vacant stare sent a shudder through him.

22

The Senate gallery was packed with spectators and family members as the senators entered a tense, final day of debate on the Iran sanctions legislation. Long was leaving the following week for a European Union meeting in Rome, and the administration hoped he could sign the bill before he departed, setting an example for European allies and carrying the strongest sanctions package possible to the conference.

Salmon Stanley had other plans. He saw the march to war with Iran as a reprise of George W. Bush urging Congress to authorize the invasion of Iraq in 2002. Stanley viewed the drumbeats of war with Iran like Iraq, driven by flawed intelligence, Dr. Strangelove scare tactics, diplomatic brinkmanship, and raw politics. Even worse, he saw Jay Noble's fingerprints. With the off-year elections looming, a vote on military action against Iran would make the Democrats look weak on terrorism.

The Senate minority leader yielded the floor to Senator Tom Reynolds, who clipped a microphone on his coat pocket and adjusted the papers on the lectern placed at his desk. The press corps rustled with anticipation. Reynolds prepared to speak to the GOP-sponsored "trigger" amendment authorizing "all means necessary" to disarm Iran if the National Security Council and CIA certified within six months that the sanctions had failed.

Wearing his best suit and a new blue tie, his thinning brown-gray helmet hair sharply parted, Reynolds's cherubic face bore the strains of fatigue and stress. He had a high bar to clear. Most viewed him as a gaffe-prone chatterbox, an inveterate camera hog, and an egomaniac possessing an outsized ambition even for the U.S. Senate. Reynolds, for his part, knew he had to project gravitas on a subject of existential importance to the United States and its allies. That was why he stayed up until the wee hours of the morning practicing his speech in front of a mirror, including punctuating the words with hand gestures.

"Mr. President," Reynolds began, his voice even, his shoulders rounded. "I want to thank my colleagues on the other side of the aisle for the bipartisan manner in which they have proceeded on the Iran sanctions bill before us." It was a calculated and disarming extension of an olive branch from one of the Senate's most dedicated partisans. "Our dear departed friend Perry Miller left some big shoes to fill, but Senator Sue Warren has done so with leadership and the ability to build consensus. I am hopeful we can pass crippling sanctions against Iran's financial sector, stop its importation of refined petroleum products, and end its pursuit of dual-use technologies and facilities."

Reynolds pointedly excluded Stanley from his lavish praise. The two men despised each other. Stanley sat on the front row, arms crossed over his chest, glaring at Reynolds, waiting for the other shoe to drop. It didn't take long.

"I say more in sadness than anger, Mr. President, that in spite of the best efforts by me and many of my colleagues, we have been unable to achieve bipartisan agreement in one essential area," said Reynolds, a expression on his face. "These sanctions must have a mechanism for ascertaining whether they have worked. Otherwise, what is the point?" He raised his arms and looked at the presiding officer, a freshman Democratic senator reveling in his moment in the sun. "After all, Mr. President, if we don't do that, these sanctions will fail, like all the U.S. and UN sanctions that preceded them, and this will have been an exercise in futility."

Reynolds dropped his chin, pausing for dramatic effect. "This is not a time for timidity. It is not a time for half measures. It is not a time for appeasement masquerading as diplomacy." He let the words sink in before looking directly at Stanley, his eyes unblinking. "None of us want war. But the question is: how best to prevent it? Some believe the way to prevent war is to project weakness and hope our enemies view that weakness as an invitation to negotiate. Like Ronald Reagan, I believe the best way to secure the peace is through strength."

Stanley glared back at Reynolds, his eyes shooting darts.

"Some forget how perilously close Great Britain came to defeat in May 1940," said Reynolds, pointing his finger toward the sky to punctuate his point. "Hitler drove across Europe in a blitzkrieg of overwhelming military superiority. Czechoslovakia, Poland, and France all fell in its wake. The United States had not joined the war effort. The British army and navy were seemingly on the verge of being driven from the European continent, their tails between their legs. In this dark hour, some urged a negotiated settlement with Hitler rather than allowing a Nazi invasion of England."

Reynolds's dark eyes darted as he reached his peroration. The entire chamber stood still. Not a single person moved.

"One person stood in the gap: Winston Churchill. On June 4, 1940, shortly after assuming the prime minister's office, he addressed the British Parliament. He said, 'We shall fight on the seas and oceans, we shall fight with growing confidence and growing strength in the air, we shall defend our Island, whatever the cost may be, we shall fight on the beaches, we shall fight on the landing grounds, we shall fight in the fields and in the streets, we shall fight in the hills; we shall never surrender.'"

Reynolds reached down and turned a page over on the lectern. His eyes scanned the text. "Mr. President, we have arrived at a similar hour of testing. It is time for all of us to take a stand for victory over Iran, the world's leading state sponsor of terrorism which now possesses the ability to blackmail other nations with nuclear weapons, or to follow the path of ignoble defeat urged by counselors of timidity and humiliation.

"History will record how we acted. Its verdict will not be forgiving. May we not be weighed in the balance and found wanting. May we, like Churchill and Roosevelt in their own time, respond to the call to save Western civilization for our children and grandchildren."

Up in the press gallery, Dan Dorman of the *Washington Post* turned to Marvin Myers. "Was he speaking to the amendment or giving a Chautauqua speech?" he asked, voice dripping with sarcasm.

"I think it was a little of both," chuckled Myers.

"I think Henry Clay is safe," joked Dorman.

"Clay? Heck, Joe Biden is safe," replied Myers. They both laughed.

IN THE SMALL ANTEROOM OFF the Oval Office, Long's inner circle watched the debate in a power clutch. Long stood in his coat and tie, rocking back and forth on the heels of his spit-shined, ostrich-skin cowboy boots, nervous as a senior waiting for his grades to be posted. Charlie Hector, dark circles under his eyes, gazed at the television with the dispassionate stare of a man halfway through a marathon. Truman Greenglass, a pensive expression on his face, hands on hips, shot an occasional glance at Long to gauge his mood. Lisa leaned forward, cobalt blue eyes staring at the image on the screen, biting her lower lip. Jay sprawled out in a wing chair, rubbing his chin, his body coiled with nervous energy.

"I never thought we'd have to rely on Tom Reynolds of all people to save the day," muttered Hector, shaking his head.

"Me either," said Long. "But beggars can't be choosy."

"When was the last time a national security vote was this polarized along party lines?" asked Jay, throwing up his hands. "I can't believe what I'm watching. This resolution should pass 95 to 5!"

"The Gulf War resolution," replied Greenglass with clinical detachment. "People forget, but it passed 53 to 47. Sam Nunn took a powder, and the Democrats followed him off the cliff. They lived to regret that."

"They'll regret this," said Long. "There are a lot of presidential ambitions going up in smoke on the floor of the Senate today. They're not being serious."

"Any chance the threat of a veto saves the trigger?" asked Lisa to one in particular.

"Possible, but unlikely," said Greenglass.

"What's our latest hard count?" asked Long.

"Forty-seven votes in favor, 45 against," said Jay.

"Even with AIPAC and all the conservative groups scoring the vote?" asked Lisa. "That's amazing."

"It's all about the far left holding a gun to the head of the Democratic caucus," said Greenglass. "No one wants to pay a price for a pro-war vote like Hillary did against Obama in 2008. Now, having said that, we're still negotiating with a few wobbly Democrats."

Long sighed. "Truman, you nailed it. The Democrats have never recovered from Vietnam, much less Iraq. It was a big part of why I finally left the party."

"The press is going to want to know if you're going to veto the sanctions bill if the trigger mechanism is defeated," said Lisa. She glanced at Greenglass. "Any guidance?"

"I'd kick that can down the road," said Greenglass. "They still have to go to a conference committee. The House bill has the trigger language. There's a chance we can save it in conference. We don't need to make a declaratory statement yet."

"That's Stanley's game," said Jay. "He's telling his guys to vote 'no' because they can still yield to the House and then vote for the conference report."

"Where are the profiles in courage?" asked Long in frustration.

"I'm not sure we can hide behind the skirts of the conference committee," Lisa offered. "The press will still want to know: if the conference report doesn't include the trigger mechanism, will the president sign or veto the final bill."

Everyone turned to Long. "It's not an easy call," said the president, his voice falling to a near whisper. "If I go to the EU meeting empty-handed, it'll be played as an embarrassing defeat, and it'll hurt us with Germany and Spain. If I sign it without the trigger, I look weak."

"The U.S. has to show leadership, or the Europeans will use it as an excuse to tread water," said Hector. "They don't want to act, and America's failure is exactly what the nervous nellies want as an excuse to do nothing."

"This is like Reagan at Reykjavik," said Greenglass. "Sometimes you have to reject a bad deal to get a good one. People said Reagan failed. So what? Had he taken Gorbachev's deal at Reykjavik, the Berlin wall probably would have never come down."

Long nodded, deep in thought, not yet showing his hand. "Keep me posted," he said. "I'll be in the living quarters. Let me know if I need to talk to any senator." He paused. "Don't worry about how late."

"Yes, sir," said Hector.

Long walked out of the room. As he passed through the door, two Secret Service agents slid beside him. Everyone headed back to their offices. It was going to be a long night, and no one knew what would happen.

IN THE PRIME MINISTER'S OFFICE in the heavily fortified Knesset building in Jerusalem, Hannah Shoval huddled with her national security team, a motley crew of Likud careerists, retired army officers, and Israeli army veterans. She sat behind her desk, a small display of an Israeli and a U.S. flag with their poles crossed behind her, a gift from an American Zionist group. All eyes were glued to the television, watching the Senate debate.

"Tom Reynolds may be a gadfly, but he's got kahunas," said Shoval approvingly.

"That he does," offered one of her advisors.

"If Reynolds's amendment loses, we're in the hot seat," said the minister of defense, a retired army general. "At that point we're down to the least bad option."

Shoval shook her head and rolled her eyes.

Shoval's communications director, a wiry man with gray, closely cropped hair and intense eyes, came into the room. He had been working the phones to the States. "My contacts at the embassy and on the Hill tell me the vote on the trigger amendment is too close to call, but their best guess is we come up one or two votes short."

"Well, gentlemen, we won't be able to count on the United States," said Shoval. She let out a long sigh. "Israel will have to go it alone."

"What if Long vetoes it?" asked an advisor.

Shoval shrugged. "I hope he does." Her face hardened, its fine, feminine features turning brittle. "This is no time for half measures. We need courage and moral clarity from the West."

"I guess we're about to find out what Bob Long is made of, aren't we?" asked the minister of defense.

"We're about to find out a lot more than that," replied Shoval.

"Like what?" asked the communications director.

"Like whether Israel survives."

Her statement landed like a howitzer round among her national security advisors. The thought of Israel acting alone militarily against Iran was a prospect so unsavory they were all reluctant to contemplate it. But if the U.S. sanctions legislation failed to authorize force if necessary, there would likely be no other option.

LEAVING THE OVAL, JAY HEADED down the hall to his own office. Suddenly he saw David Thomas barreling down the corridor, holding a piece of paper in his hands, eyes wide, looking agitated. They nearly ran into each other.

"What is it?" asked Jay.

"I just got off the phone with AP in Florida," said Thomas, his voice high-pitched. "Dolph Lightfoot is announcing he's leaving the Republican Party and is running as an independent."

Jay shook his head and laughed. "So I guess he'd rather switch parties than lose the primary to Jefferson. Ask him how well that worked for Charlie Crist."

"It gets even better," said Thomas. "He's allowing his name to be placed on the Democratic primary ballot as well."

"This guy cross-dresses more than a drag queen on Halloween," exclaimed Jay. "I don't think there's any chance it works, do you?"

"I don't know," replied Thomas. "If Stanley can get the Democrats in Florida to back down, it's possible Lightfoot could be the Democratic nominee. If he's elected, he would caucus with the Democrats, and then Stanley holds the majority even if we pick up California. Think about it. Who else do the Democrats have in Florida who can beat Jefferson?"

"No one," said Jay. "Get on the phone with Jefferson. Tell him he needs to drop a bomb on Lightfoot. Accuse him of flip-flopping. Have people show up at his rallies smacking flip-flops together."

"There is one good thing about all this," said Thomas, eyes dancing.

"What's that?"

"Now Birch is going to have to support Jefferson for U.S. Senate."

Jay burst out laughing. "That really is rich." He paused, his brain in overdrive. "We gotta win this one. Especially now. It's a two-fer. We take out Stanley and Birch with one bullet."

Thomas nodded and hurriedly headed back down the hall. They had a lot of work to do.

23

The so-called "trigger" amendment offered by Tom Reynolds to the Iran sanctions bill failed by two votes in a virtual party-line vote, as expected. Sal Stanley foiled Long again, or so it seemed. But the White House had one final card to play, and it wasted no time doing so. The morning after the Senate defeated Reynolds's amendment, the Executive Office of the President posted a "Statement of Administration Policy" on the White House Web site, which landed like a grenade on Capitol Hill.

The legislative affairs office e-mailed the statement to the press and every Senate and House office. It read in part:

Statement of Administration Policy
<u>S.R. 6, The Comprehensive Iran Sanctions
and Human Rights Act</u>
(Sen. Susan Warren (D-NV) and 59 cosponsors)

The Administration strongly opposes Senate passage of S.R. 6, the Comprehensive Iran Sanctions and Human

Rights Act, in its current form. The resolution imposes sanctions on Iran's energy, banking, financial, and import-export industries and, among other prohibitions, would bar any U.S. company, or any foreign entity doing business with a U.S. company, from importing refined petroleum products into Iran. It also would sanction leading human rights abusers in Iran, including business entities associated with the Revolutionary Guard. However, unlike the House version of this legislation, the resolution does not include a provision directing the Director of National Intelligence and the National Security Council to report to the Administration and Congress within 180 days of final passage on the efficacy of sanctions in preventing Iran from obtaining nuclear weapons. For this reason, if S.R. 6 is presented to the president in its current form, he would veto the bill.

The president strongly supports the sanctions contained in both the House and Senate versions of the legislation. However, by excluding the requirement of an assessment of the efficacy of sanctions and authorizing additional necessary measures, S.R. 6 fails to find the proper balance and will fail to stop Iran's pursuit of nuclear weapons. The president urges Congress to pass the House version of the Iran sanctions legislation.

LONG WAS SCHEDULED TO DEPART for the European Union conference just six days hence. His secretary of state urged him to accept the sanctions bill to keep the heat on the Europeans to cut their extensive commercial ties with Iran. But she lost the bureaucratic infighting battle with Truman Greenglass, who advised Long (and this was consistent with his own instincts) that he simply could not compromise on a nuclear Iran. His back against the wall, Long was doubling down.

Sal Stanley, enraged by Long's move, wisely (some said uncharacteristically) chose not to rise to the bait. Instead he dispatched Sue Warren to the Senate floor to offer the Democratic rebuttal to the administration.

She did not disappoint. Warren strode onto the floor a mere thirty minutes after the White House issued its veto statement. Her once luminous hair had faded to dirty blonde with age, her svelte figure now padded around her middle, her shoulders rounded. As she clipped the microphone on her St. John suit, her lips formed into a thin line of lipstick.

"Mr. President, the administration has issued a Statement of Administration Policy which I find deeply troubling," she began, pivoting from her hips to make eye contact with her colleagues. "On a bipartisan basis, this chamber is unanimous in its conviction that Iran must not be allowed to possess nuclear weapons. Intelligence reports indicate it either has done so in a primitive form or is on the threshold of doing so." She held her hands in front of her body, her fingers touching as though she were addressing a jury. "Time is of the essence. We must act . . . *now*. But the administration has now apparently decided to make what I believe is one of the most important national security challenges of our time a partisan issue."

She paused, measuring her words. "The president's statement is an exhibit in cognitive dissonance. It claims the administration supports the sanctions contained in this legislation, including its promotion of human rights and its support of the pro-democracy movement in Iran." She wheeled around to face the presiding officer, cocking her head in disbelief. "Yet if he vetoes this legislation, the president will delay the implementation of the very sanctions he advocates, undercut his ability to persuade the members of the European Union to adopt a similar course, and strengthen the hand of the current regime in Iran."

Tom Reynolds had wandered onto the floor since Warren began her speech. He sought recognition. "Will the senator yield?" he asked.

Warren spun on her heel, eyes aflame. "I will *not*," she said, biting off the words. "I know the senator from Oklahoma shares the president's view that there should be a trigger mechanism authorizing military action in the event sanctions fail to stop Iran's pursuit of nuclear weapons. But war resolutions and economic sanctions legislation mix like oil and water. They have never been included in the same bill, and they should not be combined in the same bill now."

Democratic senators faces lit up. Warren had moxie, unafraid to take on a sitting president on the eve of a major trip abroad. Republicans glowered.

"This is no time for us to send conflicting signals to Iran," said Warren. "America should speak with one voice. That is why I urge the president to reconsider this veto threat. Does he really want to go to Rome next week empty-handed?" She threw up her hands and arched her eyebrows. "As the lead Senate conferee with our counterparts from the House, I intend to defend the Senate's position vigorously. I continue to hope we can pass a bipartisan bill of crippling sanctions the president will sign. But if he does not"—she wagged her finger in the air for emphasis—"then his administration will have to accept the consequences for the inaction and delay that will result. And if Iran obtains a workable nuclear weapon as a consequence, it will have taken place on this president's watch, and he will bear the responsibility for that outcome."

Jaws dropped on the Republican side of the aisle. What had gotten into Sue Warren? they wondered. Warren, her face brittle, chin raised, unclipped the microphone and walked briskly up the aisle, trailed by an aide with his head down, leaving the chamber. The Democratic senators rose to their feet in applause. The battle was joined.

As the debate over military action against Iran raged on Capitol Hill, a different drama unfolded at the National Press Club, just a few blocks from the White House. Pat Mahoney's dogged investigation of Perry Miller's murder led to the arrest of Hassan Qatani and the rolling up of terrorist cells connected to Rassem el Zafarshan up and down the Eastern seaboard, from Baltimore to New York City. Meanwhile, the more mundane criminal investigation of the dominatrix service where Miller died proceeded largely unheralded. All that changed when Jillian Ann Singer, the forty-two-year-old founder of Adult Alternatives, stepped to the podium at a news conference to discuss her possible arrest on federal prostitution, sex trafficking, money laundering, and tax evasion charges. If the purpose was to make news, she dropped a bombshell.

A fount of blonde hair fell over her shoulders, chiseled by years in the gym, an occupational hazard of one who took her clothes off in front of cameras. The former porn star wore a conservative green dress with a high collar, her striking blue eyes, and shapely figure suggesting the vanishing beauty of the *Playboy* centerfold she once was. The effects of plastic surgery and age, and the dark circles under her eyes, were only partially masked by heavy makeup caked on her puffy face. The deep lines in her face and neck bespoke a life of wrong choices and bad luck. Her attorney, a feminist-activist/ambulance-chasing celebrity lawyer who regularly haunted the crime chat shows on cable, stood to her side, jet-black hair sprayed into a bouffant, mauve eye shadow matching her designer wool dress, looking as if she had just stepped out of a beauty parlor.

Singer cleared her throat nervously. "My name is Jillian Ann Singer, and until recently I was the founder and CEO of Adult Alternatives, LLC," she began in a too loud voice. Her attorney reached over and adjusted the microphone, moving it farther away. "After spending most of my career as a model and an actress, I founded the company eight years ago to give consenting adults a safe and healthy place to pursue fantasies and explore the boundaries of adult play in ways both non-judgmental and fully compliant with the law."

On the front row the press sat on the edge of their seats, their eyes lit up like Christmas trees. The thought bubbles over their heads seemed to scream: *Is this really happening? It's too good to be true!*

In the back of the room, Dan Dorman leaned over to Satcha Sanchez, never one to miss a drive-by shooting. "Actress?" he whispered. "Is that what you call a chick who starred in *Lonely Wives, Home Alone?*"

"I haven't had this much fun since Monica Lewinsky," muttered Satcha under her breath. "TMZ alert!"

"Forget TMZ, we'll have it on page 1, column 1 tomorrow," joked Dorman.

"At Adult Alternatives, we viewed ourselves as being in the entertainment business," continued Singer, her eyes fixed to her text. "We provided our clients, many of whom came from prominent positions in business and government, with an escape from the conformity and convention of their daily lives." The media perked up at the reference to prominent leaders in business and government. Might she name names? "Adult Alternatives was not a prostitution ring. Sex between employees and clients during paid sessions was strictly prohibited, and that prohibition was included in a written employment agreement. This policy was strictly enforced, and violation could lead to termination of an employee." She paused. "If employees chose to see clients on their own time, that was their right, but they were not to be compensated."

Her defense complete, Singer moved to the money line. "Discretion and confidentiality were the guiding principles of my business from the beginning," she said, her chin raised. "We always treated the client relationship as sacred and inviolable. However, if the government prosecutes me, I will release the client list to the media and the public." The press corps rustled in anticipation, seeming to beg, *Do it now!* "I will do so reluctantly, not to cause public pain for my former clients, but so those clients can verify we never provided sex for hire. This is the only way to vindicate myself and salvage my reputation and the reputations of my employees."

Singer's attorney approached the podium, barely able to repress her joy. In the back of the room, more than thirty television cameras recorded the scene. As the two women stood together, clasping their hands together in support, still camera shutters clicked and whirred. It was a media feeding frenzy.

"Before Jillian Ann takes your questions," said the lawyer. "I want to state that due to the ongoing FBI investigation, she will be unable to answer any questions about Adult Alternatives or the circumstances of his death."

"Ms. Singer, are you claiming that not a single client of Adult Alternatives had sex with an employee?" shouted the Associated Press. "You expect the American people to believe that?"

Singer leaned into the microphone. "Yes," she said. "Our employees playacted with clients, entertained them, and empowered them to actualize fantasies. They did not have sex with clients during sessions on company time."

The attorney moved aggressively, a grave expression on her face, and leaned into the microphone. "Just to be clear, the operative word here is 'during sessions.' Adult Alternatives had no control over what employees did on their own time, any more than any other employer would. If they chose to see clients after hours, which they may have, it is a free country, and Jillian Ann could not prohibit them from doing so."

"Isn't that a convenient ruse?" shouted Reuters. "So they met for sex elsewhere?"

"No," fired back the attorney, who seized control of the news conference, sucking all the oxygen out of the room while simultaneously protecting her client, who gradually assumed a deer-in-the-headlights pose. "It was a written company policy, signed by all employees, and it was in full compliance with both federal and District of Columbia law."

"I wonder if I could ask Ms. Singer a question," said Dan Dorman from the back of the room. Heads swiveled. Dorman was a bigfoot. Singer approached the microphone with obvious trepidation. "Ms. Singer, do I understand you correctly that if you are arrested on any charges, you will release the client list? Or do you hold out the possibility you will keep it confidential in exchange for reduced charges by prosecutors?"

"If arrested on any charge, I will release the client list," said Singer, her facial features hardening.

"Why not release it *now*?" asked the *Huffington Post*. "Doesn't the public have a right to know?"

Her attorney grabbed the microphone again. "We have no plans to negotiate with the Justice Department or the district attorney for reduced charges. Jillian Ann has done nothing illegal. If charged, we will fight the charges and release the client list." She allowed herself a slight smile, the ends of her mouth turned up. "If we were to go to trial, which I think is unlikely, we will call former clients to testify. Thank you all very much."

Singer and her attorney exited stage left, accompanied by two rent-a-cops with crew cuts and grim expressions hired for the occasion. They ignored shouted questions from the media.

"Will Amber Abica be charged with being an accomplice to murder?"

"Did you have any other terrorists among your clients?"

As the press filed out of the room to head back to the office and write or produce their stories, their eyes danced with undisguised glee.

"This just got a lot more interesting," said Dorman.

"You think there are big names on that client list?" asked Satcha.

"I sure hope so," replied Dorman, smiling.

PHIL BATTAGLIA LEANED FORWARD, HIS elbows on his desk, wearing his best game face. Jay slumped in the chair opposite him, his arms crossed, a studied scowl on his face, looking all the world like a middle-school cutup called to the principal's office. Lisa sat straight-backed in the chair next to him, a legal pad on her lap, thumbing through a printout of that day's page 1 mud ball from the *New York Times*. The headline screamed, "IRS Agent Resigns After White House Blocked Audit of Evangelist Ally." The story generated chatter throughout the West Wing all morning about how best to respond. This was the gathering of the war council.

"I've called this meeting at Lisa's request," said Phil slowly, his fleshy jowls hanging, his face puffy. "I feel like we're going in circles. We keep having the same meeting."

Jay glanced at Lisa. He didn't want to go next.

"The *Times* story is their usual hit piece," said Lisa. "It's based entirely on the charges of a disgruntled former employee at the IRS and anonymous sources at Treasury. It's pretty ugly. The bigger problem is the rest of the press takes their cues from the *Times*."

"I saw it," said Battaglia. "They're conflating Jay's contact with the White House liaison at Treasury with a decision by a career IRS legal counsel not to proceed with a lower-level recommendation to revoke the tax-exempt status of Stanton's ministry. They're trying to stir the pot before the Finance Committee holds its hearings."

"Look, guys, I'm a target," said Jay matter-of-factly. "This is why I didn't want to come to the White House in the first place. But I'm here now, and this is the price of doing business."

Lisa turned to Jay, her eyes open and sympathetic. He felt his stomach jump. A thought rifled through his mind: was she still attracted to him? Or was it just a combination of his imagination and his own deep yearnings?

"Jay, I know you believe I think you're a liability to the president," she said, her voice soft. "But that's not the case. I know you're being attacked because you're effective. You helped save Marco Diaz's confirmation, you've held our electoral coalition together, and you're critical to us winning control of the Senate in November."

Jay nodded, stunned by her compliment. "I appreciate that," he said.

"But whether this is fair journalism is beside the point. It's having an impact. We're off message." She turned to Battaglia, waving a press release from the Senate Finance Committee, her face and hand gestures animated. "Jay can't defend himself because he can't testify. I can say he did nothing wrong, but no one in the press believes me. We need a strategy, Phil."

"I agree, but Jay testifying ain't it," said Battaglia. "Let me see that news release." Lisa stood up and leaned over, reaching across the desk and handing it to him. As she leaned forward, Jay noticed her long legs. At moments like this, he wished she wore pants more often, or shorter skirts, but that was verboten in the briefing room.

Battaglia's eyes scanned the press release, his brow furrowed. "Who is this guy?"

"His name is Hans von Fuggers," said Jay. "He's a big lib who was chairman of the Democratic Party in the Bronx in a previous life. Part of the Cuomo machine, which tells you all you need to know." Battaglia rolled his eyes knowingly. "He's a former tax attorney who worked for the ACLU for a while, then went to the IRS and wormed his way into the bureaucracy, becoming a career civil servant."

"It would sure be nice to know if he's been talking with his friends at the ACLU," said Lisa. "Can we can get access to his government e-mail account?"

Battaglia bristled. "Absolutely not," he said curtly. "But someone on the committee could demand his e-mails be subpoenaed."

"There's going to be plenty there," said Jay. "He gave $500 to Stanley's presidential campaign. In the past he gave money to Cuomo and Schumer, among others."

"Let's get that to a friendly reporter," said Battaglia. "How about Marvin Myers?"

"Too obvious," said Lisa. "I'll get it to Merryprankster. That'll be red meat for the sharks."

Battaglia leveled his gaze at Jay. "Hang in there, champ."

The meeting over, Jay filed out behind Lisa. Phil slapped him on the back as he left. In the hallway Lisa turned to him, their eyes locking.

"Jay, I'm sorry you're going through all this," she said softly.

Jay smiled weakly, touched by Lisa's kindness. "It's alright," he said. "The irony is, if I hadn't come inside, none of this would be happening. But I know I did the right thing by coming."

Lisa nodded. For a moment Jay felt a flood of raw emotion, the remnants of their stillborn campaign romance. Did she feel it, too? She averted her eyes, perhaps sensing his affection and moved quickly down the hall alone. Jay knew right then what he had to do. He just hoped he had the courage and intestinal fortitude to actually do it.

24

Members of the Senate Finance Committee sat on the dais like a row of Ken and Barbie dolls in their best suits, hair primped, some stage-whispering to aides who sat behind them for the benefit of the cameras. They all wanted to look their best for what promised to be the riveting testimony of the man of the hour: Hans von Fuggers. More than a few senators had practiced their lines in front of the mirror. Washington dressed up for scandals the way small-town America puts on its Sunday best for a funeral. The difference was that in DC a scandal was cause for celebration, a delightful human confection of mindless entertainment, colorful characters, compelling narratives, *schadenfreude,* and ritualistic executions. Careers would be made! Some (think Woodward and Bernstein) would become stars; others would do turns on reality shows. Newspapers would sell, and cable news ratings would go through the roof!

Hans von Fuggers walked into the cavernous hearing room of the Hart Senate Building, the unlikeliest of central figures in the summer's drama. Pale of complexion with thin brown hair, a high forehead, beady eyes, and a recessed chin, he hardly seemed worthy of the advanced billing. Wearing a light gray suit with a blue paisley tie, he was accompanied by his attorney.

Senator Aaron Hayward, the sixty-seven-year-old crusty, unreconstructed liberal from Michigan who chaired the Finance Committee, sat beneath the gold U.S. Senate logo carved into the marble wall behind him. His salt-and-pepper hair, lined face, and muted demeanor seemed to belie the excitement surrounding the day's proceedings.

"Good morning, Mr. Witness, and to the members of the committee," he said in an officious voice. "Today the Senate Finance Committee continues its investigation into the improper politicization of the Internal Revenue Service. Our sole witness is Mr. Hans von Fuggers, who served as the chief auditor in the exempt division of the IRS until he resigned four months ago. For some time many have waited expectantly on the edge of their seats for today's witness to tell what he knows about White House involvement in audits conducted by the IRS. He is appearing before us without any grant of immunity and has agreed to answer all questions." Hayward rose to his feet. "Mr. von Fuggers, given the gravity of the issues we're discussing and your role in them and to help ensure there is no misunderstanding about your obligation to tell all you know, would you kindly stand and raise your right hand so I may administer the oath."

Fuggers rose. As he raised his right hand, fifty still photographers jockeyed for position, shimmying on their knees and elbows, some lying on their backs. When von Fuggers raised his right hand, the room exploded with camera shutters and flashes.

"Do you swear to tell the truth, the whole truth, and nothing but the truth, so help you God?" asked Hayward.

"I do," replied von Fuggers, his voice quiet yet firm.

"I understand you have a statement you would like to read. Please proceed."

Von Fuggers leaned toward the microphone, head down, eyes glued to the papers in front of him. "My name is Hans von Fuggers. I grew up in Peoria, Illinois, and attended Northwest University as an undergraduate and later the University of Chicago Law School," he began, filling in his biography. "After practicing law for three years with a specialty in the area of taxes and estate planning, I applied for a job with the Internal Revenue Service. I worked at the IRS for seventeen years, rising to the position of senior auditor in the tax-exempt division."

The senators sat impassively as von Fuggers read his statement, their facial expressions stonelike. A number followed along from copies of his testimony.

"Two-and-a-half years ago I was asked to supervise the audit of New Life Ministries, an international broadcast ministry affiliated with a nondenominational church in Alpharetta, Georgia." He paused, taking a sip of water from a glass on the table. "During the course of our audit, we discovered a number of irregularities and possible violations, including unreimbursed personal use of ministry aircraft, excessive compensation, for-profit entities with close ties to tax-exempt affiliates, and a number of inurement issues.

"The staff at New Life Ministries made no attempt to disguise their hostility toward me and our audit team," von Fuggers continued. He spoke in a dull monotone that forced his listeners to lean forward in order to hear him, which added power to his words. "We were placed in a cramped trailer behind the ministry headquarters with an air conditioner that often did not work. One of the staff members asked me if I voted for Sal Stanley for president. Another time a student called one of my audit team members a, quote, 'fag.'"

The media perked up at the mention of the antigay slur. The fact the alleged incident could not be verified gave them no pause.

"Last summer I received a call from Barry Bostrum, deputy director of the tax-exempt division, my immediate superior at the Internal Revenue Service," said von Fuggers. "He asked me very pointed questions about the status of our audit and pressed me on when we might be wrapping up our work. At that point I asked Mr. Bostrum if I had a White House problem. He said, 'Big time.' When I asked for an explanation, he related Jay Noble called a senior advisor to the director of the IRS and demanded to know why the department was allegedly harassing Andy Stanton, a friend of the president. A few weeks later Mr. Bostrum e-mailed me and asked me to present my report on New Life within thirty days. When I told him I could not complete the audit within that time frame, I was informed I would be reassigned."

Fuggers took another sip of water, his hand shaking slightly. "It has greatly pained me to see the agency I loved and served for seventeen years politicized in this manner. It undermines the rule of law. It violates the historic protection afforded civil servants who seek to apply that law in an even-handed manner. This administration, and in particular Jay Noble, recklessly politicized a sacred trust." He turned the page. "For that reason I resigned my position with the IRS. I could no longer participate in this farcical charade, the prostituting of our tax code to serve political ends. Mr. Chairman and members of the committee, I thank you for hearing my testimony, and I look forward to your questions."

JAY SAT IN HIS OFFICE in the West Wing, watching von Fuggers's testimony with David Thomas and a clutch of their loyal aides. Some sat at the conference table while others stood, their arms crossed, doing a slow burn.

"Talk about holier than thou," said Thomas, his face filled with disgust. "You get a call from your superior after you've been camped out at a tax-exempt organization for a year and a half asking for an interim report and your response is to . . . *quit?*"

"He's an ACLU activist masquerading as a civil servant," said one of Noble's aides. "He had Stanton in his crosshairs and dared anybody to stop him."

Jay studied the television screen with professional detachment. "You guys work up some talking points for Lisa," he said at last. "We need to push back . . . hard."

"We'll make 'em wish he'd remained a bureaucrat," wheezed one of the propeller-heads.

Jay said nothing in reply. Instead, he left his office and walked down the narrow stairwell leading to the first floor of the West Wing. He entered the suite of offices occupied by Charlie Hector and stopped at the secretary's desk.

"Charlie in?" he asked.

"Sure, go on in," said the assistant.

Jay walked in to see Hector standing as he usually did, his eyes scanning papers fanned out on his desk, brow furrowed. The C-SPAN broadcast of von Fuggers's testimony was on in the background, the volume turned down.

"What's up?" he asked, barely looking up.

Jay took a seat opposite his desk. "Did you watch von Fuggers?"

"A little bit," Hector lied.

"Charlie, we need to waive executive privilege. I need to testify."

Hector sat down, exhaling slowly, stunned.

"Look, I know it's risky. It puts me in Hayward's—and Stanley's—crosshairs," said Jay. "But let's face it, I'm there already. The more they drag me through the mud, the more it undermines my ability to serve the president. I *have* to testify."

Hector leaned back in his chair, hands folded behind his skull. "I don't disagree with you. But this is about executive privilege. It's not a political matter; it's a constitutional matter that strikes at the heart of the separation of powers. Phil's going to argue—"

"Forget the lawyers," Jay fired back. "Stanley's going to use the oversight function to go after us every single day. It's going to be death by a thousand cuts." He pointed to the television set, then leaned his entire body across the desk, his eyes pained and desperate. "Charlie, I'm begging you. *Please* . . . let me at 'em."

Hector chewed on his lip. "I'll talk about it with the president." His eyes locked on Jay's. "It'll be his decision."

"Fine. Let's talk to him."

Hector nodded. "I'll try to get with him before he leaves for the day."

"Let's just go talk to him."

"Now?

"If he's free, you bet."

Hector opened his door and stuck his head out. "Can you see if the president can see me and Jay for a minute?"

The assistant dialed the president's secretary. After a minute of conversation, she hung up. "You're good to go," she said.

Hector and Jay headed down the hall through the West Wing lobby and down to the Oval Office. They pumped hands with the Secret Service agents, greeted the president's secretary, and then opened the door to the Oval. Long sat behind his desk, scanning the day's news clips. Jay noticed he was not watching the hearing.

"What'd you guys want to see me about?" asked Long gruffly, his eyes searching. He now got defensive when aides came calling. They usually brought bad news.

"Go ahead, Jay," said Hector.

"Mr. President, I believe we should waive executive privilege and let me testify before Hayward's committee."

Long whipped his reading glasses off. "You want to walk into an ambush?"

"It's already an ambush, sir," replied Jay, hands behind his back, bowing slightly. He was in his best suck-up mode, hoping to get Long's sign-off. "Hans von Fuggers was on the front page of the *New York Times* yesterday, *60 Minutes* last night, and he's testifying today. He's attacking me frontally, and it will affect my ability to do my job."

Long studied Jay's anguished face. "Jay, I know it's no fun getting shot at," he said. "But I can't let those piranhas up on the Hill browbeat me into serving up my senior aides as the main course for dinner. This isn't about us. I took an oath to protect this office, not just for me, but for future occupants." He tapped on the desk with his index finger. "Read my lips: I will protect the right of the president to privileged advice, come hell or high water."

"Mr. President, I wouldn't do anything to compromise your ability to receive the unvarnished, confidential advice of your aides," said Jay. "But the question here is what I said to someone at Treasury. Previous White House counsels have allowed EOP staff to testify in the past, with certain ground rules. We should do the same here. If Hayward doesn't agree to our conditions, I don't go, period, end of story."

Long shot a glance at Hector. "I don't like it. What do you think, Charlie?"

"We're fighting a losing battle, sir," said Hector. "We're right on principle. But these are serious charges. My fear is if we don't let Jay set the record straight, not only will he be damaged, but your presidency will be irreparably damaged."

"That's quite a mouthful," said Long.

"It is, sir," said Hector. "It's what I honestly believe."

"Any e-mails to or from Jay that will be a problem?" asked Long.

"Not that I know of," said Hector.

Long rubbed his chin, thinking for what seemed like several minutes of silence. "You have permission to see if you and Phil can cut a deal with Hayward that circumscribes what Jay is allowed to testify about." He pointed with his index finger, eyes aflame. "Not a word of testimony about privileged communications with me or anyone else in this building, Charlie. On that point I will not bend. Understood?"

"Crystal clear, sir," said Hector.

"Thank you, Mr. President," said Jay.

"Don't thank me," said Long. "You're about to be dropped into the lions' den." He raised the corner of his mouth. "Better you than me, pal."

They all chuckled, if only to relieve the tension, and Jay and Charlie left the Oval. As they headed down the hall, Hector turned to Jay. "Well, one thing's for sure."

"What's that?"

"You're going to need to hire a top-notch criminal attorney. Phil can't be your lawyer. He works for the president."

Jay felt his heart leap in his chest cavity. "Any suggestions?"

"Yes. Walt Shapiro," Hector replied. "Call him as soon as you get back to your office. I'll have my assistant give you his direct dial. I don't have to go through a receptionist at the law firm and get the rumor mill going. People talk."

Jay gulped. He wasn't sure if he was happy or sad Long agreed to let him testify. But there was no turning back now. He would just have to grab his rip cord and jump.

IN HIS STATE-OF-THE-ART STUDIO on the campus of New Life Ministries, built at a cost of $10 million to sustain an earthquake up to six on the Richter scale without affecting the quality of the broadcast, Andy Stanton rounded his shoulders and cocked his head as he prepared another furnace blast at the unholy trinity of the media, the Democrats, and the far left. Stanton's musical intonations of syllables and sounds, his mesmerizing enunciation of seemingly ordinary words, and the metronome-like, hypnotic spell of his mellifluous voice held a weekly cumulative audience estimated at fourteen million listeners on 875 radio stations around the world.

"My friends, if you want to know the truth, it isn't what is *said* that reveals the elusive gem; it is what is *not* said. So let us review what you *didn't* hear in today's kangaroo court on Capitol Hill," said Andy, working himself into a froth. "You *didn't* hear that Mr. von Fuggers is a former hired gun for the ACLU, which wants to legalize prostitution and hard drugs and drive any semblance of faith in God from the public square. *That's* the real Mr. von Fuggers, not some disinterested public servant with no ax to grind. He's a political *activist*."

Andy adjusted his headset and wheeled around to face the control room, which was separated from the studio by a soundproof glass wall. "Mr. Producer, please play sound bite number nine from today's hearing. Go!"

Andy leaned back in his chair and rocked slightly while the audio cut played. The sound bite included a halting response by von Fuggers to hostile questioning by a Republican senator. Suddenly, Andy jumped up as if fired by a catapult, nearly coming out of his chair.

"Stop! Stop right there!" he shouted. "That's enough. There it is, my dear friends, the shocking admission! Mr. von Fuggers *admits* New Life Ministries fully complied with IRS guidelines for churches and ministries and was given a clean bill of health. *That* is why his superiors rejected his recommendation to deny our tax-exempt status, not because of political pressure by the White House or anyone else."

He spun in his chair, making eye contact with his producer, who squeezed his thumb and forefinger together to indicate time was running out before the next commercial break.

"The problem is not the politicization of the Treasury Department," said Andy, dropping his voice to an intimate, conversational half whisper. "The problem is anti-Christian bigotry. It is the last acceptable form of bigotry left in America. Like a cancer it permeates the media, the government, the courts, academia, and the opinion elites who run this country. I took them on, and Mr. von Fuggers tried to silence me." He paused, leaning into the microphone, his voice a hushed whisper. "Mr. von Fuggers, I've got a news flash for you and your friends on the radical left: I will not be silent. I will not go away. It is my *right* as a minister of the gospel and as an American to speak the truth in season or out of season. Because this, sir, by God's grace, is *still* America. You can send the IRS, the FEC, the FCC, the FTC, the SEC, and any other alphabet soup of bureaucrats you want to after this ministry.

But you will only take this microphone away from me one way . . . by pulling it from my cold, dead hands. We'll be right back."

The theme music for the program blared as they cut to a break. The producer turned on the intercom. "Wow, Andy. That was a perfect throw to break. You're the *best*."

"Can you believe we actually get paid to do this?" asked Andy with a cackle.

ON MSNBC THE PRIME-TIME HOST was in the seventh minute of the opening segment, which had been extended to twenty minutes without any commercials to accommodate the full-throated, smack-down of Jay Noble and Andy Stanton. Righteous indignation oozed from every pore of the host's body. He did his best Edward R. Murrow imitation, or at least what passed for Murrow in the postmodern world of decimated news budgets, bankrupt newspapers, and cable scream-fests produced by skeletal staffs with an average age of twenty-five.

"Corruption on a grand scale. White House manipulation. Political paybacks. Blacklisting of government employees. These are just a few of the shocking allegations leveled at the Long White House by Hans von Fuggers in testimony that riveted the Senate Finance Committee and the nation today," said the host. "Joining me now to discuss von Fuggers's explosive testimony, Dan Dorman with the *Washington Post*. Good evening, Dan."

"Good evening," said Dorman, appearing on a split screen from the *Post* newsroom, his gray hair matted and unkempt, glasses resting low on his nose, tie askew, eyelids drooping.

"I don't recall seeing anything quite this dramatic on Capitol Hill since John Dean appeared before the Senate Watergate Committee," said the host. "Mr. von Fuggers was so understated, so much the opposite of theatric, that it *was* dramatic. You've covered Washington a long time, Dan. How big was today's hearing and does it spell doom for Jay Noble and perhaps Bob Long? Isn't this so damaging Long has to fire Noble if only to save himself, as Nixon did Haldeman and Ehrlichman?"

"It's a little early to tell," said Dorman clinically. "Unless the White House can refute von Fuggers's charges, this is going to be extremely damaging. It appears—and I stress appears—that a tax-exempt organization with over $200 million in annual revenue allied with the administration got special treatment from the IRS. Recall this kind of abuse of the IRS-led Congress to impeach Richard Nixon. Whether Long can shield Jay Noble by invoking executive privilege remains to be seen. But as one prominent senator said to me today, 'Jay Noble's not going to be able to hide behind Phil Battaglia's skirts forever.'"

The host nearly came out of his chair—Dorman had used the "I" word! "Could this scandal lead to Bob Long's impeachment? . . . I mean if the facts turn out to be as sordid and unseemly as they appear?"

"Oh, it's way too early to jump to that conclusion," Dorman furiously backpedaled. "I'm simply making the point this is an explosive charge with precedent for major legal and political repercussions."

"Yet the White House continues to stonewall," said the host, growing more animated, his nostrils flaring. "Are they detached from reality, are they corrupt, or are they just plain stupid? Or is it perhaps a combination of all three?" He arched his eyebrows expectantly.

Dorman laughed. "Jay Noble can be accused of a lot of things, but stupid is not one of them," he replied. "Detached from reality? Even some of Long's friends say yes. Corrupt? I think the jury is still out. We'll have to see where the hearings go."

"Wrong answer, Dan," said the host. "The correct answer is the White House is detached from reality *and* corrupt. Stupid is as stupid does. That'll have to be the last word."

Just like that the segment was over. The television lights dimmed at the *Post* newsroom. Dorman reached for his ear, to remove his earpiece.

"Good job, Dan," said the producer into his ear. "Fantastic segment. But next time hit 'em harder."

Dorman just chuckled as he removed the microphone from his coat.

25

F ederal agents swarmed into the Dallas home of Representative Matthew "Buddy" Tisdale, chairman of the powerful House Defense Appropriations Subcommittee and the Crystal City, Virginia, offices of Aristotle Security Consulting (ASC), a defense contractor with extensive ties to the congressman. The firm received tens of millions of dollars in covert intelligence contracts annually from the CIA and the Defense Department and was arguably the most significant player in "black ops" in the war on terror. It retained a virtual shadow army of retired former CIA agents, Army Rangers, and Special Forces, deployed in Afghanistan, Iraq, the tribal regions of Pakistan, Somalia, Ethiopia, Malaysia, Indonesia, and a dozen other countries. Among its responsibilities were the infiltration, apprehension, assassination (though that word was sanitized in translation to "elimination") and interrogation of terrorist suspects on the field of battle.

The surprise raids were part of an ongoing investigation by a federal multiagency task force that included the U.S. attorney's office in Dallas, the FBI, IRS, and the Defense Criminal Investigative Service. Even more troubling for Tisdale, the FBI raided the home of his twenty-eight-year-old daughter, who managed his campaigns and ran his leadership PAC.

At ASC headquarters, federal agents carted off personal computers, laptops, smart phones, and file cabinets filled with documents. They seemed to know exactly what they were looking for in every office and at every cubicle. Clearly someone had been wearing a wire, probably for months. Police tape surrounded the building, shielding the agents from interaction with network camera crews who showed up to film the carnage, along with a few curious onlookers.

"We have no comment at this time," said an ASC spokesperson when contacted by the *Dallas Morning News.*

"This is an outrageous abuse of power and prosecutorial discretion," said Tisdale's attorney, a prominent criminal defense lawyer. "Buddy Tisdale has done nothing wrong. He has fully cooperated with this investigation, and when all is said and done, he will be fully vindicated.

Far from the raids in Dallas and DC, an opposition researcher with the Dolph Lightfoot campaign's radar went up. He remembered Don Jefferson was a member of the Defense Appropriations Subcommittee. Might he have a connection to ASC? A quick search of the Federal Election Commission database, the ASC Web site, and Google revealed Jefferson received a total of $40,500 in contributions from ASC employees, family members, and its PAC. Even more promising, Jefferson's former chief of staff was hired by ASC as a lobbyist to help the company pursue government contracts.

Within three hours of the raiding of ASC's headquarters, an influential blogger with close ties to Lightfoot's campaign (in fact, he was secretly being paid $5,000 a month in addition to the ads Lightfoot ran on his Web site), posted a blistering attack on Jefferson. "Does Don Jefferson, the baby Jesus of Florida politics, have a Buddy Tisdale problem?" screamed the post. "More to the point, does he have an Aristotle Security Consulting problem? It sure looks like it. ASC's offices were raided today by federal agents wielding a search warrant in what is a rapidly moving investigation into corruption charges relating to ASC and Congressman Tisdale. Agents have not raided Jefferson's offices—yet." The post continued: "The federal grand jury investigating this scandal will no doubt ask Jefferson some very pointed questions, such as:

1. What did he do in exchange for the $40,500 in contributions he received from ASC and its employees?
2. Did Terry Camp, his former chief of staff, have any contacts with him, his office, or his staff after he was hired as a lobbyist by ASC to drum up even more defense contracts from Jefferson's subcommittee?
3. Did he ever participate in a congressional junket overseas in which ASC staff, consultants, or officers or board members were present?
4. Did he ever submit an earmark request that benefited ASC?
5. Did he ever contact anyone at the Department of Defense, CIA, or any other government agency requesting ASC receive a covert contract?

The blogger ended his post by hurling this brick: "I have not endorsed a candidate for U.S. Senate. That is for the voters to decide. But I have said repeatedly for months that Don Jefferson is a charlatan and a fraud, a huckster, and a career politician posturing as a Tea Party candidate and a right-wing caped crusader. In truth he is a just another blow-dried (or in his case, hair dyed), self-aggrandizing, phony politician who pretends to be whatever he must to win an election. Now the mask is being pulled away. What do you think? Please let me hear your comments."

Within an hour forty-eight comments from supporters of Lightfoot and Jefferson were posted on the Web site, hurling invective and spewing venom. One typical (and anonymous) comment dripped with sarcasm: "It's only a matter of time before that crook Jefferson is doing a perp walk. When does the House Ethics Committee start looking into this can of worms? Don't hold your breath." The U.S. Senate primary pitting Jefferson against Lightfoot was about to get a lot more interesting, and bloody.

DON JEFFERSON SLUMPED IN A government-issue black leather wing chair in his office in the Longworth House Office Building, huddling on a conference call with his legal counsel, his chief of staff, and several campaign aides.

"We have two parallel issues here," said Jefferson's attorney and campaign advisor. "The first is the criminal issue. As far as I can surmise, Don, you don't have anything to worry about in that respect. You didn't do anything wrong vis-à-vis your relationship with Aristotle."

"Not at all," agreed Jefferson. "I never lifted a finger to help them."

"Unfortunately in these situations, that is not always enough. The second issue is political. Lightfoot is making hay out of this, the bloggers are mainlining crack, and the Florida media will go into overdrive to cover it. That's baked in the cake. We've got to figure out a way to push it down and insulate you from the larger story involving Tisdale and Aristotle. If you get sucked into the national story, it really gets difficult."

"How do we do that?" asked Jefferson. "Look, let's face it: I've had a great few weeks. I've led a charmed existence. The long knives are out."

"Agreed. There are certain guiding principles," his attorney said, waxing strategically. "First, whatever you say, tell the truth. I know it sounds obvious, but if I've seen it once, I've seen it a thousand times; what kills people in a situation like this is the perception they're trying to hide something. Second, I would quickly return contributions from ASC or its employees. All of it. I'd do that today or tomorrow."

"Do we give it back or donate it to charity?" asked Jefferson.

"Either way is fine. Give it to a charity providing assistance to the families of wounded soldiers. Finally, insofar as you can do it without compromising the criminal investigation, get in front of it, do a document dump to the media and be done with it. Cut off the scab."

Jefferson listened impassively. "The press is asking about contacts between us and Terry," he said. "We need to get our arms around it, and to your point we need to get it right—assuming we can tell the truth about it publicly, that is."

"Please tell me he didn't violate the one-year lobbying ban," said the attorney. "That's a felony count." Federal ethics laws forbade a former Hill staffer from having any direct contact with members of Congress or their staffs for one year after leaving government service.

Jefferson looked at his chief of staff, who shook his head. "No, we were both careful," said the chief of staff. "If he needed to communicate with us, he would have someone else call. Once the year was up, we did talk to him."

"When was that?" asked the attorney.

"January of this year," said the chief of staff.

"How often did you communicate with him?"

"Not that often," replied the chief of staff. "I'm sure he dealt with Tisdale more than us. I'd have to check, but probably once or twice a month."

"Do a quick e-mail search and make sure there's nothing problematic," said Jefferson. "We don't want to be flying blind. Run all those by the attorneys."

"We'll review every document before it goes to either the federal task force or we release it to the press," said the attorney. "Did anyone accept anything of value from Terry or any other Aristotle employee?"

"I didn't," said the chief of staff. "If Don or I meet anyone for dinner or drinks, it goes on the campaign credit card. Most of the time we just go to the Capitol Hill Club. They can't pay for it there anyway unless they're a member."

"Make sure nobody got a free meal, concert, or Nats tickets," said Jefferson. He thought a moment. "What do we do if someone did?"

"Reimburse it right away. If we're contacted by the FBI, tell them about it up front so no one thinks you're hiding anything," said the lawyer.

"Do we send a check over to Aristotle's offices?" asked Jefferson, incredulous.

"Absolutely," replied the attorney. "Who cares if anyone's there to open the mail or deposit the check? You did your part."

"Gang, we've got an immediate issue," interjected Jefferson's campaign manager, who was on the phone from the headquarters in Ocala. "The press is asking for a statement or interviews with Don. They're writing their stories as we speak. We need to get a statement up on the Web site and e-mail it to the media ASAP."

"Work up a draft and run it by me and the lawyers," said Jefferson.

"What about you appearing for the cameras and taking questions? I think we're going to have to do that at some point," said the campaign manager, his disembodied voice coming through the speakerphone.

Jefferson glanced at his chief of staff, his eyes inquiring.

"We'll have to do that eventually," said the chief of staff. "I'd let things cool down first. But if we don't get Don in front of the cameras by next week, the affiliates will fly reporters and a camera crew up here and chase you down the street, yelling out questions, airing footage of you ducking into elevators or cars."

"Announce we're returning the money today and release a statement saying I've done nothing wrong and look forward to cooperating fully with the investigation," said Jefferson. "Then I'll meet with the media when I go back later in the week."

"No news conference," suggested the campaign manager. "They all start trying to outperform one another when you do that. It's not a good dynamic. I'd do a series of one-on-ones and maybe one ed board."

Jefferson frowned. "I don't know," he said. "Maybe it's better to just bite the bullet and take the tough questions and lean into this. I've got nothing to hide."

The dead air hung as everyone absorbed the impact of the day's news. They hoped to knock Lightfoot out of the box with a quick blow. Now they were in for a long, bloody slog.

"It's unfortunate Terry's caught up in this," said the chief of staff. "It's going to make it far more difficult for us to stay out of the story."

"It's a stinking mess," said Jefferson. "Not just for him, but me. Who knew?"

"He needs to keep his mouth shut and stay out of the paper," observed the chief of staff.

"If it's any consolation, I've seen people survive a lot worse than this," said the attorney. "Lightfoot's going to have his problems. And it was unrealistic to think we'd have smooth sailing." He paused, adding brightly: "Hey, Don, look on the bright side . . ."

"What's that?" asked Jefferson.

"You're not Buddy Tisdale."

Everyone allowed themselves a morbid laugh. It wasn't that the joke was funny—far from it. But laughing was less painful than crying.

TRUMAN GREENGLASS STARED AT HIS computer screen, his stomach doing flips, the pain of a migraine headache shooting through his skull like hot knitting needles being twisted slowly in his brain. The news accounts splashed across the Internet of the raid on ASC headquarters by federal agents filled him with panic. The photographs of FBI and DOD investigators carting out boxes, computers, and file cabinets sent a shudder through him.

What worried Greenglass was the most explosive aspect of the ASC probe wasn't the campaign contributions, bribes, or gratuities the firm paid to Buddy Tisdale, or any other member of Congress for that matter. It was the fact that Aristotle was the main conduit for covert aid to the Green Movement in Iran, including the elimination of key members of the nuclear program and the Republican Guard, a program so secret it was known by only a handful in the entire government. One of them, Senator Perry Miller, was dead.

Greenglass picked up the phone and dialed the direct number of his main day-to-day contact on Iran at the State Department: Michael Moyle, undersecretary of state for Middle Eastern Affairs. Moyle answered on the first ring.

"I assume you saw the story regarding ASC?" asked Greenglass.

"Yes," replied Moyle. He let out a pained sigh. "I'm afraid it's going to get choppy."

"Choppy?" asked Greenglass, his voice rising. "This is a cluster. We already have the FBI asking questions about my involvement in covert aid to the Green Movement. Now we've got an interagency task force and a U.S. attorney with every phone and hard drive at Aristotle."

"I hope their shredder was working overtime."

"You and me both," replied Greenglass. "Were they encrypting their e-mail?"

"I don't know."

"Me, either. If they didn't, it's not good."

Silence hung on the line as they mulled their options.

"Someone's got to alert the DNI, the SecDef, the SecState, and POTUS," said Moyle.

Greenglass thought a moment. "I'll tell Charlie and the president."

"I'll handle my boss and the SecDef," said Moyle.

"Listen, Michael, it's absolutely critical you and I stay simpatico," said Greenglass.

"Don't worry," said Moyle. "I won't let any daylight between us."

Greenglass hung up the phone, staring at it for moment. Could he trust Moyle? He didn't know. When the artillery started to fly, people tended to look out for themselves.

LISA ROBINSON BREEZED INTO JAY'S office without announcing herself. Engrossed in a phone conversation, he motioned for her to grab a chair. When his call was done, he turned to face her. "What's up, sunshine?" he asked. "I hope it's not about me again."

"Shockingly, it's not . . . for once," said Lisa, twirling a pen in her hand as she scanned notes on her legal pad. "What do you know about this Jonah Popilopos?"

Jay shrugged. "He's a televangelist who wears a white suit and bears a striking resemblance to Yul Brenner. Shameless self-promoter. Claire apparently attended his revival in New York City recently, and he pulled her up on stage."

"I know," said Lisa. "Who can forget the white dress? Anyway, Dan Dorman called and is asking about Popilopos's relationship with Claire. Specifically, he wants to know how many times he has visited the White House. He's asking to see the visitor logs."

"Great," said Jay. "Dorman's such a jerk."

"You don't have to convince me. But what should I say? I mean, this is fairly delicate insofar as it involves Claire's personal faith."

"Kick it to the East Wing," said Jay. "Don't give Dorman the time of day. Have Claire's press secretary give him some innocuous statement about how she knows a lot of evangelical, Jewish, and Catholic leaders, and she has met with many of them on interfaith issues, et cetera."

"What about the visitor logs?"

"Put in the records request and then slow-walk it. Maybe after the piece runs, Dorman will forget about it."

"Alright," said Lisa. "But Dorman's a jackal. And from what I hear, this Popilopos guy is a bit of a nut."

Jay smiled. "Yeah, but he's our nut," he said, laughing. It was becoming an increasingly common saying around the West Wing.

Lisa just shook her head and left.

26

S al Stanley sat in his spacious, elegantly appointed office in the
Capitol surrounded by his leadership team, known informally
as "the Sanhedrin." They sat on twin green Queen Anne
sofas anchoring the room: Democratic Whip Leo Wells; Chuck Clay,
chairman of the Democratic Senate Campaign Committee and a
prodigious fund-raiser; and Pat Broome, chairman of the Democratic
Policy Committee. In the past, Michael Kaplan would have attended
the meeting, but he was currently on trial just a few blocks down
Constitution Avenue. Also joining was Aaron Hayward, chairman of
the Finance Committee, to give an update on his investigation into the
Long administration politicizing the IRS.

"We're not always the best in the world at staying on message,
especially when we don't have the White House's megaphone," said
Stanley, his hands grasping the arms of his thronelike, wingback chair
as though strapped into an electric chair, his long legs crossed, his foot
slipped half out of a black loafer, leg bobbing the shoe from the end
of his toes in a nervous tic. "But in this case we've done a good job

pounding home Long's abuse of power. The narrative is hardening that Long promised to change the way Washington works, and instead he's treated the sewer like a Jacuzzi." He allowed himself a low, satisfying chuckle. "The *Times* editorial today was devastating. Have you guys all seen it?"

Several heads nodded.

"No, I haven't," said Broome, her fair skin drained of energy by a long day of work, her auburn hair chiseled with flat iron and hair spray to the rough texture of hewed granite. "I've been in meetings and hearings all day. What did it say?"

Stanley turned to one of his ever-present staffers, several of whom sat against the wall in chairs scribbling notes, scrolling through their BlackBerries. "Get today's *Times* editorial and make a copy for everybody," he said. "It called Long out for promising the most ethical administration in history and now tolerating corruption on a Nixonian scale. Said Noble was Long's Bob Haldeman. As I recall, the headline was, 'Noble the Ignoble.'"

Everyone laughed at the skewering of their nemesis and former Democratic wunderkind. Their laughs formed a symphony of nasal guffaws, low wheezes, and high-pitched cackles.

"That's rich. That's classic," said Broome, her knees bouncing.

"Just goes to show you, if you want to stick it to your enemies, sometimes the best thing you can do is let 'em win," joked Clay.

"Don't remind me," said Stanley with a mock grimace. He held open his hands and shrugged his shoulders.

"Now the shoe's on the other foot. Can you say 'subpoena power'?" asked Wells, his lips curled into a sardonic grin.

"I don't want to rain on the parade, Mr. Leader," said Hayward, who had been holding back during the fun and games. "But I got a call from Phil Battaglia today. He's ready to deal. They're going to send Noble up to testify."

"What?" asked Stanley, incredulous. He shot forward in his chair, the veins in his neck protruding, his nostrils flaring.

"That's what Battaglia said," replied Hayward crisply. "He asked me to come over to the White House tomorrow and work out a deal."

"What *kind* of deal?" asked Stanley, his voice rising to a squeal. "There is *no* deal with this White House. Noble's been subpoenaed. He will appear before the Finance Committee pursuant to that subpoena, answering all questions truthfully and honestly, under penalty of one year in prison for each count of perjury. *Period!*"

Hayward recoiled from Stanley's blast. He was the senior member of the group, having served on the Finance Committee for twenty-four years and chaired it for six years. He didn't like being told how to run his committee.

"It's not that simple, Sal," he said firmly. "The only way to get the Republicans to agree to issuing subpoenas to the White House and the IRS was to hold a fair hearing. I got a full day with von Fuggers as the sole witness. His testimony was devastating."

Several grunted their assent.

"We have to give Noble the opportunity to respond. If this investigation looks partisan, it will backfire."

Stanley methodically tore a mint from its foil wrapper as Hayward droned on self-righteously, his face turning a deep shade of red. "Don't tell *me* about *partisan witch hunts!*" shouted Stanley, hurling the wrapper at the candy bowl. It bounced off the bowl, skittered across the coffee table, and fell to the floor. "A good friend of everyone in this room is on trial right now on trumped-up charges," he said. "Mike Kaplan is staring at twenty years in federal prison. He faces disbarment. What was his crime? Paying consulting fees to delegates in Virginia! Do you think for *one minute* this Justice Department hesitated to throw the book at him?" Stanley's voice quavered. His facial muscles twitched. "Jay Noble blocked an IRS audit of illegal activity by a tax-exempt organization, including the personal enrichment of the head of that organization, forced a career civil servant into retirement, and you tell me to *be fair!?*" He shook his head. "Aaron, I feel like we're operating in parallel universes."

Hayward maintained his composure, his poker face unmoving. He let his silence speak louder than words: *I am not budging.* Everyone else stared at the floor, studying the carpet or gazing into space, discomforted by Stanley's outburst. The pressure of Stanley's reelection campaign (caused, not incidentally, by Noble's recruiting Kerry Cartwright to challenge him) and the still-painful loss in the presidential campaign exploded to the surface.

"Amen," said Clay, a notorious brownnoser and Stanley dead-ender who was the majority leader's handpicked choice to run the campaign committee. He rapped his knuckles on the coffee table. "They've gone after Kaplan and the leader. Let's fight fire with fire. Noble should not get any special treatment."

"Look, I *loathe* Noble and everything he represents," said Wells, who positioned himself to Stanley's left within the caucus and made no attempt to hide his desire for his job, secretly hoping he was defeated in November. "But I don't see the White House agreeing to waive executive privilege without ground rules. If we compromise, we still get him in front of the committee."

"And not just the committee," said Stanley, seemingly calming down. "The media, too. They hate him."

"Let's not get carried away. Noble will be lawyered up," said Broome. "Besides, he's too smart to out-and-out lie. He'll review every call and e-mail. Unless we have a witness to directly contradict his testimony, he could be a problem."

Stanley glowered, his eyes smoldering. "He's a problem either way," he said.

"Pat's right," said Hayward. "Noble's agreeing to testify is not necessarily a gift. He'll be well prepared. He'll dissemble a lot. The Republicans will have their talking points—"

"Dictated by the White House," said Wells.

"Agreed. Which is why I need to work out a deal with Battaglia," said Hayward. He leaned forward, resting his elbows on his knees, leaning into Stanley. "I'll depose Noble and everyone around him.

They'll be plenty of contradictions if only because people have fuzzy and selective memories. It's unavoidable." He arched his eyebrows, his eyes scanning their faces. "I've run this investigation to our benefit so far, haven't I?"

Stanley appeared to soften, his fleshy jowls sagging. "Of course, Aaron," he said. "Hans von Fuggers was brilliantly played. I just want to make sure we don't let Noble hide a crime, and a felony at that, behind executive privilege."

Wells cleared his throat. "I think Aaron should go down to the White House tomorrow," he said. "Let's see what Battaglia proposes. If we can force Noble to give sworn testimony without unreasonable restrictions, I don't see how we lose." Always looking for a way to undermine Stanley—and curry favor with the bulls of the caucus like Hayward, who held the key to his future aspirations to be Democratic leader—Wells stuck in the knife.

"The key is he has to be sworn. He must be under oath," said Broome. "The only way to force him to tell the truth is if a perjury rap hangs over him like the sword of Damocles."

"Agreed," said Hayward. "I'll tell Battaglia that's nonnegotiable."

"Okay, that's the game plan," said Stanley. "One final question: what about Stanton? Do you call him?"

"We've discussed that. I lean no," said Hayward. "It'll only make him a martyr. He's on television and radio four hours a day, and he has a big audience." He shrugged his shoulders. "Besides—and I never said this—in spite of his bluster, he's cooperated. He veered into gray areas, but I doubt he broke the law."

"Don't let that leave this room," joked Stanley, to knowing smiles.

"He'll raise $10 million on the radio and over the Internet if we call him," said Clay. "You know the drill: we need a legal defense fund to fight the IRS."

"Right," said Stanley. "But we should highlight his opulent lifestyle. He flies around in a G-5, lives in a mansion, all paid for by little old ladies sending in their Social Security checks."

"Don't worry," said Hayward. "That'll all get into the record. And we're planning to depose Ross Lombardy."

"Good," said Clay. "Make that deposition last three days. Run up his legal bills and keep him off the campaign trail. He's putting the hurt on our candidates."

"Alright, Aaron will drive a hard bargain on Noble's testimony and drop the dime on Stanton with timely leaks to the *Post,* the *Times,* and other media outlets without ever calling him to appear as a witness," said Stanley. "Everybody agree?"

They all nodded.

Stanley rose from his chair, the meeting adjourned. He glanced at his body man, who pointed to his watch. They were pressed for time to get to the first of three fund-raisers scheduled that evening. He calculated he would need $45 million for the reelect, not counting union efforts and independent expenditures. He could thank Noble and Long for that.

JAY'S ASSISTANT STUCK HER HEAD in the door of his office. "It's Walt Shapiro," she said in a low voice, cupping her hand over her mouth to make sure no one overheard her mention the name of the most prominent criminal lawyer in town. "Line two."

Jay motioned for her to close his door. He placed a call to Shapiro's direct line at his law firm about an hour earlier. With the Kaplan trial in full swing, he did not expected to hear from him so quickly. His stomach filled with butterflies as he picked up the phone. "Walt, it's Jay Noble. Thanks for returning my call so promptly."

"Certainly," he said. "It was good to hear from you."

"I assumed you had your hands full with the trial and all."

"I would have called earlier but couldn't for that very reason. I've got a couple of clients who are witnesses," said Shapiro smoothly. "How can I help you?"

The guy's involved in the biggest corruption trial in DC in a decade and he's got ice in his veins, thought Jay. "Well, I don't know if you have a conflict or not," said Jay slowly. "And I would certainly understand if you felt you needed to refer me to another attorney." He swallowed hard. "But if you've been following the news regarding Hans von Fuggers, who recently retired from the IRS, he's leveling some serious charges against me."

"I'm familiar with it," said Shapiro. "I don't have a conflict. Now, obviously, I'll have to check with my partners and make certain there isn't anyone else in the firm representing someone else in this matter." He paused. "I'm trying to remember, who's representing von Fuggers . . . isn't it Ted Stricker?"

"I think that's right," said Jay.

"Ted's a good lawyer, but I thought he was an odd choice," said Shapiro obliquely. "It signals more of a media play than litigation."

"That's my impression," said Jay. "Shopping a book and doing *60 Minutes* isn't about winning a legal settlement. That's someone looking for an advance."

Shapiro sighed. "I'm afraid that's the way the game is played by too many."

"Still, I need to err on the side of caution and defend myself, so I need a criminal attorney who knows how to handle a high-profile case that generates a lot of media interest." Jay did not mention that he decided to testify before the Senate Finance Committee, fearing it might scare Shapiro away. *Better to drop that on Shapiro after he's on board,* he thought.

"That's smart," said Shapiro, his voice calm, his tone soothing. "If more people contacted me before they ever talked to the FBI or prosecutors, there would be a lot fewer people in trouble. Someone's natural instinct at a time like this is to prove they've done nothing wrong; and by trying to disprove a negative, they make mistakes, some of which are fatal."

"Exactly," said Jay. "I know the feeling. All I did was give someone at Treasury a heads-up about complaints I'd received about selective enforcement by the IRS. I didn't ask for special treatment for anyone. But of course that's not how it's going to be portrayed."

"Not when it's you," said Shapiro. He paused. "So have you decided whether you're going to have to testify before the committee?"

Ouch! Jay hoped to dodge that touchy subject. "Not yet," said Jay slowly. "But frankly, I may have to testify, or at least agree to be interviewed by committee staff. We're war-gaming that now."

"Well, I'm not your attorney, at least not yet," said Shapiro. "But as a general rule I'd try to avoid appearing before the committee."

"I agree," said Jay. "But why?"

"I'm not worried about your telling the truth," said Shapiro. "But I don't want to give them the money shot."

"You mean the photo of me raising my right hand, being sworn in?"

"Exactly."

"I'm beginning to think it might be better to go ahead and testify rather than be crucified in absentia," said Jay.

"What's going on now is still less problematic than testifying," said Shapiro. "To a certain extent, von Fuggers gets discounted as a disgruntled former employee."

Jay grunted in acknowledgment. "How soon do you think you can determine whether or not your firm has a conflict? Obviously this thing is moving pretty fast."

"We can do our due diligence by tomorrow. I'll call you then. Assuming there are no unanticipated issues, maybe we can sit down tomorrow afternoon."

The two men exchanged contact information and hung up. Jay was now more confused than ever. His head told him to listen to Shapiro's advice and ignore the committee's subpoena, while his heart told him he could no longer serve Long effectively unless he cleared his name. He didn't know which to follow, his head or his heart.

27

L isa Robinson approached the podium in the White House
briefing room trailed by a coterie of grim-faced aides, wearing
a black skirt, white blouse, and aqua jacket. Her flowing black
hair, turned-up nose, blue eyes, lush lashes, milky-white complexion,
and immaculate makeup gave her the appearance of a china doll, but
she was all business. "I have a message from the president. I'll read it
and then take your questions," she said crisply.

Late-arriving reporters scrambled to their seats. In the front row,
Dan Dorman of the *Washington Post* glanced at a colleague expectantly
as if to say: *Here it comes.*

"I am returning herewith without my approval S.R. 6, 'The
Comprehensive Iran Sanctions and Human Rights Act,'" said Lisa,
reading. "The bill fails to address the danger posed by Iran's nuclear
weapons program, its designation by the State Department as the
leading state sponsor of terrorism in the world and its involvement
in the proliferation of nuclear technology to terrorist organizations,
including the network of Rassem el Zafarshan." Lisa's recitation was

punctuated by the *click-whir* of still photographers recording the scene. "The House bill instructed the Director of National Intelligence (DNI) to report to the Executive Office of the President (EOP) and the Congress on the efficacy of the sanctions within 120 days. It also authorized 'any and all measures deemed necessary' to disarm Iran of nuclear weapons."

Lisa pressed her lips into a thin line of lipstick. "However, this provision is not included in the final conference report. Its absence endangers the security and vital interests of the United States, which I cannot countenance as commander in chief. The bill fails to deal adequately with one of the most serious national security issues facing our nation, and for that reason I return it without my approval. Signed, Robert W. Long."

Finished, Lisa grabbed the podium as though bracing for battle. "Any questions?"

"Lisa, how disappointed is the president that he has been effectively humiliated by the Congress on the eve of the European Union meeting?" asked CBS. "Doesn't this weaken him just before one of the most critical meetings with U.S. allies in years?"

"No," said Lisa firmly. "This isn't about who's up or who's down. The issue is: the overwhelming preponderance of evidence indicates Iran has weaponized a nuclear device. The intelligence community has concluded it possesses long-range missile technology capable of striking many capitals in Europe. This bill did not adequately confront that threat."

"But the president is asking the EU to enact crippling sanctions when he has failed to do so himself," said FOX News.

Lisa bristled. "This has nothing to do with the sanctions. The president supports the sanctions in the bill. The problem is the failure to include a certification process on their efficacy and an explicit authorization for 'all necessary measures.' The president previously pledged to veto the bill if these two provisions were not included. He has now done so."

"Why not sign the sanctions bill and then seek military authorization in three to six months?" asked Reuters. "Why throw the baby out with the bath?"

"This is not a time for half-measures. Iran has a uniquely dangerous combination of nuclear weapons and ties to terrorists," replied Lisa. She glanced down at Dan Dorman, whom she had deliberately passed over for the first few questions. "Dan?" Everyone braced for fireworks; Lisa and Dorman famously despised each other, a legacy of their frosty relationship during the campaign.

"Lisa, if the president doesn't persuade the European Union to enforce strict sanctions against Iran, then it seems clear that, along with this defeat in Congress, he's completely failed to stop Iran's nuclear weapons program, hasn't he?"

Lisa's face hardened as Dorman asked his question. "I can't address a hypothetical, Dan. Your question presumes a lack of action by the EU. I reject the premise of your question."

"But the U.S. isn't doing what the president wants the EU to do, so why should they?"

"My answer is identical to my answer to your original question," said Lisa, her voice jagged. Ever the pro, Lisa stayed on message. But it didn't change the fact that Long was headed to Rome empty-handed, hoping his European allies bailed him out. Lisa was just glad the press didn't know the worst part: Air Force One was wheels up in three hours, and the president still didn't have the votes in the EU to pass sanctions.

KERRY CARTWRIGHT LUMBERED INTO THE Hispanic Family Center of Southern New Jersey in Camden, serving one of the largest Puerto Rican communities outside of the island, as well as Mexican-Americans. The Garden State boasted the seventh-largest Hispanic population in the nation, and Cartwright was on the hunt for their votes. He loped to the front of the room and stood behind a small podium wearing a crooked grin, a five o'clock shadow, and the searching eyes of a statewide candidate. A banner behind him read: "Viva Familiar Hispano!"

A group of Latino children enrolled in the center's preschool program sat in a circle around Cartwright, bright-eyed, youthful props for the cameras. Their mothers stood beneath the banner, wearing expressions ranging from bemused pleasure to stage fight. In the back of the room stood a row of reporters, their faces reflecting their boredom with Cartwright's disciplined, cash-rich, consultant-driven campaign.

"Thank you so much for having me, Jose," said Cartwright, nodding in the direction of the center's executive director. "As governor, I've made partnering with the Hispanic community a major priority of my administration. I believe strongly in the idea that parents, families, grassroots groups, and faith-based organizations can do a better job of caring for our children and seniors than government. I believe the main duty of government is to assist what Edmund Burke called these 'little platoons,' and then largely get out of the way." He spoke easily and freely, without a note, his right hand chopping the air, the other hand stuffed in his pocket. "I believe we've established a model of how to do that here in New Jersey. It's a model I want to take to the entire country, should I be fortunate enough to be elected as the next U.S. senator from our state."

Cartwright spun on his heel and turned to face the mothers behind him. "Are some of you ready to tell us how the Hispanic Family Center has helped you?" he asked, arching his eyebrows theatrically. They shifted nervously. "Don't worry about the press . . . they don't bite." His eyes twinkled. "At least not you, only me!" Everyone laughed.

Finally, one woman raised her hand. "I say something," she said.

"Come on up," said Cartwright, waving her to the podium.

"I work as a dispatcher for a local trucking company—"

Cartwright leaned forward. "Tell everyone your name."

"Oh—sorry," she said, rolling her eyes. "My name Mercedes Bonilla. I am from Puerto Rico. I am a single mother raising two children, a six-year-old daughter and a four-year-old son. The preschool program at Hispanic Family Center has been an answer to prayer for me and my family." Her eyes welled up. The other moms nodded knowingly. "I couldn't be as good a mother without it." She turned to Cartwright. "I thank God for you, Governor, for understanding the needs of families like mine." She began to cry.

Cartwright instinctively enveloped her in a hug. She sobbed on his shoulder as he patted her back with the palms of his hands. In the back of the room, Bill Spadea, Cartwright's campaign strategist, was beaming. Several of the reporters rolled their eyes.

The remarks concluded, the video of the event duly recorded for the campaign Web site, Cartwright pumped hands and hugged necks, heading for the door. As he walked, the press surrounded him like bumblebees around a daisy. Cartwright's press spokesman moved to his side to play defense.

"Governor, Sal Stanley has a new ad up accusing you of breaking your promise to lower property taxes for homeowners," said the *Bergen Record*. "Do you have a response?"

"You *bet* I have a response!" blurted Cartwright, stopping dead in his tracks. "Sal Stanley attacking me on property taxes is like Paris Hilton lecturing someone on modesty," he said, his face animated. "Sal was governor for two terms, and over those eight years property taxes in New Jersey *doubled*. When I took office, they were the highest in the nation. So it takes real *chutzpah* for Stanley to attack *me*."

The reporters' faces lit up like children on Christmas morning. The Latino photo op was over. . . . Now they were getting the juicy stuff. This was fun!

"You promised to hold annual property tax increases to no more than a percent or the rate of inflation, whichever was lower," pointed out the *New York Times*. "But property taxes are up 14 percent since you were elected. So what about Stanley's ad is inaccurate?"

Cartwright's nostrils flared. His lip quivered. "That's a flat-out lie," he said, his voice brittle. "The annual increases have been lower than I promised in some years, and there was only one year in which the increase was higher than I pledged. When Stanley was governor, property taxes doubled. Actually, *more* than doubled." He turned to his spokesman. "What was the actual number again?"

"One hundred and eight percent," said the aide.

"One hundred and eight percent!" exclaimed Cartwright. He did a quick calculation in his head. "So the average increase in taxes on New Jersey home owners was more in just *one year* under Stanley than in the entire five years since I became governor."

"But the fact is taxes have risen more than you promised," said the *Gazette Herald.*

"Are you a reporter or Sal Stanley's press secretary?" shot back Cartwright. "The ad is a lie. If Sal were Pinocchio, his nose would be growing."

The press corps could barely repress their smiles. As Cartwright lumbered past them to a state Town Car warming on the curb, they surrounded his press spokesman. "Can we get an official quote from you on Stanley's ad?" asked the Associated Press.

"I think you just got one," deadpanned the spokesman.

"No that was from the governor," said the *Times*. "That's different."

"Sure," replied the spokesman. He paused, wheels turning. "How about this: Sal Stanley is a desperate, big-spending Washington politician trying to change the subject from his abysmal record on taxes and ethics. This ad is just his latest failed attempt to distract from the massive property tax hikes that took place during this governorship and the corruption staining him as senator, for which his top aide is now on trial." He flashed a nasty grin.

The reporters nodded and laughed, closing their pads and shuffling away.

Cartwright lowered his bulky frame into the Town Car, pulling the door closed. Spadea sat to his left, looking crestfallen. He knew the footage of the emotional embrace with the Latino mother would now be subsumed by his candidate's unscripted swipe at Stanley.

"I know you didn't like what I said," said Cartwright, staring straight ahead. "But I learned a long time ago, when someone hits you, you hit back twice as hard."

Spadea shrugged. It was just another day at the office for him. "Guess what Jose, the center's ED, told me as we were leaving?" he asked.

"What?"

"He got a call from Stanley's chief of staff yesterday when they saw the event on the calendar. Asked him if it was true. When he said it was, the chief of staff told Jose not to count on any further help from them on federal grants. Basically tried to muscle him into canceling."

"He threatened to try to torpedo his federal grants?" asked Cartwright, incredulous.

"Yep. Tried to intimidate him into bailing out of our event."

"I wish we had that on tape."

"Me, too," said Spadea. "Jose was so insulted he said he's going to redouble his efforts for us in the Puerto Rican community."

Cartwright stared out the window. "Stanley's feeling the heat. Look at his new ad." He turned to Spadea. "We're really in a knifefight, aren't we?"

"Yes, we are, Governor," said Spadea.

LONG LEANED BACK IN THE leather captain's chair in his private office on Air Force One wearing a blue jacket bearing the presidential seal with "Air Force One" stenciled in gold thread. Truman Greenglass sat directly across from him wearing a pensive expression on his face. They were somewhere over the Atlantic Ocean, heading for Rome.

"Anatoly, time's up for the Iranians," said Long. "We're done playing hide the ball. We know they've got the nuke. Now I need to know . . . can I count on your vote?"

He sat impassively, rocking slowly in the chair, listening to the Russian leader's response. "Mmmm-mmmm," he said quietly.

Another long pause. "Iran's nuclear program will be dismantled or disabled," he said forcefully. "That decision is made. The only question is how. EU sanctions are our last chance to avoid war. If they work, we may be able to avoid military action."

Long's face flushed red. "Anatoly, I'm not surrendering any options in dealing with Iran. Now having said that, I don't have war plans on my desk." He brushed a piece of lint off his pants with a sweep of his hand. "If we don't pass EU sanctions, I may have no other choice. Do I make myself clear?" A final pause. "Alright, do all you can. I need your support."

Long hung up the phone.

"Well?" asked Greenglass.

"The Russians have convinced themselves anything that hurts the Iranian civilian population is counterproductive," Long replied. "That rules out serious sanctions. They're also arguing it's never been verified independently that the Iranians weaponized a nuclear device."

"Did he say he won't vote with us?"

"No," said Long. The side of his mouth turned up. "Anatoly knows without sanctions, we'll go full out on missile defense—and share technology with the Israelis and moderate Arab states. That is not good for him."

"He's also conflicted by the fact a military strike would put some Russian-built nuclear facilities in danger of being hit," said Greenglass.

"Outside of the Brits and the French, the Europeans have got no backbone for this fight," said Long, letting out a sigh. "We need the Italians."

"That's why you're meeting with Brodi as soon as we land."

"Good. Let's get him on board."

"I'll get a bottle of wine and invite over a couple of dancers," joked Greenglass. "That'll get his vote."

"It's like lobbying the Olympic site selection committee, isn't it?" replied Long. He got up from behind the desk, pacing the floor, his hands on his hips. "This is the greatest threat since the end of the Cold War, Truman, and we're hunting down go-go dancers and bottles of vintage vodka for people. Where are the Churchills and the De Gaulles?"

"Dead and gone, sir."

"You got that right." Long turned and headed for the small bedroom off the office. "I'm going to try to get some shut-eye," he said. "Keep working it."

"Yes, sir." As Greenglass headed for the conference room, he glanced at his watch. They would touch down in Rome in four hours. If the EU rejected the U.S.-backed sanctions package, they faced more than just public humiliation. They faced a possible military strike against Tehran, and they still didn't have congressional authorization.

28

Sal Stanley sat bolt upright in the witness box in the Federal Court House, ending months of speculation over whether he would endanger his own reelection by testifying on behalf of Mike Kaplan. Wearing a blue suit with muted pinstripes, white shirt, and blue patterned tie, Stanley appeared confident. He was never one to shrink from a fight.

The defense counsel was wrapping up his softball questions. He stood facing the jury, one hand in his pocket, his face expansive and inviting. He turned to face Stanley. "Senator, how long have you known Mr. Kaplan?"

"Twenty-seven years," replied Stanley.

"Twenty-seven years," repeated the attorney, punching the syllables for emphasis. "And how would you describe your relationship?"

"Mike is a good friend and a trusted advisor."

"And since you knew him so well over so many years, I would imagine there are few people other than his immediate family who know him better. How would you describe Mike Kaplan's character?"

Stanley looked directly at the jury. "Mike is an unselfish public servant and a trusted advisor who gave me sound counsel. He is a man of discretion and integrity."

The defense counsel smiled. "That's quite an endorsement, Senator."

"Mike is a rare individual. He is a fine man."

"Thank you." The defense counsel turned to the prosecution table as he sat down. "Your witness," he said.

The lead prosecutor rose from his chair and walked directly to Stanley, stopping no more than two feet from the witness stand. Stanley shifted in his seat, anticipating blows.

"Senator Stanley, Mike Kaplan was your campaign manager when you ran for governor of New Jersey the first time, is that correct?"

"Yes."

"He directed your transition, and you then named him chief of staff."

"That is correct."

"How long did he serve as chief of staff?"

"I believe it was a little over three years. He ran the day-to-day operations of the office, scheduling, policy development, and the budget."

The prosecutor ignored the embellishment. "After which you appointed him to chair your reelection campaign."

"Yes."

"After you were reelected, you appointed Mr. Kaplan to become the head of the New Jersey Port Authority."

"Yes."

"Previous testimony before this court has indicated that after four years as head of the port authority, he joined an international export-import law firm."

"Yes," said Stanley.

"To your knowledge, there were no state ethics rules or regulations preventing him from interacting with the New Jersey Port Authority in his new capacity?" asked the prosecutor.

"Not that I am aware of." Stanley's face hardened.

"I see." The prosecutor paused, turning to make eye contact with the jury. "Do you have any idea what Mike Kaplan's net worth was at the time of his indictment?"

"No," replied Stanley icily.

The prosecutor approached Stanley, placing his hands on the rail of the witness stand. "Senator, it's not an exaggeration to say that Mike Kaplan owes his entire career to you, is it?"

The question landed like a howitzer. "I think that's an exaggeration."

"Really?" asked the prosecutor, feigning surprise. "I just went through every position he held for more than a dozen years, and you appointed him to every one of them. Isn't that right?"

"Yes, but I appointed a lot of people. Very few excelled on the level Mike did."

"Indeed," said the prosecutor. "His net worth at the time of his indictment was eighteen million dollars. Not bad for someone with an unselfish commitment to public service who had little personal wealth at the time he came to work for you."

"Objection!" shouted the defense counsel. "Counsel is leading the witness."

"Sustained," said the judge.

The prosecutor stared at Stanley more in pity than anger. "No further questions," he said.

OUTSIDE THE COURTROOM, STANLEY STOOD before a mountain of microphones on a small podium, a phalanx of reporters gathered around. His attorney stood immediately behind him, a look of profound discomfort plastered on his face. The majority leader rejected the advice of his political advisors to avoid the media. He didn't want to look like he was hiding.

"Senator, how do you think it went?" shouted CNN.

"Well," said Stanley, his face drained of color, his lips pressed together. "I was glad to be able to testify on Mike Kaplan's behalf. I believe he's an innocent man."

"How do you think this will impact your reelection campaign?" asked *Politico.*

"I don't know. Sometimes you have to do the right thing, regardless of whether it helps or hurts you politically. This was the right thing to do."

"Without being critical of Mr. Kaplan, surely you would admit you would have preferred not to be here today?" asked AP.

"Unlike a lot of people in this town, I'm not a fair-weather friend," said Stanley, his chin raised defiantly. "Mike Kaplan is my friend. I will not turn my back on him."

Within minutes the headline rifled across news Web sites, "Stanley: I Won't Turn My Back on Mike Kaplan." There was little surprise when a few days later a poll conducted by a consortium of newspapers in New Jersey showed Stanley trailing Kerry Cartwright by four points. The Dele-gate scandal and the Kaplan trial were an albatross around the majority leader's neck, and a growing chorus of chatterers in DC doubted he could survive.

IN THE PRIME MINISTER'S OFFICE in the Palazzo Chigi, just off the Piazza Colonna in the heart of Rome, Lorenzo Brodi and Bob Long sat in thronelike chairs, flanked by translators. In diplomatic-speak, their visit was the first "bilateral" of the European Union conference, an honor accorded to Brodi as the head of state of the host country.

Renaissance frescos and decorative stuccos depicting biblical scenes on the ceiling and walls gave their encounter an almost sacred ambience. Staff lined the wall, among them Jay, Lisa Robinson, and Truman Greenglass. Ironically, it was Jay's first visit to the prime minister's office since he engineered Brodi's victory the previous summer. He gazed at the frescoes, impressed by the palace that resembled an Italian Versailles. It was quite a rush watching two of his winning clients plotting the future of the planet. It was a long way from running state legislative races in the San Fernando Valley, which is how he began his career.

"Thank you for letting me borrow the brain," joked Brodi. "Isn't that his nickname?"

"We call him something else," volleyed Long, lips curled. "It can't be printed in a family newspaper." He shot Jay a mirthful look. "I hope he didn't charge you as much as he did me."

"I paid in euros, so I came out ahead," said Brodi, flashing his white teeth.

"I don't comment on currency exchange rates," laughed Long.

Jay shifted uncomfortably in his seat. He knew Long didn't like it when he got too much glory or publicity.

"Lorenzo, I need your help on the Iran sanctions package," said Long, shifting gears, reaching across to place his hand on Brodi's broad shoulder. "We're going to have to drag the Russians and the Spanish to the water. I've always been there for you. I need you on this one." It was a veiled reference to the CIA's role in Brodi's election. He paused as the translator spoke in Italian, his eyes locked on Brodi's.

When the translator finished, Brodi's eyes flashed with recognition. "Mr. President, you have my support. We sent troops to Iraq and Afghanistan. We lost men on the battlefield in the struggle with terrorism. Italy will be there. We must not allow Iran to gain nuclear weapons."

Long's face broke into a wide smile. "I knew you wouldn't let me down, Lorenzo." He glanced at Greenglass, looking for stage directions. "What about the Spanish?"

"We will push them," said Brodi. "We will push the other EU members. We must present a united front. Anything short of that will be seen as weakness by the Iranians."

"Time's running out," said Long.

"What do you think the prospects are the sanctions will work?" pressed Brodi.

Long's face grew somber. "Fifty-fifty."

"I was hoping you'd say better than that."

Long sighed in frustration. "The only thing left are bad options and worse options," he said. "Our intelligence says we've got six to nine months. After that, who knows?"

Brodi leaned forward, his black eyes intense. "I'm with you until Salami is gone or Iran is disarmed, Mr. President." They rose and shook hands. Brodi pointed to the paintings surrounding them. "This was once Mussolini's office," he said proudly. "He survived an assassination attempt in this very room. He delivered speeches from the balcony."

"I wouldn't mind giving a speech off that balcony myself, but the media in my country already thinks I'm Il Duce," joked Long. They both enjoyed a laugh as official photographers snapped photos. The advance staff and Lisa Robinson moved in to choreograph a joint news conference with the Italian and U.S. press.

Brodi walked over to Jay and pulled him close, clasping his hand. "Look what you got me into," he said.

"It's better than the alternative, sir," fired back Jay.

"What's that?"

"Losing."

Brodi laughed. "Have fun while you're back in Rome," he said with a wink.

"I'll do my best." During the meeting he had been texting Gabriella Felissi, the fetching wine goddess who was his flame during the Brodi campaign, but she had not responded.

"Let me know if you need any help," said Brodi. He was notorious for his retinue of exotic dancers, singers, models, and aspiring actresses known collectively as "Brodi's bimbos."

"I think I can handle it," said Jay.

Brodi spun on his heel and slid to Long's side as they left the room to face the press. It was then Jay noticed his old CIA handler standing in the corner. Their eyes locked. The CIA handler turned to leave, heading down the hallway of the prime minister's suite. It was the first time Jay had seen him since the Agency dispatched him to Israel on a government jet to advise Hannah Shoval's campaign. Jay decided it was unwise to greet him.

At that instant a text message came in from Gabriella. "Hey, babe. R u in town? Can we get together or r u too busy?"

Jay felt his heart skip a beat. "Sure. Drinks or din din?"

"Mmmm," came her reply.

Jay texted, "1. Save Western civilization. 2. Hook up with Gabby."

"Not sure about the order . . . but I'm impressed," Gabriella texted back.

Jay smiled. Truman Greenglass walked over. "What's so funny?" he asked.

"Nothing," lied Jay. "Just an e-mail from a friend."

ED DOWDY WAS A BOTTOM-DWELLER among lawyers, specializing in those who lost at love and life: divorces, DUIs, and debtors. But Dowdy did not pine away in anonymity. A few years earlier, he read about a female Hill staffer who had an affair with a U.S. senator. On a lark, he cold-called her. The sexual harassment suit he filed against the senator fizzled, but a small fortune followed as he negotiated a book deal and reality TV show contract for the woman. He now represented Jillian Ann Singer, the former CEO of Adult Alternatives.

Dowdy sat with his feet on his desk, chewing on an unlit cigar. "Ed Dowdy. D-O-W-D-Y," he said smoothly into the telephone receiver. "Tell Mr. Myers I represent Ms. Singer."

Marvin Myers came on the line, his voice singsong. "Mr. Dowdy, what can I do for you?"

"It's not what you can do for me," said Dowdy. "It's what I can do for you."

"I'm listening."

"Mr. Myers—"

"Please, call me Marvin."

"Alright. Marvin, as you know, Ms. Singer founded Adult Alternatives, LLC, and was CEO for seventeen years. It specialized in providing legal entertainment for consenting adults. It is *not* a prostitution ring."

"I know who Ms. Singer is, believe me. How could I not?"

"Ms. Singer is a very savvy businesswoman. She's made millions, frankly. But her business has been destroyed by the publicity surrounding Perry Miller's death, even though neither she nor her employees had anything to do with it," said Dowdy, in full sales pitch mode. "Once the FBI determined a terrorist murdered Miller, that should have ended the investigation. But prosecutors are threatening Jillian Ann with jail time."

"I sympathize with your client, Mr. Dowdy, but I don't know if this merits a column," said Myers, swatting away the pitch.

"I agree. It merits several columns."

"How so?"

"We are prepared to provide you with the complete client list for Adult Alternatives . . . for consideration, of course," said Dowdy. "This will be one of the biggest stories of the decade."

"I'm interested," said Myers, intrigued and repelled at the same time. "If it appeared in my column first, it would certainly guarantee prominent coverage."

"That's why I called you first."

"I'm afraid we have a challenge."

"What's that?" asked Dowdy, sounding disappointed.

"I have a policy against paying my sources," said Myers. "I think that works in your favor. There are plenty of other ways for your client to realize monetary benefits without me compensating her." His brain shifted into overdrive. "Book deals, magazine exclusives—there are a lot of options. Lots."

"I respect that, Marvin, I really do. But Jillian Ann's ability to support herself in the short terms is ruined. I have to look out for her interests. I hope you understand."

"Certainly," said Myers. "Does she have a literary agent?"

"Not yet. That's on our to-do list."

"I could help . . . if you wanted. I'm good friends with Bob Simms." Myers could almost hear Dowdy's heavy breathing on the other end of the line. Simms was the biggest literary agent in New York for political authors, steering a long string of presidents, pols, and cabinet officials to mid-six and seven-figure contracts.

"I'd be deeply grateful for an introduction," said Dowdy.

"Sure," said Myers. "Happy to." Having gained the upper hand, he moved in for the kill. "Why don't you, me, and Ms. Singer meet for lunch and discuss this further?"

"You bet," said Dowdy. They penciled in a date for the next day. Hanging up the phone, Dowdy put the unlit cigar between his teeth and smiled. If he could negotiate a print and broadcast exclusive with Myers (hopefully for six figures) and get Singer a book and a movie deal, he'd be in tall cotton.

29

Gabriella walked into the lobby of the Hotel Hassler looking purple-licious in a black bustier and purple-striped Dior skirt, volleyball player legs seeming to extend forever to Ferragamo heels, brown hair flowing to sun-kissed, bare shoulders. She blithely ignored male gazes that followed her as she headed for the bar. Preternaturally confident and alluring, she slid to a table in the back where Jay sat alone, sipping an espresso.

When Jay caught sight of her, a thought hit him: did she wear this killer outfit for him? Or was it just his imagination? He hoped for the former but feared the latter. They embraced, pecking cheeks. She looked down at his coffee and frowned. "Espresso?" she asked disapprovingly. "What, no wine?"

"Jet lag," said Jay. "I'm running on caffeine."

A waiter appeared. "Ms. Felissi, what can I get you?"

"Mmmmmmm," she said, cocking her head and narrowing her eyes. "Bring me a bottle of the '99 Reserve."

"Two glasses?" asked the waiter.

"Yes, and a decanter. I want it to breathe." She talked with her hands in a characteristically Italian way, making a shape of a decanter with her fingers and then twirling her hand under her nose. The waiter nodded and departed.

Jay grinned admiringly, shaking his head.

"What?" asked Gabriella.

"I forgot you own any room you walk into," said Jay. He downed the espresso. "I missed you, darn it!"

"You have no one to blame but yourself," fired back Gabriella with a regretful lilt in her voice. "You're the one who left."

"Because the president asked me to."

"Don't spin me, lover. You had a choice."

Jay threw his head back and laughed. "So you outrank the president of the United States? That's your story?"

"Who's better, me or him?" she asked with a wicked grin.

"At what?"

"You know what."

"Gabby, we had a Supreme Court confirmation going south," said Jay. "We're about to go to war with Iran. And on top of all that, the midterm elections are in seventy-two days, and we have to win control of the U.S. Senate."

"What's going to happen?"

"Honestly, I don't know," said Jay in a rare moment of candor. "We've got good candidates. We've spread the field. We've got Sal Stanley, the Senate Majority Leader, playing defense." He shrugged. "We have a shot."

"Don't be so modest. You'll win."

"Speaking of winning, how's Brodi doing?"

"Well, let's see," said Gabriella sarcastically. "His trade minister is about to get indicted for taking bribes from companies in exchange for trade missions. His legislative agenda is dead on arrival. His latest round of plastic surgery was botched, making him look eternally surprised, and he got caught cheating with an underage actress who once did a porno." She made quotation marks with her fingers when she said "actress," giggling. "Other than that, he's doing great!"

"Ouch!" exclaimed Jay. "That's worse than I feared." He noticed the Tuscan sun had bronzed Gabriella's shoulders and chest, giving her skin a bronze glow. Freckles flecked her nose, which he found endlessly attractive. A rush of memories flooded his mind: sipping wine on the terrace at the Hassler watching the sun set over St. Peter's, a lazy afternoon spent at Ufizzi gallery in Florence, a midnight swim under a full moon at the Felissi family villa in Carmignana. *Why*, he wondered, *had he ever left?*

"You elected him, baby," said Gabriella.

"Yeah, well, the other guy was a fascist."

The wine steward approached with the bottle, presenting the label to Gabriella, who glanced at it and nodded approvingly. He methodically inserted the corkscrew, pulled out the cork, opened the bottle, and poured a small amount into a glass. Gabriella twirled it in the glass, lowered her nose to inhale the aroma, and nodded again. The steward poured the bottle into the decanter and left.

"I haven't had a bottle of your wine since I was in Italy," said Jay.

"But you took five cases home with you."

"I know. I'm saving them for a special occasion."

"Like what?"

"A visit from you."

Gabriella blushed. "I want to come. But I've been *so* busy with business."

Jay reached over for the decanter and poured wine into their glasses. He picked up his glass, clinking it with Gabriella's. "After the election," he said, raising his glass. "I'll come to Italy or you come to DC. Deal?"

"It's a deal."

After two days with virtually no sleep and an eight-hour flight across the Atlantic, the wine hit Jay's bloodstream like grape moonshine. He felt light-headed. "Boy, I forgot how good your wine really was."

"And what about me?" asked Gabriella, leaning forward. Jay felt her shoeless toes tickling the back of his calf. "Did you forget how good I was?"

"No," Jay heard himself say. Their eyes locked as they drank.

Jay knew Gabriella wasn't real. Her world was artificial, a world of five-star resorts, house servants and cooks, private jets, good food, great wine, . . . and . . . she was an escape from the take-no-prisoners, smash-mouth politics that was his life. He might hook up with Gabriella for a night of romance, but then he'd be back on Air Force One with Long heading back to the political wars. But as he took another long sip of Brunello, he decided to worry about that tomorrow.

MARVIN MYERS HELD COURT IN a private dining room at Tosca Ristorante, the power lunch spot for the K Street crowd in downtown DC, joined by Jillian Ann Singer and Ed Dowdy. Given the speculation rocketing around town about Dowdy shopping the client list, it was a dangerous time to be seen in public. Taking extra precautions, they arrived separately before the lunch crowd. Singer hid her face behind a scarf and large designer sunglasses.

"So tell me, Ms. Singer, have you been interviewed by the FBI?" asked Myers as he took a bite of mushroom risotto. "If you don't want to answer, I understand."

"I don't mind," said Singer. "They interviewed me the day after they found Perry Miller's body." Myers noticed the puffiness of Singer's skin. Black roots were visible beneath a mountain of bleached blond hair. A life spent in illicit pleasure had taken its toll, but underneath, like the bright colors in a master's painting obscured by years of smoke and dirt, she still possessed a smoldering beauty.

"That happened before I was representing Jillian," said Dowdy in self-congratulation, his face glistening with summer sweat. "They're getting nothing from her now, I assure you."

"What did they want to know?" asked Myers.

"Mostly about Amber and Senator Miller," said Singer. "They also wanted to know about any Muslim clients."

Myers perked up. "So they suspected a terrorist connection from the beginning?"

"That was my impression," she replied. "They also asked if I knew who Miller was."

"And did you?"

"Oh, sure. We all did."

"Were you surprised?"

"Nothing surprises me, Mr. Myers," said Singer. She took a sip from her vodka martini. "When you've been in my business as long as I have, you're not surprised by people's secrets." She shook her head. "You wouldn't believe some of the things I've seen."

"It's what keeps me in business," said Myers drolly.

Singer smiled knowingly. "Anyway, the FBI didn't ask about other clients beyond the Muslims or Arabs. At least not at first. Only about whether Miller had a regular time for his appointment and if someone might have been able to observe him coming and going . . . that kind of thing."

"They were trying to figure out how Hassan Qatani tracked him," observed Myers.

"I believe so, yes."

Myers looked at Dowdy. "When did you realize the FBI was zeroing in on Jillian?"

"When I got a call from Patrick Mahoney," said Dowdy. "He wanted to ask Jillian a lot of questions. He said they would agree none of what she said could be used against her if they chose to prosecute her down the road. It's called, 'queen for a day.'"

Myers nodded. "A common prosecution strategy when lacking leads."

"Yes, but we declined," said Dowdy. "That's when they started to turn the screws."

"And that's why you've decided to release the client list," said Myers.

"It's the only leverage I have," said Singer. "It's hard because I've always protected my clients. But the feds destroyed my business. They've ruined my life." Her eyes welled with tears.

"I know it's tough," said Myers, reaching out to touch her arm, awkwardly trying to comfort her.

"I'm sorry," said Singer. She dabbed her eyes with her napkin. "Now my mascara is going to smear."

Dowdy jumped in. "Marvin, I know you don't normally compensate sources. But I have to secure Jillian Ann's future. She may not be able to work for some time."

"I can't pay Jillian," said Myers. "But there's more than one way to skin this cat. With the right literary agent, you could get a book contract in the mid-to-upper six figures." He dropped his chin. "That is assuming you're willing to tell everything. And I mean *everything*."

"I am," said Singer, her voice brittle and defiant. "I've got nothing left to lose. I did nothing wrong, and they still took everything from me."

Dowdy pulled a note card from his pocket and wrote something on it. When he was done, he slid it across the table to Myers. "Here's a little down payment," he said. "Off the record."

Myers picked up the note card and put on his reading glasses. The card had two names on it. One was Rick Roberts, a high-ranking Democrat in the House. The other was Mike Fannin, Republican U.S. senator from Arizona. Myers felt his heart rate quicken. He tried to keep his cool.

"That's just the appetizer," said Dowdy. "The main course is *mind-blowing*. There's one name on the list that will blow sky high. I'm talking Nagasaki." He made a low, muffled noise and raised his hands from the table, simulating a mushroom cloud.

"It's in your interest for me to be the one to break this story," said Myers smoothly. "You don't want the tabloids getting it. It'll be like Gennifer Flowers—cash for trash. There's no future for Jillian Ann in that scenario besides a Vegas lounge act."

"We know that," said Dowdy. "If you can help her get a book deal or a magazine deal, the list is yours. But there are other sharks circling. They're hungry . . . and they're waving a lot of cash under our noses."

"Understood," said Myers. "I'll get back to you this afternoon." His mind raced. He didn't like dealing with a sleaze like Dowdy, but he couldn't let the client list slip away. He still had the mojo, of that he was certain. Now was the time to show the bloggers and the pseudo-news Web sites who was boss.

HOURS AFTER EU HEADS OF state passed the most crippling sanctions ever slapped on Iran after two days of nonstop lobbying and cajoling by Long, Jay was awakened by a sharp knock on his door at the U.S. embassy, where the American delegation was staying. He stumbled across the floor wearing a T-shirt and his underwear, cracking the door slightly.

"What is it?" he asked groggily.

"Mr. Noble. I need you to get dressed and packed. We're leaving," said the dark-suited Secret Service agent.

"What? Now . . . in the middle of the night? Why?"

"The president and the delegation are in extreme danger. There's been an assassination attempt on Brodi. We believe the president may be a target as well."

Jay let out an expletive. "Are you serious?"

"Yes, sir. There are also reports the French foreign minister has been assassinated. Two members of our delegation are missing."

"Who's missing?" asked Jay, now fully awake, adrenalin hitting his bloodstream.

"One of Truman Greenglass's deputies and Victor Levell," he said. Levell was assistant secretary of state for Middle Eastern affairs. "Get packed and put your bags outside the door. We leave in ten minutes."

The door closed. Jay felt his adrenal glands open. The clock on his bed stand read 4:35 a.m. He had only left Gabriella an hour earlier. He put on a shirt and suit, fumbling with the buttons with shaking hands. He threw his clothes in his suitcase, not even bothering to fold them, and placed it out in the hallway. He tried to call Gabriella on her cell phone but it went straight to voice mail. Thinking she might still be at the Hassler, he dialed the operator and asked for her room. She answered on the second ring.

"Hello?" she asked, half asleep.

"Gabby, it's Jay. There's been an attempt on Brodi's life and two members of our delegation missing. The Secret Service is ordering us to leave tonight."

"Mama mia!" exclaimed Gabriella. "Are you okay? Are you sure you're safe?"

"Yes, I'm inside the embassy compound," replied Jay. "We're covered up with security. But I didn't want you to wake up in the morning and hear the reports and be worried."

"Thanks, baby. Be safe. Call me when you land in the States. I'll come see you soon."

"I can't wait," said Jay. "I had a great time."

"Me, too, sugar."

Jay hung up and stepped out into the hallway, where pandemonium unfolded. Helmeted military police in Kevlar vests jogged up and down, semiautomatic rifles drawn, barrels in the air. Air Force stewards grabbed luggage from staff, some of whom were half-naked or still wearing their pajamas. As Jay stood there unsure of what to do next, he saw Truman Greenglass walking past, panic-stricken.

"Truman!" shouted Jay. "What's going on?"

"They tried to kill Brodi," said Greenglass, his eyes like saucers. "Pingeon is dead. Levell and Daniels are missing." Pingeon was the French foreign minister, Norm Daniels was Greenglass's deputy for the Middle East.

"Who's behind it?" asked Jay.

"It's Zafarshan, which means the Iranians," said Greenglass. He leaned into Jay. "Levell was running all the covert aid to the Green Movement. This is payback." With that he scurried down the hall. As he rounded the corner, he shouted, "Get downstairs or you'll be left!"

Jay felt a shudder go through him. He could not believe Zafarshan was brazen enough to murder U.S. officials on foreign soil. Then again, he had already assassinated a U.S. vice president and engineered the murder of Perry Miller. Just then Jay felt someone grab his arm. He turned to find a Secret Service agent in a dark suit, his gun drawn, leading him to an elevator.

"Mr. Noble, come with me."

They stepped onto the elevator, already jammed with staff, Secret Service, embassy employees, and soldiers. As the elevator descended, its passengers were eerily silent. When the doors opened, they stepped into the parking garage, filled with flying bodies, moving vehicles, and total chaos. As Jay headed for one of the staff vans, he caught sight of the president stepping into the armored presidential limousine, surrounded by gun-toting Secret Service and military police. *What a surreal scene,* thought Jay.

30

T he presidential motorcade traveled to the airport at speeds approaching ninety miles an hour. Rome resembled a city under siege. Police set up roadblocks at every exit and major intersection in the city, flashing blue lights piercing the darkness. No one could enter major highways from either direction. The route from the city center to the airport was lined with police water cannons, tanks, armored personnel carriers, and soldiers. U.S. AWACS surveillance aircraft and NATO F-18 fighter jets flew overhead, ready to fire at anything suspicious. Police choppers flew overhead, their searchlights scanning buildings and side streets.

Air Force One took off with its lights darkened to make it more difficult for a terrorist to launch a shoulder-fired missile at its fuselage. For Long and the White House staff, it was eerie departing Italy under the cloak of darkness. Whether declared or not, the U.S. was at war with both Iran and Rassem el Zafarshan, and it wasn't entirely clear who was winning.

When Americans awoke the next morning, they did so to blaring headlines and melodramatic morning news shows reporting the shocking news: terrorists blew up a car bomb outside the French embassy, killing the foreign minister, one member of his security detail, and two civilian embassy employees. A second bomb intended for Lorenzo Brodi failed to detonate, at which point a terrorist tried to run a police barricade wearing an explosive vest and was killed in a hail of bullets.

Had Long been a target? No one knew. A top secret Special Threat Task Force was created after the murder of Perry Miller, housed at the Justice Department, staffed with FBI and Secret Service agents as well as CIA and counterintelligence operatives from the Pentagon. They tracked intel, assessed threats, and evaluated assassination plots, particularly from terrorist sources. Miller's murder ratcheted up the number of government officials with Secret Service protection to more than fifty. The task force assessed the European Union conference as a major security threat for the president, but the Secret Service was so focused on protecting the president it was blindsided by the assassination and kidnapping of lower-level officials.

On Air Force One, Long convened a meeting of his national security team. The atmosphere was tense, the scene bizarre. Vice President Whitehead, Charlie Hector, William Jacobs from CIA, and the secretary of defense joined via video conference from the Situation Room in the White House. Everyone was jumpy.

"Can we lay this at Zafarshan's feet?" asked Long. "If we have proof, we can take retaliatory action." He wore gray slacks and a blue Air Force One jacket with a presidential seal. He was tired but calm, fully in control.

"Yes, but against whom?" asked the secretary of defense. "Iran or Zafarshan?"

"Both," replied Long, not missing a beat. "But it depends on the evidence. We need the FBI and the CIA to get us a readout on who's behind it."

"Mr. President, Norm and Vic Levell were the ones keeping the spigots open for both materiel and financial support to the Green Movement," said Greenglass, his eyes narrowing. "The Iranians knew. They were targeted."

"They're hitting us back for what we're doing inside Iran," said Jacobs.

"Related to the nuclear program, you mean?" asked Long. "Like the assassination of the engineer in Damascus."

"Yes, and much more," said Jacobs, his face visible in a grainy color mage on a big-screen TV in the plane's conference room. "The elimination of human assets within the nuclear program has taken a toll. Some of Salami's top advisors have been taken down. Plus general unrest within the country."

"I get Brodi, but why the French?" asked Long.

"They've been partners on a lot of the black ops," said Jacobs. "They're very good at that sort of thing."

"Well, that explains it," said Long.

"Mr. President, you'll need to make a statement when you land," said Charlie Hector over the videoconference.

"Should I do it at Andrews or wait until I land on the South Lawn?"

"Andrews," replied Hector. "I don't like the idea of you leaving Air Force One and getting in Marine One without saying anything."

"Have the speech writers work something up and get it to Lisa and Truman," said Long. "It's going to have to be more firm but probably not name any names, given the fact we're still in the fog of war."

"Mr. President, anything short of a military response is going to be perceived as insufficient," said Whitehead, who had hung back until now, as was his usual custom. "This is coming on the heels of the murders of Flaherty and Miller. This is a killing spree."

"I agree," said Long. "The problem is Zafarshan's in a cave in the mountains of Pakistan. I don't want to drop five-hundred-pound bombs on a pile of rocks."

"What if Levell and Daniels have been kidnapped?" asked Hector. "Zafarshan could hold them as hostages."

Long looked at the video screen, his facial expression worried. "Bill, if that's the case, can we find them?"

"The first twenty-four hours are critical, Mr. President," said Jacobs. "We've got hundreds of FBI, CIA, and Special Forces crawling all over Rome," replied Jacobs. "The Italians are helping."

Long nodded. "Good. Find them."

"Charlie raises a good point," said Greenglass. "If they're hostages, it's a different situation. The vice president is correct. If they've been murdered, we must retaliate militarily. But if they've been kidnapped, our first priority is to get them back alive."

Everyone waited for Long's response. He got up from his chair and stood behind it, his hands resting on its back, his face a portrait of determination. "Either way, Zafarshan must pay. And not just him, but his Iranian paymasters. Find Levell and Daniels. Prepare actionable military options." He turned to leave, then stopped. "This is a declaration of war, not just against the United States, but against the civilized world."

With that, he walked out of the conference room, the door closing behind him. Everyone had their marching orders. It was going to be a long night.

AIR FORCE ONE LANDED AT Andrews Air Force Base at a little after 8 a.m. Broadcast and cable news outlets broke in to record the aircraft on approach and landing, then taxiing to a stop. The doors opened, and Long, accompanied by the First Lady and his national security team, descended the stairs and walked to a small podium bearing the presidential seal. In a brief statement he condemned the attacks, calling them "an evil and despicable act of terrorism committed by cowards and butchers against the innocent." He mentioned each victim by name, his voice choking when he reached Pingeon, the French foreign minister, who was a hero on the EU sanctions vote. "While we mourn their loss, we vow they will not have died in vain. Our grief is accompanied by a determination to confront state sponsors of terrorism and those who seek to threaten nations with the most dangerous weapons on earth." Without making a direct connection to Iran and the attacks (yet), Long added: "If these attacks were intended to undermine our resolve to stop Iran's pursuit of weapons of mass destruction, they will have the opposite of the intended effect. We will bring Iran to its knees until it suspends its nuclear program and complies with its international obligations."

When Long and his traveling party arrived back at the White House, they found it resembled a bunker. Security was tight. Staff were not to leave the building without a Secret Service escort. Meetings outside the White House complex were cancelled. Everyone was glued to the cable news channels and gathered in hallways, speaking in hushed whispers. Still, Charlie Hector, acting at Long's direction, told everyone to remain at their desks and work as normally as possible. Long rejected the Secret Service's request to surround the White House with tanks, fearing it would give Zafarshan a propaganda victory.

Three hours after returning from Italy, Jay walked into a previously scheduled meeting with Phil Battaglia and Walt Shapiro to go over the status of negotiations with the Senate Finance Committee staff over his possible testimony in the IRS flap.

Shapiro rose from his chair, his eyes projecting concern, and shook Jay's hand. "Welcome back. How are you holding up? You've had a pretty wild time."

"It was crazy," said Jay, shaking his head in disbelief. "We were roused out of bed at 4 a.m. and told to get downstairs in ten minutes. We could hear explosions in the streets. There were rumors Brodi was dead. No one knew what was going on."

Battaglia let out a sigh. "I hope we find our guys."

"If we don't, there's going to be hell to pay," said Jay.

"Look, I know you're busy and jet-lagged," said Phil. "This will only take a minute. Walt and I want to bring you up to speed on our discussions with the committee."

"Sure."

"Overall, we're making progress. But there's one issue on which they refuse to budge. They're adamant your testimony is sworn."

"That's bad, right?" asked Jay.

"You'll be under oath. It puts you at risk for a perjury rap if you make a material misstatement of fact," said Shapiro, his face long, his fleshy jowls giving him the look of a bulldog. "Not that you would be, of course. But it's a risk."

Jay shrugged his shoulders. "I know it's your job is to keep me out of jail, Walt, but—"

"It's a job I take very seriously," said Shapiro.

"Good. But as long as I can review the documents and e-mails, and we can do a murder board, I'm really not worried."

Shapiro and Battaglia exchanged worried glances. "We can agree to that," said Walt. "But it gives them what they want."

"The money shot," said Jay.

"Correct," said Shapiro.

Jay frowned as they sat in silence. Finally, he stood up and began to pace the room in a highly agitated state. "To hell with 'em!" he shouted, throwing up his arms. "Give 'em the money shot. I'll ram it right down their throats." He wheeled to face them, placing his hands on the table, his face animated. "Let me tell you something, Stanley's going to rue the day he called me to testify."

"Alright," said Battaglia. "We'll agree to sworn testimony. You okay with that, Walt?"

"Not entirely, but it's Jay's call."

"Alright," said Battaglia, reviewing his notes on a legal pad. "We've gone back and forth on the parameters of the questions the senators can ask. Our waiver of executive privilege will be limited. We're only agreeing to have you answer questions about communications you had with Treasury and IRS."

"What are they asking for?"

"They want access to any communications between you and anyone at any agency or cabinet department."

"Forget that," said Jay dismissively.

"If we agree Jay will testify under oath, I assume we can hang tough on other issues, including the parameters of which questions will be allowed," said Shapiro.

"Yes," said Battaglia. "That's from on high." He pointed in the direction of the Oval.

"What if a member of the committee just ignores the agreement?" asked Jay. "What do I do . . . refuse to answer?"

"That's what Walt's there for," replied Battaglia.

Shapiro smiled like a Cheshire cat. "We have ways of dealing with such transgressions."

"We should get Republican senators teed up to object," said Jay.

"Sure. We can have leg affairs handle that," said Battaglia, making notes.

"When is this going to happen?" asked Jay.

"We haven't finalized negotiations, but my guess is a week or ten days."

Jay nodded. "I'll be ready. And I may have a few allies out there with big audiences who may have something to say around that time as well." He winked.

"I have no doubt," said Battaglia with a smile. "Can you spell, S-T-A-N-T-O-N?"

As the meeting broke up, Shapiro turned to Jay. "You got a minute?" he asked.

"Sure," Jay replied. They walked down the hall, through the West Wing lobby, and up the narrow stairwell leading to Jay's office. Once inside, Shapiro closed the door.

Shapiro's eyes bore into Jay, lids hooded. "Do you remember ever meeting a woman named Samah Panzarella?"

Jay felt his stomach flip. "Why?"

"I got a call from her attorney. She claims you had sex with her in LA a few months ago. Seems she's pregnant."

"Oh, is that all?" replied Jay.

Shapiro did not flash a smile. "Between us, did you sleep with her?"

"This is protected by attorney-client privilege, right?" asked Jay.

"Yes. Anything you say to me is privileged," replied Shapiro.

"Okay," said Jay, with a sigh. "I met her at a party in LA when I was hanging out with Satcha Sanchez. I was there for a fund-raiser with the president. Layla—that's her nickname—and I had a few drinks. We danced. A few months ago I went out to do a fund-raiser in Orange County and I texted her. We met for drinks at the Chateau Mamont and then to a club."

"I don't hear an answer to my question," said Shapiro, his eyes piercing.

"We fooled around, made out, that kind of thing," said Jay. "But I didn't have sex with her. There was no intercourse. At least not that I recall. Of course, I did have a lot to drink."

"It would seem to me you'd remember that."

"I would sure think so."

"Well, it's not good," said Shapiro with a heavy sigh. "Her attorney wants a DNA test and is threatening a paternity suit."

"It's a shakedown," said Jay. "They know I can't have the negative publicity, so they're looking for a pay day." He scrunched up his face, deep in thought. "Should I call Satcha and see if she can talk this chick down off the ledge? She's her friend."

"I don't recommend that," said Shapiro. "I'll write her attorney a letter, tell him you have no such recollection. Then let's see what happens."

"Alright," said Jay, his face drained of color, looking like he had been hit by a bus. "If this comes out before I testify, it'll be very bad."

"You lead an interesting life," said Shapiro.

"Tell me about it." He stared at the wall, shell-shocked. "What do we do if you can't back this guy off the plate? He could go to *People* magazine . . . or worse."

"We're not going to be passive in dealing with her," replied Shapiro. "We'll threaten her with a libel suit if she goes public with knowingly false charges. And you can offer to take a DNA test. That'll call their bluff."

"Good Lord," muttered Jay. "Let's hope it doesn't come to *that*. There are two words you never want in the same sentence: your name and DNA."

"You might want to party less when you're in California," deadpanned Shapiro.

Jay walked Shapiro to the stairwell and watched him descend the stairs to the lobby. As he staggered back to his office, his head spinning, his assistant said something about a conference call waiting, but he couldn't make out the exact words. His mind raced. He hoped Shapiro could work his magic. If not, he was about to go into the barrel with a box of razor blades—and the president was going to be royally ticked.

31

The senators stood in front of a podium covered with microphones outside the Senate Majority Leader's office, faces hardened, lips pressed. The press gathered round feigning interest, exchanging knowing smirks. Everyone knew the news conference was going to be a clubbing, and Jay Noble was the piñata.

Sal Stanley stepped to the microphone as his colleagues jockeyed for position behind him, craning their necks to get in camera range. Television lights illuminated them, causing tourists to gather.

"Today I have sent a letter to Attorney General Keith Golden signed by forty-one senators calling on him to appoint a special prosecutor to investigate whether Jay Noble obstructed an IRS investigation of a political ally of the president," said Stanley, his face stretched like putty. He held up the letter to a flurry of camera flashes. "These are serious charges. The Finance Committee's investigation has revealed a level of corruption that is frankly shocking. Not since Richard Nixon was impeached in part for using the IRS to harass political enemies have we seen such an abuse of power." He paused, his eyes intense. "Only an independent counsel can conduct a fair investigation of the White House's politicization of the IRS free from any further hint of political manipulation." He folded up his statement and placed it in his coat pocket. "Any questions?"

"Senator, the independent counsel statute expired years ago," said *Roll Call.* "Why not just pass the statute and force the appointment of an independent counsel?"

"It's a fair point," said Stanley, raising his chin, projecting confidence. "But given Republican control of the House, passage of an IC statute is highly unlikely. This investigation needs to be conducted now."

"But you haven't even tried, Senator."

"I'll be sure to check in with Speaker Jimmerson to gauge his interest and report back to you," Stanley deadpanned to chuckles.

"What do you say to those who claim you're the one with serious ethical challenges, given the indictment of Michael Kaplan?" asked the *Washington Post.* "Your critics say basically people who live in glass houses shouldn't throw stones."

Stanley's eyes shot darts. "That matter was investigated by a *Republican* Justice Department," he said through clenched teeth. "A grand jury voted to bring an indictment, which is an accusation. Mike Kaplan deserves the same presumption of innocence any other citizen is granted under our laws. The charges related to Jay Noble are entirely different. The Long administration can't investigate itself."

"If I may briefly comment," said Senator Craig McGowan, a notorious camera hog and Stanley stalwart, sliding to the podium. His jet-black hair and cherubic face projected earnestness mixed with shameless self-promotion. "I believe the charges against Mike Kaplan were a textbook case of the criminalization of political differences, but that is a debate for another day." Stanley stood beside him, staring into space. "The charges against Jay Noble are contained in sworn testimony by three IRS employees about White House interference in an audit of a prominent supporter of the president. Let me be clear: if the president had knowledge of this, it is an impeachable offense. That is why Attorney General Golden should name an independent counsel, and he can do so without any additional authority by Congress. He has that authority now."

The press largely ignored McGowan. He was windowdressing. They hungered for Stanley trying to take down Noble, who thwarted his presidential ambitions in the recent campaign and was even now trying to defeat him for reelection in New Jersey.

"Question for Senator Stanley," said *Politico.* "What is the status of negotiations with the White House over the president's waiving executive privilege and allowing Jay Noble to testify before the Finance Committee?"

Stanley stepped back to the podium. "We are hopeful those negotiations proceed and Mr. Noble appears before the committee," said Stanley. "Previous presidents waived executive privilege in similar cases. Remember Condaleeza Rice, who was then national security advisor to President George W. Bush, testified before the 9/11 Commission. But because the allegations by Mr. von Fuggers were made under oath, Mr. Noble's testimony must be sworn and take place in public. So we just don't know what the White House will do."

"If Jay Noble does appear," asked *Politico,* "and he addresses these questions in a way the committee finds satisfactory, isn't it possible an independent counsel is unnecessary?"

"In a word, no," said Stanley. "I don't anticipate that happening." His colleagues smiled and the press contingent chuckled. The news conference over, Stanley headed back to his office, trailed by staff and the other senators.

"Do you think there's any chance Golden takes the bait?" asked Leo Wells, the Democratic whip.

"I doubt it," said Stanley, head down. "He's on a short leash to the West Wing. Battaglia says, 'jump,' Golden asks, 'how high?'"

Within minutes the *New York Times* posted an update on its Web site beneath the headline: "Senate Democrats Demand Special Counsel in Widening Investigation of Key White House Aide, Jay Noble."

SENATOR KATE COVITZ TRIED TO reach her husband for two hours on his cell phone but got no answer. She was on her way to yet another fund-raiser, a reception for gay supporters at the Mark Hopkins Hotel in San Francisco. The fund-raisers were a blur now. Her husband was at their weekend place in Carmel-by-the-Sea, a two-bedroom cottage three blocks from the beach they purchased a decade earlier. She was scheduled to drive down from San Francisco after the fund-raiser and meet him for a late dinner at a favorite restaurant and a rare day off. She was looking forward to it.

Frank Covitz was a wealthy commercial real estate developer who helped finance his wife's early campaigns for Congress. His $200 million fortune and controversial investments became an issue in this and other campaigns. An avid golfer, he loved the Monterey peninsula, was a member at Pebble Beach Golf Links, and he and Kate spent as many weekends there as their busy schedules allowed. He sent her a cryptic text message earlier in the day that read, "You're the best. Miss you. Love to you and the children. Forgive me." He had recently been the target of a hit piece in the *LA Times,* and was feeling down.

Unsettled, Kate tried to call him repeatedly. As they entered the lobby of the Mark Hopkins, she turned to her finance director, eyes fearful. "I can't get in touch with Frank," she said. Outwardly, she looked terrific, sheathed in a lavender St. John pantsuit, matching Stuart Weitzman heels, dark brown hair feathered to her shoulders.

"Really? That's odd," said her finance director. "Want me to try him?"

"No," she said. "Call the Carmel police and ask them if they can run by the house."

The finance director nodded stoically. Everyone on the campaign staff was used to what they called "Frank management." She stepped into the corner of the lobby, out of earshot, to call the police while Covitz walked into a reception and click line for those who gave or raised at least $5,000.

Covitz kept her game face on, a frozen smile affixed and teeth bared, greeting donors and bundlers as if each was the only person in the room. After brief remarks, she went into a holding room before they headed upstairs for the large reception. She sat at a table with several glasses, a pitcher of water, and a plate of mints.

Her finance director entered the room and closed the door. "I got a call back from the Carmel police."

"Did they find Frank?"

"No," replied the finance director. "They went by the house and he wasn't there. Or at least he didn't answer."

"He's probably on the golf course," she said. "I swear he'd play in the dark if they strung lights on the course."

"I don't think so. His car is in the driveway. So if he went somewhere, he must have walked."

"Maybe he went with someone else," said Covitz. "I'll call Pebble Beach and see if they've seen him." She scrolled through her BlackBerry for the number and dialed it. "Hello," she said. "This is Kate Covitz. I'm trying to reach Frank. Have you seen him out there this afternoon?" She paused, listening to the answer. "I see," she said, her facial expression disappointed. "Well, if he turns up, would you mind having someone call me, or have him call me?" She gave the person in the golf shop her phone number and hung up.

"Not there?" said the finance director.

"No," said Covitz quietly. Her growing concern was palpable. But 150 donors were upstairs waiting for her to speak to them. She'd deal with it after the fund-raiser. "Let's go upstairs," she directed. "I'll work the room, hit the marks, make brief remarks, and then I need to get down to Carmel."

She and her finance director left the hold and headed for the elevator, which was held open by a campaign advance man. They rode silently up the elevator to the top floor. When the doors opened, she walked down the hall toward the Top of the Mark, the bar at the top of the hotel offering beautiful views of the city and the San Francisco Bay.

"Ladies and gentlemen," intoned an announcer. "The senior U.S. senator from the state of California, Kate Covitz!"

The crowed broke into loud applause and cheering. Covitz bounded on to a stage, her plastic smile masking her inner turmoil, pointing to familiar faces in the crowd, her body bathed in the flashes of cameras.

AN APB FOR FRANK COVITZ went out from the Carmel Police Department at 5:42 p.m. The dispatch was sent to all local law enforcement, including the Carmel-by-the-Sea Beach Patrol. Half an hour later, one of the beach patrol officers who remembered seeing a man who fit the description strolling on the beach jumped on an all-terrain vehicle, its large tires giving it the appearance of a moonwalker, and gunned the engine, hurtling toward the end of the beach. It was a beautiful late summer day, the sun low in the ocean mist, seagulls flying and squawking overhead, children running to and fro, couples holding hands as they walked on the white sand.

Reaching the end of the beach, the patrol officer got off the ATV and stepped gingerly across the large rocks separating the ocean from the marshlands inland. He could make out Clint Eastwood's Mission Valley Inn in the distance. The waves crashed against the rocks, sending white foam and spray into the air. He stood on top of a high rock, surveying the surrounding landscape. That was when he spied the body.

He was a white male, approximately mid-sixties, dressed in a white-and-blue checkered shirt, brown belt, khaki chinos, and Gucci loafers with no socks. The police report would record that the victim had suffered "severe head trauma." In less clinical terms, the top of his skull was blown off, his scalp hanging by a flap. His torso rested against a rock, his left arm lay across his chest, his hand closed tightly in a fist. His legs were splayed underneath him in opposite directions. His right arm lay on the sand, also with a closed fist. A .38-caliber Smith & Wesson revolver lay on the ground. The blood from the wound covered the side of the rock and sand at its base. The cylinder of the revolver held three bullets. One shot had been fired.

The beach patrol officer picked up the revolver with a Bic pen so as not to leave prints and sniffed the barrel. The pungent odor of fresh gunpowder filled his nostrils. He touched the victim's neck with his index and middle finger. There was no pulse, but the body was still warm. He pressed the button on his walkie-talkie. "I got a body," he said. "End of the beach by the Mission Inn." He paused. "I'm going to need an ambulance and a Crime Scene Unit."

BACK AT THE MARK HOPKINS, Kate Covitz wrapped up her speech and dove into the crowd, hugging necks, signing autographs, pecking cheeks, and posing for photos. The scene took on the feel of a night-club, with thumping music and a surging mass of humanity, with some bodies bumping and grinding. Everyone was having fun. And why not? Covitz was up six points in the polls and raising dough by the bucketfuls. Best of all, from this crowd's perspective she wasn't afraid to embrace the gay community. When she finished working the room, Covitz headed for the elevator, walking purposefully, eyes straight ahead. When she saw the stricken face of her finance director drained of color, she knew something was terribly wrong.

"What?" she asked.

"I need to tell you something," she said. "Not here."

The advance man guided them down a narrow hallway to an office, apparently for the manager. Without asking anyone if they could use it, he turned the knob and opened the door. Covitz and her finance director closed the door.

Her face etched with anxiety, Covitz asked, "Did they find Frank?"

"Yes," said the finance director. "He was on the beach." She began to choke up. "Kate, he's dead."

"Oh, God!" screamed Covitz, sobbing. "No! No! No!" She fell into the arms of her finance director and sobbed uncontrollably.

AN AMBULANCE TRANSPORTED FRANK COVITZ'S body to the Monterey County coroner's office for an autopsy as required by state law. The Carmel Police Department went into lockdown, maintaining silence on the death of one of the town's most prominent residents until Kate Covitz could arrive from San Francisco. They also searched the beach cottage, where police found a suicide note. As she hurtled down the 101 Expressway, Covitz called her two adult children to relay the tragic news.

The next morning at 8:00 a.m. Pacific time, Covitz's office released a statement. "We may never fully understand what caused this vibrant, loving, and joyful man to feel his life was no longer worth living. We will remember him as a loving husband, devoted father, and a visionary who impacted countless lives for the better. In this early hour of our grief, we ask for the prayers of the people of California and request the media respect our privacy during this time of mourning."

Covitz immediately suspended her campaign, pulling down television and radio ads and cancelling public events indefinitely. Heidi Hughes followed suit within the hour. In characteristic fashion, Covitz's grief propelled her into a whirling dervish of activity, meeting with attorneys to handle the couple's complicated financial affairs, cleaning out Frank's office, lovingly boxing up his personal effects, and making funeral arrangements. Her grief soon gave way to anger. *How could Frank abandon her like this?* she wondered. *Why would he take his own life when he had so much to live for . . . the children, the grandchildren, their life together?*

One of the most high-profile Senate races in the nation ground to a halt. The entire political class was thunderstruck. The macabre details of his suicide only added to their morbid curiosity. But an anonymous blogger in Carmel put a post up on a community Web site that held forth a clue to the mystery: "I know a real estate agent specializing in the Monterey peninsula who recently spoke with Frank about putting the Covitz beach property up for sale, reportedly for $5 million. Their house in DC was already on the market. I know he was having financial difficulties, and it may have led him to end his life."

32

As reporters descended on Carmel to cover Frank Covitz's suicide, another bombshell dropped in Los Angeles. In LA Superior Court, Grand Central Station for Hollywood celebrities behaving badly, Samah Panzarella's attorney filed a lawsuit accusing Jay Noble of paternity, abandonment, and emotional and mental cruelty. Panzarella's suit sought $20,000 a month in child support and $8 million in damages. Within minutes, Merryprankster. com posted the news under the head-snapping lead: "Jay Noble's Baby Mama Sez: Pay Up or Else!!"

The news landed in DC like a howitzer. Jay's cell phone went off at 6:10 a.m. as he rode in a government sedan to the White House. It was a thoroughly unhappy Charlie Hector.

"Jay, I want to see you and Phil as soon as you get in," he said with clipped efficiency, his voice jagged. "We're going to get a lot of press inquiries about this lawsuit, and I want to make sure we have our facts straight."

"Phil knew this was coming," said Jay, trying to sound calm. "But the timing's horrible."

"What?" screeched Hector. "Phil knew? Why wasn't I told?"

Jay pulled the receiver away, protecting his ear from Hector's blast. "I don't know," he said haltingly. "I assumed Phil told you. This bimbo was trying to shake me down, and Walt was talking with her lawyer to try to keep it out of the media."

"We'll deal with why I was not informed later," snapped Hector. "But something of this magnitude should have been brought to me by *you*. What were you thinking?"

Jay's heart pounded. Hector was no fan of Jay's. This screwup was going to give him more ammunition he needed to clip Jay's wings in the White House, where their power struggle was an open secret. "I'm sorry, Charlie," said Jay, backpedaling furiously. "I should have come to you. That's my bad. But I was so distracted by the preparations for my Senate testimony, I thought Phil and Walt could handle it."

"Terrific. Now I get to inform the president. He's not going to be happy . . . *at all.*"

"Charlie, I'm sorry to cause heartburn for the president," said Jay, his body quivering with fear. "I met this girl when I was in Caly raising money. It's a stickup. She hired a liberal, ambulance-chasing personal injury attorney I defeated for a state assembly seat eighteen years ago. The guy's had a vendetta against me ever since. I'm telling you, it's *total* nonsense."

"I hope for your sake that's the case," said Hector. "You're already in the penalty box for the IRS flap. Jay, you're becoming a distraction."

Jay wanted to scream into the phone: *Are you threatening me? Have you forgotten I got you your job as chief of staff?* Instead, he kept his temper in check.

"Walt's all over it," said Jay. "He says she has no case, and he doubts she's even prego. The timing alone is suspicious and ought to tell us what this is about."

"Nevertheless, you need to get off the front page," said Hector. "We're burning too many calories cleaning up your messes. Get your sorry rear in my office as soon as you get in."

The line went dead. Jay knew if it was up to Charlie, he'd probably be out. Would the president stand up for him? He hoped so, but it wasn't like the old days. Long had to protect himself. He was supposed to testify in three days. His stomach churned, sending acid reflux running up his throat and into his mouth. He smelled a rat. He was sure either Sal Stanley or the Covitz campaign dropped the dime on him.

THE LINE OF MOURNERS FILING into St. Bartholemew's Catholic church in downtown San Francisco stretched for half a block. The guest list for the funeral of Frank Covitz read like a who's who of the financial and political elite of California: Governor Mack Caulfield, the mayors of San Francisco and Los Angeles, most of the state's congressional delegation, major donors, CEOs, and a sprinkling of Hollywood stars. Presided over by the bishop of the San Francisco diocese, it featured eulogies by Frank's eldest son, his brother, and one of his business partners.

As people filed out after the service, Kate stood in the foyer wearing a black dress and white pearls, accepting condolences. Many were in shock. For her part, Kate kept up a brave front—planning the funeral and dealing with the estate and lawyers preventing her from having to fully confront her grief. She was running on adrenalin.

A friend and her husband approached her, their faces sympathetic. "Kate, we're all pulling for you," said the woman. "Frank had too good a heart for this world."

Kate nodded in the direction of the casket. "Frank never wanted a political life," replied Kate sadly. "He finally found a way out, didn't he?"

"SATCHA SANCHEZ ON LINE TWO," announced Jay Noble's assistant.

Jay closed the door to his office and picked up the receiver. "Well, at least you can't say I lead a boring life," he quipped with morbid humor.

"Honey, I'm so sorry about this," said Satcha. "I can't believe this gold-digging witch."

"Yeah," said Jay. "She's bad news."

"I feel horrible. I mean, *I* introduced you to her."

"I remember," said Jay. "It was at that party at The Standard in LA."

"I only invited her because I thought she'd be fun. I wanted you to have a good time and blow off some steam. I never thought it would lead to *this*."

"Don't worry about it, Satcha. It's not your fault. Who knew?"

"The lawsuit is complete bull, isn't it?"

"Total," replied Jay, trying to sound confident. "My attorney thinks it'll be dismissed. But it's going to cost me an arm and a leg in legal bills. Not to mention a PR beating."

"Should I call her and urge her to drop the suit before Shapiro gets his pound of flesh?"

"Bad idea," said Jay. "We can't rewind the tape. . . . The suit has been filed. Given our relationship and your profile, you need to steer clear."

"Alright," said Satcha, her voice filled with regret. "I just wish I could do more to help."

Just then the door opened, and Jay's assistant stuck her head in. She mouthed in a half whisper: "The First Lady is on the phone."

Jay did a double take. He cupped his hand over the receiver. "Claire?" His assistant nodded. "Satcha, I have to grab another call. But thanks for your call. You're the best."

"Hugs and kisses," said Satcha, making a kissing sound.

He picked up the other line. "Hello, ma'am. To what do I owe this honor?"

"Jay, I just wanted to call and tell you I'm praying for you. In fact, my entire Bible study group is praying for you," said Claire. "We're lifting you up before the throne of grace and asking for God's protection as you endure all these attacks."

"Thank you, Claire. That means the world to me. It really does."

"Jay, the Holy Spirit has shown me this is a Satanic attack. The enemy is trying to destroy you because you're important to Bob and the country. This is a spiritual battle."

Jay didn't quite know what to say. "This woman's lawyer is some trial lawyer I helped defeat for state assembly. It's a political hit job."

"It's more than that. We wrestle not against flesh and blood but against the principalities and powers of darkness in the heavenly realm," said Claire, her voice firm. "Second Corinthians 5:10."

"I hear you," said Jay politely. He had heard about Claire's Christian faith, but he feared she might be drinking the Kool-Aid. Still, he appreciated her reaching out and supporting him. It was a good sign there was no daylight between him and the president.

"Jay, do you mind if I pray with you?"

"No, not at all. I'd be honored."

"Father, I pray for my brother Jay," Claire began. "You have placed him in a strategic position at the highest level of government. The enemy would love nothing more than to destroy and discredit him. Surround him with Your love and grace. I pray against those who would seek to destroy him, that they would be destroyed instead and, as was the case with Mordecai in the book of Esther, his enemies would be hung on the scaffolds they built for him. When Jay enters that Senate hearing room, I pray You will surround him with Your angels, and I ask that he would sense Your presence and rest in Your strength. In Jesus, Amen."

Jay choked up. Through his tears he chuckled at the line about his enemies being hung on the scaffolds. "You're hard-core, Claire," he laughed. "I haven't been prayed over like that in a long time."

"Just because I became a Christian doesn't mean I'm a wimp. I never shrink from a fight," said Claire.

"How well I know that's true," said Jay. "I've always liked the fact you have a little vinegar in you."

"I came to Christ, Jay. I didn't have a lobotomy."

Jay laughed.

"Jay, one other thing."

"Yes, ma'am?"

"In the future keep your pants on. Bob and I love you like a son, and we think you're brilliant. But Bob's the president. For his reputation if not your own, you need to clean up your act. Find a nice, Christian girl and make her your wife would be my advice."

"I'll take that under advisement, ma'am."

"You do that. Good-bye."

Jay hung up the phone and shook his head. *When the good Lord made Claire,* he thought, *He sure broke the mold.*

THE *WALL STREET JOURNAL* HAD been working on story for weeks, chasing down leads from New York to DC, San Francisco to Boston, Switzerland to the Cayman Islands. Ironically, the story was about to go to press when Frank Covitz killed himself. Confident of their exclusive, *Journal* editors resisted competitive pressure and held the story until after the funeral. It would have looked mercenary to publish it while the body was still warm.

The day after the funeral, the story ran on the *Journal*'s front page under the headline, "Husband of U.S. Senator Faced Criminal Charges at Time of Death." Relying on securities filings, real estate records, and analysis by tax lawyers, and a former IRS commissioner quoted on the record, it reported Frank Covitz evaded tens of millions of dollars in taxes by relying on illegal tax shelters, offshore accounts, and phony trust funds. Settlement negotiations between the IRS and

Covitz's lawyers dragged on for months. Days before Frank's suicide, the IRS threatened to make a criminal referral to the U.S. attorney's office in Los Angeles.

All told, Covitz owed $42 million in taxes, penalties, and interest at the time of his death. Beyond the eye-popping amount of money, the most politically explosive revelation was that trust funds used in the course of the alleged fraud were jointly held by Frank and Kate Covitz. Her signature appeared on many documents the IRS alleged were part of a sophisticated ruse to evade paying taxes.

Heidi Hughes was at the FBO at the San Diego airport, having just wrapped up a speech to a local chamber of commerce, when the *Journal* posted the story. She stepped into a conference room to join a hastily arranged call with her campaign team.

"Everyone's here, Heidi," announced her campaign manager.

"Good. I've only got a minute before I have to get on the plane," said Hughes. She was focused. "I hate to benefit politically from such a personal tragedy, but this *Journal* story is a bombshell."

"It's a game changer, Heidi," said her general consultant, a grizzled veteran of twenty years of statewide campaigns in California.

"It's only a matter of time before the *LA Times* piles on," observed Hughes.

"They've already called," said the campaign press secretary. "Twice."

"The answer is, 'We have no comment,'" said Hughes. "We don't know where this is going, and I don't want to get in front of any cameras . . . at least not yet."

"Roger that," replied the press secretary. "I can hold them for a day."

"This is going to be hard for Kate to explain," said the general consultant. "Tax evasion, fraud, money laundering. She can't hide behind her husband. She signed the documents. She's an accomplice to multiple federal felonies."

"She can claim ignorance, but that just makes her look worse," said Hughes.

"I think the election is the least of her problems," said the campaign manager. "The IRS could claw back some of the money they moved offshore or put in trusts, go after their houses, even the insurance money. She could end up bankrupt and in prison."

"Do you think she knew what Frank was up to?" asked Hughes. "I can't imagine she did."

"*Of course* she knew," said the general consultant. "Kate may be a lot of things, but dumb is not one of them. She's going to have a hard time convincing voters she didn't have a clue what was going on."

"Well, today we can keep our heads down. But at some point, this takes on a life of its own, and I'm going to have to comment on it," observed Hughes.

"It's a grenade going off in a lunch box," said her consultant. "The media will take the lead, but we can't ignore it. At some point you're going to have to take a position. Let's face it, we'll probably end up hitting her with an ad."

"I should express sympathy for her loss but say she's an elected official, these are serious charges, and the people of California deserve an explanation."

"We demand . . . an explanation," said the campaign manager, his voice mocking.

"What if it turns out she participated in a scheme to evade taxes?" asked the press secretary. "Should she be prosecuted?"

"I'm not going there," said Hughes.

"That's up to the IRS and prosecutors," said the consultant.

"I got to go," said Hughes. She sighed. "First, Frank's suicide. Now this. I wouldn't wish this on my worst enemy. I wonder how this affects the race. I guess it's hard to know."

"She'll drop seven points in seventy-two hours," said her consultant.

"You really think so?"

"Count on it."

Hughes hung up and headed for her plane. She wondered: *Was she on her way to the U.S. Senate? And given the price Kate Covitz paid, was it even worth it?*

THE HIGH COMMAND GATHERED IN Charlie Hector's office to plan the White House's response to the Panzarella paternity suit. Joining Hector and Jay were Phil Battaglia and Walt Shapiro. Jay sat slumped on the couch, his face pale, looking crestfallen. Shapiro sat next to him, holding a gold-embossed leather pouch like a shield. Hector and Battaglia sat in wing chairs. Everyone was tense.

"I've talked to the president," said Hector, shamelessly playing the POTUS card for leverage. "He suggests Jay settle with this woman and admit no wrongdoing. Get it off the front page." He turned to Shaprio. "I assume that's doable, Walt."

"Too early to tell," said Shapiro. "The attorney is a partisan Democrat who's taken the case on contingency. If this were about the legal merits only, I'd say yes. I'm not sure it is."

"Paula Jones, call your office," said Battaglia.

"The guy hates my guts," said Jay. "I defeated him—"

"Hold that thought, Jay," said Hector, holding up an index finger. "Anything can be settled, right? It's just a question of how high is the price."

"We can't have Jay deposed and be asked detailed questions about intimate relations with the woman," said Battaglia. "It opens him up to perjury or a leak."

"I don't think we'll ever get there," said Shapiro.

"But you could," fired back Battaglia. "I know LA Superior Court. Been there, done that. You get the wrong judge in the draw, you're shafted."

"What happened with this girl?" asked Hector, his eyes boring into Jay. "I mean, is she just making this up out of thin air?"

Shapiro leaned forward in his seat. "Don't answer that, Jay."

Hector nearly came out of his chair. "What? You're instructing a White House employee to take the Fifth? Come on, Walt, we're all on the same team."

"Charlie, this meeting is subject to discovery. This very conversation is discoverable," said Shapiro, his face hardening. "I can't have Jay say something in this meeting that appears to contradict what he might say in an affidavit in the lawsuit."

"This conversation is protected by executive privilege," shot back Battaglia.

"Oh, you mean like Jay's conversations with Treasury about Andy Stanton?" asked Shapiro. "That he's going to testify about under oath? Like that?"

Jay had heard enough. "Walt, I appreciate your concern, but Charlie has to know the facts." He looked directly at Hector. "I took her out a couple of times. We made out. Fooled around a little bit. To the best of my recollection, I never had sex with her."

"To the best of your recollection?" asked Hector, incredulous. "You sound like Clinton."

"There was a lot of drinking."

"Jay's going to offer to take a DNA test," said Shapiro. "That will call her bluff."

Battaglia raised his eyebrows. "You sure you want to do that, Jay?"

Jay shrugged his shoulders. "No. But if it gets this behind me, I'm willing to do it."

"Alright, here's the deal," said Hector, bringing the meeting to a close. "Phil, you and Walt work up a statement Lisa can read in the press briefing. I don't want a bunch of lawyer-speak like, 'There is no controlling legal authority,' or 'It depends on what the meaning of *is* is.' Got it?"

"Got it," replied Battaglia.

"Walt, we want this thing settled," said Hector, his eyes boring in on Shapiro. "Make it go away. That's what you do, right?"

"I'm not a magician," said Shapiro. "But that's the objective. If it's doable, we'll do it."

"Good," said Hector. He stood up, signaling the meeting was over. Everyone looked drained. "Well, hasn't this been fun?"

Everyone filed out, Jay heading back to his office, Shapiro joined at his hip. Jay's mind raced. He wondered: if he made it through the Senate Finance Committee hearing alive, would he survive the Panzarella flap? He wanted to kick himself for being such a fool. He sure hoped Claire's prayers were answered.

33

J ay's bimbo eruption gave the media a field day. The crawler at the bottom of FOX News read: "She's Having My Baby: LA 'Party Girl' Accuses WH Aide Jay Noble of Fathering Her Child." In a play on the old Bob Dylan song, the *New York Post* headline read: "Lay, Layla, Lay!" Inside the issue were splashed paparazzi photos of Samah Panzarella arriving at her apartment in West Hollywood, wearing a sheer top, black leggings, and a denim miniskirt, her face obscured beneath a floppy hat and large sunglasses.

Jay tried to ignore the storm raging around him. He e-mailed Lisa the statement Phil and Walt worked up but received no reply, then called her direct dial and got voicemail. She did not return the message. She was giving him the silent treatment.

It didn't take long after Lisa walked into the briefing room for the shooting to start.

"Lisa, are you going to comment on the paternity suit filed by Samah Panzarella, a.k.a. Layla?" asked ABC News as he vainly attempted to wipe the smirk off his face.

318

"This lawsuit is a personal, legal matter between Mr. Noble and Ms. Panzarella. It does not relate to Mr. Noble's official duties as a member of the White House staff," said Lisa. "The administration does not comment on pending legal matters or purely personal matters."

The briefing room broke out in laughter. "Oh, come on!" someone shouted. Lisa ignored the outburst and pointed to Dan Dorman of the *Washington Post,* who was puffed up like a blowfish. "Yes, Dan? I assume you have a question," she deadpanned.

"Without commenting on the specifics of the lawsuit, can you tell us if the president continues to have confidence in Jay Noble?" asked Dorman, head cocked.

"The president has confidence in all his staff," said Lisa, quick on her feet. "They are working hard to serve the American people. That includes Jay Noble."

"It's a yes-or-no answer, Lisa."

"I answered it. I just didn't answer it the way you wanted me to," she said, her jaw tightening, the muscles in her face hardening with hatred.

"Let me rephrase the question," said Dorman. "Is the president personally aware of these allegations, and does he continue to have confidence in Noble?"

"I don't think that's a rephrasing of your original question. I think it's an entirely different question."

"Aaaaah," moaned the press corps in protest. "Answer the question!" shouted a disembodied voice from the mob.

Lisa shook off the zinger hurled from the cheap seats. She held up her watch. "Folks, you can ask questions for twenty minutes about this topic," she said with a smile. "You'll get the same answer. The answer's not going to change. The White House does not comment on personal, legal matters."

"Is Jay going to grant any press interviews?" asked *Politico.* "Or is he going to hide behind his lawyers?"

"If Jay decides to address these issues, we will certainly make that known," said Lisa. "In the meantime we have provided you with a copy of his statement. Any further questions should be directed to his personal attorney, Walter Shapiro."

Jay sat in his office watching the carnage unfold on the TV screen. The cable networks covered the briefing live, which was a bad sign. The only good news: his Senate testimony would blow the Panzarella scandal off the front page, if only for a day.

THE HEARING ROOM ON THE second floor of the Hart Senate Office Building was packed. Hundreds were in line since before dawn to get one of the coveted seats. Members of the Finance Committee sat on the dais beneath a gold U.S. Senate seal carved into the white marble wall, contrasting with the wood paneled walls on either side. They chatted among themselves as they awaited Jay's much anticipated arrival.

Suddenly Jay entered the room accompanied by two Capitol police and Walt Shapiro. The senators snapped to attention and cameras flashed. Jay stepped across the dais to shake hands with Aaron Hayward, chairman of the committee, and went down the dais, shaking hands cordially. He then walked to the witness table and sat down.

Hayward banged his gavel, his white hair combed immaculately, his facial expression grave. He came loaded for bear. "This hearing of the Senate Finance Committee is hereby called to order," he said. "The witness will please rise."

Jay stood to his feet. Dozens of photographers crouched on the balls of their feet or on their knees jockeyed for position. "Mr. Noble, please raise your right hand." Jay lifted his arm. "Do you swear to tell the truth, the whole truth, and nothing but the truth, so help you God?"

"I do," he said as camera shutters exploded. *Well,* he thought, *they got their money shot. Now it's my turn.*

"Mr. Noble, I understand you have an opening statement."

"I do, Mr. Chairman," replied Jay. "I will read only portions and would ask that the entire statement be entered into the record."

"Without objection, so ordered," said Hayward.

"Chairman Hayward, members of the committee," Jay began. "I appreciate the opportunity—"

"Excuse me, Mr. Noble," interrupted Hayward. "Could you please introduce your legal counsel to the committee? I mean for those few who don't already know him."

The crowd chuckled knowingly. Jay had one of the most famous white-collar criminal lawyers in the nation by his side.

"Walter Shapiro with the Webster and Puck law firm," said Shapiro.

"Thank you, Mr. Shapiro. Please proceed, Mr. Noble."

"Yes, Senator," said Jay. "I appreciate the opportunity to appear today and testify about the events this committee is investigating. There is a great deal of misinformation and misunderstanding about my role in the Internal Revenue Service's audit of New Life Ministries and other charitable organizations. I am grateful for the chance to set the record straight."

The committee members stared down from the dais impassively. Some of them flipped through copies of Jay's prepared statement, following as he spoke.

"Last August, the president held a meeting in the White House with religious leaders about the nomination of Judge Marco Diaz to the U.S. Supreme Court, which I attended," said Jay. "After the meeting, Ross Lombardy, the executive director of the Faith and Family Federation, asked if he could meet with me briefly. He informed me of the concerns his boss, Reverend Andy Stanton, and other evangelical leaders had about what he characterized as politically motivated and highly invasive audits of conservative ministries and alleged bias by the IRS agents conducting them. He asked me if anything could be done to ensure greater fairness, as he felt the audit process constituted harassment. I told him I would pass on his concerns."

Jay reached for a glass of water, taking a sip. "Two days later I called David Thomas, political director of the White House, and asked him to check in with Carl Bondi, the White House liaison at the Treasury Department. I related my conversation with Mr. Lombardy to David. I told him I heard similar concerns during the presidential campaign from religious leaders. I told Mr. Thomas to ask Mr. Bondi to make the appropriate individuals aware of the fact the White House was receiving complaints." Jay lifted his head, looking directly at the senators, his eyes like lasers. "At no time did I ask anyone at the Treasury Department to modify its audit procedures to reduce scrutiny of tax-exempt organizations." His leaned into the microphone, his voice rising. "I instructed Mr. Thomas to tell Mr. Bondi that we were confident the decisions regarding the audits of tax-exempt ministries were being determined on the merits alone." He paused for dramatic effect. "There was no attempt by me or anyone else at the White House to influence any audit.

"Mr. Chairman, I know some have claimed I interfered with the audit of New Life Ministries," said Jay, his voice firm and resonant. "That is a lie." A few of the Democratic senators flinched. "I never spoke with anyone at the Treasury Department regarding this issue. I never tried to influence any decision by the IRS. These allegations have more to do with partisan politics prior to an election in which control of the Senate hangs in the balance than they do with my conduct as a White House employee." Jay paused. "I am happy to take your questions."

The entire room held its breath; Jay's denial was categorical. He had all but accused the committee of conducting a witch hunt. Everyone waited for the fireworks.

Hayward leaned back, eyes narrowing as a staffer whispered in his ear. He nodded silently, then pulled his microphone close.

"Mr. Noble, I read your statement with great interest. You claim you never spoke to anyone at the Treasury Department and thus could not have influenced the outcome of the audit of New Life Ministries." Hayward hunched his back, rounding his shoulders. "But Mr. Thomas did it for you. Mr. Thomas is your deputy, correct?"

"Senator, he is one of them," said Jay, his voice even. "I have many people who report to me, including the head of public liaison, the director of policy planning—"

"I don't need the White House organizational chart," said Hayward, his voice withering. "When someone at the Treasury Department or any other cabinet-level department gets a call from Mr. Thomas, they know they're really getting a call from you, right?"

"Not necessarily," said Jay, fouling off the pitch.

"Not according to Mr. Bondi. He testified Mr. Thomas said he was calling on *your* behalf." A staffer quickly produced a transcript. Hayward put on his reading glasses. "Mr. Bondi said, and I quote, 'David said Jay asked him to call and relay the concerns of Andy Stanton and other conservative religious leaders about the IRS.'" He snapped off his reading glasses. "Mr. Thomas delivered your message, didn't he? And your message was: we're getting blowback from the evangelicals. Back off. Isn't that what happened here?"

"Senator, my message was to make all decisions on the merits alone."

"Then why, pray tell, have the White House political director call?" asked Hayward, his face animated, throwing up his hands. "If the audits were so fair, and you fully concurred with the way the IRS was conducting the audits, why not send the message by . . . the tooth fairy?"

The room exploded with laughter. Jay sat stoically.

"I suppose I could have, Senator," he said with a wry smile. "But I wouldn't want the tooth fairy to have my legal bills." The crowd laughed appreciatively. A few Republican senators enjoyed a chuckle. On the majority side of the dais, they just glared at him.

"Is it that, or you don't want the tooth fairy to file a paternity suit against you?" asked Hayward, flashing a wicked grin. There were gasps and guffaws at the reference to the Panzarella scandal.

Jay's lips turned up and his eyes twinkled. "Senator, I can state categorically and without fear of correction, I have never partied with the tooth fairy in Los Angeles."

The room exploded in laughter. Even Shapiro's face stretched into a rubbery smile.

Hayward glowered over the top of his glasses. Jay's testimony was turning into a comedy routine. He'd had enough. "When the political director of the White House, whose job it is to oversee the *political interests* of the president, calls an agency on the carpet that is supposed to be free from any political influence, it speaks volumes about what the president's advisors want, does it not, Mr. Noble?"

"With all due respect, Senator, the only message we conveyed was that we were receiving constituent complaints regarding audits of ministries," said Jay. "Given the vital work these ministries do helping the poor, feeding the hungry, educating the illiterate, and helping people find jobs, if they had concerns about selective enforcement, it was entirely appropriate to pass them on to the relevant individuals in the government. Indeed, it was my job to convey their concerns. Had I failed to do so, I would have been delinquent in my duties. The agencies deal with that information however they deem appropriate based on the merits alone."

"I see. You would have been *delinquent*," said Hayward sarcastically. "Is that particularly true if the organization in question turned out millions of votes for Bob Long?"

"No, sir. But they raised the concerns, and I passed them on. That's my job."

A staff member handed Hayward a sheet of paper. His eyes scanning the contents. "Mr. Noble, please turn to Exhibit 450-A." He waited as Jay and Shapiro flipped through a large binder to the page. "This is an e-mail from Mr. Thomas to Ross Lombardy on November

20. It reads, 'OPP sent nomination of Lee Fenty for IRS commish to Hill. Solid guy. Andy will be pleased.'" He stared down at Jay, his eyes accusing. "Obviously a reference to Reverend Stanton getting more favorable treatment from the new commissioner of the IRS. I suppose this would be another example of something being decided solely on the merits?"

"Yes, sir. Mr. Fenty was a career civil servant with impeccable qualifications."

"You see nothing unusual about the White House political director telling a prominent supporter being audited by the IRS that he'll be pleased with the new management?"

"Senator, Mr. Fenty has already testified no one at the White House encouraged him to give favorable treatment to Andy Stanton," fired back Jay. "If you're suggesting this e-mail was part of a White House attempt to influence the IRS, then apparently Mr. Fenty disagrees."

"Mr. von Fuggers agrees," said Hayward impatiently. "So do two other IRS agents who have testified to White House interference." He picked up a stack of papers, waving it for the cameras as still photo shutters fluttered. "How would Mr. Fenty know? He was not confirmed until after von Fuggers was reassigned and resigned in disgust."

"If that is the case, then according to your time line, Mr. Fenty could not have been part of a conspiracy to influence an audit if he came to the IRS after the fact. You can't have it both ways, Senator."

"Don't tell me what I can and can't have, Mr. Noble," bellowed Hayward, his eyes narrowing to slits. "You're the witness. Keep that in mind?"

"Yes, Senator."

Walt Shapiro nearly came out of his chair. He leaned into the microphone. "Mr. Chairman, with all due respect, is this a hearing or an inquisition?"

"Counselor, I've served in the senate for twenty-four years and chaired this committee for eight years. Are you trying to tell me how to conduct a hearing?"

"No, Senator, but I believe this is known in a court of law as browbeating the witness," said Shapiro, eyes aflame, his jaw firm.

"You're not in a court of law!" shouted Hayward. "You may well be in court before this is over. But today you are at *my* hearing before *my* committee, and your client will answer *my* questions."

"He has answered all your questions, and he will continue to do so pursuant to the White House's agreement with this committee, Senator," said Shapiro. "I'm only asking that he be treated with a modicum of decency and respect."

"Well, I see my time is up," said Hayward, ignoring Shapiro. "I'll turn it over to the other side of the aisle."

IN THE RADIO STUDIOS OF New Life Ministries, Andy Stanton spun in his chair, clapping his large hands together. "Ladies and gentlemen, you heard it yourselves! Aaron Hayward didn't lay a *glove* on Jay Noble. This isn't a fair fight. It's child abuse! I'm waiting for a referee to call the fight before someone gets hurt."

He pressed a button on his console, playing a tape with the sound effects of a flurry of punches landing. "Is this it? Is this all they have? Some innocuous e-mail and the testimony of a disgruntled government bureaucrat with liberal sympathies who's flogging a book on CBS and MSNBC?" He leaned into the microphone, lowering his voice to a silky baritone. "Brothers and sisters, we are at war. The chairman of the Senate Foreign Relations Committee is dead. The French foreign minister is dead. Both murdered by terrorists working for Rassem el Zafarshan. Two U.S. officials are missing. Iran has a nuclear weapon. Zafarshan has enough yellowcake to build a dirty bomb and blow up a major U.S. city." He dropped his voice to a hush. "In the midst of the worst national security threat since September 11, who do the Democrats target? Momar Salami? Not on your life! Zafarshan? No . . . *me!* Poor little old me, someone who pastors a church and a ministry. Imagine *that!*"

He roared with laughter. "It would be funny if it were not pathetic. It should tell you all you need to know about their priorities, their worldview. Are the Senate Democrats holding the hearings on the murders at the European Union conference in Rome? No! They *ignore* the terrorists, but they are scared to *death* of evangelical Christians. If an evangelical ministry simply asks to be free from the harassment of the IRS, get on your helmets. Hire lawyers! Alert the cable news bookers! Everyone get dressed up in your best pin-striped suit for a kangaroo court!" Andy worked himself into a lather, but his producer held up his thumb and index finger, closing them together. A hard break loomed.

Andy nodded at the producer. "My friends, that's why we need the biggest turnout of freedom-loving, Constitution-defending, God-fearing patriots we've ever seen in November. Starting with Sal Stanley, we need to show this crowd the door. Now, I want you to do something. Call the Senate switchboard. Do it right now. Ask your senator if he agrees with this charade of a hearing, and don't take 'no comment' for an answer. Back after this."

The program's theme music played over the speakers in the studio. Andy pulled his headphones off his gigantic skull, smoothing his hair with the palm of his hand. Impulsively, he checked e-mail on his laptop. He spied an e-mail from Ross Lombardy. It contained only one word: "Wow." Andy chuckled.

THE WHITE HOUSE WAS INSISTENT Jay would testify for only one day. Get your pound of flesh, but get it all at once, it vowed. The committee interpreted this as a biblical "day," dragging the hearing into the night, hoping Jay would crack. But Jay held his own, crossing swords with the Democrats and hitting softballs lobbed by the Republicans. A little after 8:40 p.m., after answering questions and deflecting accusations for eleven hours with only a short break for lunch, he emerged from the Hart Building. When he appeared on the curb, a crowd numbering more than one thousand turned out by the Faith and Family Federation began to chant as if on cue.

"We love Jay! We love Jay! We love Jay!" they shouted. Many held signs of support. "Jay is Noble! Senate is NOT!" read one. "Noble, 1; Senate, 0." read another.

Jay flashed a broad grin and gave the crowd a thumbs-up before stepping into the Town Car. They roared with approval. Inside the sedan, he speed-dialed Ross Lombardy on his cell phone. Lombardy answered on the first ring. "Jay, you were terrific! Congratulations."

"Thanks, buddy. Hey, that's quite a rent-a-riot. Appreciate it, pal."

"My gift to you, friend," said Ross, suck-up juices flowing. "We bussed them in from Liberty University, Trinity University, and New Life. They chanted for ten hours. They made all the network news broadcasts."

Another call flashed on Jay's cell phone. "Hey, I got to grab this call. Say hi to Andy for me." He answered the other call.

"Jay, I have the president on the line," came the voice of the White House operator.

"Okay, put him through." He felt his heart leap.

"Jay?" came Long's voice over the line, crisp and clear, as if he were in the next room.

"Yes, Mr. President?"

"Claire and I are up in the living quarters," said Long. "We've been watching you on TV while we ate dinner. I just wanted to tell you it was a home run. You put the honorables right in their place. Very impressive."

"Thank, you, sir. I wasn't sure testifying was the right thing, but I'm now convinced it was. We had to hit back."

"One hundred percent," said Long. "You were flawless. Unflappable. We're proud of you. And listen, I've got your back. Don't let those SOBs get you down."

"Yes, sir. Thank you, sir."

"See you tomorrow."

Jay hung up the phone. A wave of emotion rushed through him. In the back of the car, cloaked behind smoked windows and bulletproof steel, he broke down and cried, his shoulders shaking with sobs, the tears falling in drops on his suit pants.

34

Ed Dowdy sat in the lobby of the W Hotel in Times Square sucking on a black Starbucks with two shots of espresso. Wrapped in a blue pin-striped suit with a blue tie and a tailored shirt with flashy gold cuff links, he looked a little like the Pillsbury doughboy dressed for a *GQ* cover shoot. He was in Manhattan to escort Jillian Ann Singer on a series of book pitch meetings to major publishers. The elevator opened and out stepped Singer, looking resplendent and ready in four-inch heels, black skirt above the knee, black spectator jacket, and a tight-fitting navy blue silk blouse. She flashed a nervous smile.

"You look great," said Dowdy effusively, bouncing to his feet.

"Really?" she asked. "My outfit's not too much?"

"Noooo," said Dowdy. "You look sexy . . . but in an understated way."

"I've been accused of a lot of things," she replied, laughing. "Understated is not one of them."

Dowdy blushed. "You look great, really."

"So do you. Love the tie!"

"Got it at the Hermes store yesterday," said Dowdy. "A hundred and eighty-five bucks! Can you believe it? For a tie."

"You'll be able to afford it if these meetings go well."

"We'll both be rich after today."

"Let's hope," she replied. She sat and crossed her legs, placing her hands on her lap. "Okay, give me my last-minute instructions."

"Just be yourself."

She frowned. "Anything but *that*!"

"No, that's what they want. Tell them what you want to accomplish with the book. Titillate them a little, but don't give it all away. You want to leave them begging for more."

"I'm good at that, honey," said Singer, dropping her voice to a husky female baritone.

"Well, there you go! You'll do great." They walked to the elevator and rode down to the motor lobby, where a Town Car waited on the curb. They were scheduled to pitch five publishers in one day. The goal: sparking a seven-figure bidding war for Singer's tell-all.

After a short drive across town, the Town Car pulled up in front of a glass and granite skyscraper, headquarters of Alex Lane Books, an imprint of Regency Publishing, which, like all publishing houses, had been swallowed up by a media conglomerate. The drive for best-sellers and fat profits took its toll on Regency's once-legendary editorial staff—all good news for Singer and her team. Bob Simms, who signed on as Singer's literary agent after a referral from Marvin Myers, met them in the cavernous lobby. He wore a stylish brown suit, his face cracking with a crooked grin, black hair flecked with gray.

They rode up the elevator together and walked into the lobby of Alex Lane Books. A tall, willowy African-American receptionist escorted them to a modern conference room with glass walls, white leather chairs, and a black granite table. A large spread of bagels, cream cheese, and fruit sat in the center of the table, along with coffee dispensers, bottled water, and pitchers of orange and grapefruit juice.

"They rolled out the red carpet," said Dowdy. "Good sign."

"Alex is a hustler," said Simms with professional detachment. "She wants this book, I assure you, if only to keep a competitor from getting it."

Dowdy grinned and tore into a raisin-cinnamon bagel slathered with cream cheese. The door opened, and in walked Alex Lane, the famously aggressive, strikingly attractive publisher who made hundreds of millions for Regency. She made a career signing offbeat books like the memoir of a professional wrestler and the heartrending story of a mother who lost three sons in the wars in Iraq and Afghanistan. She was accompanied by the house's publicist, two editors, general counsel, and a couple of eager-beaver deputies.

"Hello, Bob," she said, greeting Simms with a peck on the cheek. Trim with the figure of a professional tennis player, she wore a black leather skirt, Dior heels, and a leopard-patterned sleeveless blouse. Dowdy noticed her flawless skin, almond-shaped brown eyes, lush lashes, and feathered brown hair. *She's hot*, he thought. Everyone took a seat.

"Welcome, Jillian," said Lane, her eyes warm and inviting.

"Thank you," said Singer.

"Tell us why you want to write this book." She paused for effect. "Besides money." Everyone laughed appreciatively. The joke broke the ice.

"I want the American people to know who I am," said Singer. "I'm not a prostitute. I'm not a criminal. I want to shatter the stereotypes about bondage and domination. It's not a bunch of weirdos in dungeons spanking one another. It's about overcoming inhibitions, exploring the boundaries of convention. There's nothing dirty about it."

Lane raised an eyebrow suggestively. Her aides shifted uncomfortably in their seats. "So you're thinking of this as . . . the apologia of a dominatrix?" she asked, wrinkling her nose.

"Somewhat."

"That's not a bad title," said Simms with a grin.

Alex shook him off. "I understand that's a motive for you," she said. "But as an author, if you want this book to break through the clutter, it has to settle some scores. It should be a postfeminist manifesto about the empowerment of women. Think Gloria Steinem meets the Happy Hooker, with a sprinkling of Naomi Wolf."

Singer gave her a blank stare. Simms jumped in. "We can do that," he said eagerly.

"And sex," offered one of Lane's deputies, cocking his head suggestively.

"Sex sells," said Lane.

Singer smiled. "Don't I know it."

"That's what people will want to read about. It has to be tastefully done, of course."

"I get that. Totally."

"Can I ask a question about the writing?" asked another one of Lane's deputies, an earnest young man with tousled black hair wearing a designer watch that looked like it belonged on an astronaut. "Do you plan to write this book yourself, or will you want help?"

Jillian shot a glance at Simms. He nodded. "I'm best at telling the story," she said. "I could sit down with a writer and relate anecdotes. I'll need help organizing them in chapters." Her eyes scanned the faces of her suitors. "I've got some amazing anecdotes. Me and my girls have been with movie stars, politicians, some of the most famous CEOs in America."

The deputy nodded, his lips curled up, satisfied.

"We'll have you talk into a tape recorder for a few days, and then we'll take it from there," said Lane. "If need be, we can bring in a book doctor." She rolled her eyes. "We had one author, very famous but I won't say who, suffering from writer's block. He was coming up on the pub date and had written *nothing*. I moved into his basement for three weeks. He would come home after doing his TV show, drink scotch, and dictate while I typed away on a laptop. I slept four hours a night. It was murder, but we got the book done."

"As I recall, it sold two million copies," said one of the editors. Everyone chuckled.

"Bob," said the general counsel, jumping in. "I don't have to tell you this book could be a legal land mine. Once it gets out Jillian is writing, we're going to get cease-and-desist letters from every libel law firm in town. Have you thought about that?"

Simms leaned forward, clearly prepared for the question. "Yes. A couple of preliminary observations. First, Jillian's got the credit card information on almost all her clients, so it's going to be hard for them to deny they utilized the services of Adult Alternatives. Second, we could obtain affidavits from former employees. We may ask the publisher to share in some of that expense, which will be minimal, and could save us a lot of legal bills down the line."

"You're ready to name names?" asked Lane, her eyes boring into Singer.

"Yes," said Singer. "If the price is right."

"Good," said Lane brightly. "I knew I'd like you."

They all rose from the table shaking hands and making small talk as Simms, Dowdy, and Singer breezed through the lobby.

"Bob, we'll discuss this internally and get back to you," said Lane.

Simms nodded and hugged Lane good-bye. She shook Simms's and Dowdy's hands as they stepped onto the elevator. When the doors closed, Singer turned to Simms. "How do you think it went?"

"Home run," said Simms. "Alex loved you. My guess she'll bid in the mid-to-high six-figures. If we're lucky, maybe seven figures."

Dowdy's face broke into a wide grin. "Now we're talking," he said.

AT CIA HEADQUARTERS IN LANGLEY, William Jacobs sat behind his desk wearing a frown as he reviewed the latest top secret intelligence reports on Iran. As was usually the case, they were simultaneously encouraging and disturbing. Refined gasoline imports were cut by two-thirds by EU sanctions, creating gas shortages throughout the country. Targeted assassinations of key Republican Guard and nuclear engineers continued apace. But so did Iran's rush to the bomb.

The intercom on Jacobs's desk buzzed. It was Phil Brookings, the deputy director of the Agency and Jacobs's number two. "Bill, Zafarshan has posted a video of Daniels and Levell on a Web site he's used in the past for propaganda purposes. It'll hit the press in a matter of minutes."

"They're alive?" asked Jacobs.

"They were when the video was shot," said Brookings. "I'd like to bring some of our top analysts from the Zafarshan Task Force and watch the video together. They can give you a briefing so you can in turn brief the president."

"Good," said Jacobs. "Get up here STAT." He buzzed his assistant. "Brookings is on his way up with a group. Cancel everything else on the calendar this afternoon."

Five minutes later Brookings walked into Jacobs's spacious office, accompanied by three senior members of the Zafarshan Task Force, an interagency group headquartered at CIA that included FBI, Homeland Security, and Pentagon personnel. They sat at the large conference table by the window. Jacobs took his usual seat at the head of the table, his jacket buttoned formally, a cup of hot tea in his hand, his deep-set eyes scanning each face.

"Well, gentlemen, what have you got?" he asked.

"This video just went up on a radical Islamic Web site," said Brookings. "Rather than prejudice your response with a play-by-play commentary, let me play it. It's not very long." He picked up a remote control and turned on the sixty-inch video screen on the wall opposite the table. Also using the remote, he pulled up the Web site. The video appeared as a frozen screen. He hit "play."

The visages of Norm Daniels and Victor Levell appeared, their images grainy and slightly out of focus. They looked pale and disheveled, with a stubble of beard growth. Daniels spoke first. "We have been told by those holding us we are being held captive for the crimes of the United States against the Islamic Republic of Iran," said Daniels in a dull, flat monotone. "Specifically, they complain that the sanctions imposed by the West against the sovereign nation of Iran constitute an act of war. We have been treated kindly. But they say that if the sanctions are not lifted, we will become casualties in this war." He stared into the camera, his eyes hollow and fixed. It sent a chill down Jacobs's spine.

The camera, which appeared to be on a tripod, turned to Levell, who seemed more nervous and agitated. "We hope our government will make a good-faith effort to negotiate with our captors. We believe the best outcome of the current conflict is a settlement with the Islamic Republic that would allow us to go home and Iran to develop peaceful nuclear power." He squinted his eyes, apparently reading. "We apologize to the innocent people of Iran for the difficulties we and the U.S. government have caused. Please give our love to our families."

A man wearing a white turban and a beard stepped in front of the camera, brandishing an Iranian flag. His brown eyes were fiery, but he looked more like an accountant than a dangerous killer. He wore glasses, his cheeks hollow, his smooth skin giving him a youthful appearance.

"Who's that?" asked Jacobs.

"Rajab Ali Marjieh," said Brookings. "He's Zafarshan's top lieutenant."

"Bad guy," said one of the analysts.

Jacobs turned back to the video, where Marjieh was droning on in Farsi about the United States, the Great Satan, and its oppression of the Iranian people. One of the analysts translated.

After a few minutes Jacobs had seen enough. "Where are they?"

"They're no longer in Rome," said one of the analysts. "Our hunch, based on the clothes they're wearing, the time elapsed since their capture, and the background of the video, they're either in Zafarshan's network of caves along the Pakistani-Chinese border, or they're in a safe house in southern Waziristan, in Pakistan."

"How can we be sure?" pressed Jacobs. "They could have shot this in a warehouse in Italy, right?"

"Possible, but unlikely. We know of no case where they've recorded a video outside of their network of camps and safe houses."

"How did they get out of Italy without being detected?" asked Jacobs. "The place is crawling with agents."

"They probably got help from the inside," said Brookings. "These guys have no shortage of money from the opium trade. They probably paid someone off."

"Will they kill them?"

"Yes," said the lead analyst. "There's only one way to get them out alive and that's diplomatic pressure on Iran from another country. If Zafarshan thinks he's going to get in trouble with the regime, he might release them."

"Yes, but who?" asked Jacobs, rocking in his chair. "China? Russia?"

Brookings shook his head in disgust. "Good luck."

"What about a rescue operation?"

"We'd obviously try, assuming we can get White House authorization," replied Brookings. "But first we have to find out where they are."

"Ali Marjieh is a killer," said the lead analyst. "He's not a negotiator. They're in great danger. We don't have much time."

Jacobs let out a sigh. "Alright, thanks everybody. Keep working it. Do everything you can to find out where this video was shot and get a team in there." The analysts filed out. Brookings hung back, closing the door behind him.

"It doesn't look good," he said quietly.

"No," replied Jacobs. "The good news is they're alive. And as long as they're alive, we've got a shot." Brookings nodded.

Jacobs picked up the phone on the conference table and dialed a number. "Truman, it's Bill," he said. "I need to see the president. Zafarshan's released a video of Norm Daniels and Victor Levell. They're being held as hostages and Zafarshan is threatening to execute them both if the West doesn't lift sanctions." He paused, listening. "Yes, I can jump in a car now. Should get there in fifteen minutes."

DON JEFFERSON SAT AT THE head of the table in a private dining room at The Caucus Room, one of the more popular watering holes in DC for members of Congress and the K Street Crowd, where everyone gathered to drink too much, harden their arteries, and see and be seen. Gathered around the table were Jefferson's chief of staff, his campaign consultant, his wife Lila, and Max Stampanovich, his election-law and ethics lawyer. Stampo, as he was known, numbered Speaker of the House Gerry Jimmerson and Andy Stanton among his clients.

The timing of the meeting was urgent. Two days earlier Jefferson received a document request from the House Ethics Committee asking for e-mails between him, any member of his staff, any individual on his campaign, and any family member with his former chief of staff (a top lobbyist with PMA), employee of PMA, or any consultant or registered lobbyist hired by PMA. The Ethics Committee was not taking a backseat to Justice in the mushrooming scandal surrounding PMA, and Jefferson threatened to get sucked into its vortex.

Jefferson dug into a New York strip steak floating in its own juices, creamed spinach and sautéed mushrooms piled high on his plate. His wife ate a salmon Caesar salad. The dinner conversation alternated safely between small talk and campaign gossip until Jefferson signaled he was ready for the strategy session to begin.

"Rut-roh! Rut-roh!" Jefferson suddenly exclaimed. "Scooby Dooby Doo!"

Everyone at the table stopped eating, a few frozen in midchew. Lila shot him a look of disapproval seasoned with the experience of a veteran candidate's wife who was no stranger to her husband's occasionally juvenile outbursts.

"Well, what do we do, Stampo?" asked Jefferson, his eyes fixed on Stamponovich.

"You talking to me?" asked Stamponovich.

"Yeah, Bobby DeNiro, I'm talking to you," replied Jefferson. "I'm paying you a lot of money to keep these guys off my back while I'm running for the Senate. What's your plan?"

"I've talked to Gerry about it," said Stamponovich, who dropped the Speaker's name at every opportunity. "He says more than likely the committee will bring in an outside investigator, take several months on discovery, and take another two to four months interviewing people. He doesn't think any shoes will drop until after the first of the year."

Jefferson smiled. "I love Gerry! The guy's got gonads."

"Totally," said Stamponovich, beaming. "By then, you'll no longer be in the House, so it won't matter. The Ethics Committee has no jurisdiction at that point."

"We still have banner headlines that Don's under investigation," said Jefferson's consultant, staring morosely at his steak. "Common Cause has filed a formal complaint with the committee. Lightfoot's going to plaster television with it."

"Understood, but it's highly confidential," said Stampanovich. "Unless and until the committee staff makes a recommendation, it's locked up tight as a drum."

"The editorial boards will kill me," observed Jefferson. "Is there anything that can be done in the interim?"

Stamponovich furrowed his brow, thinking. "Well, I had a client who was running for governor when he got hit with something similar. The campaign asked three retired federal judges to review the evidence. They issued a report saying he was innocent." He shrugged. "It's a thought."

"I guess it depends on who the judge is," said Jefferson.

"Did he win?" asked the chief of staff, a brainy, pale, and wan whiz kid who ran Jefferson's life and kept the trains running on time while he campaigned.

"No," said Stamponovich.

"Great strategy, Stampo!" shouted Jefferson. "You got any other brilliant ideas from losing campaigns?"

"I'm just brainstorming," protested Stampanovich.

"You can't trust Gerry, and you can't trust the committee," said Lila, who had hung back while the others dominated the conversation. Her brown hair was pulled back behind her ears, which were studded with diamond earrings. She had feline eyes, fine features, and thin lips.

"Why do you say that?" asked Jefferson, surprised.

"Gerry's focused on holding the House. Your seat is safe. Whether you go to the Senate is no concern of his," answered Lila, her features hard, eyes fixed. "Smith has the backbone of a chocolate éclair. He won't stand up to the Democrats. He's a quiche eater. He'll throw you under the bus so fast your head will spin." Arthur Smith was the ranking Republican on the Ethics Committee.

"Wow," chuckled Jefferson. He put his hand on Lila's shoulder. "How does a woman who looks so *nice* and *petite* pack so much acid?"

Lila smiled. "Someone's got to watch your back."

"It's hard to argue with Lila," said the consultant. "Worst-case scenario they drop a staff recommendation on you two weeks before the election and we're toast."

Jefferson nodded, his wheels turning. "Well, counselor," he asked, turning to Stamponovich. "What do you think?"

"It could happen," said Stampanovich slowly. "We have some backdoor lines of communication into the committee. We can monitor it. If it looks like the process could go sideways on us, there are other options."

"Such as?"

"Resign from Congress."

Jefferson's face went slack. "You think I should consider that?"

"If we're going to get hit with a reprimand or worse, yes," said Stampanovich. "It's not my first, or even my second or third choice. But it ends the investigation."

"What's my reason for resigning? Avoiding prosecution?"

"Of course not. It's this: you need to devote your energies to campaign for the Senate, and the people of the Fifteenth District deserve a full-time congressman," said the consultant. "Make it a virtue. You don't feel comfortable serving in Congress when you're spending your time running for higher office."

"You okay with that, honey?" asked Jefferson, turning to Lila.

"I'm okay with doing what we have to do to win," she said.

Jefferson raised his wine glass. "Good answer!" he exclaimed. "That's why I married you, Lila. You're not only beautiful; you're smart!"

The table exploded in laughter. Lila gave him the bored look of a tolerant spouse. The campaign team got a big kick out of their repartee, which often resembled a Sonny and Cher routine. But resigning from Congress to avoid ethics charges was no laughing matter. All of their careers were on the line. They were staring into the abyss.

"SHOULD I CONFERENCE JILLIAN ANN in?" asked Ed Dowdy, who was in his DC office. It was going to be a tough call. He wanted moral support.

"Sure," said Bob Simms, who was on the phone from New York.

Dowdy dialed Singer's number. She answered on the second ring.

"Jillian Ann? It's Ed. I've got Bob on the line. We just got a fax from Alex Lane and wanted to give you the news."

"Okay," said Singer expectantly.

"I've got some good news and some not-so-good news," said Simms. "Alex took a pass on the book proposal. Ed can forward you her letter, but the gist is she feels there's not enough human-interest narrative; and in terms of the salacious material, the legal department fears publication could be delayed indefinitely by litigation or by the threat of litigation."

"Oh," said Singer softly, her voice disappointed. "I'm surprised. That's too bad."

"It is," said Dowdy. "Alex was clearly interested. I don't think she's just hiding behind the legal department. They have legitimate concerns about libel lawsuits, and a lot of publishers will just shy away from the legal uncertainty."

"The good news," said Simms, "is we do still have one publisher who is interested. They're not known for their big advances, but they do sell a lot of books."

"I suppose that's good. But I was hoping for an advance."

"So were we, Jillian Ann," said Dowdy. "But the publishing business just isn't what it used to be. Between the rise of Amazon, digital books, cost cutting, and consolidation, everyone's scared. Outside of big-name, established authors, it just isn't what it used to be."

"I see," said Singer.

"Anyway, we haven't given up by any stretch of the imagination," said Simms, trying to buck Singer up. "We'll keep plugging until we get you a book deal. Hang in there."

"I appreciate that," said Singer. "I'm so grateful for all you guys have done."

"Our pleasure," said Dowdy. "Just wanted to give you an update. Sorry it wasn't better, but keep your chin up. It ain't over 'til it's over."

Singer signed off and hung up. Simms and Dowdy stayed on the line.

"Well, what do you think?" asked Dowdy.

"Honestly?" replied Simms. "I don't think a New York publisher is going to touch this thing with a ten-foot pole as long as the FBI investigation is still going on. I had hoped otherwise, but Jillian Ann is radioactive. She could go to prison."

"It's too bad," said Dowdy. "Bob, I appreciate your giving it your best shot."

"Happy to do it. Sorry it didn't work out. Maybe we can revisit this once the scandal blows over."

Dowdy hung up the phone and stared into space. The big payday he imagined for himself and Singer turned out to be a mirage. Now what would they do?

35

Pat Mahoney's unmarked car pulled up outside a three-story, brick, townhouse in a nice neighborhood on the outskirts of Arlington. Mahoney noticed the lawns were well manicured, the homes were properly maintained, and school-age children rode by on bikes. It didn't feel like the scene of a crime. There were two police squad cars out front, drawing curious looks from passersby.

He opened the front door and walked on to the main floor. He scanned the room with professional detachment, seeing nothing awry, no sign of a struggle or forced entry.

An Arlington police detective peeked down the stairs from the second floor. "Are you the FBI guy?" he asked.

"That would be me," replied Mahoney.

"Come on up," said the detective. "She's up here."

Mahoney walked up the stairs and into the master bedroom. It was sparsely furnished, with a white carpet and a queen-size bed covered in a pink bedspread with matching comforter. The bed did not appear slept in. A big-screen TV was mounted on the wall. He greeted the two detectives. One of them pointed to the bathroom with his index finger.

Mahoney stepped into the bathroom. The nude body of Jillian Ann Singer dangled from the curtain rod, an electrical extension cord wrapped around her neck. Her unseeing eyes were open, her mouth slightly agape, her arms dangled at her side. Her feet were no more than four inches from the floor.

One of the detectives approached. "So she's the madam?" he asked.

"Yes," said Mahoney. He glanced around. "Assuming you have no objection, I'm going to have an FBI Crime Scene Unit come out and sweep the townhouse. I want every fiber, every fingerprint, every footprint captured."

The detective shrugged. "Suit yourself," he said. "But this looks cut-and-dried. The woman was bankrupt, and she was facing time in prison, so she killed herself."

"Maybe."

"Maybe? What do you mean?"

"Well," said Mahoney. "Is there a suicide note?"

"No."

"Don't you find that strange? She's got two grown children. Her mother is still alive, living in Florida. Don't you find it odd she didn't give them the comfort of an explanation?"

"Not everyone who kills themselves leaves a suicide note."

"No. But while about half of the men who kill themselves leave no note, two-thirds of women do. It's unusual."

"That's not enough for a murder investigation."

Mahoney's black eyes bore into the detective. "She was shopping her client list to the highest bidder," he replied. "Careers and reputations were about to go up in flames. There are some very powerful people on that list. Somebody wanted her dead."

"Okay, that's motive," said the detective. "Who's the suspect?"

"I don't know yet," said Mahoney evasively. "But when I arrived at the townhouse in Georgetown where Perry Miller was killed, all the physical evidence pointed to a dominatrix who supposedly asphyxiated him. Guess what? It turned out he was killed by a terrorist operating in a cell trained by Rassem el Zafarshan." He pulled out an unlit cigar and put it in his mouth. "Things aren't what they appear." He turned to leave.

"So what do you want us to do, G-man?" asked the detective.

"Sit tight," said Mahoney. "The crime scene unit will be here shortly. In the meantime don't touch anything."

He walked down the stairs, dialing the number to his office as he walked. He wondered if Singer cracked under the pressure of threatened prosecution, or had someone on the client list decided it could never see the light of day? He felt a twinge of guilt. He pressured her to testify before the grand jury, hoping it would lead to more information on the Zafarshan network. Now she was gone.

NEWS OF JILLIAN ANN SINGER'S death rocketed across the Internet within minutes. "MADAM OF MILLER DOMINATRIX RING COMMITS SUICIDE!" shouted Merryprankster.com. "DOM DEAD: Jillian Ann Singer, dominatrix to the powerful, whose clients included the late Senator Perry Miller, hangs self," read the news feed on FOX News. The story was catnip for cable news outlets and gossipy Web sites trafficking in rumors and the unknown.

In the denizens of DC, along K Street and on the Hill, people spoke in hushed whispers about the political implications. Did it signal the end of the threatened leaking of the client list for Adult Alternatives? Or could it mean just the opposite—the list sat in a safe deposit box, and her will stipulated it would be released upon her death? No one knew. Official Washington didn't know if Singer's ex-clients could now breathe easily or wait for the next shoe to drop.

People were still absorbing the news about Singer when another update flashed across the wires. At the E. Barrett Prettyman Federal

Courthouse, where jury deliberations in the trial of Mike Kaplan dragged into their twelfth day, the jury foreman sent a note to the judge asking for clarification of what the jury should do if it found itself deadlocked on some counts but not others. There were eleven counts for perjury, obstruction of justice, destruction of evidence, and providing misleading information to FBI agents. The judge replied pointedly, "I urge the members of the jury to make every possible and conceivable effort to reach a verdict on each count in the indictment of the defendant. Until all such efforts have been exhausted, you should continue your deliberations."

Kaplan's supporters and Stanley's bitter-enders read the jury's cry for help as a hopeful sign of a hung jury. Court reporters, on the other hand, trained their gimlet eyes on the development and saw bad news for Kaplan. It seemed likely the jury had reached a verdict on some counts. But everyone was guessing.

In the Senate majority leader's suite of offices at the Capitol, the staff pretended it was business as usual even as they surreptitiously surfed news Web sites. Sal Stanley was in hiding, huddled behind closed doors with his chief of staff and top advisors. In a running meeting interrupted by an occasional phone call, he held court, his ruddy skin freckled and lined, his graying hair combed and sprayed, his blue tailored suit and patterned red tie contrasting with a crisp, cuffed white shirt.

"Well, what does it mean?" he asked, reclining in his favorite chair, his hands clasped behind his head. "We're just reading tea leaves, aren't we?"

"Afraid so, sir," said his chief of staff. "On the other hand, after eleven days without a verdict and they send a flare to the judge. That's not good for the prosecution."

"Mmmmmmmm," grunted Stanley. "What do you think, Nathan?"

Nathan Tabor, Stanley's long-time personal attorney and stand-in consigliere, joined by conference call from New York. "Well, I'm an armchair quarterback insofar as I wasn't involved in jury selection," came his voice over the speakerphone. "But I've got to believe their focus groups helped them get one or two jurors strongly inclined to acquit. It's an educated guess, but I'd say they'll acquit him on some counts and convict on others."

Stanley frowned. "That's not particularly helpful."

"No," agreed Tabor.

"A mixed verdict is better than a conviction on all eleven counts," said Stanley's chief of staff. "He can claim partial victory and vow to appeal."

"There's precedent," said Tabor. "Oliver North, Ted Stevens, to name just two, had convictions overturned."

"They both lost Senate races," said Stanley, the worry lines in his forehead deepening. "Unless he's acquitted on all or all but one count, I'm going to drop in the polls like a rock."

"I don't disagree," said the chief of staff. "But we can claw our way back. There's still time. I'd rather have it happen now than the week before the election."

"Been there, done that," said Stanley. "DOJ indicted Mike the week before the House voted for president."

"Probably cost you the presidency," said Tabor clinically.

"No question, which is why they did it," said Stanley, rolling his eyes. "Nathan, what if it's a hung jury? Could DOJ retry the case before election day?"

"No way," said Tabor. "How many days are left before the election? No judge will let them impanel a jury and hold a trial in that amount of time."

Stanley stood up, leaning toward the phone so Tabor could hear him. "Let's hope for that outcome. A hung jury and then slug it out with Long all the way to election day. I'll be like Ulysses S. Grant during the Wilderness Campaign. Blood, guts, and mud until one side bleeds more than the other."

The chief of staff winced at the metaphor. Stanley signed off, hanging up the phone, and walked silently to the bay windows overlooking the Mall, crossing his arms across his chest, and gazed at the Washington Monument and Lincoln Memorial in the distance. In his campaign's nightly tracking poll, he trailed Cartwright by one point, with 7 percent undecided. Given his high name ID and long tenure in the Senate, the undecided were unlikely to break for him. The thought hit him: if Kaplan were convicted, he'd lose and his political career would be over.

IT WAS A LITTLE AFTER 9:00 p.m. and Jay sat at his desk in the book-lined study of his apartment at the Four Seasons, compulsively catching up on e-mail. A television built into the wall of the oak book-shelves was tuned to FOX News, the volume turned down so it was only faintly audible. The phone rang. It was Walt Shapiro, calling from the offices of his firm in LA, where he was attempting to negotiate a settlement with the attorney for Samah Panzarella.

"Well, it's been a long day," Walt said with a sigh, his voice tired. "But I think we have a deal. I wanted to call you and make sure you felt comfortable with the direction this is going before we draw up the papers."

Jay picked up the wireless receiver and stepped to the wet bar, pouring a scotch into a tumbler with no ice. "Okay. What does it look like?" He opened the door to the terrace and stepped outside, watching the lights of DC twinkle against the black. A light breeze cut through the late summer humidity.

"She started out at a million dollars," said Walt.

"*What!?* That's nuts. No way!"

"I know. I told her attorney hell would freeze over first. It's been like chipping away at granite with a toothpick, but after hours of back and forth, I got them down to $300,000."

"Three hundred grand?" he squealed. "Jeez, that has to be the most expensive date in human history."

"Actually, that was Monica Lewinksy."

"I'm sick to my stomach, Walt. Are you sure you can't get the price down?" He took a deep swig of the scotch to settle himself.

"I don't think so," replied Walt. "They're dug in. They know the election is in twenty-four days, and you can't afford the bad publicity. Believe me, they wanted a lot more."

"I've certainly got the money. But I hate to give it to *her*. What a sleazy, bottom-dweller this chick is."

"Her attorney's worse. I'm going to have to take a shower as soon as I leave here."

"Trust me, I know. The guy should be disbarred."

"Now, you want the good news?"

"Please."

"They've agreed to a joint statement in which she states you engaged in no wrongdoing and there is no evidence of paternity. And—this is the big concession from our standpoint—neither she nor her attorney can make any public comment about you or this episode beyond the joint statement, or they have to return the entire settlement amount."

"That's good. That's very helpful. But if I'm going to fork over that kind of money, she has to drop all claims of paternity, period."

"I agree, if we can get it," said Walt. "But if we buy her silence and she admits no proof, you're home free. She can't ever talk about this again, or we sue her to claw back the settlement. And we'll win."

"Yeah, Walt, but what are the odds I'll want to do that?"

"Slim and none. But she doesn't know that. We'll have a sword over her neck forever."

Jay leaned on the rail and stared into the night, his eyes narrowing as he thought through his options. "You think this is the best deal we can get?"

"I do. I think you should take it and move on with your life. You can't have this thing hanging out there, not with the IRS matter still going on. That's not over yet."

There was a long pause. "Alright, make the deal," said Jay at last. "But e-mail me the draft joint statement before you sign the papers so I can approve it."

"Will do."

Jay hung up the phone. *Three hundred thousand dollars!* It was after-tax income, so it was really closer to a half a million bucks. He felt a mixture of anger and self-pity welling up inside. He downed the scotch and hurled the empty glass against the wall, shattering it. The only consolation was Sal Stanley might be in even worse shape. If Kaplan was found guilty, Sal would be dead politically. If he wasn't, Jay had a problem, and getting the Senate would be that much harder.

36

Lisa Robinson sat in her office in the West Wing, her high heels kicked off, hosed feet on her desk, spinning one of her favored reporters at the *Washington Post.* Christine Featherstone was an up-and-comer in the DC sisterhood, with a string of page-one scoops to her credit and a commentator slot at National Public Radio and PBS. More importantly, she was not Dan Dorman. Lisa relished stabbing Dorman between the shoulder blades by leaking to other *Post* reporters. She hoped his editors would figure out he was in the journalistic equivalent of Siberia and replace him as chief White House correspondent.

"You claim the president isn't mad at Jay," said Featherstone, working her prey and betraying a colleague at the same time. "But he has to be disappointed, right? You guys are trying to make the midterm election about Sal Stanley and the Senate being a graveyard for reform, and all you read about instead is Jay's zipper and his Machiavellian machinations."

Lisa kept her guard up. She might have grown weary of Jay, but he still made her. Loyalty was the currency of the realm in Long-land. "I can't speak to private conversations between the president and Jay," she said, staying on message. "But no one in the White House believes Jay attempted to influence the IRS audit of New Life Ministries. That includes the president. And, off the record, no one believes Jay fathered Panzarella's baby."

"Why not?" pressed Featherstone.

"Which one, the IRS flap or Panzarella?"

"The LA party girl."

"Simple. She's not his type."

Featherstone let out a cackle. "Well, you would know. . . . You dated him, right?"

"Ooooh," said Lisa, drawing out the syllable. "Low blow, sistah."

"I'm just sayin'."

"Well, I'm not his type either."

"So his type is somewhere between classy, smart, tough woman and skank?"

Lisa burst out laughing. At that moment one of her deputies burst in, his body vibrating with the kinetic energy of a five-year-old. Lisa cupped her hand over the phone. "What? You look like you need to pee."

"The Kaplan verdict is in," he said, eyes wide, pupils dilated.

"Christine, did you hear?" Lisa said into the phone. "The Kaplan jury's reached a verdict."

"Wow. What is it?"

"We don't know yet. The jury is coming into the courtroom now."

"So . . . whaddayathink? Will he go to prison or walk?"

Lisa dodged Featherstone's question as if it were a grenade. "I don't know and I wouldn't want to speculate. Let's talk after we hear it." She hung up the phone and spun her chair in the direction of a bank of five television sets on the wall tuned to Fox, CNN, MSNBC, Bloomberg TV, and CNBC, the volume turned off. "Turn up the sound."

Her deputy picked up a remote and unmuted FOX. A blonde reporter stood outside the Prettyman Federal Courthouse holding a cell phone to her ear and a microphone in her hand. "We are awaiting word from inside the courtroom, where FOX News has a reporter standing by. As soon as the jury foreman makes the announcement—" She held up her finger to the camera. "Wait . . . wait!" she said excitedly. "The foreman is addressing the judge. We have a verdict."

The male anchor leaned into the camera. "What is it?"

The court reporter nodded. "I'm being told now . . . Kaplan has been acquitted on five counts, including the most serious charges of obstruction of justice. The jury was unable to reach a verdict on two counts of conspiracy. On three counts of perjury, GUILTY. On one count of lying to the FBI, GUILTY. Mike Kaplan . . . GUILTY of four counts. A shocking development here in the nation's capital that promises to make this hard-fought midterm election even more interesting and hard to predict."

Along with everyone else in the communications shop, Lisa sat in stunned silence. After two-and-a-half years, the scandal that propelled Bob Long to the Oval Office was over. Barring a successful appeal, Mike Kaplan was on his way to prison. And Sal Stanley? Well, stick a fork in him.

SAL STANLEY HAD JUST WRAPPED up a speech to the Jewish Community Center MetroWest in Whippany, a forty-minute drive from Manhattan. He delivered his usual stump speech, seasoned with a predictable recitation of pro-Israel bromides and his Jewish bona fides. A crowd of about three hundred sat in a steamy room on metal-backed chairs, arms crossed and lips pursed, looking like they were about to play bingo.

"I've talked long enough," said Stanley, slipping off his coat and handing it to his body man. He paced the floor, his eyes darting, holding a wireless microphone, one hand stuffed in his gray pants pocket, looking a little like a game show host. "Any questions? I've debated Tom Reynolds on the floor of the Senate, so there's nothing you can say that will offend me."

The crows laughed appreciatively at the barb slung at Reynolds, Stanley's chief nemesis and the most camera-hungry right-wing blowhard on Capitol Hill, which was saying a lot.

A short, wiry woman with a bubble of hair dyed fire-engine red stood up. "Senator Stanley, given the failure of the sanctions bill and Iran's threat to Israel, I hope we can count on you to support Israel if it attacks Iran's nuclear facilities. So, can we?"

"Well, you certainly didn't start off throwing softballs, did you?" joked Stanley to chuckles. "I strongly supported sanctions legislation. We *cannot* allow Iran to obtain a nuclear weapon. President Long insisted on an unconstitutional 'trigger' for military action that killed the bill." Stanley's rivalry with Long was the elephant in the room, and Stanley had so far tiptoed around it. "I say this with no animosity: elections have consequences. It was the most shameful failure of presidential leadership I've seen in my career." There, he said it! Murmurs of agreement filled the room. Then Stanley seemed to catch himself. "Now, I say all this more in sadness than anger." No one believed him.

"I hope the EU sanctions will work," said Stanley. "There are a lot of things I can't talk about because they are classified." It was a clear reference to the CIA's not-so-secret war inside Iran. "Certainly Israel is a sovereign country, and it has a right to defend itself."

A man with beady eyes and a bulbous nose stood up. Stanley vaguely recognized him as a Republican plant. A "tracker" from the New Jersey GOP stood in the back, his digital video camera trained. Stanley braced for the question.

"Senator, you've said Mike Kaplan is your best friend," the man began in a firm voice. He was instantly greeted with a chorus of hisses from the overwhelmingly Democratic crowd.

"It's alright," said Stanley, holding up his hand. "Let him ask his question."

"If Michael Kaplan is convicted of perjury and obstruction of justice, will you repudiate him and condemn his conduct?"

More boos. Stanley face turned to stone. "Let's welcome our friend from the Cartwright campaign," he said sarcastically to jeers and laughter. He pointed to the tracker. "And in the back of the room is one of Jay Noble's minions, recording this for the White House and FOX News." Stanley waved theatrically to the camera. "Everyone wave to Jay." More laughter. Then Stanley spoke in bullet points. "Mike Kaplan is innocent until proven guilty. I'm not going to prejudge the case. I testified to his character, not the evidence, which is up to the jury to decide. Mike is a good friend, but I'm not going to comment on a pending legal matter."

"I didn't ask you to comment on the case," pressed the man. "I asked you if you would condemn his criminal behavior if he is convicted."

Stanley's posture stiffened. "He hasn't been convicted," he shot back.

"Yes, he has," said the questioner. "I just got a news alert on my iPhone. He was convicted of four counts of perjury and lying to the FBI." There were audible gasps. Stanley went white. "So tell us . . . will you condemn Mike Kaplan *now*, Senator?"

Stanley struggled to answer, his lips moving, but making no audible noise. He turned to his body man. "Is there a verdict?' he asked. The body man nodded. Stanley's eyes were desperate. "If that is the case, all I can say is that I will keep Mike and his family in my thoughts and prayers. I believe an innocent man has been wrongly convicted in a case poisoned by politics from the beginning. I retain my faith in our criminal justice system, and I believe he will ultimately be cleared on appeal."

With that Stanley headed for the exit, trailed by a mob of reporters. They followed him into the parking lot where a black SUV with tinted windows waited on the curb.

"Senator, are you disappointed by the verdict?" shouted the *New York Times*.

Stanley stopped on the curb. "I've said all I have to say," he said, biting off the words. "I continue to believe Mike Kaplan is innocent. I hope he is cleared. But for me this closes a painful chapter, and I am moving on." With that the doors closed, and the SUV sped away.

"Where's he heading next?" asked the *Bergen Record*.

"Fund-raiser in the city," replied AP. "Closed press."

"We'll find him," said the *Times*. "This is one issue he can't duck."

"If he does, he's dead meat."

"He may be dead anyway," chuckled AP.

MARVIN MYERS SAT ON A television set five blocks from the Capitol. He pulled the flap of his jacket down, sitting on his buttoned coat, checked his tie, and removed a throat lozenge from his mouth. He took a sip of water from the bottle and cleared his throat. The floor director talked into a headset. "Thirty seconds," she said. "Fifteen, ten, five, four, three." She pointed at the anchor, then made eye contact with Myers, pointing her finger to Camera Two to indicate which camera he should look when speaking.

"Joining us now for reaction on the Kaplan verdict is syndicated columnist and regular contributor Marvin Myers," said the anchor, his spray-tan nearly matching a wave of brown hair that billowed from the back of his head, peaking at his forehead. "Marvin, you've covered Washington's political scene for decades. How do you think the conviction of Michael Kaplan today is likely to impact the midterm elections?"

"Actually, I'm entering my fourth decade covering politics in this town," said Myers smoothly. Like all insiders, he referred to DC simply as "this town."

"Forgive me," said the anchor deferentially.

"No offense taken." Myers turned to the camera, rattling off his points in staccato bursts. "If past is prologue, Kaplan's conviction could very well spell doom for the Democrats. Just as Watergate foreshadowed big Republican losses in 1974, Iran-Contra the loss of the Senate for the GOP in 1986, and personal scandals contributed to Republicans losing control of Congress in 2006, the Kaplan conviction could not come at a worse time. It contributes to a larger narrative about Sal Stanley and the Democrats as partisan and corrupt."

"How will this impact Sal Stanley? Is his seat now in serious jeopardy?"

"It was in jeopardy before this. Unless he can make the election about Kerry Cartwright's spending cuts, he's in real trouble. If the election is about Mike Kaplan and corruption, he's going to have a very hard time."

"Really?" queried the anchor, his eyebrows arched. He glanced at the camera. "You think it's that bad?"

"Oh, yes," said Myers. "There are only nineteen days until election day. There's not a lot of time to bounce back. Mike Kaplan was Stanley's alter ego. This is a devastating blow. One Democratic official I spoke with today said this is like Stanley having his right arm amputated without the benefit of anesthesia."

The anchor smirked. "But what about the Republicans? They have their own problems. Allegations Jay Noble interfered with an IRS audit of Andy Stanton. The ACS bribery scandal. Congressman Don Jefferson, the Republican nominee for U.S. Senate in Florida, is entangled in that investigation. Could this counter the effects of the Kaplan conviction?"

"It's possible," said Myers in a professorial tone. "Certainly the Democrats will try to make hay with it. But it lacks the proximity to

Speaker Jimmerson the Kaplan scandal has to Sal Stanley." He leaned forward, appearing to confide in the anchor, seemingly oblivious to the television audience. "My sources tell me Jefferson has been urged by the Republican leadership to resign his seat, thereby removing the threat of ethics charges."

"Really? Resign?"

"It would be a dramatic step," said Myers, chuckling. "For the record, Jefferson is denying he plans to resign."

"We'll keep an eye on that one, to be sure," replied the anchor drolly. "Final question for you Marvin. Jay Noble has settled with the California woman who sued him for paternity. How might his troubles impact the elections for the White House?"

"It's a wild card," said Myers. "But the Senate hearings on the IRS are over, and Noble acquitted himself well. The lawsuit is now behind him, so Jay is now free to focus on what he does best, namely winning elections. As one senior administration official put it to me, 'No one is indispensable around here except Long, but Jay is a close second.'"

"So you think his job is secure . . . for now?"

"Yes."

The segment wrapped and Myers unclipped the microphone, breezing through the makeup room to remove the powder from his face with a baby wipe. He headed down the elevator and was walking across the lobby to the hired car that would whisk him back to his office when his cell phone buzzed. He answered it.

"Marvin! It's the indispensable man," came the booming voice at the other end of the line.

"Jay?"

Jay let out a burst of rat-tat-tat laughter. "I'm calling to say thanks for all those nice things you just said about me on TV."

"I always look out for my best sources."

"Speaking of sources, who was that senior administration official you quoted?"

"I could tell you, but then I'd have to kill you."

"Oh, come on, you can tell *me*."

"You really want to know?"

"Yes."

"I made it up."

Jay was stunned. "But I thought everything you said was true."

"It is true," said Myers. "Let's just say it's a composite of a lot of different people."

"Oh, I get it," said Jay, laughing. "Hey, come by and we'll grab lunch in the mess."

"Sure. I'll have my girl call to schedule."

"Terrific. We need to catch up."

"Oh, one last thing."

"Yes?"

"If you want me to keep being your unpaid PR agent, you better have some nuggets for me at that lunch, and I don't mean chicken nuggets."

"Anything in particular you're on the prowl for?"

"Yes. Can you find out if Jefferson is going to resign his House seat?"

"Let me do some checking around."

"Feed the beast, Jay."

"I get it."

Myers hung up the phone and stepped into the back of the hired Town Car. Gazing at the pedestrians as he sat at a red light, he allowed himself a smile. His suck-up cable chatter had worked like a charm: Jay was going to feed him intel from the campaigns all the way until election day.

G. G. HOTERMAN GOT THE news flash on WTOP over his car radio as he pulled up to his townhouse on North Carolina Avenue a few blocks from the Capitol. The sun was beginning to slip behind the

Library of Congress, casting shadows from the trees whose leaves were beginning to turn bright yellow and orange with the onset of fall. He parked on the curb and bounded up the steps, anxious to watch the verdict live on television.

Once inside he grabbed a cold Heineken from the fridge in the kitchen and padded his way down the hall to his study, flipping on the television and settling in to his favorite leather chair. He braced himself, hoping Kaplan would beat the rap but fearing the worst. Hardly a disinterested observer, G. G. played a major role in the trial with his testimony, and his lobbying practice would take a major hit if Stanley lost his seat. Sal was his primary pipeline in the Senate for the care and feeding of his clients.

CNN assembled a panel of legal eagles to comment on the verdict. "What can you tell us?" asked the anchor expectantly of the court reporter in DC. "Does Kaplan's legal team have any insight into the jury's decision?"

"Not at this time," replied the court reporter. Someone off-camera handed her a sheaf of papers. Her expression shocked, she read from the paper on top. "We have just received the jury's verdict. It is a mixed verdict. Guilty on three counts of perjury and one count of lying to the FBI. But the good news for Kaplan, if one can call it that, is he has been acquitted on the most serious charges of obstruction of justice."

"As we are just learning the news, it may be difficult to know, but what are the political implications of this verdict for Sal Stanley and the Democrats?" asked the anchor.

"Kaplan's lawyers are already vowing to appeal," replied the reporter. "Democrats will argue this trial represented the criminalization of politics. Kaplan will claim partial vindication in the failure of the jury to find him guilty on the most serious charges. In nineteen days, we'll know whether the voters bought their argument or not."

On the set the faces of the commentators were long. Their stumbling attempts to find good news for Stanley were painful to watch. G. G. knew better. He felt as though the wind had been knocked out of him. He turned down the sound and walked back through the kitchen, turning the knob on the door and entering the courtyard in the back.

It was a crisp fall evening, and he breathed deeply. G. G. paced back and forth, the memories rushing through his mind like a motion picture: Stanley's presidential campaign, the blowup with Long in Chicago that split the party, Kaplan's indictment, his own brush with being indicted, and now this. Suddenly he began to cry. Catching him by surprise, the tears welled in his eyes and spilled down his face, burning his cheeks. His nose ran. He choked back sobs. Always the tough guy on the outside, G. G. was relieved no one could see him in this pathetic state.

He sat down at a cast-iron breakfast table and pulled out his cell phone. He hit the speed dial.

"Hello?" came the voice of his estranged wife, Edwina. They had tried to maintain a measure of civility since their separation, if only for the sake of the children.

"Hi," said G. G.

"Oh, hi."

"Did you hear the news about Mike?"

"No. What happened?"

"He was convicted on four counts of perjury and lying to the FBI."

"I sorry to hear that, but I can't say I'm surprised."

"Me, either. As Walt Shapiro said to me, there were some bad facts."

"Are you okay?" asked Edwina, concern in her voice.

"Not really," he replied, downcast. "I feel partially responsible for this whole thing. I was involved in the campaign, helped raise the money, then I testified against him. This is not going to help my business either, I'm afraid."

"You weren't responsible for what Mike did. He used you. So did Sal."

"I know. But I never wanted Mike to go to prison."

"Well, he shouldn't have lied. If he couldn't tell the truth to the grand jury, then he should have taken the Fifth. That's his fault, not yours." She paused. "You told the truth. You paid a heavy price for it, but you're not going to prison."

G. G. winced at the reference to his grand jury testimony—later leaked—in which he acknowledged a sexual relationship with Dierdre. His honesty cost him his marriage and family. He began to tear up again.

"G. G.? Are you sure you're alright?"

"No," said G. G., his voice catching. "I want to come home."

There was a long pause. "I don't know if that's possible."

"Edwina, I wouldn't blame you if you said no," said G. G. "If you want to go ahead with the divorce, I certainly have no right to object. I made a terrible mistake. But I'm willing to change. I want to come back to you."

"I know you say that now," said Edwina. "But if I take you back, you'll just go back to your old ways once the danger of losing everything is gone."

"I won't," protested G. G. "I would have at one time. But I've seen what it's like out there. It's not better."

"I won't do anything unless you agree to go to see a marriage counselor."

"Absolutely," said G. G. "I'll do whatever you want."

"Let me think about it," said Edwina softly.

"Okay. I love you."

"I love you. I just don't know if there's enough love left to sustain a marriage. I have to go. Good-bye."

G. G. hung up and sat in silence, the only noise the chirping of birds in the trees covering the courtyard with a leafy canopy. With Kaplan's conviction Stanley was toast. G. G. feared the Democrats might lose control of the Senate. If they did, Hoterman and Schiff would take a major hit. But if his business and political contacts were crumbling, G. G. thought, maybe he could still save his marriage.

It was a pleasant fall evening in New York City, the air crisp, a breeze whistling among the skyscrapers. Jay took the shuttle from DC and now sat in the back of a Town Car wrapping up a call with David Thomas, watching as couples walked arm in arm down Fifth Avenue. He wondered what their normal, happy lives were like and sometimes yearned for one himself. It had been so long, he couldn't remember what it was like.

"What are the overnights?" he asked, using the shorthand for polls. "I'm going to see our candidates in a few minutes, and I want to give them some good news if I can."

"In New Jersey, KC and the Sunshine Band was up 7. In the three-day roll, he's up 4," said Thomas, using their nickname for Kerry Cartwright. Their shorthand for his political team was "The Sunshine Band."

"That's a good trend line."

"Stanley's fav-unfav is 42–49 with a hard-name ID 96 percent," said Thomas, using pollster speak for Stanley's cratering popularity.

"Wow, he's upside down. The Kaplan conviction is killing him."

"Yeah, but it's still Jersey."

"Right. Who knows how much walking-around money Stanley will put on the street?" He paused. "What else?"

"Jefferson down 2, Hughes down 3."

"Ouch. I can't believe Covitz's husband's death and scandal hasn't hurt her."

"Incredible. There's a sympathy factor," observed Thomas. "She's up 7 among women over fifty. She's a widow and a woman in distress. They identify with her."

"What keeps you up at night?"

"Florida. Jefferson's going sideways, the ACS scandal is hurting with indies," said Thomas. "Birch could help him, but of course he won't lift a finger."

"Don's bleeding from every artery," said Jay. "Pedal to the metal, pal. Keep the gas on."

"Yes, sir."

The car pulled up to the curb in front of the $28 million Fifth Avenue apartment, home for Fred Fincher, the hedge fund billionaire hosting the blow-out fund-raising for Cartwright, Holly Hughes, and Jefferson. Jay was the headliner. The driver hustled to the passenger side and opened the car door. Jay stepped out on the sidewalk. Heads turned as pedestrians recognized him. A campaign staffer stood on the sidewalk with a clipboard. She motioned him to an elevator in the lobby.

The elevator opened, and Jay stepped into the foyer of Fincher's apartment, beautifully appointed with marble floors, priceless antique furniture, Oriental rugs, and a massive shimmering crystal chandelier. Fincher was an avid collector of modern art; the paintings on the walls, gave the apartment the feel of a museum. Waiters floated through the room balancing silver trays of champagne, white wine, and sparkling water. Two open bars anchored the main living area, which was already jammed with more than two hundred donors.

Jay approached the registration table. "Jay!" exclaimed Angelica Manning, who handled all Fincher's political projects. Jay did a double take. She was distractingly beautiful. Stiletto heels and black patterned hose adorned her long legs, and her jet-black hair fell to her bare shoulders. Rumor had it that she and Fincher were an item, which Jay assumed was more than a minor complication, since he was married.

"Hey, gorgeous," said Jay, embracing her. "Talk to me. What's the take?"

"It's 1.9 million," said Angelica, beaming.

"You're the best."

"So I'm told," said Angelica, batting her eyes. "Ready for your victory lap?"

"Take me to your Kasbah, baby," said Jay flirtatiously, holding out his arm. "By the way, what victory lap? We haven't won yet." As a waiter hustled by, he grabbed a sparkling water with lime.

"Who are you kidding, boyfriend? You're a rock star." Angelica curled her arm through his and led him into the living area. The crowd broke into spontaneous applause and surged forward. "See?"

Jay braced himself as a short, balding man wearing designer glasses approached. "Jay, you *killed* at the Senate Finance Committee hearings," said the man, his Chablis-and-brie breath nearly knocking Jay out.

"Thank you," he said. Someone tapped him on the shoulder. He spun around to see a man he vaguely recognized as a former senator. He was struck by how much the man had aged.

"Jay, do you remember me?" asked the senator-turned-lobbyist.

"Of course," Jay lied. "How do you stay in such great shape?"

"I work out. I can use the Senate gym as a former senator." He smiled. "I also got remarried . . . to a thirty-two-year-old."

Jay laughed. "That'll keep you young. Now I know your secret."

People were thrilled Jay survived his combat with the press, the Democrats, and the floozy in LA. . . . What was her name again? Who cared? . . . Her fifteen minutes were up, just the latest in a string of tabloid tarts throwing darts at their hero. Jay's rendezvous with power had only begun. He was back in the cockpit for the closing weeks of the election. He was brilliant, a master strategist, a genius, really—and he was theirs!

"Fred!" shouted Angelica over the crowd. "Jay's here."

Fincher sauntered over, a one-hundred-watt smile plastered on. Tall and lanky with a boyish demeanor belying his seventy-six years, his blue eyes fairly sparkled. "The man of the hour," he exclaimed. "Boy, have they ever been gunning for you."

"I hadn't noticed," deadpanned Jay.

"Baloney! Sal Stanley, Aaron Hayward, the *New York Times, Time,* NBC News . . ."

"Fred, what did Winston Churchill say?" asked Jay, baring his teeth. "There's nothing more exhilarating than to be shot at without effect."

Fincher shook his head. He turned to Angelica. "See why I love this guy?" He draped an arm over Jay's shoulder. "He's got brass gonads. I love it!"

"Alright," said Angelica. "Enough male bonding. Let's get the program underway."

Kerry Cartwright lumbered over from across the room, sweat beading on his forehead, his suit rumpled. "Hey!" he said, pointing at Jay with his index finger. "You're the one who talked me into this campaign. I oughta slug you."

Jay grinned sheepishly. "Actually, it was the president who talked you into it."

"That was only because you put him up to it."

"Guilty as charged. You can thank me later, Senator."

"Whoa! Hold on just a minute. I'm not a senator yet."

"You will be in fifteen days," replied Jay. He leaned into Cartwright. "You're up 7 in our tracking, pal. Stanley's unfav is 49. He's in a tailspin, both engines blown."

Cartwright cupped his hand and stage-whispered, "Thank God for Dele-gate, huh?"

"Tell me about it!" roared Jay. They both laughed. "My guy's in the White House because of it, and you're on your way to the U.S. Senate."

Angelica grabbed Cartwright and Jay and hustled them to the front of the room, where they stood beside a massive marble fireplace with a Kandinsky hanging over the hearth. Heidi Hughes and Don Jefferson joined them. They all hugged and air-kissed as Fincher banged a fork against a champagne glass.

"Thank you all for coming," said Fincher as the crowd hushed. "When the White House asked if I would be willing to host a fund-raiser for not one, not two, but three"—he held up three fingers—"future United States senators, I foolishly agreed." The crowd, lubricated with wine and champagne, laughed and clapped. "Then they told me Jay Noble was coming. That's when I knew this was really important." (More laughter.)

"Anyway, Jay needs no introduction. He is the senior advisor to President Long and has been his chief political strategist since he ran for governor of California. Please welcome the most brilliant political mind in America, our friend, Jay Noble."

Jay walked to the front of the fireplace wearing a sheepish grin as the crowd applauded loudly. "Thank you, everybody," he said, raising his hands to quiet them. He turned to Fincher. "Fred, next time you host a fund-raiser, could you do it some place a little more uptown?" (Laughter.) "I mean, come on!"

"I would have used my yacht," volleyed back Fincher. "But it's in Nova Scotia."

"Likely story," joked Jay as he folded his hands in front of him. "It's great to get outside the Beltway and be with real people, if I can call you that." (More laughter.) "Seriously, we are two weeks and one day from one of the most important midterm elections of our lifetimes. The issue is whether a Senate poisoned by partisanship and corruption will be able to block every reform measure this president puts forward, or whether we're going to have a Senate that serves the American people." He glanced in the direction of Hughes, Cartwright, and Jefferson. "These candidates are among the finest public servants in the country today. They are taking on some pretty tough customers. I've gone toe-to-toe with Kate Covitz and Sal Stanley, and it isn't pleasant." The crowd nodded knowingly. "Politics ain't beanbag. These are all close, hard-fought races. With your help they will change more than just the arithmetic of the Senate. They will qualitatively change a dysfunctional chamber in desperate need of new blood."

Jay stabbed the air with his index finger for emphasis. "The president and I are deeply grateful for your support. Make no mistake. These three races will determine control of the U.S. Senate." He turned to Angelica. "If we win two of these three seats, we'll control the Senate. I think we're going to do better than that. I think we're going to win all three." He raised his right hand in a friendly wave. "Thank you again."

One by one, the candidates gave abbreviated versions of their stump speech. The donors listened respectfully, but their eyes glazed over. Grizzled and cynical by years of writing checks, they had heard it all before. When Jefferson wrapped up his remarks, people began to head for the exits, Jay included. He had to catch the last shuttle back to DC.

"Jay?" came a voice behind him. He turned to see Don Jefferson barreling down on him like a lynx.

"Congressman!"

"Can I talk to you . . . in private?"

"Sure. Step into my office." Jay led the way onto the apartment's huge terrace, which offered a breathtaking view of Central Park. The two men stepped into the corner to keep from being overheard, huddling in a power clutch. "What's up?"

"I need to tell you something in confidence," said Jefferson, his face somber.

"Sure. Fire away."

"I'm resigning my congressional seat tomorrow."

Jay maintained a poker face. "Are you sure you need to do that so close to the election?"

"The Ethics Committee is demanding I agree to an admonishment for bringing dishonor on the House," said Jefferson, his eyes piercing. "If I do that, my campaign is finished."

"I see," said Jay, absorbing the blow. "If that's the case, there aren't a lot of good options. You gotta do what you gotta do."

"One other thing," said Jefferson, moving in closer, their bodies nearly touching. "I'd like the president to come down for me the weekend before the election. This race is going to be close. It could make the difference."

"We haven't made a final decision yet on the last week of his travel," said Jay noncommittally. "Where would you want him?"

"Jacksonville and Orlando."

"Both places?" asked Jay, incredulous.

"You want me to win, right?"

Jay laughed. "Yeah, but I don't know if I can put Air Force One on two tarmacs in Florida when we also have to go to California for Heidi."

"Do what you can," asked Jefferson, his voice pleading.

"If we can, we will," said Jay. "We're with you all the way."

"I'm sorry about this ACS nonsense," said Jefferson.

"Don't worry about it," said Jay dismissively. "If it wasn't this, it'd be something else. It's the price of doing business, pal."

With that Jay breezed through the foyer on his way to the elevator, hugging necks and grabbing shoulders as he moved. He was the portrait of confidence. But inside his stomach was churning. If the ACS scandal took out Jefferson and Covitz benefited from an outpouring of sympathy over her husband's suicide, they'd miss control of the Senate by one seat.

MARVIN MYERS BELLIED UP TO the bar at a right-wing confab at Charlie Palmer's, the DC steak joint and inside-the-Beltway watering hole. Everyone was walking on pins and needles, mainlining *Real Clear Politics, Politico,* and other Web sites for the latest polls and gossip emanating from the key House and Senate races.

A top Republican leadership aide sidled up next to Myers and ordered a double vodka on the rocks. He was all forehead and cheeks with a flattened nose, as if someone hit him with a frying pan. Myers recognized him as an occasional source. "How's it look out there on the House front?" he asked.

The aide took a swig of vodka as he pondered the question. "*Comme ci, comme ca.* It's plus or minus 5 right now. There's plenty of blood in the water but not many seats in play."

Myers nodded.

"Our problem right now is some of our own guys won't man up."

"What do you mean?"

"Follow me," said the aide. "This is confidential." They maneuvered their way through the crowd, walking out on a patio overlooking Constitution Avenue and leaning against the rail. "I had lunch today with a good friend of mine who used to be on staff at Energy and Commerce. He's now the lead counsel for the Ethics Committee."

Myers nodded.

"He said the Don Jefferson case is about to blow sky high. They've got e-mails proving his former chief of staff violated the lobbying and gift bans. If Don doesn't agree to an admonishment by the House, there's going to be a trial."

"I'd heard it wasn't going well for Jefferson. Is it the Rs or the Ds on the committee?"

"Both," said the aide, grimacing. "That's my point. We're two weeks from a midterm with the House and Senate on the line, and we're shooting our own guys on the battlefield. This could cost us the Senate. It's nuts!"

"The timing is atrocious."

"Do you think the Democrats would do something this stupid?" asked the source, his face twisted with anger, vodka breath belching forth.

"Probably not."

The aide polished off his vodka. "Don't burn me on this one, Marvin."

"Oh, don't worry. I could have gotten this anywhere." The source disappeared into the crowd. Myers glanced around to make sure no one overheard the conversation. He decided it was time to make his exit. The party was a dud anyway. Now that he had a scoop, he needed to start working the phones to see who could confirm Jefferson's impending ethics charges.

38

Secretary of Defense Jock Healey walked to the podium in the Pentagon briefing room, trailed by grim-faced aides. At his side was the chief of naval operations, a jug-headed admiral with a shock of black hair who commanded an aircraft-carrier group during the second Gulf War and was known for a near-theological belief in naval superiority. He wore dress blues and spit-shined shoes, a rack of ribbons on his chest. The press was alerted there would be a big announcement.

"After extensive consultation with the president, the Joint Chiefs, and NATO allies, we are beginning a series of measures designed to enhance our military presence in the Persian Gulf," said Healey, eyes narrowing to slits, jaw jutted, a five-o'clock shadow evident on his face. Reporters cocked their heads and craned their necks as if responding to the call of a dog whistle.

"Today I have ordered the USS *Harry S. Truman* and the USS *Ronald Reagan* from the Arabian Sea and the Mediterranean to the Gulf," Healey continued in an even voice. "They will participate in previously scheduled training maneuvers. Each carrier group includes three guided missile destroyers and a frigate. They have a combined total of thirteen thousand sailors and marines. We are dispatching the additional carrier groups in anticipation of responsibilities flowing from recent developments related to the Iranian regime, including the need to protect our allies and to keep these vital waterways open and free for commerce and trade."

The room exploded with shouted questions. "Secretary Healey, is this a direct response to Momar Salami's threat to close the Strait of Hormuz?" asked NBC News.

"I would not call it a *direct* response," replied Healey, gripping the lectern, glowering. "We are aware of President Salami's intemperate remarks on a wide range of topics. But this action is broader in nature. We have many vital security interests in the region. In the event we need to protect those interests, it's much easier if our forces are in the area."

"What will the United States do if Iran closes the Straits?" asked FOX News. "Is it prepared to take military action?"

"That's a decision we will make at the time," said Healey, his face expressionless. "Suffice it to say, we have made clear our intention to keep them open."

"Including force if necessary."

The chief of naval operations stepped forward. Healey stepped to the side, happy to share the spotlight with his naval Top Gun. "Each of these aircraft carriers has eighty-five fixed-wing aircraft, including the F-18 Super Hornets and the F-35 Joint Strike Fighter wings. Each guided missile destroyer in the carrier group can launch five guided missiles at a target." He bobbed his chin for emphasis. "We will have sufficient firepower to carry out whatever military or other objectives we are given by the president and Secretary Healey. Of that I am totally and completely confident." The reporters scribbled furiously.

"How soon will the aircraft carriers be in the Gulf?" asked the *Wall Street Journal.*

Healey stepped back to the microphone. "They're traveling a relatively short distance, from the Arabian Sea and the Med," he replied. "Two days at the most. The training maneuvers will take place this week."

"How long will they stay?"

"As long as the situation requires it," said Healey, stone-faced.

Within minutes the press reported the USS *Harry S. Truman* and USS *Ronald Reagan* were steaming to the Gulf, armed to the teeth, ready to use force against Iran to keep the Strait of Hormuz open. Cable news networks had a field day, displaying maps of the region (with Iran highlighted in blood red) and showing stock footage of navy fighters catapulting off carrier decks. The usual retired generals and admirals did a bum's rush to television sets to predict the outcome of a conflict as war clouds threatened. Political commentators, meanwhile, wondered what the impact of Long's October surprise would have on the elections, now only twelve days out. Democrats smelled politics. But they were helpless to do anything about it.

DON JEFFERSON'S CAMPAIGN BLAST E-MAILED his resignation letter to the media shortly after noon. His advisors batted around the idea of a news conference but ultimately decided not to subject their candidate to hostile questions. Better to let the letter speak for itself.

"Dear Governor Birch," the letter began officiously. "It has been my great privilege and honor to represent the people of Florida's Fifteenth Congressional District for six terms in the House of Representatives. Over these years I have worked to rein in out-of-control federal spending, reduce taxes on small businesses, grow our economy and create jobs, and ensure a national defense posture second to none." Shifting gears, the brief letter offered an apologia of Jefferson's decision to leave the House. "Because of the rigorous demands of a statewide campaign for U.S. Senate, I am no longer able to devote my energies to my few remaining congressional duties and believe it is best to pass the baton to my successor. In order to give Florida the advantage of seniority in the next Congress, I hereby resign from the House of Representatives, effective at noon tomorrow. I respectfully ask that you fill this vacancy by appointing the person chosen by the voters of the Fifteenth District to represent them in Washington."

The looming ethics charges were conspicuous by their absence in the statement and news release. When a reporter for the *St. Petersburg Times*, perturbed at being robbed of the chance to interrogate Jefferson at a news conference, asked if the Ethics Committee's pending charges played any role in his resignation, a Jefferson spokesman said without hint of irony, "For Congressman Jefferson, this had nothing to do with politics. This was about giving the people of Florida an effective voice in Congress by ensuring his successor has the greatest seniority of any new member elected this year."

Newspaper editorials rained down on Jefferson, demanding either he or the Ethics Committee release its findings before the voters went to the polls. Such goo-goo protestations were all for naught. The Ethics Committee had no authority over Jefferson as a former member, but the voters still did. How they would react was anyone's guess.

KATE COVITZ SAT IN THE conference room of the *Los Angeles Times* wearing a pensive expression on her face. The room was filled to overflowing with editors and reporters who crowded around the table and sat in chairs lining the wall. Covitz had an entourage as well: her longtime personal attorney, tax accountant, press secretary, and campaign manager. The stakes were high. With ten days left before the election, the largest newspaper in the state had yet to issue an endorsement in the Senate race. A tape recorder lay in the middle of the table, and Covitz occasionally eyed it as if it were ticking bomb. The editors announced their intention to post the entire audiotape and transcript on the *LA Times* Web site.

"Let me start at the beginning," said Covitz. She spoke haltingly and slowly, as though trying to avoid making a mistake. "When my husband started working as a developer twenty-five years ago, I helped with the books. I was treasurer of the company. Over time, as his business grew, it became more than I could handle, with the children, managing the house, and my other responsibilities. When I was elected to Congress, I backed out of the picture even more. But I continued to sign documents when asked."

"So even though you remained legally an officer—"

"Allow me to finish, if I may, and I promise I'll take questions for as long as you want," said Covitz firmly. "When I signed the various trust documents, I was told by the attorneys it was for purposes of estate planning. I had no knowledge tax avoidance was a factor beyond the obvious, which was to establish nontaxable trusts for our children and grandchildren. That was my only role in the trusts. I had no involvement in my husband's other businesses for the past fifteen years, and I was surprised when I learned of their financial condition. With that I'm happy to take any questions."

"So you were not aware the trusts were designed to evade income taxes?" asked a reporter at the end of the table.

"No. Estate taxes, yes, as allowed by federal law. I did not know my husband's attorneys were using those same trusts to avoid income taxes," said Covitz. "I did what any other person would do under similar circumstances. We hired lawyers and accountants and I told them to err on the side of making sure I paid my fair share of taxes. Period."

"How do you respond to critics who ask how you can make tax policy for the taxpayers of California and the nation if you were ignorant of your own personal taxes for so long?" asked one of the editors.

Covitz visibly flinched. "I would say there are many spouses in California who sign tax returns and rely on their accountants to make sure they are fully complying with the law."

"But the IRS and SEC both say you didn't comply with the law."

"That is a legal matter between the trusts and the IRS," said Covitz. "I have instructed my attorneys to make every effort to settle this matter as expeditiously as possible and pay every dime we owe under the law."

The editor arched his eyebrows. Faces fell in shock. "You mean you're prepared to pay $40 million in back taxes and penalties?"

Covitz's attorney jumped in. "The senator has inherited this situation as the sole beneficiary of her husband's estate. I can't get into a specific dollar amounts, but we are making every effort to reach a settlement. Without speaking for the IRS, let me just say they are open to reaching an amicable and mutually acceptable arrangement." He smiled tightly.

"Do you feel betrayed by your husband?" asked a smart-aleck reporter with a disheveled look and brillo-pad hair. Covitz knew him as one of her tormentors at the paper.

"No, not at all. We had a wonderful life together. Frank was a loving husband and father. He was in an impossible real estate market and tried desperately to turn it around," said Covitz, keeping her game face on. "When he couldn't, he was overwhelmed by a sense of failure and did not feel he could go on. I do not feel he let me down, but I wish he had confided in me, and I will always wonder why he didn't."

Covitz answered questions for nearly two hours, occasionally helped by her attorney or the accountant. It was a virtuoso if slightly stilted performance, showing grace under pressure and toughness. When the grueling session was over, once they were safely out of earshot in the parking garage, Covitz turned to her press secretary.

"Well, what do you think?" she asked.

"I think it begins the process of putting it behind us. The editorial page editor told me after today they'll likely either endorse you or stay neutral. They can't stand Hughes."

"Do you think hating Hughes will be enough?" asked Covitz.

"It better be. It's going to have to be."

They piled into a black Chevy Suburban and headed out of the parking garage, turning right on Sepulveda and heading for the next stop, a speech to college Democrats at Occidental College. Covitz yearned for the *Times'* endorsement. If she didn't get it, she wasn't sure she would win.

KERRY CARTWRIGHT LUMBERED FROM HIS pew and walked up the steps to the pulpit of the Ebenezer Baptist Church in Newark, a portrait of political humble pie. The pastor, Bishop Eugene Sheets III, a cherub-faced man with blindingly white teeth, was a fierce advocate of education reform and school choice who battled the teachers unions and Democrats in Trenton for years. Now he was doing what he could to help Cartwright in the African-American community. He put his arm around Cartwright's ample waist and pulled him close in a hug of great symbolism.

"Our guv-a-nah doesn't just talk the talk; he walks the walk," said Sheets, his brow glistening with sweat. He picked up a folded white handkerchief from the pulpit and wiped his brow. "We thank Ga-awd for him!"

"Amen," the congregation replied in unison.

"He has been there for our community through thick and thin," Sheets exclaimed. "He offers a hand up, not a hand out."

"Hallelujah!"

"Those who tried to keep black folk down used to stand in the schoolhouse door to keep us out," shouted Sheets, his voice rising to a raspy shriek. "Well, we got in. But today they stand in the doorway of crime-ridden, drug-infested, gang-plagued school houses where children can't read and write and try to keep us in!"

"Preach it!"

"We're tired of second-class citizenship. We're tired of the wealthy folk in the rich suburbs sending their children to the good schools while other young people—and let's tell the truth, Hispanic and black children—are left behind. We're tired of the powerful special interests taking precedence over the most precious resource in our community . . . our children!"

"Amen!"

Sheets dropped his voice to a whisper. "Governor Cartwright is our brother. He is my friend, he is your friend, and I believe by God's grace, he is going to be the next United States Senator from New Jersey. Give him a warm Ebeneezer Baptist welcome."

Cartwright held a microphone in his hand and bowed his head modestly as the entire congregation stood to its feet and applauded. After everyone took their seats, he cracked, "I have nothing further to add, pastor." Everyone laughed.

"As I see it, education is the ultimate civil rights issue," said Cartwright, his standard talking point when addressing minority audiences.

"Amen!"

"If our children can't read and write, then they can't get a good-paying job, and without a good job and economic empowerment, what good is the vote?" The approving murmurs of the crowd lapped over him like waves of affirmation. "The reason you want the vote is to be able to get better schools, good jobs, and opportunity!"

"Hallelujah!"

Cartwright gripped the pulpit with his free hand as though steadying himself. "This isn't about white or black, Republican or Democrat, rich or poor, liberal or conservative," he said, now on a roll. "It's about right and wrong. It's *wrong* to force children in New Jersey to stay in a school that is not safe and where they cannot learn." The crowd broke into loud applause. "If you send me to Washington, I'll deliver that message to the nation's capital and every corner of this nation." He held his hand in the air as though delivering a benediction. "May God bless you and the great state of New Jersey."

Bishop Sheets jumped from his thronelike chair on the stage and wrapped Cartwright in a manly hug, his sweaty face leaving a smear of perspiration on his cheek. He then grabbed him by the shoulders and pulled him close, whispering something in his ear. Cartwright laughed and waved once more to the crowd, bounding down from the stage in a jog and heading for the exit, shaking hands on either side as he walked up the center aisle.

A New Jersey state trooper stood at attention in the parking lot, holding the rear door open. Cartwright removed his coat and slid in. Bill Spadea, his political strategist, joined him the back.

"That guy's a stud," said Cartwright to no one in particular.

"Big time," said Spadea. "I don't think we'll get a lot of votes out of Newark, but all we have to do is hold down Sal's vote. Every vote we get out of here comes right out of Stanley's hide." He flashed a wicked smile. "And this is playing major head games with Sal."

"I hear you, Kemo Sabe." Shifting subjects, Cartwright asked: "We gave Sheets a grant, right?"

"Absotively. Thirty-five grand from the Department of Faith-Based and Community Affairs."

"What was it for?"

"He's got an after-school program for latchkey kids. It's won some national awards. Clean as a whistle, boss."

"Good. And what about the other money? We took care of him, didn't we?"

"One of our donors gave a hundred grand to Children First, his school choice group. He earmarked 50K of that for the ground game. But you don't know anything about that."

Cartwright chuckled. "Is a 50 percent commission the going rate?"

"Whatever works, right?"

Cartwright shook his head. "As long as he stays bought."

The trooper deftly guided the car on to the freeway. It was not yet 11:30 a.m. and Cartwright had two more church services to hit.

39

A retired Florida State University professor was puttering around in his backyard when he heard the buzz overhead of a small plane. Looking into the overcast sky, he could hear the engine but couldn't see the plane through the clouds. Then he heard a popping noise, like a gun going off, followed by the roar of a plane's engine. The man glanced up at the sky again, just in time to see a small aircraft hurtling toward the ground in a death dive, its nose pointing downward. The plane was no more than four football fields away. He lost it behind the tree line but heard the sickening noise of impact. He ran inside to call 911.

AT A HOLIDAY INN AROUND the corner from the state Capitol in Tallahassee, a group of business leaders waited patiently for the arrival of Dolph Lightfoot. There were 150 people in attendance at the monthly networking lunch, a frequent stopover for candidates. When the entrees were served and Lightfoot was still not there, organizers put it off to the vicissitudes of a busy campaign schedule. But once waiters began to put desserts on tables, they began to get nervous. Where was their speaker? Efforts were made to contact Lightfoot's advance staff to no avail. Finally someone heard back from the campaign, and the news was shocking.

"Could I have your attention, please," said the business group's chairman, his face pale. Table conversation came to a stop, and the ballroom fell silent. "I'm afraid I don't have good news. I am sorry to report that the airplane carrying Dolph Lightfoot to Tallahassee has apparently been involved in an accident." There were audible gasps. "I don't have any further information, and we do not want to speculate beyond what we know. We are in touch with his campaign, and we will give you more information as we receive it. Please keep former Governor Lightfoot and the others who were on the plane in your prayers. Thank you."

He left the podium hurriedly as slack-jawed businessmen and women stared at one another in disbelief. Several devout Christians gathered in a corner and held hands, murmuring in prayer. Others drifted out of the room, some talking on cell phones.

Within minutes Florida news organizations reported Lightfoot's King Air had gone down in bad weather after clipping a cell phone tower. In the fog of confusion, there were conflicting reports about whether anyone survived. The initial footage of the crash scene didn't look good, but the hospital where the passengers were taken refused to release any information.

Then, at 1:41 p.m., forty-five minutes after the first reports that the plane went down, the Lightfoot campaign issued a statement. "We regret to announce that Dolph Lightfoot, his forty-two-year-old son Bill, his pilot, and a campaign aide died this morning when the plane carrying them to a campaign event in Tallahassee crashed. We ask all Floridians to pray for the Lightfoot family and the families of the other victims. We are devastated by this loss of one of Florida's towering giants and finest public servants."

A U.S. Senate race that began with Perry Miller's murder had now been turned upside down by the untimely death of his successor. With only nine days to go before the election, tens of thousands of Florida voters had already cast their ballot for a dead man in early voting. A campaign birthed in tragedy became even more bizarre and potentially unpredictable.

"ARE YOU WATCHING TV?" ASKED David Thomas, who was in his office in the Eisenhower Executive Office Building across the alley from the White House.

"Yeah," replied Jay. "I didn't have much use for Lightfoot, but this is terrible." He was in a holding room at a Marriott, two blocks from John Wayne Airport in Orange County, California. The president was about to do a campaign rally with Heidi Hughes.

Thomas studied the aerial footage of the crash site, which was airing constantly on cable news. Lightfoot's King Air looked like a bird with broken wings, its charred fuselage broken into three pieces. A black mark in the grass marked the point of impact.

"The poor guy never had a prayer," said Thomas.

"What happened?"

"They're reporting the pilot tried to land in the rain with a low cloud ceiling. He flew right into a cell phone tower. That was all she wrote."

"Good, Lord. What an idiot."

"It's criminal. So what happens now?"

"I don't know," said Jay. "We need to find out. Does Birch appoint someone to fill out the rest of the Miller/Lightfoot term? Can Lightfoot's campaign committee choose a stand-in, like his wife? I assume the votes already cast for him don't count."

"It's a mess," said Thomas. "I'll get answers."

"We also need to release a statement from POTUS. Better yet, he should make some remarks of condolence when he speaks at this rally for Hughes."

"If he doesn't, the press will smoke us."

"I'll work something up."

"I'll get on the horn with Jefferson's folks and get my arms around whether they can replace Lightfoot on the ballot or not."

"Good," said Jay, his voice somber. "I know it's hard to focus on politics at a time like this, but we've got a Senate race to win."

"Roger that."

Jay hung up his cell phone and stared at the television. He felt a slight tug of guilt. Part of him was glad Lightfoot was gone—it made it easier for Jefferson to win. Another part of him repulsed at having to make political calculations when a man, his son, and two others were dead. But he had no choice.

"HEIDI! HEIDI! HEIDI!"

A crowd of four thousand screaming campaign volunteers and grassroots activists jammed into the ballroom of the Marriott, chanting at the top of their lungs. They waved green "Heidi for Senate" signs and snapped photos with flip cameras. Hughes stood at the podium bearing the presidential seal, flashing a relaxed smile and exuding confidence. She wore a form-fitting orange sleeveless top that drew the eye like a neon tangerine against her sun-kissed shoulders and wave of brown hair. Long stood directly behind her wearing a bemused expression.

"I don't want to hold you from our featured speaker," said Hughes. She was under strict orders from the White House to hold her introduction of the president to under two minutes. In the West Wing they called this the "Underwood rule" after U.S. Senate candidate Josh

Underwood of New Hampshire, who froze at the stick and blathered for fifteen minutes before finally calling the president to the podium. After that, the word went out: two-minute intro or you die.

"I have such great admiration for this man," she said, oozing sincerity. "He is one of the greatest leaders California has ever produced—which is saying a lot because it includes men like Ronald Reagan." (Applause.) "When he ran for president as an independent, Bob Long put his country ahead of his party, principle ahead of ambition, and he is leading our nation with courage and clarity. Please welcome the president of the United States, Bob Long!"

Long gave Hughes an affectionate hug and stepped to the podium, his steely blue eyes sparkling, flashing his best "aw shucks" smile.

"Six more years! Six more years!"

Long let out a theatrical chuckle at the chant, his shoulders gyrating. "Not yet," he said, holding up his hands. The crowd quieted down. "I'll tell you who we want to have six more years is Heidi Hughes in the U.S. Senate." The crowd cheered lustily. "She's the reason we're here." He paused for effect. "We can talk about me later. What's that old Toby Keith song . . . 'I Wanna Talk about Me'?" Everyone laughed.

"Really, it's great to be home," said Long, warming to the moment. He stared at the back of the room, where a riser held bloggers, print reporters, and forty television cameras. "We're now just days from a really important election, so I'm doing a little politicking around the country." (Applause.) "Being with you and Heidi here in Orange County is a particular pleasure for me." He leaned on one elbow on the podium, his posture relaxed. "You see, I know Heidi well. She was the minority leader in the state senate when I was governor." He twisted his lips into a comic smirk. "That was back before I got religion. I was still a Democrat." (Laughter.) "I got to know this woman well. I saw what she was made of, and I'm here to tell you she is a person of character, smart as a whip, with a backbone of solid steel; and she will do California proud in the U.S. Senate." The crowd erupted into loud cheers and applause.

"Heidi! Heidi! Heidi!"

Long kept his eyes down, his facial expression serious. The chants died. "We're going to need her because the Senate suffered a great loss today. Senator Dolph Lightfoot of Florida, a good man and an outstanding legislator, lost his life earlier today in a tragic accident." The crowd fell silent. "Earlier today I spoke with Mrs. Lightfoot, who also lost a son, and offered Claire's and my sympathy as she mourns her loss. The Lightfoot family is in our thoughts and our prayers at this very difficult hour, and we ask for God's comfort as they grieve." The crowd offered applause muted by the gravity of the remarks.

On that solemn note Long cut his remarks short, delivering a truncated version of his stump speech about jobs, health care, terrorism, and Iran. The entire time Hughes stood like a creamsicle mannequin, her hands clasped in front of her, facial expression frozen in a gaze of sycophantic admiration. She knew her pollster had her down by one point. But she was confident Long's appearance in Orange County, along with a later stop in her home turf of San Diego, would put her in the lead. The question was: could she hold that lead until election day?

DON JEFFERSON WAS IN A holding room at a Sheraton convention hotel in Kissimmee, a stone's throw from Disney World, when news flashed that Dolph Lightfoot's plane had gone down. He was scheduled to speak to a local Republican women's club—the GOP women had been the shock troops of his campaign. Not knowing whether his opponent was dead or alive, he delivered emotional, abbreviated remarks, worked the room, and left before the media arrived. Now he sat in a suite in the hotel, on a strategy conference call with his shell-shocked campaign team. Joining him in the room were his campaign manager and body man. Everyone else was at headquarters. A corned beef sandwich sat on a paper plate in front of him, untouched.

"Congressman, have you heard the latest on the crash?" asked his press secretary.

"No. I was downstairs. What's the latest?"

"AP is reporting both Lightfoot and his son are dead. No word on anyone else. But I don't see how anybody could survive. Someone caught a few seconds of the plane on a video camera. It dropped out of the sky like a rock."

Jefferson sat silently. His campaign manager scrolled through his BlackBerry in search of more updates. "What do we do now?" asked Jefferson. "It's a very delicate situation."

"I think we flood the zone," said his campaign manager, who had a Rasputin-like hold over Jefferson's fragile psyche.

"Meaning what?" asked Jefferson.

"Take every interview you can, local as well as national, and express deep remorse and sympathy for the Lightfoot family, and say you are praying for his loved ones. Refuse to answer any political questions at all," said the manager.

"I'd be a little more careful," said Jefferson's consultant over the speakerphone. "You don't want to look like you're grandstanding."

"If I'm mugging for the cameras, it'll backfire," said Jefferson firmly.

"What? It's the opposite!" shrieked his campaign manager, his voice rising to the rough audible level. "A former governor is dead. You've got to hang black crepe. This isn't about politics. This is about a human tragedy. If you don't express sympathy, *that* will look cold and calculated."

Jefferson looked torn. "What do you think, Melissa?" he asked his press secretary.

"I've already got a stack of press calls," she replied. "My concern is if you don't get out there, the Democrats can soak up the earned media. Then they get the independents who were with Lightfoot, not us."

Jefferson frowned. "We can't do everything. But we can do some on a selective basis, a mix of national and local."

"Guess who's on hold?" asked the press secretary.

"Who?"

"*Meet the Press.* They want you Sunday."

"Holy smoke. That could be big."

"If you take that and knock it out of the park, it'll be over," said his campaign manager.

"Ask who else they're booking," said Jefferson. "And tell them if we do it at all, it's one-on-one in the first segment. No panels. Not if I'm there primarily to talk about the grief of our state."

"Got it."

"Alright, let's talk about the politics of this, awkward as that is," said Jefferson. "Can Lightfoot's campaign put someone else on the ballot? Max, are you on the line?"

"I'm here," said Max Stampanovich, Jefferson's legal counsel. "The short answer is yes, they can. Even though he was running as an independent, Lightfoot's campaign committee is technically a third party. The official name is the Florida Independent Party. Their executive committee can meet and select a new nominee."

"Who's on that committee?" asked the campaign manager.

"We're pulling those names now," said Stampanovich.

"What about the early votes he's already gotten?" asked Jefferson.

"They're invalid," said Stampanovich.

"How many do we think that is?"

"There were 652,000 early votes through yesterday," said Jefferson's campaign manager, who had a mind like a computer. "Assuming his share was consistent with where he was polling, it would have been 250,000 votes."

"Wow," exclaimed Jefferson. "That's a lot."

"Under the law those voters can go back to the county board of elections and request a replacement ballot through election day," said Stampanovich.

"Really?" said Jefferson. "I never knew that."

"Yes. But they must show up in person. My guess is most of them won't. So Lightfoot's replacement, if there is one, will be down one hundred thousand votes the day they get in."

"So, what's our best guess?" asked Jefferson. "Will they do it? Lightfoot's executive committee, I mean."

His campaign manager shrugged. "I don't know. But strategically we should assume they do. Even worse, we should assume it's his widow. That's what the Democrats did in Missouri in 2000 when Mel Carnahan's plane went down."

"Actually, they nominated no one," corrected Stampanovich. "But the new governor announced he would appoint Carnahan's widow if the voters elected Carnahan, which they then did. So John Ashcroft lost to a dead man."

"I'm not sure that will play the same here," said Jefferson. "But whatever they decide, we should assume Marie runs in his place." He shook his head. "How crazy would it be if I lost to her?"

"We're not going to let it happen," said his campaign manager with bravado. "That's why we flood the zone. You want to soak up as much earned media as you can, look senatorial, show a lot of gravitas."

"You convinced me," said Jefferson, rising from his chair. The rest of the campaign team occasionally took to calling the campaign manager Geppetto behind his back. "But nothing today. The state is traumatized. People are in shock. Nothing until tomorrow."

"I'll start calling back the stations and networks and report back with a game plan," said the press secretary.

Jefferson signed off and reached for the corned beef sandwich. He was suddenly hungry. *What a crazy campaign,* he thought. At the beginning he was given no chance, then he was leading, then he was written off when Lightfoot bolted the party, then he was leading again, then he was dead because of the ACS scandal. Now he was alive again. If he was a cat with nine lives, he pondered, how many did he have left?

40

Bob Long sat in the small anteroom off the Oval Office, eyes locked on the television screen, straining to hear every word. Joining him were Charlie Hector, Truman Greenglass, and Lisa Robinson. They were watching live coverage of Momar Salami ranting before the Iranian parliament in Tehran.

"The imperialist empire of the United States, completely under the spell of the Zionist entity and Jews in the American media, thinks it is the boss of the entire world," said the English translator in a calm, measured voice. It was a stark contrast to the image of Salami in a brown suit, white shirt, and no tie, cutting the air with a clenched fist, his eyes aflame. "Does every nation in the world have a right to a nuclear energy except Iran? We are signatory to the nonproliferation treaty. Israel is not. Is that a problem for the U.S.? No!" Salami preened for the cameras, even as the mullahs seated behind listened impassively.

"We will not allow America to dictate the destiny of our civilization," Salami shouted, his face flushed. "I have ordered our military commanders to take steps to stop commerce with the U.S. and its hirelings from flowing through Iranian waters."

Long arched his eyebrows. "Well, there it is. He's closing the Strait."

There was silence for a moment as the gravity of the situation sunk in. Greenglass spoke up. "We should get Jock and the Chiefs on the phone to assess options."

"Tell them to come to the Situation Room," said Long. "If I take military action, I want to look them in the eye. Charlie, I assume we can do that before the end of the day?"

"Yes, sir," said Hector.

"Should we alert the media you're meeting with the national security team?" asked Lisa.

Long frowned. "No. I don't want to play cowboy. Or show my hand just yet. We've been clear in saying we will keep the Straits open." He stood up. "Our actions will speak for themselves when we're good and ready."

"Yes, sir," said Lisa.

The phone on the end table rang. Hector walked over and picked it up. He turned to Long. "It's Dart," he said, referring to Bryan Dart, the secretary of the Treasury.

"Put him through," said Long. Hector handed him the phone. He listened intently, grunting occasionally. "Thanks, Bryan. Keep me posted." He hung up.

"What did he want?" asked Hector.

"He said west Texas crude has already shot up to over $60 a barrel," said Long. "Bryan says it could go to $85, maybe higher."

"That's $5.00 a gallon gasoline," said Greenglass.

"That's why Salami's doing it," said Long. "Oh, and Bryan also said the Dow's down three hundred points already."

"That's the market's reacting to a possible war with Iran," said Greenglass.

"That didn't take long," said Hector.

"Nope," said Long. "Fasten your seat belts, everybody. We're in for quite a ride."

Everyone filed out. Long gazed at the television, deep in thought. Lines at the pump and skyrocketing gas prices could cost him control of the Senate and the House, both of which were on the bubble. And it wasn't just Congress that hung in the balance. Unless the U.S. military reopened the Strait of Hormuz, the U.S. economy—not to mention Europe—would be on the brink of recession. Forty percent of the world's oil passed through the narrow passageway of Hormuz. Cutting off the world's oil supply would send the entire global economy into a tailspin.

MARIE LIGHTFOOT STEPPED IN FRONT of a bank of microphones at her late husband's campaign headquarters in Miami, surrounded by beaming supporters who held up yard signs bearing the words, "Marie Lightfoot for U.S. Senate." The ink on the signs had barely dried.

Lightfoot seemed strangely composed and confident for someone still absorbing the news of the death of her husband and eldest son. Her demure mouth and high cheekbones suggested a feminine softness, while steely blue eyes revealed inner resolve. She wore a proper black dress at the knees with black pumps. Her trim figure and black hair with light brown highlights to hide the gray made her look younger than her sixty-two years.

"I have never had political ambitions, and this campaign is not about me," said Lightfoot, her voice filled with pathos. The emotion filling the room was palpable. "This is about the things my husband stood for throughout his career and devoted his life to advancing. It is about the people of Florida." She glanced down at her notes, collecting her thoughts. "The more I thought about it, the more I realized the only thing worse than losing Dolph was allowing the things he believed in to perish with him. I can't let that happen. So with a heart still heavy with his loss but inspired by his example and determined to finish the work he began, today I announce my candidacy for the United States Senate."

The supporters waved their signs and cheered and applauded. Still cameras flashed to capture the image.

"We want Marie! We want Marie!"

"I look forward to carrying on Dolph's work in Washington," said Lightfoot, seeming to gain her footing as she talked. "Should I be fortunate enough to be elected to the U.S. Senate, I will work hard to grow the economy, bring about a new era of fiscal responsibility while preserving our solemn commitment to our children and seniors, especially in the areas of education, Medicare, and Social Security." She raised her finger to the *click* and *whir* of camera shutters. "I am not running to be a placeholder. I am running to be an advocate for Florida. I may be a grandmother, but I haven't forgotten how to clean up a mess. Washington is a mess, and it needs a grandmother to clean it up."

More cheers and applause all lapped up by a press corps hungry for the narrative of the widow slipping on the brass knuckles to honor her husband's memory. The election was only five days away. With Marie Lightfoot's entrance, the campaign took another bizarre turn into the unknown.

KATE COVITZ STOOD IN THE foyer of a large home in Beverly Hills, surrounded by a crowd of about two hundred women. The women drank Chablis and sparkling water and nibbled on sushi appetizers. Emily's List endorsed Covitz and bundled individual contributions totaling over $500,000 to her campaign. It was all about the money now. Covitz and Hughes blanketed the state with a blizzard of television and radio ads. The campaign invited the media to the event, which stood to the side, video cameras, microphones, and steno pads poised. They wanted to highlight Hughes's antiabortion views and boost Covitz's support among women. No one saw coming what happened next.

Covitz, in a pastel blue pantsuit with heels and a white blouse, wielded a handheld microphone in both hands. Her buttoned coat pinched her waist, her make-up was flawless, her hair coiffed. But her eyes were tired, with dark circles, and her crow's feet showed.

"Thank you all for coming," she said into the mike. "It's become a cliché, but I truly believe next Tuesday is the most important election of my lifetime. And not just because my name is on the ballot." She pivoted on her heels, chin thrust forward. "Arrayed on one side are forces that want to take us backward. Back to a time when women's rights were not part of the agenda, when women could not control their own bodies. On the other side is a future based on freedom of choice, economic opportunity, and caring for the least among us. In the end this is not about me and my opponent. It's about California. It's about America."

Someone started to applaud and others joined in. Covitz nodded in acknowledgment. "Now I don't want to make this personal with either my opponent or the president," she said. The mention of Bob Long's name elicited scattered hisses and moans. "I worked well with the president when he was governor of California. He was pro-choice then, you may recall. Apparently he changed his mind." The room laughed knowingly. "Everyone has a right to change their opinion. But when it comes to something like the Constitution, people are looking for consistency and character. When it comes to reproductive rights, I have never wavered, and I never will as long as I am in the U.S. Senate."

The room broke into loud and sustained applause. Covitz glanced at her aides, tapped her watch, and raised her eyebrows to signal she wanted to take questions. "The staff is going to give me the hook here in a minute because I have to get to another event," she said. "But I'll be happy to answer or dodge any question you might have for me."

Several hands shot up. Covitz pointed to a middle-aged, demure woman in a chocolate business suit that matched her brown eyes. A staff member handed her a microphone. "Senator, there seems to be a double standard for women in politics. Women are asked different questions, they are held to a different standard, and they are forced to deal with things in a campaign male candidates are not. I wonder how you deal with it?"

Covitz leaned forward slightly, her eyes focused. "There is a double standard," she said, her voice soft and vulnerable. "I've never complained about it. It's a price I'm willing to pay for women who cannot run themselves but need a voice." Her eyes locked on the questioner. "It's been hard not only for me but for my family." Her eyes began to well and her voice cracked. "It's hardest on my children. They didn't sign up for this. They don't like seeing their mother attacked." She paused, choking back tears, patting her heart. The media contingent snapped to attention, sensing a possible meltdown. "But I keep going. And you know what keeps me going? The knowledge that as tough as it is on me, it's tougher on so many other women who live paycheck to paycheck, who work two jobs, who take care of their children or parents, often without the benefit of anyone to assist or support them, and they never, ever get any credit for it. I have lived their life. I know what it means. I want to fight for *them*. And with your help I will continue to do so."

"We love you, Kate!" shouted someone in the back of the room.

"Thank you," she said as the room broke into loud applause. "I love you, too."

Several reporters hustled out of the room to tweet the audio of Covitz's emotional answer, which would soon run on every television station in the state and every news network in the country. Her allies praised her for showing her softer, personal side, while critics accused her of making a final play for a sympathy vote. Covitz's emotional display would dominate the airwaves and the blogs for two days. Would it help or hurt her? No one knew.

The following day the *Los Angeles Times,* which broke several front-page stories about her husband's financial troubles, weighed in with its endorsement at last. "We have made no attempt to disguise our disfavor for the business practices of Senator Covitz's late husband. But we never viewed his misdeeds as grounds to disqualify her," the editorial stated. "While Mrs. Covitz was an officer of her husband's companies for a time, there is no evidence she had knowledge of or participated in any attempt to evade income taxes. Indeed, her attorneys have announced plans to settle with the IRS. Senator Covitz has accomplished too much for the people of California to remove her now, especially when the alternative is someone with little to recommend her except her fidelity to an extremist agenda and her unquestioning loyalty to Bob Long."

It was a backhanded compliment, but it was the endorsement Covitz needed. Her media consultants dropped her existing closing TV ad in LA and replaced it with a spot built around the *Times* endorsement.

ANDY STANTON'S G-5 DESCENDED INTO Pensacola as the sun set over Florida's panhandle, the lodestone of social conservative voters in the Sunshine State. The sun hung low over the Gulf in the distance, its rays of orange and red dappling the seemingly endless expanse of pine trees. Andy looked out his window, gazing at the beauty, and felt the adrenalin kick in. It was Sunday night before the election, and the Faith and Family Federation was turning out the pro-family vote for Don Jefferson. The plane taxied to a stop and the ladder lowered to the tarmac. Andy, Ross Lombardy, and the rest of his entourage loaded into a line of black Cadillac Escalades, which whisked them the short distance from the airport to their destination, Calvary Chapel, the largest evangelical megachurch in the panhandle, with more than six thousand members.

When the motorcade arrived, Stanton ducked into a holding room, its door guarded by security. The room echoed with the sounds of hymns being sung in the packed sanctuary. Even through the walls Andy's party could make out the familiar words.

"In my life, Lord, be glorified! Be glorified!" sang the congregation.

Andy sucked on a throat lozenge and downed a bottle of water, hydrating for his speech. "When do we go?" he asked. He was getting antsy.

"We hold here for five minutes," said Ross, tapping his watch.

"But I want to go *now*. I want to join the praise and worship," said Andy plaintively.

"The pastor doesn't want to distract the congregation." Ross shrugged. "Andy, you're the featured speaker at the biggest church in the panhandle two days before the election. Please humor me!"

Andy laughed. He glanced at his body man. "He's got an answer for everything."

The door opened a crack. It was one of the associate pastors. "Dr. Stanton, we're ready."

They filed out of the holding room and walked down a carpeted hallway, then stepped through a side door into a darkened wing off the main stage. The pastor was leading the congregation in prayer. From the shadows a female figure appeared. Andy recognized the woman instantly as Twinkle Starr (her real name), a female country singing sensation of yesteryear whose career had since faded. At one time she sold millions of records and packed concert arenas throughout the country.

"Pastor Stanton, I'm Twinkle Starr. It's an honor to meet you," she said. She wore a form-fitting, sequined gold top, skinny jeans embroidered with matching gold thread, and black cowboy boots with gold-tipped toes.

"I know who you are, and the honor is mine," Andy gushed, his eyes drinking her in. "I've been a big fan of yours for years!" He was struck by how tiny she was in person and how artificial her appearance, with fiery red hair, large eyes, and china-doll makeup. "One of my wife's favorite songs is 'Well-Behaved Women Ain't Never Made History.'"

Starr smiled, revealing gleaming white teeth. "That was a good one for me."

"I'm surprised to meet you here. What are you doing here?"

"I'm good friends with Don Jefferson through my first cousin, who lives in Florida," Starr replied. "So I'm singing here tonight and then performing on Don's fly-around tomorrow."

"Good for you! God bless you, sister." He leaned over, whispering in her ear. "I think we're going to win."

"Me, too." She hugged him, then she and Andy posed for some quick photos. Other members of Andy's entourage lined up for pictures as well.

A voice came out of the semidarkness. "Dr. Stanton, this is your cue."

Andy snapped to attention in time to hear the pastor say, "Please welcome one of the most influential men in America today, an advisor to presidents, a pastor, a broadcaster, and, most importantly, a man who preaches the gospel in season and out of season, when it's popular or unpopular, ladies and gentlemen, Dr. Andy Stanton!"

Andy bounded up on the stage as the crowd rose to their feet in a standing ovation. He hugged the pastor and stepped to the pulpit, soaking in their love. In the back of the sanctuary, there were several cameras on sticks, including FOX News, CNN, and ABC. Andy made a mental note to himself: *don't say anything stupid.*

"Thank you, thank you, God bless you!" He raised his hands, signaling for the congregation to sit down. "What a privilege to occupy the pulpit, if only for an evening, of one of the greatest churches not only in the Florida panhandle but in America. And what a joy to share this evening with my good friend and your pastor, one of the finest pastors of any church in the country today. You are truly blessed to have this man." He pointed at the pastor as the congregation broke into appreciative applause. The pastor nodded and smiled.

"Brothers and sisters, in thirty-six hours the American people will go to the polls," said Andy, his hands gripping the edges of the pulpit, his face a portrait of earnest zeal. "Actually, here in Florida you've already started voting. But before we cast our final ballots, we need to pray."

"Amen!" shouted several voices.

"We need to pray for forgiveness. Before we point the finger at the liberals, the radicals, and secularists, if we want to know how our country got into such dire straits, we need to look in the mirror." The crowd murmured in assent. "*We* allowed this to happen. *We* failed to be the watchmen on the wall. *We* cowered in the comfort of our stained-glass ghetto while our cities were on fire and families disintegrated and marriages broke up and our children were swept up by drugs and crime. It is we who must repent, brothers and sisters."

A smattering of applause rippled through the sanctuary. Andy was just warming up.

"After we humble ourselves, we must pray for God to forgive us and heal our land," said Andy, now on a roll, stepping to one side of the pulpit. "We need modern-day Esthers and Nehemiahs who will stand up and rebuild the walls of our society, which have been broken and violated because of our disobedience and failure to honor God." The applause built to a full-throated cheering. People began to rise to their feet and raise their hands to the heavens. "Now is the hour of decision! We must fall to our knees and rededicate ourselves to restoring ourselves, our homes, and our country to dependence upon Almighty God through Jesus Christ, the strong Son, our Savior and Redeemer!"

"Amen! Hallelujah!"

In the back of the sanctuary, Ross stood in the shadows studying Andy and the congregation like the seasoned political operative he was. He knew from the Federation's nightly polling that Marie Lightfoot was closing fast. Would she overtake Jefferson in the closing hours? He feared the worst.

Ross turned to one of his harried staff members, who parachuted into the state for the final two weeks. "How many volunteers do we have knocking on doors here?"

"Four thousand, most of them deployed in the panhandle and along the I-4 corridor. Half of those are being paid. At fifty doors knocked per day per volunteer, that's four hundred thousand doors in the final weekend."

"I sure hope it's enough."

"We've done all we can. Now it's in the hands of the Lord."

"That's what worries me," said Ross.

41

A black Town Car carrying Sal Stanley and his wife pulled up in front of an elementary school in a light drizzle. Stanley stepped into the rain without an overcoat, wearing a charcoal suit and a light blue tie. His reddish-gray hair perfectly combed, a pocket square flawlessly folded, his pasty face looking like a marathon runner at the finish line, he wore a forced smile. Mrs. Stanley walked beside him, her weathered face wrinkled, her hand covered with age spots and blue veins and curled over his arm.

Stanley entered the school through a side door as photographers snapped away. He approached the table where poll workers issued cards for the voting machines. He signed the voter register, took his ballot, and walked to a voting booth, pulling the curtain.

A few minutes later he emerged from behind the curtain, flashing an awkward smile as the camera flashes exploded. He stepped out on to the sidewalk to hold an impromptu election-day news conference.

"How do you feel, Senator?" asked AP.

"I feel good," said Stanley in a hollow voice. "It's been a hard-fought campaign. I believe I made a strong case to the people of New Jersey." *Click-click, whir-whir, flash.* "Now it's in their hands. They've never let me down before. I don't think they will now."

"Did Mike Kaplan's conviction hurt you politically?" asked ABC News.

Stanley stiffened. "That's for others to decide. I think the campaign will be decided on the issues, and I expect to win." He paused. "This is my tenth time on the ballot in New Jersey, and I've never lost. I don't intend to start now." His eyes began to well with tears. His lower lip trembled. A tear trickled down his left cheek and he pulled the handkerchief out of his pocket and wiped his eyes, slightly regaining his composure.

"You seem emotional," said CNN, sticking the knife in. "Is it because this could be the last time your name is on the ballot?"

Stanley's eyes shot darts. "I expect to be on the ballot and in the U.S. Senate for many years to come. And I expect to be majority leader when the new Senate organizes in January." He lowered himself into the Town Car. The car pulled away and he was gone.

The stakeout over, the press drifted to their own cars and vans in the parking lot. They had their money shot: a tearful Sal Stanley overcome by emotion on the day that might mark the end of his storied political career. How great was that!

MARVIN MYERS'S ASSISTANT BROUGHT A UPS package into his office and set it on his desk. "I thought you might want to open it yourself," she said. "It's from Ed Dowdy."

"Jillian Ann Singer's lawyer?"

"Yes."

Curiosity piqued, Myers stared at the overnight package. A book proposal, perhaps? No one would want it with Singer dead. He tore open the package and pulled out a two-inch thick stack of papers, his eyes scanning the contents. When he realized what it was holding in his hands, he nearly fell out of his chair. Dowdy sent him the complete client list for Adult Alternatives, complete with names, credit card numbers, cell phone numbers, and supporting documentation. He tried to breathe but felt no air reach his lungs.

A simple act of self-interested faux generosity, helping Singer obtain a literary agent, nabbed him one of the biggest scoops of his career. When his eye paused at a name on the third page of the stack, he wanted to jump on his desk and do a victory dance.

"Hold my calls for the rest of the afternoon," he said into the intercom to his assistant.

KERRY CARTWRIGHT HUNKERED DOWN AT Drumthwacket (Scottish for "wooded hill"), the Governor's Mansion in Princeton. He sat in his study nursing a sore throat with a cup of herbal tea laced with honey. On his laptop he pecked away at what he hoped was a victory speech.

The phone rang. The butler entered the room. "Governor, Jay Noble from the White House is on the line, sir."

Cartwright picked up the phone. "Jay?" he asked.

"Governor, I just left the Oval and the president wanted me to check in with you," said Jay smoothly. "How's it going up there?"

"We feel good," said Cartwright guardedly. "No guarantees, but it all looks good."

"We're going to have a big night tonight, and it wouldn't have happened without you stepping up to the plate," said Jay. "I wanted to call and say thanks. The president and I are going to be watching the returns from New Jersey with a great deal of interest."

Cartwright felt warm fuzzies passing through his body. "I was happy to do it," he said in a raspy voice. "And I'm glad I did it, regardless of what happens."

"Well, it's going to be a good night. For whatever it's worth, we think you're going to win."

"Just remember . . . it is New Jersey," joked Cartwright. "You know, where dead people vote and Jimmy Hoffa disappeared?"

Jay laughed. "This time the good guys are going to win."

"We left it all on the field, brother, that's for sure." He shifted gears. "What about Florida? What are you hearing?"

"It's going to be close, but Don should win," said Jay. "Lightfoot's widow may win on election day, but she's lost too much ground in the early vote and absentees."

"What about the House?"

"It's on the bubble, but Gerry and his guys should hang on by five to seven seats," said Jay, his voice like melted butter. "Anyway, we'll wait until the votes come in. The president will call you later."

"I look forward to it."

"We're happy for you and for New Jersey. Have fun tonight."

Cartwright hung up the phone and looked out over the manicured grounds of the Governor's Mansion. If he got lucky, he was going to be only the third person in history to defeat a sitting Senate majority leader. And when Long's presidency was over, he might be running for president himself. Cartwright took a sip of herbal tea and allowed himself a smile.

Jay hung up the phone and turned around to see Lisa standing in the doorway, her face etched with terror. "What's going on?" he asked. "You look like you've seen a ghost."

SHE CLOSED THE DOOR AND sat down across from his desk. "I just got a call from Marvin Myers."

Jay knew that wasn't good. "What does he want?"

"He says he's got proof Whitehead was a client of Adult Alternatives."

Jay leaned back in his chair and let out a pained sigh. "I was afraid this might happen." He spun around to face her. "It's true."

"What?" Her facial expression was complete shock. "Is this some kind of joke?"

"I wish. Johnny told the president shortly after Perry Miller was murdered."

"Why didn't anyone tell me?" asked Lisa, her eyes aflame.

"The president told me and Charlie. He wanted a lid on it. We were hoping it wouldn't break."

"That's ridiculous. Something like this always comes out."

"Lisa, the president was adamant. He wanted to try to protect Johnny. He wouldn't let us get in front of the story." He shrugged. "It is what it is."

"Well, now what? Needless to say, Myers will post something on his Web site within the hour, whether we confirm it or not."

Jay looked at his watch. "Can you get him to hold it until the polls close?"

"I doubt it."

"We have to. Make it happen. Offer him an exclusive with Whitehead. Heck, offer him the president. We can't have this break until the polls are closed on the West Coast."

"And what if he agrees?"

"Whitehead gives Marvin a statement saying he made an error in judgment, it was years ago, he's reconciled with his wife, he's forgiven, yaddah, yaddah, yaddah," said Jay.

"That's it?"

"That's it."

Lisa gulped. "So . . . does Whitehead stay on the ticket?"

"That's above my pay grade," said Jay. "Just freeze Marvin for a few hours. We can deal with the fallout later. If we're lucky, it's a speed bump, and we can get through it."

Lisa rose from her chair, slightly dazed, and headed down the hall to the vice president's West Wing office. She thought Jay was delusional. This wasn't a speed bump; it was a multi-car crash. She wasn't looking forward to facing Whitehead. And if she couldn't persuade Myers to hold his scoop until after the polls closed on the West Coast, Hughes would lose in California and they would lose the Senate in the process.

IT WAS JUST AFTER 8:00 P.M., and Ken Klucowski hunched over a laptop in the count room at the Gaylord Hotel in Orlando staring at the county-by-county vote returns on the secretary of state Web site. Klukowski was worried. Jefferson was holding his own along the vote-rich I-4 corridor, but his margin in the panhandle counties was not what he hoped for. If Lightfoot swamped them in Birch's home turf of Pinellas and Hillsborough Counties (Tampa and St. Petersburg), along with her expected lopsided victories in Dade and Broward, they would lose in a cliffhanger.

Jefferson was climbing the walls, calling his cell phone constantly. Klukowski ignored his calls. The truth was he didn't have anything to tell him.

One of the propeller-heads on the campaign bounded over, studying his BlackBerry like a talisman.

"What?" barked Klukowski.

"I've got some potentially good news," said the staffer.

"I need some. Feed me."

"You know how we're up only 942 votes up in Bay County?"

"Yeah. That can't be right."

"It's not. I just found out that total doesn't include early votes or absentees."

"Now we're on to something. What do those look like?" asked Klukowski.

"According to our county chair up there, we won 62 percent of the early vote. But all the votes cast before Friday for Lightfoot were thrown out. So apparently it's going to be closer to 75 percent." The staffer's eyes widened. "We're talking four thousand more total votes."

"Good. We're going to need them." Klukowski's cell phone rang again. It was Jefferson. Klukowski decided to answer it. "Hello, Congressman," he said abruptly.

"What's going on?" asked Jefferson. "The numbers on the television don't look good."

"They're going off AP," said Klukowski. "We're looking directly at the secretary of state's Web site."

"What does it look like?"

"It's going to be close. It'll be a long night. The good news is they haven't accounted for all the early Lightfoot votes that are going to be thrown out."

"What do you think?" pressed Jefferson.

"We've got a shot. If Marie hadn't gotten in, it was over. But now we're in a fight."

"I assume you've got the lawyers on full alert?"

"Are you kidding?" said Klukowski, laughing. "I've got attorneys pre-positioned in every county in the state. We're ready to file injunctions tonight in federal court if it comes to that."

"Good. Keep me posted."

Klukowski fixed his gaze on the laptop screen and refreshed the secretary of state Web site. He kept a close eye on Duval County, which was Jacksonville. They had a good ground game there. He hoped it was enough.

THE PRESIDENT WAS IN THE residence on the second floor, monitoring the returns on television as they flowed in from around the country. Claire drifted in and out of the room, occasionally pausing to watch the talking heads. Jay stood in the corner of the room, speaking in hushed tones on his cell phone.

The phone rang in the living quarters. Jay cupped his cell phone with one hand and answered the hard line with the other. It was his assistant.

"I've got Bill Spadea on the phone calling from New Jersey," she said. "Do you want to take it?"

"Yes. Put him through."

Spadea came on the line. "Jay, the governor's going to win, and it looks like it won't even be close. It's five points now, but with most of Bergen County still out, we may hit seven. And we're going to pick up the congressional seats in the Sixth and the Eighth Districts, too."

"That's fantastic, Bill. Congratulations."

"Who is that?" asked Long, overhearing the conversation.

"Bill Spadea with Cartwright," Jay whispered. "They're going to win, and they're picking up two House seats."

Long motioned for the phone. "Bill, I've got someone who wants to talk to you," said Jay. He handed the phone to the president.

"Bill, you've done a great job," said Long enthusiastically. "Well done."

"Thank you, sir," said Spadea, his knees going weak. The leader of the free world was thanking *him!* "I'm just glad we could deliver one of the two seats we need to gain control of the Senate. It was an honor. Beating Stanley was icing on the cake."

"It's huge," said Long, pumped. "You guys did a fantastic job."

"Is Don Jefferson going to make it?" asked Spadea. He was talking shop with the president of the United States!

"We don't know, but we think so," said Long. "It's close."

"I sure hope he hangs on."

"So do we, but it may go to a recount." Long handed the phone back to Jay.

"Bill, don't wait for Stanley to concede. Have the governor declare victory," he instructed. "We need the momentum for Hughes in California and the House seats on the West Coast."

"Will do," said Spadea. "I'll get the governor downstairs ASAP."

Jay hung up the phone and turned to the president. "Well, it took two years, but we got him," he said matter-of-factly. For Long and Jay, it was sweet revenge. Stanley stole the Democratic presidential nomination from them and was a thorn in Long's side ever since. Now he was finished.

Long seemed conflicted that the end had finally come. "I'll give him this: he was an able adversary. The word *quit* was not in his vocabulary."

Claire walked into the room just as the networks cut to Kerry Cartwright walking on stage. Red, white, and blue balloons fell from the ceiling, the crowd punching them into the air with their fists as "I've Got a Feeling" by the Black Eyed Peas blared from loudspeakers.

"I've got a feeling that tonight's gonna be a good night!" the crowd sang along.

"Did Sal lose already?" asked Claire.

"Yes, ma'am," said Jay. "He's toast."

"Serves him right," said Claire, her voice withering. "He is positively the most evil person I've ever met in my life. Oh, thank *goodness* he lost."

The phone rang again. Jay answered it. "What?" he asked. "Why?" He paused listening. "I'll call him right now." He hung up.

"Who was that?" asked Long.

"Lisa," said Jay, his face white. "She's been trying to get Marvin Myers to hold the story about Johnny until the polls are closed on the West Coast. He says he's got all he needs, and he's going to post it on his Web site in the next ten minutes."

"Oh, no," said Claire.

"Call Myers," said Long. "See if you can stop him."

"What if he wants to talk to you?" asked Jay. "He's knows I'm with you."

Long scrunched up his face. "Tell him I'm otherwise occupied."

"Alright," said Jay. He stepped into the kitchen, the semidarkness partially illuminated by a fluorescent light over the sink. He dialed Myers's cell phone. He answered on the first ring.

"Marvin, it's Jay," he said, barely pausing. "Listen, I know what you've got, but the veep isn't going to have a statement tonight. We're focused on the elections. If you hold off until first thing tomorrow morning, I'll give you Johnny exclusively."

"I can't do that, Jay," said Myers, brushing off the offer. "I don't know who else has the documents. I've got the story and I'm posting it. It'll be on my Web site and the *Washington Post* Web site in minutes."

"Marvin, come on! Give me a few hours," Jay pleaded, his voice shaking. "After all I've done for you, if you cost us the California Senate seat, you won't get directions to the washroom after tonight. You'll be persona non grata around here."

"Let me tell you something," said Myers, his voice dripping like acid. "I've been in this town for forty years. *No one* threatens me . . . not even you. I was here before you got here, Jay, and I'll be here long after you're gone."

"Good night, Marvin. I'm sorry it's turned out this way." He hung up and walked back into the den.

"Well?" asked Long. "Any luck?"

"No," said Jay, beside himself. "He's shafting us."

Long let out a sigh. "Once this breaks, the late vote will turn against Hughes. Now we really need Jefferson to hang on."

Jay gazed at the image of a beaming Kerry Cartwright delivering his victory speech, his stomach churning. Florida was hanging by a thread, and once Myers posted his story, the world would turn upside down. *At least we beat Stanley,* he thought.

42

The sun rose at 7:12 the day after the election, the dawn stirring a sleep-deprived, confused capital. In California, Kate Covitz rode a wave of sympathy to victory despite legal and financial woes. In Florida Don Jefferson clung to a thirty-four-hundred-vote lead out of more than seven million votes cast, with a recount looming. Meanwhile, as all eyes were on the Senate, the Republicans lost the House by five seats. Finger-pointing in the GOP was rife, most directed at Gerry Jimmerson, who was certain to be ousted as Republican leader.

Most shocking, Johnny Whitehead was outed on election night as a client of Adult Alternatives, the dominatrix service where Perry Miller lost his life. "BAD BOY WHITEHEAD GOT SPANKED!" sneered Merryprankster.com, never known for subtlety. The White House reeled at the revelation.

Jay walked out of the West Wing after pulling an all-nighter and crossed the alley to the Eisenhower Executive Office Building. He entered the ornate Indian Treaty room, which was turned into a war room. Folding tables covered with phones and laptops stretched the length of the room. A few staffers stared at computer screens or surfed Web sites. David Thomas presided like a general at Gettysburg, surveying the carnage with dispassionate discipline and cool detachment.

"What's the latest?" asked Jay. "POTUS will want an update."

"We're buttoning down Florida," said Thomas, dark circles under his eyes, sleeves rolled to his elbows, tie loosened, giving off the aroma of body odor. "Max Stampanovich has a veritable SWAT team of lawyers. We've got attorneys on the ground in all sixty-seven counties, and they'll be present for the recount. We're flying in reinforcements with experience in recounts this morning on charter jets. They're killers."

"Any word yet on how Lightfoot plans to play it?"

"She's in the bunker. But our guys think three thousand plus votes will be hard to overcome."

"If they can steal it, they will," said Jay.

"No question. We're loaded for bear, legally and politically."

"Good." Jay grunted in disgust. "I still can't believe Gerry lost the House. We did our job. We assumed he'd do his. That was a *huge* mistake."

"Worst run midterm I've ever seen."

"If it weren't for the pain it will cause us, I'd say good riddance."

"Total," agreed Thomas. They stood in silence for a moment. "Too bad about Heidi. I hate that Covitz got away."

"Me, too," agreed Jay. "You know what's funny? She probably would have won if Covitz's husband hadn't killed himself."

"Yeah, it was that blasted sympathy vote," said Thomas. He stared into space for a moment. "The Whitehead story didn't help."

"No."

Jay turned to leave, signaling the meeting was over. "Thanks, guys!" he shouted to pasty-faced aides hunched over their laptops. They waved and smiled wanly. His assistant opened the door. Jay turned back to Thomas. "Make sure Jefferson hangs on," he said. "Don't let him play nice under any circumstances."

"Don't worry. He's not in charge anymore, thank goodness. It's in the hands of the lawyers now, and they're junkyard dogs."

"There are three big losers from last night," said Jay, ruminating. "The biggest is Stanley. After that, Jimmerson. He'll probably resign. Finally, Mike Birch. He tried to get cute by appointing Lightfoot, and it blew up in his face. I don't even think the guy can run for president now."

"He's done," said Thomas. "The question is, who will the Republicans run now?"

"If we're lucky, nobody," said Jay. With that he was gone.

IT WAS A FEW MINUTES after 9:00 a.m. when Johnny Whitehead strode to the end of the driveway of the vice-presidential residence at the Naval Observatory wearing a blue suit and a blue patterned tie, an American flag pin visible on his lapel. A small podium with the vice-presidential seal affixed to the front was set up with two microphones on top. A press pool awaited consisting of the chief AP White House reporter, two broadcast and cable network reporters, and Dan Dorman with the *Washington Post,* who had by sheer luck made the draw. It was Whitehead's first public comment since Marvin Myers's story broke about his having once been a client of Adult Alternatives.

Whitehead approached the podium and pulled a sheaf of papers from his coat pocket. His eyes were tired, his facial expression somber. Cable news and broadcast networks preempted regular programming to cover the event live.

"Good morning," he said in a firm voice, his chin raised defiantly. "Five years ago, after my term as governor of Kentucky ended, I went through a difficult time personally. I had been in public office almost continuously for a quarter century and found the adjustment to private life extremely difficult. During this period, when I was a private citizen holding no public office, I visited Adult Alternatives. At no time did I have sexual relations with any employee. Nevertheless, it was a serious error in judgment, and I deeply regret the pain it has caused my family and my colleagues."

The only sound was the *click-whir* of cameras. "I take the trust of public service seriously. That is why as soon as my friend Perry Miller's body was found at a townhouse leased by Adult Alternatives, I informed both my wife and President Long of my prior mistake." He paused, clearing his throat. "Both Janice and the president forgave me and have been totally supportive. For that I am deeply grateful. My marriage has never been stronger, and I have never been more in love with my wife. Nor have I been more committed to Bob Long's agenda for this country." He glanced down, as though bracing himself. "But this revelation will make it difficult if not impossible for me to serve effectively as a senior member of the Long administration. Therefore, it is with great regret I announce I will resign the office of the vice presidency of the United States, effective at noon tomorrow." He smiled tightly. "Thank you all very much for the honor of serving this great president and the country I love so much. May God bless you and may God bless America."

The press pool and the viewing public watched in shock as Johnny Whitehead strode back toward the vice-presidential residence. His wife stood on the porch waiting. They embraced briefly, then disappeared from view.

Dan Dorman turned to the AP White House correspondent. "You can't make this stuff up."

"It gets better," said the AP reporter, his face lit up like a one-hundred-watt bulb. "I hear White House aides are on the client list."

"Oh, *please* tell me Noble is on the list."

The AP reporter laughed. "If we get that lucky, there's truly a God in heaven."

"This could be Sal Stanley's revenge," said Dorman.

"How so?" asked AP.

"If the Senate doesn't confirm a new vice president during a lame duck session and Jefferson hangs on in Florida, the Senate is tied 50–50. There'll be no veep to break the tie."

"Sal's never been known to pull a punch. He may just hold up the nomination of a new vice president for spite."

"Exactly. And it would result in my favorite state of affairs," joked Dorman, his lips curled into a grin.

"What's that?"

"Total chaos."

ON A TELEVISION SET TWO blocks from the Capitol, a blow-dried anchor with makeup caked on his face turned to Marvin Myers. "Marvin, you broke this story. Did you ever in a million years expect Vice President Whitehead would resign this quickly?"

"No, I did not," said Myers, turning down the corners of his mouth, trying to express regret. In fact he was ecstatic. Whitehead's was the latest scalp on his wall. *Take that, bloggers,* he thought to himself. "I assumed since this took place years ago and he had the confidence of Long, he would remain in office, at least until the end of his term."

"Any possibility he was pushed out?" asked the anchor.

"Yes, it's possible, but I doubt it," said Myers. "Look, Johnny Whitehead's a savvy guy. He knew he would not be on the ticket in two years. I think he made a cold-eyed calculation that it was better to leave now on his own terms than twist in the wind for a year and a half while the press speculated about who might take his place."

"Better to jump than be pushed?"

"Something like that."

"Marvin, I must ask you this," said the anchor. "Washington is rampant with rumors about who else might be on the client list. One report making the rounds on the blogosphere is there are prominent members of the White House staff among them. What can you tell us?"

"Stay tuned," said Myers smugly.

"We certainly will," said the anchor, his eyes dancing. He turned to the camera. "And you stay tuned right here as well. Vice President Whitehead has resigned after revelations he patronized a dominatrix service where former Senator Perry Miller lost his life. Back after this."

WHITEHEAD WAS STILL WALKING UP the driveway of the Naval Observatory when Jay buzzed Charlie Hector. Hector's assistant put him right through.

"Charlie, what the heck?" Jay asked without a greeting. "What is Johnny doing?"

"He called me at seven this morning and said he slept on it and this was his decision," said Hector somberly. "He was adamant. I conveyed it to the president, and the president said he respected Johnny's decision and accepted his resignation with regret."

"I sure hope you tried to talk him out of it."

"It was a done deal. He was worried about his family. How do you argue with that?"

"Okay, I get it. But noon tomorrow?" said Jay, his voice rising. "That means we have to push a veep nominee through a lame-duck session. Why can't Johnny just wait until January when the Republicans take control of the Senate?"

"I asked him that," said Hector. "Johnny said, 'If I'm going to go, I need to go now. I don't want to die a slow death.' When I pointed out the implications of Johnny's resigning now, the president said if Stanley blocks his veep nominee, it will look like sour grapes."

"I don't blame Johnny for wanting to pull the rip cord, but this puts us in a real bind."

"It's not an ideal scenario."

"What other shoes are going to drop?"

"I don't know, do you?"

"Not a clue."

"Well, the president wants to see you, me, and Phil in the Oval in fifteen minutes. He wants to review the veep selection process, which Phil will quarterback and discuss a strategy for dealing with additional names on the client list."

"Roger that," said Jay. "See you there."

He hung up the phone, his head spinning. What if Sal Stanley did block Long's veep pick? The country would be without a successor to Long—at the very moment intelligence reports suggested Rassem el Zafarshan was targeting the president for assassination.

JAY LEFT THE OVAL OFFICE and headed through the West Wing lobby. It had been a no-drama meeting with Long, who seemed to draw energy from adversity. They threw out a long list of potential candidates from both parties—Jay had more than thirty names written down on his legal pad. As with Whitehead's selection, it would winnow down quickly to the top half-dozen candidates. Long stressed with the nation at war and facing possible military action against Iran, he wanted someone ready to serve from day one.

Jay's view was that Long had proven his mettle in twenty-one months as president. He was the commander in chief now. His greater worry was domestic politics. Should they choose a centrist Democrat in Long's image and make a run for the middle? Or should Long make his common-law marriage to the GOP official and pick a conservative Republican? If so, perhaps the GOP would nominate him as their standard-bearer as well. It was a bold stroke, one Jay suspected Long would find attractive for its brilliance and audacity.

As Jay headed to the stairwell to his own office, he passed Truman Greenglass, who mentioned Whitehead was in the building.

Apparently he decided to stop by and say good-bye to his staff in person. No surprise there. Johnny was a class act to the end.

On a whim Jay turned left and headed for the vice president's West Wing office, first used by Walter Mondale and coveted ever since by future vice presidents for its proximity to the president. Whitehead's assistant sat at her desk fielding calls from old friends and well-wishers.

"Is he in?" asked Jay, afraid he was imposing.

"Let me tell him you're here." She disappeared for a minute and then reemerged. "Go on in. He's just wrapping up some things and getting some personal effects."

Jay walked up the few steps and opened the door. Whitehead sat at his desk, shuffling through some papers. He stood. "It's the maestro," he said affectionately, face cracking into a smile. "Nice of you to come by."

Jay felt a wave of emotion. He fought back tears as he extended his hand, which Whitehead shook firmly. "Johnny, I just wanted to say you've been a valued colleague and an invaluable asset to this president. You covered yourself with glory today. It made me even prouder than I was when the president first asked you to join the team."

"Thanks, Jay," said Whitehead. "If I was going to go out, I wanted to go out with dignity. I hope I did."

"You did, sir." An awkward silence hung in the air for a moment. What does one say at a political funeral? Jay reached for humor. "Of course, I do wish you'd waited until Stanley was no longer Senate majority leader."

"Well, sometimes you have to do what's best for the country first and let the politics take care of itself," said Whitehead, his eyes boring into Jay. "I did the right thing. That will become more evident with time."

"I know," said Jay softly. "We're going to miss you." He turned to go.

"Jay?"

"Yes, sir?"

"Make sure you get Long reelected," he said, pointing to the Oval. "You sure know how to pick 'em. He's far better than I ever knew. The country needs him." He paused. "The world needs him."

"Thanks, Johnny. Don't you worry, we'll get it done."

"I have no doubt."

With that Jay exited and headed back to his office. His head spun. He had almost grown immune to the human toll, and yet Johnny going down hit him harder than he expected. Johnny was Jay's personal project, and now he was gone. At least they gained control of the Senate. There wasn't much time to mourn Johnny's departure. In quick succession they had a risky veep pick to execute, followed by a dicey confirmation battle in the lame-duck session. Then it was on to the reelect, which Jay had no intention of losing. That, he vowed, would be his final campaign.